Mindoro
and Beyond

Mindoro and Beyond
Twenty-one Stories

N. V. M. GONZALEZ

The University of the Philippines Press
Diliman, Quezon City

THE UNIVERSITY OF THE PHILIPPINES PRESS
E. de los Santos St., UP Campus, Diliman, Quezon City 1101
Tel. Nos.: 9282558, 9253243 E-mail: press@up.edu.ph

First published by the University of the Philippines Press in 1979
Second Printing 2008

The National Library of the Philippines CIP Data
Recommended entry:

Gonzalez, N.V.M.
       Mindoro and beyond: twenty-one stories/
N.V.M. Gonzalez.—Quezon City: The University
of the Philippines Press, c2008.
296 p.; 23 cm.

1. Short stories, Philippine (English). I. Title.

PR9550.9 899.210301 2008 P082000122
ISBN 978-971-542-567-4

Book Design by Nicole Victoria
Printed in the Philippines by EC-tec Commercial

Once again for
Narita; and for Boye,
Sel and Ces, Mike and Pat,
Laksh and Jim; Bangbang
and Chittychitty—whose
book this is.

And for Charles Burton Fahs.

Contents

Part Five

Part Six

Appendices

A Note by the Author

THIS BOOK GREW out of the 1978 University of the Philippines Summer Writers Workshop which I was privileged to attend as its writer-in-residence. This ended a nine-year absence from the campus and entailed catching up with what was going on. Easily remarkable was a fever of activity in the air; and the idea, suggested by President O.D. Corpuz himself, that I should have my stories "around" seemed attractively appropriate. It is to him that we are indebted for this collection.

Since the publication of *Seven Hills Away* (1947), out of Alan Swallow's home in Denver, Colorado, a number of my stories have been anthology-hopping, as it were. Wasn't it time to hold them down, to cage them all in one book? Four of such favored pieces from *Seven Hills Away* are therefore in this collection; six are from *Children of the Ash-Covered Loam and Other Stories* (1954) and six more from *Look, Stranger, on This Island Now* (1963).

The five remaining stories have not so far appeared between book covers but at no time have they been fugitive pieces, since I have had many a plan for them. In any event, they are here to tarry for a while. Three of them deal with the American scene—providing, I trust, a modest justification for our title as well as an earnest of work in the future.

It will be noted that the Mindoro of the early stories appears to have become the Sipolog of the later ones, a transmutation that is inevitable since the imagination must grapple with the appearance and essence of things. Neither one place nor the other is intended, in any case, to refer to the geographical counterpart. Horizons, too, have shifted.

I might add that over the years I have tried, but have somehow failed, to get my thoughts on this work of writing organized. On occasion I would jot down a note or two. It was, for instance, while looking over some manuscripts for this collection that one item turned up—asserting quite without the least hesitation, as jottings go:

> It is because of our access to story-telling that the confusions and the incomprehensible realities round and about do not overwhelm us with despair. We find in due course a way of ordering the experience we go through (as, indeed, others do), and we somehow come to understanding Reality as we live it—until swamped once more by fresh confusions and perplexities. Then comes a new surge of hope, and, again for him who must give an account of how things are, a search for form.

How I wished at the moment that I had cribbed those lines from someone; for to a sentiment so high-minded I felt somewhat a stranger. I had obviously set it down thinking that someday there might be some use for it.

Has that time come? I do not know. The essay "In the Workshop of Time and Tide" tells how others have tried to work out the problem from way back. The effort appears to be never-ending.

May I, in closing, express my thanks to the University administration, perhaps beginning from the days of President Bienvenido M. Gonzalez up till today, for its generous support of imaginative writing on the campus. The policy allowed my teaching (and writing) at the University from 1950 to 1968. And if my misadventures, such as they have been, are understood as details borrowed from myth, the policy may be said to have arranged last April for my return as well.

There are others that need special mention at this juncture. In the list where we find President O.D. Corpuz's name are those, too, of Dean Francisco Nemenzo, Jr., and Associate Dean Pacita Guevarra Fernandez, of the College of Arts and Sciences; Professor Josefina Mariano, Head, Department of English and Comparative Literature; and the staff of the 1978 UP Summer Writers Workshop, chaired by Professor Amelia Lapeña-Bonifacio. They made my summer visit possible. Thanks should also go to PAL Board Chairman and President Roman A. Cruz, and to the Philippine Air Lines, for providing round-trip transportation. To Dr. E.J. Murphy, Chairman, Department of English, Hayward; and to California State University, Hayward, for the courtesy of allowing my travel and participation at a writers' workshop eight thousand miles away from our own workshop, which at that time was also in progress; to Mrs. Cheryl Olsen, who was kind enough to meet my students during my absence— to them go my deep appreciation.

Without research by Professor Damiana L. Eugenio, I would not have been able to write "In the Workshop of Time and Tide"; and for this I should like to thank her. To my son Michael M. Gonzalez and my daughter-in-law Patricia Araneta Gonzalez; to my wife, Narita, and others in the family, whose assistance took many forms and, in every instance, has been steady and invaluable; to Acting Director Luis D. Beltran of the University of the Philippines Press and his staff; and to Professor Gémino H. Abad, who took full and personal charge of the project, transforming material from thousands of miles and a couple of decades away into a happening called a book—I am grateful to them all.

July 25, 1978
Hayward, California

Acknowledgments

To THE MAGAZINES where these stories first appeared our thanks are due, and particular mention is made of the following: *Solidarity*, for "On the Eve"; *Asia-Philippines Leader*, for "The Tomato Game"; and *Philippines Free Press*, for "The Lives of Great Men" and "Serenade."

Thanks are also due Berkeley Unified School District and the Asian American Bilingual Center for permission to reprint "In the Workshop of Time and Tide," from *The Well of Time: Teacher's Handbook*, compiled by Teresito M. Laygo (Berkeley, California: Asian American Bilingual Center, 1978).

Part One

On the Eve

WE LIVED THAT year in Manila, in an *aksesoria*—which sounds a whole
lot better than "tenement house"—on Lakas-Loob St., about three blocks
from Commonwealth Publishing Co., where I worked. My job was that of
proofreader. We managed to pay the rent, Father and I, keep the house
in groceries, and send my brother and sister to school—a not particularly
outstanding performance, in short. But, then, you realize that this was
1939. We had made the decisive move from San Roque, in the province of
Sipolog, only the year previous; and the wars in Europe and China were
soon to change our lives. As a salesman, Father was endlessly speaking of
prospects, of commissions; he was involved in the future. As proofreader,
with lines of type before my eyes, or galleys in my hand, my commitment
was to the present. It is now rather easy to see things in this light. I stood
for the text of the day, Father the pages of tomorrow. But this we hardly
understood in those days. We were in Manila "to eke out a living," as Father
liked to put it. He had been a schoolteacher and had picked up the phrase
somewhere, favoring it as his grudging recognition of the present.

Lakas-Loob seemed all too appropriate as the name for our street.
The word translates as "initiative, with a good measure of self-confidence
thrown in." Small wonder that the street was in actuality an oversized alley,
one of several in that quarter of Sta. Cruz that began from Azcarraga and
ended haphazardly with clapboard dwellings clustered along an *estero*,
or canal. Our tenement was some distance away, and we were spared the

sight of the greenish blue and viscous pool. The stench hardly reached us.

Directly across our doorstep was a furniture factory owned by a Chinese, and here was much vigorous activity. From some place within welled up the fragrant smell of narra wood shavings laced with shellac; and through a large window covered with wire netting we could watch the feverish movement of men and tools that resulted in tables, chairs, commodes, and clothes chests. These were hauled away to a display store on Dasmariñas St., off Escolta. The craftsmanship and the prices passed muster for most people, many of whom would make purchases and arrange for deliveries on the spot and, feeling good perhaps over having struck a bargain or two, hie away to one of the nearby restaurants. There headwaiters would hurry to greet them and then continue calling out in singsong Cantonese, from behind the backs of some departing diners, the prices of the food that the latter had ordered.

The furniture factory employed a watchman, or perhaps an overseer-in-residence, who, in the evenings, celebrated for his part his own good fortune by providing our neighborhood with music from a Chinese fiddle. My untrained ear could not grasp the melody, which resembled tortured cries and yearnings; but I imagined that it told some enchanting story inspired by the exotic aroma of narra wood and the unarticulated patience of the lives round and about, those in the aksesoria across the street included.

> Something is lost,
> The world is grieving;
> Grieved over, ungiving . . . .

I tried to put the sentiment in a poem that opened with these lines. The three stanzas came movingly, unbidden. And thinking that the effort might serve toward my advancement on the *Daily Observer*, I decided to show it to Mr. Campo, our editor. Hardly did I realize that in so doing I was transgressing my commitment to the present, that I was in fact making a dubious step to the future, a territory of promises—Father's country.

I have told this episode elsewhere, and I have no excuse for repeating it other than that it might put succeeding events in perspective. My submission of the poem to Mr. Campo was a moment attended by mysterious quiverings of butterfly wings in my throat. "Well, now—" he said, kindly enough. "What in heaven's name have you got there?" But this generosity was short-lived. "Do take a look at this—first!" he said next, handing over a copy of this week's *Observer's Folio*, the thirty-two-page rotogravure supplement to the Saturday edition for which I did all the proofreading. And there they were: underscorings of misspelled words, letters in their wrong fonts, initials standing askew or upside down. "The muse has kept you preoccupied, it seems," Mr. Campo remarked with some acerbity, waving in front of my nose the sheet on which I had presented my poetic effort. For the first time, in all the months that I had worked for him, I noticed the green eye-shade he wore. Whenever he thrust out his chin, the way he did just then, the eye-shade looked like the blade of a knife.

Surrounded by huge rolls of newsprint, in a corner of the printing plant on the ground floor, my desk smelled of ink and woodpulp, which to an up-and-coming poet ought to have been a source of inspiration. But there was also Mr. Campo's buzzer to reckon with. Its imperious commands sounded as many as thirty times a day, which meant my running up three flights of steps to the editorial floor that same number of times. The eager jinni that I was, as the new boy on the job, had become short-winded, with calf muscles intermittently knotted up by pointless fatigue. And now my offer of poetry had one effect: the boss began to keep a closer watch on me. Both poet and proofreader now attracted Mr. Campo's special attention; as often as the fledgling Milton dashed up the stairs was the proofreader faulted for something or other. Before the week was over, the watch culminated in a summons.

"Now, if you don't mind, Mr. Padua, we might begin by your wiping that stupid smile off your face!"

More I could not bear. The gala dressing down took only three minutes of Mr. Campo's precious time, a pointless expense considering that I had already willed myself into feeling that nothing should faze me ever. To this day I can still see Mr. Campo loosening his tie the better to be relieved of outpourings that seemed about to choke him; and I recall how, restored to my corner table amongst the rolls of newsprint, I became acutely conscious of a great stillness that had descended on the scene.

The machines had not stopped turning out the afternoon edition of some 15,000 copies. The rotary was the same gathering of gears and wheels and cylinders that seemed hell-bent on tearing at each other and yet never succeeding. In and out of the flat-bed tray, sheets of paper slipped in a rhythmic and otherwise senseless regularity. And all this was cast in silence. Perched on his stool beside the rotary was the foreman enjoying his cigarette. Surely nothing could be wrong. Upon the conveyor belt of the stitching machine marched an Independence Day parade: the week's comic strips in all their lurid colors.

And then suddenly the spell was broken; the rotary called out: "Stay on!"

"Aren't you being foolish, boy?" added the flat-bed press. "Be a little more patient!"

Someone at that time happened to be operating the paper-cutter, which had an odd resemblance to a guillotine, and the blade, having emerged also from that otherworldly quiet, hissed teasingly, calling my attention: "*Ssssst*, you there! It'll be your neck soon!"

I brought my hand to the back of my neck. Gooseflesh was all over me, and beads of cold sweat were gathering on my brow. My knees seemed to give way. I reached for the banister that fenced off my desk at one end of the compositors' section. Batches of page-proofs had been tossed over to me from that direction, and even now numerous galleys lay scattered, uncorrected, on my desk. I saw them all, however, as mere strips of paper, the print on them awash with bleak gray. What a state I was in, I thought. I had indeed to pull myself together, and collecting the galleys into a bundle helped to ease my discombobulation. I had been in the habit of reading novels whenever the work was slack or when I got too tired to apply myself to proofreading with any kind of care; and now soon enough I was getting out of my desk drawer D. H. Lawrence's *Love Among the Haystacks*, Hemingway's *The Sun Also Rises*, and Hudson's

Green Mansions. The very feel of the books in my hand enabled me to further regain my composure. I leafed through Hemingway's book in particular, as though I had hidden something somewhere between those pages. A letter? A message from someone?

The decision had not come all that suddenly. I had had it there in the back of my head, a weapon that I had been carrying along with me, a Batangas-crafted knife, a *balisong* to use in self-defense. I would not return to work the next day. Nor the day after! Mr. Campo would buzz for all the world, and no Greg Padua would appear at his command. No one by that name would run up those steps and, proofs in hand, stand before the green eye-shade, saying, "Yes, sir!" His Smiley had decided not to give a hoot to all that. Let them search high and wide for him. Yesterday had been payday; therefore, they owed him a good day's wage. He would forego that. Let them be that much richer . . . .

It was not quite six-thirty, judging by the big Osaka Bazaar clock across the way from State Theater, on Rizal Avenue. Surely, Father would still be at school. This was the National College of Law and Government, located off Escolta, which he attended as a freshman. The classrooms were in an old building directly overlooking the Pasig River, and there was scarcely any water traffic now. I was conscious of a quickening of my senses, an attentiveness to all the bustle around me; and yet my entire being was as if driven by one purpose: to talk with Father.

Near the embankment, snug against one of the rows of classrooms on the second story, was a makeshift gasoline station. Someone was tooting a horn when I arrived, obviously a car-owner anxious for service. Laughter broke out from one of the rooms overhead, the jollity eddying about like a squall moving along a stretch of island shore. Elsewhere, a lecturer was diligently holding forth, his palaver like the sound that waves make tirelessly raking up seaweeds, driftwood, shards of seashells, coral and pebble.

For all that, the place reeked of oil fumes from the gasoline station and the rotted waterlilies piled against the river embankment not far away. I ran up the steps, leaving the hallway which opened directly upon the street. The steps had the smoothness of the inside of a seashell—how they had borne the weight of thousands of eager feet!—and the last rung, at the threshold of a parlor that served also as an exhibition hall of sorts, was a particularly much-scalloped slab of molave wood such as might have graced a temple door.

I knew that I had time to spare before Father's class ended. To occupy myself, I went to the bulletin boards that were ranged along the length of the hall. Donations from past graduating classes, these were elaborate glass-enclosed cabinets for sundry announcements; the light of the naked electric bulbs dangling from the ceiling struck a garish shimmer on them. One sheet on display read "Wanted at the Cashier's Office," listing some fifteen names of students who had been delinquent in their tuition payments. Had the list been that of three months before, I said to myself, surely my name would be there. For I still shared at that time Father's sense of the future. He had wanted me to remain in school and that I did, putting in three semesters' work altogether, meeting the fees with my meager proofreader's pay and leaving hardly anything for Mother and for my own pocket expenses. I had doubted even then whether the sacrifice would be worth it. And then the evening came when in the middle of a mid-term exam a proctor stepped into our room asking for one Greg Padua—a visit the meaning of which was all too clear. Before taking my last two monthly exams I had had to produce stubs from the Cashier's Office, proof that I had not been in arrears with my tuition, that I was a student in good standing. "Let me keep an eye on your books, if you have to go," a seatmate had offered. To which I replied: "Thanks, let me take them with me. I am not sure I'll be returning here." The remark took him by surprise. "You have been exempted! What luck!" he had said; and jauntily I had left my seat, saying, by way of a parting shot: "Take care now—don't crib!"

Father said afterward that I could have done better than that. He had found me home early that evening and had thought I had needlessly cut my classes. "You could have walked straight to the Cashier himself and asked for a note that would tell the professor to allow you to go ahead with the exam, to simply not report your grade until the bill was paid. They do that, don't they? You could have done that. Which class was this?" Patpat's, I had told him, a piece of information that could work in my favor. But he went on: "In which case, you'll need a special exam—that's all. We'll pay the bill—the fee and the fine as well." I braced up, summoning all my courage, all my sense of reality. "But, Pa," I said. "Don't you see? It's nothing but a big hold-up! That's what it's been all the time! A racket! What's to be gotten in a place like that anyway? All that they're after's our money!" He didn't listen, though. "So you believe you can't learn a thing out there? You really believe that? I'll show you. I'll take courses myself. I'll show you what I can do, so we'll have something to fall back on in the future." He had never been that way before. In fact, he sounded angry and was trying very hard not to show it. I said I was sorry, that I knew what he had expected of me, but that the work at the printing plant really got me pooped out when the day was over, where was I to get the energy to sit through Professor Patpat's Political Science, or Torts and Damages, and take down notes besides? "Don't make any excuses now." His voice was trembling. "I'm not making any—for the kind of life we're living. We weren't born into money; so we take things in our stride. We try hard, that's all. The harder it gets, the more we try—that's all. So we aren't able to produce tuition money! But poverty's not anything to get embarrassed about. We'll pay up, we will! With you, it's a different story. You can't even talk . . . ." He meant, of course, my failure to present my case before the Cashier. It had been a matter of pride. And to think, I told myself, that as a boy I used to recite "Out of the night that covers me . . ." at the offer of a centavo. "It's no use, Pa," I said, weakly. To which his reply was a spirited one: "Let me show you what I can do! No point getting terribly ashamed of you—you know that . . . ."

Which was what hurt. If it had been Mother's opinion of me, it might have been less painful to bear. It was as if Father had prepared to write me off as an asset to the family, as a helper in the making of a future. It was well past nine o'clock in the evening, the neighborhood was quiet. Yet I could hear, it seemed, the noises of the furniture factory in full gear. My imagination was getting the better of me. The sounds of hammering and sawing, of wood being planed, of planks falling to floor, even of a truck hauling off to Dasmariñas St. the day's production—all these swelled into a nightmarish cacophony that my imagination conjured, insisting upon holding on to the present. I now know that this was the intent. For, as if that did not suffice, the sounds of mid-morning—the crash of a zinc washtub against the adobe wall, the rush of water in the kitchen faucet— emerged as well. That would be Mother out there doing the laundry in the washtub she had insisted we bring along with us to the city all the way from San Roque. And to this access of vividness was added the alley population of cats rampaging about, running the length of the aksesoria roof, their feet continually slipping on the galvanized iron shingles and getting caught in the trough of the rain gutter.

The school had been prospering all along, serving as it did the likes of us part-time students, hopefuls after inconsequential posts in the government bureaus, or for middling shares in the practice of the professions. Our number had certainly increased. Wooden partitions had been set up at the far end of the hall, making new lecture rooms. I took a peek through a crack in the wall-board. The good professor happened to be on the point of putting his notes away. At this signal the class let itself be overwhelmed by a weariness that each one tried to conceal. Sighs and yawns filled the air momentarily, followed by much commotion as benches and desks were being pushed out of the way. Students from all directions now swarmed the place. I held my ground behind the partition, stepping back on occasion so as not to be in anyone's way.

Father was standing in the middle of the hallway when I saw him, and a classmate had been calling his name. "Oh, Mr. Vivo," I heard Father speaking, turning to this other person. ". . . And what have you got that I can borrow myself?"

"*Government.*"

"What I need very badly's *Persons and Family Relations.*"

A batch of mimeographed sheets changed hands. Mr. Vivo gave Father a folder, saying: "As you can see for yourself, Mr. Padua, I've fastened the pages together . . . ."

"A great idea. I should do the same with mine. Don't you lose a single sheet, please!" Mr. Vivo promised he wouldn't. "I've carefully inked in the places where the print's a little too difficult to read," Father said. "Ah, those thieves! Why can't they change the stencils? . . . You'll see what I mean."

"Good!" said Mr. Vivo.

A touching optimism was shared by the two. I could sense it in their cheerfulness. In the meantime, Father had already noticed my presence. "Mr. Vivo," he said. "My son, Greg. You know each other, don't you?"

"Of course, of course! A chip off the old block, eh?"

Father was pleased by this. "Rather!" he said.

"And where've you been all this time? Weren't you once here with us?"

It was Father who replied. "He's lost interest."

"You shouldn't have," said Mr. Vivo, addressing me directly. "Look at the two of us, your father and myself. Aren't we old enough to be *politicos*? I'm pushing forty as it is and still making the effort."

"He thinks he's all the time in the world for whatever it is that he wants to do," Father said.

"I can't seem to put my heart into it, that's all," I said. At which remark, Mr. Vivo laughed. Father went on:

"He's with the *Observer*, that's why." Without perhaps trying, he made it sound so important. The note of pride he affected was unmistakable.

"I know what that is," Mr. Vivo said. "Your father told me. Professor Patpat took you to task once, didn't he? For scribbling verses in the course of his lecture, I recall. Wasn't that it? I can't blame you. He used to come late to class. Pale and exhausted usually, after a full day at the Municipal Court. Class was just something extra for him. A diversion, or perhaps grocery money for his *querida*. Explains why those lecture notes look so mouldy, in folders the color of corn husks."

How, indeed, could I have missed it? Mr. Vivo had simply put into words what had been in my mind for a long time. I couldn't bring myself to regret the incident, of course. The more I thought of it, the more I felt justified about having dropped out. Like most of his colleagues, Professor

Patpat (Introduction to Criminal Law, MWF, 6:30–7:30) sold his notes to us at twenty centavos a page—a goodly sum, for they ran to three hundred poorly typewritten pages. Sheer felony, considering that the stuff came straight out of *Philippine Reports*. Father overlooked it all, so concerned he was about preparing for what he liked to call "the days ahead."

Now turning to him, Mr. Vivo said: "Can't blame your son here at all—no, I can't. Youth nowadays—ah, they have their own plans! As for oldsters like us—well, how about lending me your *Roman Law*, eh?"

What was behind all that palaver had suddenly become apparent. Would that Father could wise up to it!

"Sorry, Mr. Vivo," he said presently. "I haven't the book here with me. Next time, perhaps . . . ."

I felt relieved although somewhat disappointed.

"Now, there's a real scholar for you," Mr. Vivo turned to me again. "Won't settle for mere notes when the real text could be got. Especially in so basic a subject as Roman Law. Yes, sir! Nothing like the real text, if you can get hold of it."

He was talking about a twenty-two-peso book, and Father said: "You make sacrifices, as you know."

"Right. That's your Father for you, young man," Mr. Vivo said to me.

A sudden chill ran down my back. What could he be up to next? I felt there might just be no end to this. And it was just like Father to be good-natured and helpful. But, in any case, we should be on our way.

We were on Escolta now and walking in the direction of the little bridge that led to Plaza Sta. Cruz. People were hurrying about, and it was Father who asked:

"A black-out practice, isn't it?"

"You bet," said Mr. Vivo. "I've got to run . . . ."

And with that he slipped away and was soon lost in the crowd.

I asked Father where Mr. Vivo lived, and he said Parañaque. It would be a full hour and a half before Mr. Vivo could get home then. He was a real glutton for sacrifices.

A hundred yards ahead, to our right, was Plaza Goiti. It was a lump of gray; *calesas*, streetcars, people—they were all one blurred mass that merged with the buildings and the night.

"He seems to be an earnest, hardworking fellow," I said.

"That's why I like him," Father said. "He manages a bakery."

This did not strike me as unusual. Besides, I was thinking about something else. "Pa," I began, as we turned toward Plaza Sta. Cruz, "do you really have to lend him the *Roman Law* book? Can't you find a good excuse not to?"

"Oh, I know!" Father said quickly, as though he had understood what I meant. "I'll simply say that you'll be needing the book yourself—that, in fact, on your own initiative you've started reading it. Sort of in preparation for the time when you go back to school and enrol in the subject yourself. How's that? Convincing enough?"

He had taken me by surprise. "You really want him to believe that?"

"Unless I have to tell him the truth."

"Which is that—"

"That I sold the book a week ago," Father said.

He had tried encyclopedias, the *Corpus Juris* and other law books, even leather-bound Bibles that contained blank pages for family histories. He had had his crack at insurance as well. "Objectively speaking," he would say, "the end is all that we can be certain about. It's the only event worth providing for, isn't it?" This, with a disarming smile, although as everyone knew, it was a chilling subject to bring up in the first place. His getting into real estate was a relief; he did not have to bring gloom into his conversation with friends and acquaintances. Yes, East Security Insurance was sophisticated anxiety at best, but Gold Star Homes definitely was hope in three simple words. And then there were the Sunday morning outings in the company car, which Mother enjoyed. She would come home aglow with accounts of each excursion to the suburbs, as if she had returned from a vacation in some foreign country and now everything looked different in the native land. She would also have her own bungalow, come fifteen years or so of faithfully remitted amortizations. Whenever she talked in that vein, a lawn with bermuda grass materialized before our eyes, neatly laid out and trimmed and, beyond, a gravel-washed terrace with clusters of periwinkles and sunflowers all the way to the steps. On a bad week, the sunflowers wilted.

I couldn't bring myself to ask Father how much the *Roman Law* fetched. Even as a "used" book, it should command a good price. But perhaps this was not the time to think of it, I said to myself. We were entering the patio of Sta. Cruz church and the siren was wailing in that pointlessly heart-wrenching way it always does.

In an instant all lights were out, and what had been the grey of a distended twilight had become simply pitch-black. Yet I was struck by the ease with which my eyes adjusted to the change. Father did not quite get used to the darkness readily. Progress for him was hampered at every step. He bumped against one of the fruit-stalls ranged along the sidewalk and overturned a basket. I heard it fall as if from a platform or counter and roll over to one side. It must have been empty; but, all the same, the stallkeeper was very much around—he had been the lump of black against the lamppost! He let out a frightening "Who's there?" and a belligerent "Don't you see where you are going? Well, well, use your eyes, friends! Use your eyes!" And from that moment on Father and I avoided the sidewalk like the plague.

Only a few people seemed to be up and about. On Ongpin St., which was the fringe of the Chinese district, the moving shadows were less easy to pick out. The Chinese shops along Misericordia St. were open, though; the shopkeepers had brought out their stools. They'd sit through the black-out in the open. Voices filled the air; in their forced idleness, all that the Chinese women could do was talk. It was like wading across a river of gossip.

"We lost precious time on account of Mr. Vivo," I said.

"Did we?" Father didn't seem eager to concede it.

The sidewalk was narrow and the street itself was pitted with holes— could I manage well enough?—made by calesas. I assured Father that I certainly could, we should be home in a matter of minutes. Already, as we approached Dulong Bayan Market, the stalls exuded all too heavily the oppressive smell of chicken dung.

Someone had brought out a flashlight, and all at once police whistles pierced the air. We crossed an alley to get to a bakery, which reminded me of Mr. Vivo. But wasn't that the smell of oven-fresh *pan de sal*? And then something darted across our path. A cat, Father said. I knew then that the next turn would take us directly to our street, Lakas-Loob.

Darkness had transformed the tenement houses into gossamer black—in which aksesoria did we live?—the line of sky a filament that might have been also the long sweep of tenement roofs. While our aksesoria was in the first building from the street corner, it was difficult to distinguish which one among so many, and so similar, was our doorstep. There were the windows to go by; but the grills to these were all of the same design, I knew. Now the curved iron bars were like protuberances on the back of some monstrous wall lizard.

Our place would be the seventh doorstep, Father said, or the seventh pair of grilled windows. That meant retracing our steps. Only then did we start counting, making certain not to miss the first unit at the corner. A tom called from one side of the alley; at our approach, it scampered away. It seemed to have run toward a wall of webbed wire and was now climbing it. I heard it fall on some overhang or zinc roofing.

The furniture factory! I was certain of it now. I could smell the narra wood shavings and shellac.

"Gregorio—Eugenio!"

The voice—Mother's!—came from the dark void to my right.

"And there's Papa! Don't you see him?"

My sister Celia, obviously. I reached out my hand. The iron grill seemed to have far too many sharp edges. But was this now Celia's hand? No, it was Mother's.

"We thought we've gotten lost! Is that you, Mama?"

"The door! The door!" Mother called out to my brother Ben.

From where I stood at the doorstep, I heard a chair crash to the floor. Ben's clumsiness, no doubt. "Can't we even light a candle?" he protested.

"You may not," Mother said. And to Father, she called out, frantic: "Eugenio, where are you?"

He was, in fact, already standing behind me at the doorway. "It's darker here inside than in the street," he said as we entered.

"I've already gotten used to it," I said.

"So have I," said Celia, and proved it by reaching out to me.

"So have I," said Ben—only to hurt himself again as another chair went tumbling to the floor.

"Did you two come together?" Mother wanted to know.

The tenement looked quite different in the blaze of lights that came with the "All Clear" siren. A small living room and two equally small bedrooms and a kitchen with a hallway in which a dining table and five chairs and a cupboard all fitted in somehow—but we've been happy here, I said to myself. The window in my room gave a view of the adobe wall that enclosed a three-by-four-meter all-purpose yard. In one corner was the water faucet; its bent and, I thought, rather brooding head often fascinated me. And out of nowhere tonight leapt one memory: the joy of that morning, years back, when we first came to the aksesoria, Father saying then, "You see, we were quite sure you'll like it!" and Mother saying next, "It's so small; but I think it's all right, really . . . ." and Ben asking, "Did you really live here, you and Papa, for three months all by yourselves?"—because, indeed, we did, we thought we had to try it out somehow before writing to Mama to get ready for Papa to fetch them and take along the washtub that had been in the family all these years.

The "All Clear" continued, and the glow of the bare electric bulb in my room washed the grilled window clean, letting the light drip to the yard.

Dinner was nothing unusual—dried fish and tomatoes and fried rice—but Father had a surprise for dessert, something really especial, a promise, a hope: he had made a sale, he announced.

"Which one is it, Papa?" I asked.

"A piece of property we saw three Sundays ago, your Mother and I. Near the San Juan River, just off the road to Antipolo. Do you still remember the place, Pilar?"

"Go on," said mother.

Father was runabout with the story of his success. It was as if every detail must be correctly reported and, in the telling, every truth appreciated. He avoided mention of it, but I knew: his client had hedged and wavered. The property was for a mistress, a querida, an earnest to keep her happy and be set up comfortably for life. Father must have had second thoughts about his complicity in the affair, yet the commission that would be forthcoming was much too real for him. It would be cold cash for us all. He did collect an initial portion of it, he said.

"And it was as if someone said to me: 'Don't you lose any time now. Don't you waste that money on trifles now!' " Father said. "So straight off to school I went—this noon—"

"Oh, no." I said.

"And there I was at the Cashier's window. But, no, they won't take the money. It was too late, they said. I appealed to the Bursar personally— offered to pay the fine, if a fine was to be levied. But it was no use. You just have to start your third semester in school all over again—"

"You mean, Pa," I said, "that you tried to get me enrolled again, to get me back in good standing? After all this time—late in the semester as it is? Oh, what a thing to do!"

"Because you aren't that slow, you'll catch up—easily."

"And the Bursar himself said they didn't want the money."

"Yes, he said so himself."

"Then that's great of him, really great."

"You don't have to feel so righteous about it," Father snapped back.

At this point Mother put in: "You two have that thing about school in your heads. But what about us here? The bills, I don't know what's to be done . . . ." And having said that, she rose from the table.

The smell of cheap cigar reached my room, and I said to myself: "This is perhaps the best time for it. Papa will be in a good mood."

Ben was preparing to go to bed. He had no canvas cot like mine but only a sleeping mat which when not in use stood, rolled up neatly enough, against the pillow rack in the other bedroom. He usually spread the mat in a corner in the room that he shared with me. But tonight he preferred the *sala* instead. It was not at all that warm, although November evenings are not in any way that cold either. Ben must be beginning to learn to feel himself alone against the world, what with Azcarraga and Avenida Rizal for his classrooms where harsh lessons of this sort were taught. I smiled at the notion, pleased that I had figured it out.

His could not have been a more appropriate beginning, here in this aksesoria on Lakas-Loob St. Mine had begun in San Roque, the same one celebrated in the song about four beggars who made merry—

> The mute began to sing,
> The deaf listened:
> While the blind watched
> The lame danced the *maskota* . . . .

There I had tried selling magazine subscriptions, contributed news items to the *Daily Observer*—the effect, no doubt, of the earnestness in Henley's "Invictus" which, along with Longfellow's "The Psalm of Life," I knew by heart even as a boy in grade school. Armed with a homemade scrapbook of clippings of those tidbits that I had gotten into print, I presented myself before the manager of Republic Publishing Co., in Intramuros, and thus landed my first job.

A thriving house, Republic Publishing Co. promised for a fee the publication of one's picture and biography in an annual, bound in buckram and with gold-lettered titles. Already the firm had produced several of these. The two-inch volume called *Men of Justice*, for example, had been devoted to municipal justices of the peace. The other volumes in the series had equally glowing titles: *Leaders of Youth* (for schoolteachers), *Pillars of Society* (for landed proprietors), and *Beauties of the Land* (for society ladies and club women). My job had nothing to do with the making of the volumes, however. I had been involved merely in the routine of their getting to the post office at Plaza Lawton.

Just off the press at the time of my employment was a book on town mayors, a five-hundred-page compendium of pictures and flattery called *Leaders of the People*. Ten volumes each trip to the post office had been about my limit. Arrived at the stamp-vending window, I found usually a long queue. There would be considerable jostling about while I awaited my turn. From fear of getting in other people's way and being shouted at, I always tried to get done with my business as fast as I could. This entailed licking the stamps instead of using the sponge on the counter, since either somebody would be busy with it or it would be simply quite out of my reach. Invariably, I came away with a funny taste in my mouth.

As Mr. Campo later said: "You worked for that Montiero, did you?" For I had taken some pride in the job at first and had given Mr. Campo the name of my earlier employer. "You stayed on three weeks! Imagine having to sweat for a gang of racketeers that long! But then you've just come from the sticks, so that's understandable . . . ." And, in the end, praised for having had the good sense to quit the Republic, I was duly hired. The pay was three times that of the short-lived messenger whose mouth had run dry from having had to spit out the taste of glue, hurrying down the sunlit steps of the Plaza Lawton post office. It was, in short, out of that spit that Mr. Campo's Smiley was born.

On my desk was the pile of *Weekly Observer* copies that I had brought home and accumulated, tokens of my industry under Mr. Campo's patronage. I had seen at least five times over every single printed word in those pages. Some of them had given me nightmares, even. How could I tell Father now that I would have nothing more to do with work of this sort?

On the rough paper-covered lauan board which was my desk-top, modelled after the one I used at the printing plant, were a dictionary and a few other books. I had placed one of them as a weight to hold down a folder labeled "Work in Progress"—a presumptuousness! But why not? Others had used the phrase before. And it hurt no one. I read my own heavy blocked letters, appalled by the frankness of the words, though. Three stories and the drafts of four others: this was my entire œuvre to date. It had as yet no working title, but already I had written at the bottom of the folder:

"To My Father."

Whenever he and I talked about books and things of the sort, Mother often felt left out. "What are you both having such fun about?" she might ask, knowing exactly the answer. Then, leaving behind whatever it was she might be doing in the kitchen, perhaps to remind us breadwinners that there was some urgent shortage in the larder that must be attended to, that indeed the two of us might do well finding the time for work that would fetch some more money instead of indulging in idle talk; or, coming to the sala and standing before us, smiling so as to hide her jealousy, annoyance, even exasperation, and quite simply unable to hold back speaking up, or merely voicing a whim, she would say: "Why don't you two worry instead about the rent? About the gas bill? About the electric iron that I've to have if you want your clothes pressed neatly so you'd both look like *señoritos*? Yes, why not do something? Oh, do something!" To which there was never quite any reply. For what words could be found to match her truths? Mother would then throw up her arms and return to whatever it was that she had to do, and I myself might remain in my room and continue scribbling at my desk, while Need moved about the house like an otherworldly being, disembodied but capable of taking that chair or of looking out that window, of listening to our conversation and at times reading our very thoughts. And Father would get his cigar because It hated the smell of tobacco, trembling even at the sight of smoke . . . .

I brought out my folder now. The inscription bothered me. I wanted to erase it and did get out my eraser and begin to work it vigorously. Yet the traces of the dedicatory phrase remained. The letters became all the more readable.

I was being drawn, nevertheless, as by a powerful force, toward where Father sat in the sala, the window to his left and a strip of roofing—the factory's—across the street glinting there in the dim glow from the corner lamppost. With my folder in hand, I said:

"Pa—"

"What have you got there?" Father said.

"Pa," I tried again. "I've quit my job."

It was Ben, and not Father, who responded to this announcement. From his sleeping mat in the corner of the sala, Ben stirred and sat up. Putting a pillow between his back and the wall, he hugged his knees. He had been awake all this time, judging by the look in his eyes.

And it was he who broke the silence. "I heard you," he said. In those eyes something flitted by that meant joy. "If you've quit," he said, "then— then I can go near around there now—with my shoeshine box, can't I— can't I?"

It had been forbidden territory. I had decreed that. For as long as I worked at the printing plant, the area was out of bounds for Ben. My reasons were sound. The Azcarraga traffic was never light; that one street, any street, for that matter, wouldn't be safe at all. And more so for him, who was hardly as tall as an automobile, and who would be dodging those trucks with huge rolls of paper. Safe on the sidewalk, and after recovering his breath in good order, he would shout his calculated challenge to the world: "Shine! Shine!" I had been able to serve him only the mildest warning: "There are always roughnecks around there, you know." For I could not have said then what I really meant.

"Don't be foolish," I said to him now.

"Can't I, Pa?"

But this appeal only made the full force of my earlier announcement more overwhelming, and Father could only remain all the more silent.

"Look, Pa," I persisted, offering him the folder. "Do take a look at this, Pa. Don't you think this will be simply great?" My voice sounded strange; my hands were trembling. "From now on, I'll be working on this. This will be my life! Look at what I've already got!"

Silence, though, was Father's only answer.

The Chinese fiddle across the street began once more to wring its heart out. Father and I had now changed places.

1970

Part Two

Far Horizons

ON A TIME it happened that a sailboat sank off the coast of Sta. Cruz, Marinduque. Of its crew of six, only one survived, picked up by a passing steamer and forthwith brought to Manila. It was some time before he got back to his home-port Maricaban. Then, when he related the story of his disaster, people did not at once believe him, some even saying that he was so young and, perhaps, was simply fooling. Only after months had passed did the owners of the vessel give it up for lost and the women say their prayers for the souls of the departed.

Now it occurred to Juancho, for that was the name of the young survivor, that among his companions who drowned was one not a native of Maricaban Island, but of some distant barrio in Mindoro. Gorio was his name, and Juancho thought that certainly no news of the man's ill fate could have reached his village. And how then could the women of his family say their prayers for him? Juancho was troubled by this, for Gorio had been his friend.

At one time he thought of writing to Gorio's father, but he did not know the man's name, and besides, his letter would not bear much weight, or might not even be believed, Juancho thought. Afterwards, however, he met a fellow-sailor, one named Bastian, who claimed he was from Mindoro. Would he be good enough to look up Gorio's people and tell them what had happened? When Juancho mentioned the name, Bastian was filled with sorrow—for Gorio was his own brother.

But it was not until May that Bastian thought of going home. It was only then that the chance came. The sailboat *Pagasa* was then on her way to Bulalacao in southern Mindoro, and off at a point called Dayhagan she was becalmed. Bastian's barrio was not a long way off from there, and on that calm morning he could see the sandbars lying off the mouth of his home river. In the clear bright sunshine, it seemed to rise like a huge polished arm above the sea.

A strange feeling swept over him. There came some kind of itching in the soles of his feet and his heart began to throb wildly as though trying to get out of his mouth. At his age it was almost funny to feel this way, he thought. Then it occurred to him that it was some seven or eight years since he had left home.

So he could not help talking with the *piloto*. At first he said naively that he wanted to see his village, for it had been years now that he was away. *Ka* Martin listened indifferently. Then Bastian told him about the disaster off Sta. Cruz, in as detailed a manner as Juancho had related it to him. Ka Martin was suddenly moved. Certainly, he said at last, Bastian might go ashore. With this kind of weather it would be about dawn of the next day when the vessel would reach the river's mouth. Bastian must be back on the beach when the *bodiong* sounded.

"But you must be the one to blow it," Bastian said to the sailing master. "For, when you blow, it is like the whistle of a steamer, and surely nothing else can waken me from my sleep."

The remark flattered Ka Martin, and he bullied the boy who sculled Bastian to the shore.

Bastian was hours on his hike to his village, and on the way he thought of how he would break the news to his mother. For, surely, *Aling* Betud would be grieved. But was he not there strong and very much alive still and willing to take care of her?

Perhaps it would be better to tell her nothing at all. Should she learn of his brother's death, it might prove difficult for him to go to sea again. And how he loved the sea though it might claim him too.

It was hot most of the way. He passed two villages before noon and two more in the afternoon. About dusk he reached Paclasan, but though he knew many people there, he did not stay for the night. Ah, my barrio is just the next one ahead, he kept thinking.

He came now on the beach and just then the moon was rising. Far away on the horizon he could see the *Pagasa* with her sails unfurled as though trying to catch the moonbeams rather than the wind. It occurred to Bastian that he could be home early enough and so he hastened. He hoped he could be in time for supper. At last he reached the riverbank and called for the boatman. On the cold sand he sat and waited. On the opposite shore, the houses were sounding with much bustle of folk. Strains from guitars and the stamping of rice pestles reached his ears. Bastian remembered it was Maytime.

When he met his kin he wondered why they were all in the barrio. He had thought they would be in the country preparing their *kaingins*; planting time was near. But now it seemed they had known of his coming.

One after another, they asked:

"Why is it that you have come only now?"

"And how long will you stay?"

"Are you married now, and have you any children?"

Bastian could only smile at these questions, for it was beyond him to answer them all. Women tugged at his elbow and chattered in gleeful voices. "What a tall man he has become," they would say. "Ay, how handsome with his curly mop of hair! How like a hero!"

Presently they dragged him out to his mother's hut. The old woman could not contain herself with gladness. She laughed loudly, saying how fortune had been good enough to bring him back. She had two sons and, at least, one of them was back, she said. Several old folks brought in *tuba* in long bamboo containers and soon every one was drinking. The moonlight was bright in the sandy front yard.

"But now you must stay with us for a while," Aling Betud said.

"Oh, no. Only tonight," replied the son. He drew her to a corner and spoke at length about his agreement with Ka Martin, the sailing master of the *Pagasa*.

That night he was given a finely woven sleeping-mat on which to lie. He could feel with his back the delicate designs of colored *buri* leaves woven into it. How many moons must have been spent in the weaving of it, he thought; before any answer came to him he fell asleep.

Some time after midnight he was wakened by a dream, and rubbing his eyes he could not remember what it was. This made him restless. The night wind came in through an open window carrying many sounds, even the noise of the rising tide in the river. He also heard the cry of some lonely bird—and the sound of a sea horn. It came full and clear, but how soft! It was as though but lightly borne by the wind.

He got up and tiptoed to the door. It was still dark. He stepped on his mother's sleeping-mat and almost knocked against her feet.

By the river, *Mang* Tiago the boatman had built a night fire. The man sat within the circle of the light and Bastian went up to him. At first the two were silent, but as soon as Bastian had warned himself he began to talk. He told of the *Pagasa* and of his lost brother, Gorio. When he had finished, he said:

"You are the only soul who knows about this in the whole village," and he laid his hand upon the man's bony shoulders.

The sound of the horn reached his ears for a second time and he stood up now and bade the boatman goodbye.

"You can go and tell the others what I have told you, for I am going now, you see," said he.

Off at the river's mouth the *Pagasa* swung at anchor. Her sails were still unfurled as before. As the day was breaking, flashes of light spread on the empty canvas.

Left alone by the fire, Mang Tiago sat wondering. Bastian had told him a sad story, indeed. And he felt sorry for the lost brother Gorio, and in his own mind he told all the barrio folk about it. He thought it wrong of Bastian to keep such tidings to himself.

So it was through Mang Tiago, the boatman, that the story spread, for he told it to every one who came to cross the river on his banca. Soon people came to Aling Betud, hoping to console her.

But the old woman had little to say. Sadness came slowly to her, and for days she sat at the window simply thinking and thinking. Then one day, the idea came to her: it must have been Bastian himself who had died and what had come was his ghost. And she went out to her close friends and relatives and told this.

"Ah, really, how can we tell?" said one.

"Nothing else can be true, it seems. For why did he not wait for day before departing?"

"Ghosts are like that," easily explained another.

It irritated Aling Betud to hear these others speak as though with a doubt. So she managed to smile dryly when she said:

"We shall know all, we shall know all. For my other son Gorio will come—and we shall ask him, and he will tell us."

1938

Hunger in Barok

DURING TWO OR three months of the year in Mindoro there is hunger, a kind of half-famine, as it were; and riding homeward down the empty riverbed of Barok one afternoon, Cesar Manao was thinking of this very phenomenon. He had just come from his coffee plantation and had been displeased over how ill-kept it was. He had had a long talk with Selmo, the man in charge, and had demanded that the undergrowth be cleared away within a fortnight.

Selmo, honest fellow, had said that he could not possibly do that; in fact, he said, he had not as much as passed by the coffee grove lately. Why, he had to go to the other clearings, of course—to search for sweet potatoes, cassava, and such other tubers as might put some weight into the stomachs of his seven little boys!

"Could it be," *Mang* Cesar asked himself, "that all these days I have not realized the whole country has been half-starving again?"

He rode on, slouchily. The horse, a grey *potro*, or stallion, lifted his head and sniffed the cool, late afternoon air, shook his mane, neighed a little, then lifted and switched his tail, swatting away at mosquitoes that had begun to buzz behind his master's ears.

Smoke smudged the sky, for someone had been busy in his clearing, burning the felled trees and the underbrush. "There's one hopeful soul, I must say," said Mang Cesar to himself.

He owned some land and a house in the town of Mansalay, but was considered different from most landowners. People would come to him and ask for a hillside to clear, and later pay him in rice after each harvest. He was about forty-eight; and it was good indeed, he felt, that at that age he had some property and was esteemed by people.

Potro sniffed the air and shook his shoulders again. Tall cogon grew in the sandy riverbed, forming a number of grass-islands around which the path wove, then climbed up the low bank and turned into a coconut grove where Mang Cesar's house stood.

Before he reached his gate, a man came to him. "*Pare* Crispin?" asked Mang Cesar.

"Ay, it's your pare Crispin," replied the man, looking up at Mang Cesar in the saddle and timidly stroking the horse's mane. Potro pranced about haughtily as Mang Cesar dismounted. The horse almost stepped on one of Pare Crispin's flat, veiny feet.

"Any news?" asked Mang Cesar. Pare Crispin rented that part of his land which bordered Bonbon creek, in the northeast, and a troublesome neighbor off and on had trespassed on the land. A loyal tenant, Pare Crispin reported every untoward incident at the creek-side: the cutting down of a prize *ipil* tree, the hauling off of rattan, the gathering of honey . . . "Any news?"

"No, the place is quiet this time," replied Pare Crispin, but he added, as if it were only an afterthought: "I've a mind to leave the clearing."

Mang Cesar said: "You—leaving?"

Pare Crispin hesitated. Leading Mang Cesar's horse by the bridle, he walked with the landowner toward the house.

"You're leaving your clearing and three boys and a wife?" asked Mang Cesar.

"I can't help it any longer," replied Pare Crispin.

"Now, come, come," said Mang Cesar, "something is in your head. Probably it's the drought. The rain seems lost this year, indeed."

"Ay, the rain will come no more, it seems."

Both of them fell silent.

"I'm thinking," broke in Pare Crispin, "I'm thinking of going back to my old trade. I was a carpenter once, see? And before that, a fisherman. I can go to Sumagui and work there."

"That would be foolish," said Mang Cesar. "Sumagui isn't the place for you."

Sumagui was a big lumber camp, he knew, where the men worked like carabaos six days a week and gambled away their earnings on Sundays.

"Besides, you are a fellow who has a way with the soil," Mang Cesar added.

Pare Crispin looked away at the trees. Cuckoos began to call from somewhere in the grove. "But there's nothing a man can do, with the rains coming late like this," he said.

Mang Cesar had a clear picture of Pare Crispin's *kaingin* in his mind. He had been there only the week before. A whole hillside was now clean and ready for planting, only the ground was too dry; even the logs had cracked in the heat of the sun.

"But you are a fellow," repeated Mang Cesar, "who has a way with the soil. When the rains come you'll have the best kaingin in all Barok. You and your wife and children—why, you'll have a good harvest. There's not a drop of lazy blood in you!"

Pare Crispin's eyes narrowed. For a while he didn't say a word but seemed to listen to the cuckoos in the grove. It was a slow twilight.

A servant had come for Mang Cesar's horse and had taken off the saddle. Potro now stood at the back of the house, a wet sack on his back, his muzzle inside a bucket of rice-husks mixed with water and molasses.

"You're not on your way somewhere else, Pare Crispin? Or, is it me you want? Why, man, tell me what you've come for!" said Mang Cesar, patting the tenant on the back.

Pare Crispin looked sideways, in the direction of the horse, Potro, enjoying his feed. Almost shyly, like a young girl, he said: "Ay, it's about some rice."

"But I've just given you a loan," said Mang Cesar.

I've my children and my wife. You know how it is," said Pare Crispin.

Mang Cesar shook his head, grumbled a little, and began slapping the side of his pants with his leather horsewhip. Payments were hard to collect; usually he had to send out somebody with a carabao and a cart to get his due. And Mang Cesar did not have much rice to give. He had sold all his *palay* except several cavanes for his own household supply during the rest of the year. And Potro, and yes, three other horses, needed rice-husks for feed every day.

"Your sweet potato patch did not yield this year?" he asked Pare Crispin.

The tenant looked up at Mang Cesar, gaped, and then said: "For three weeks now we've eaten nothing but sweet potatoes. Providence wills it so, perhaps."

"I'm afraid," said Mang Cesar slowly, "I can't let you have any."

"I'll pay you double next harvest," offered Pare Crispin.

"That's a long time off, and besides I've no rice to give to men like you.

"Ay, it's really hard with men like us," agreed Pare Crispin.

Potro had emptied his pail of rice-husks and molasses and now kicked it away. The horse attracted Pare Crispin's attention once more and, as if speaking to himself, repeated: "It's really hard with us . . . . If only the rain comes."

As though he had not heard, Mang Cesar turned to his horse. Leaving the pail where it lay overturned on the dry dusty ground, he tied the horse to a coconut tree nearby, pulled off the wet sack that covered the animal's back, and with this gently rubbed his flanks. Addressing Pare Crispin, he said: "I've nothing to lend anyone any more, I'm afraid."

Then he walked to his house and told a boy to prepare supper. Twilight had deepened into evening. The fire burned brightly. The cuckoos were no more, but crickets hummed in the grove.

Pare Crispin did not go. For a while he stood all by himself near the fence, looking vaguely at the night about him. Then, he joined the boy who was cooking Mang Cesar's supper and tried to make conversation with him. Mang Cesar himself came into the kitchen to light his cigar. As though knowing what he wanted, Pare Crispin picked up a kindling and handed it to Mang Cesar. Mang Cesar half-looked at his tenant in the glow and he saw Pare Crispin's thin, wrinkled face, the gaping mouth, the turned-up nose.

"Can you stay and have supper with me?" he asked.

"Ay, I've a long way to go tonight," replied Pare Crispin. "I've to see a man up the riverbed, about some sweet potatoes. There are no more of them to dig in my clearing."

He coughed strangely, like a sick man.

"I've only seed rice, that is—should it suit you," suddenly offered Mang Cesar. "It's seed rice, I say . . . . But you don't have to plant it if you need rice so much."

"I could bring home a cavan of that?" asked the other.

"And you need not plant it—if you want the rice so much, that is," Mang Cesar repeated.

That night after supper, Mang Cesar watched the moon rise over his coconut grove, and seeing his horse Potro in the yard, standing in the moonlight, he was reminded of Pare Crispin. Mang Cesar decided he would ride up the empty riverbed again and go to Pare Crispin's place.

And this was the first thing he did the next morning. There was heavy dew on the grass and the ground seemed moist. It was as if sometime during the night the rain had stealthily come.

Mang Cesar rode leisurely, playing with his leather horsewhip. When he reached the turn of the road that led to Bonbon, and his horse climbed up the riverbank and then slowed its gait as they passed through the wild banana groves, Mang Cesar, with his whip, began slapping at the leaves and trunks, making loud crackling sounds. Soon he began to whistle.

He thought he would find Pare Crispin in his hut at the edge of his new clearing. He thought he would see the man and his wife pounding rice while three hungry boys looked on. But when he came to the hut it was empty. The three skinny boys and the thin, though strong-limbed woman, as Mang Cesar knew them all, were not there but were away up in the clearing. Mang Cesar did not see them at first, but he heard voices in that direction and recognized one of these as Pare Crispin's. Then he saw—first the father's head, then those of the boys, then the wife's—bobbing up and down, behind the huge trunks of felled trees. They were planting upland rice.

"That's a good cavan of rice seed he has," said Mang Cesar. "And the man has a way with the soil."

With his horsewhip he struck a big banana leaf and it made a sound like laughter.

1939

Seven Hills Away

JOVITO WATCHED HIS mother working quietly by the stove. With a handbroom she brushed all the bits of burning firewood to one corner and then sprinkled water over the little mound of glowing charcoal and hot ashes. The wood sizzled and the sound made the boy sleepy. Covering his mouth with the back of his hand, he yawned several times. It was still early, but he was tired. He had been to the well and, earlier, to the coconut grove and brought the milch cow home.

His mother turned and looked at him with her big kind eyes, as if to say: "Why don't you go to sleep now, son?" No, thought Jovito, he would not go to the *silid*—bedroom—where his two young sisters were already safely tucked under a mosquito net. He would not leave his mother alone in the kitchen. Besides, his father might come home from the ranch any time now. If only it was not a moonlit evening: then his father would come home earlier. He would doze until his father arrived, Jovito decided. He would ask his father about the white yearling he had given him on his last birthday.

He yawned again. His eyelids began to droop. He tried to shake sleep from his eyes and succeeded. His mother had almost finished tidying up the kitchen. Now she placed a small oil lamp on a shelf of the stove near the wall, so that it threw a circle of light by the water jar. She began to wash her hands and asked Jovito for a clean dry rag. The boy reached out for the rag that had been tucked in the palm-leaf wall to his left.

"Shall we wait for your father?" his mother asked when she had dried her hands.

She stood for a moment by the window and looked out at the moonlit sky. The tops of the trees glowed radiantly under a moon three-fourths full. White-grey clouds raced past the moon until they faded away toward a dim and distant horizon where lay, in daytime, a pale-blue mountain range.

Jovito watched the sky, raising himself on his toes beside his mother as she looked out of the window. His chin touched the window sill. Gently his mother pulled him away and led him to the silid, holding him by the hand. He wished he were fifteen instead of six years old so that he would not have to stand on his toes when he looked out of the kitchen window.

He crept under the mosquito net; his mother followed after him. He lay down beside his sister Maria who was four years old; his mother lay down between her and his baby sister Tita. Tita had not yet been weaned, although she was almost two years old, and the mother's coming had awakened the child. She began to stir restlessly and his mother gave Tita her breast. Jovito closed his eyes as his mother mumbled endearing words to Tita, the little one, and at the same time reached out with her left hand to see if Jovito had covered himself with a blanket.

An oil lamp flickered on top of a small wooden table at the far end of the silid. Although Jovito tried hard to close his eyes tight, he still could see the light. It shone through his eyelids as though it were composed of a thousand illuminated threads. Jovito's sleep had vanished and he tried hard now to get it back. He turned on his right side and buried his head in a pillow behind his sister Maria's back.

He felt something warm at his feet and thought it was Maria's feet. How could it be, since he was bigger and taller than she? he asked himself. He gently pushed the warm thing away. It was the cat which tried again to snuggle in between him and Maria. Jovito shooed the cat away, and it darted from under the mosquito net.

"What was that?" asked his mother, startled; for the fleeing cat had almost jumped upon the table where the oil lamp stood.

"The cat," replied Jovito. Sleep had come to him again. He began to dream of a day in the woods when he saw a white cat—no, not the one in the house, but a stray one, with a cut-off tail. The cat mewed and stared at him in a friendly though clever manner, and he followed the cat till it brought him into the deepest and darkest part of the woods. There, he saw a big black house.

Jovito turned on his left side so that he lay back to back with his sister Maria. The warmth eased his fears, as he dreamed of the black house in the woods. Suddenly the black house vanished from his mind, and he began to dream of other things. He dreamed of a long road and of a carabao upon whose broad back a man was riding. From the distance the man looked young, but as he approached he grew older and older. The man coughed as he stopped to ask Jovito where the road to the river was. It was twilight and Jovito pointed to the footpath which went into a hemp plantation and finally ended at the riverbank. Jovito pressed closer against Maria.

He heard sounds from outside—like the old man's coughing. Then, it seemed as if some big tree nearby was being pulled out of the earth, its roots crackling. Then, Jovito heard what seemed like the falling of the tree. His right leg jerked.

"What was that?" asked his mother softly. Then because Jovito did not answer, she said to herself: "Maybe it is the cat in the kitchen. Maybe it's the lamp . . . ."

Fear seized her. She pulled her breast away from the little one. The child did not give it freely but struggled to keep the nipple in her mouth. When at last her breast was free, she whispered to the little one to keep still. "Hush, little one, there's a witch outside . . . . Don't you hear?" Then she got up.

Jovito dreamed the tree had pinned his tiny and helpless body to the earth. He tried to move but it seemed every bone and muscle of him was in great pain. He began to cry in his sleep.

When he awoke, he thought it was morning. Then a great blaze blinded his eyes for a moment. He thought it was the midday sun and time to tether his milch cow in a shadier place in the coconut grove. Standing under a coconut tree, he looked around him and saw the cow, her full round body and skin of mottled dun; and she was standing as still as a log or a tree-stump in the light. The cow stared at the burning house and mooed softly.

Jovito felt someone tugging at him from behind. It was his sister Maria. She was crying with fright. Soon Jovito himself began to shout for help. Dazed, he saw his mother dart in and out of the fire. He called out to her repeatedly, but she would not listen. Now she shoved a trunk out of the window; now she hurled out pillows and mats, some stools and a small table; and then another trunk . . . .

The fire, like a hideous giant, ate up the house, making a weird crackling sound. But for this sound, nothing could be heard for stretches of moments. Even the woods nearby were silent; the insects were awed, as it were, by the spectacle. No wind blew and yet the flames moved quickly, sprightly, and reduced almost at once the entire kitchen to a gory little hill of fire. The uprights of bamboo and wood, not all aflame, began to tumble one by one, and one after another, making a heap on the ground.

The nearest neighbor lived in another coconut grove about five hundred yards away. Help had come at last. Jovito saw the figures of one—two—yes, two other persons besides his mother, fleeting in and out of the burning house. It seemed she had forgotten him. Again and again, he called out to her but she would not listen. The thought that his mother had forgotten them—him and his two sisters—threw him into a panic.

He half ran towards the fire, but Maria clung to him, shrieking. Then his mind grew clear and he began to ask himself where the little one was. Grief clutched at his throat this moment: he trembled in his knees and he stumbled on the grass. Then, as he rose to steady himself, he found his two arms had been protectingly holding the little one close to his breast and he had been holding her thus for long minutes, without knowing it. The little one's feet were cold, and he noticed she gave the fire a questioning stare, then turned her eyes away and looked out at the shrubbery and the thickets and the coconut trees in the distance, all bathed in moonlight.

The figures sped about the burning house as though each were in a race with time. Jovito could see his mother's spare body, her features sharply distinct, now in the midst of a glare of ruddy light, now etched against the very crimson of the flames. He could hear her excitedly giving orders to the two neighbors who had come to help. As his hearing grew clearer, Jovito recognized the familiar timbre of his mother's voice. Intermittently she asked, shouting: "Where are the children? Where are the children?" as if she did not know where they were. And, also, as if she knew, she would not stop to wait for an answer. It seemed the asking was enough, as though by instinct she knew they were safe. Jovito called back to say that they—the three of them—were all safe and that they were over there, huddled together under the sky; and he would open his mouth wide and try to shout at the top of his voice. But the only words he could utter were "Mother!"—Mother!"

Rafters turned to glowing splinters of wood, and the nipa thatch burned into bits that flew about like the fiery wings of frighteningly large insects. The fire had spread in all directions now. The kitchen was completely gone, and the silid was smouldering and falling into a heap. For a moment, nothing remained whole but a square piece of wall with a window in it. It was a ghastly sight; it was so unreal. Then even this wall caught fire and slowly disappeared in flames.

Scattered about the yard were all the effects which had been wrenched from the fire. Jovito recognized the shape of trunks, and he saw that one of the bundles must be the sleeping mat and the mosquito net. He remembered now that these were the first things his mother had gathered up. He remembered that after she had hurled this bundle out of the window, she had pulled him and Maria out of the house and, as though they were inanimate objects, had deposited them, little Tita included, under the nearest coconut tree.

Was that she—now coming towards them? Her small head was ruddier than ever in the shimmering light of the fire. Suddenly she did not look like his mother any more. She was suddenly a stranger to him. She was not the woman he knew, the one who looked out in the moonlight, thinking his father would be on his way home.

Tears rolled down her wet cheeks when she took the little one from him, into her own arms. "Don't cry," she said gently. "The house is gone, don't you see? The house is gone." She pointed at the fire, as though it were something that could make the little one stop crying. Maria too had begun to cry.

But no matter. They were now together again.

Said one of the neighbors: "When I first saw the fire I thought it was nothing."

"But I heard the children's voices," said the other.

"When I heard the children shouting, I was already on my way here," continued the first one. "Had it not been for the shrill cries of those children—"

Jovito recognized the two men. They were old Mang Pepe and his son-in-law Ponso, the widower, who had once helped him find his milch cow when she strayed away one April morning. Jovito remembered the incident; how he and Ponso combed the hills for the cow, and how he followed Ponso down the valleys and into thickets and along the edge of the woods. Ponso was wearing a *buri* hat frayed at the brim, and when they came to the valley and the sun began to get hot, he gave his headgear to Jovito to put on. When they had found the cow, they took a shortcut through the valley and up the hill, beyond Mang Pepe's new clearing. Ponso and Jovito had found the old man busy cleaning his patch. The old man had stopped work and had taken Jovito to an adjoining clearing where he grew sugarcane. Then he had given Jovito an entire stalk for himself.

Mang Pepe joined Jovito and his mother and sisters gathered under the coconut tree. "Don't cry, don't cry," the mother repeated. "The house is gone, see? There, it's gone." The little one continued to whimper, and Maria sobbed like a big girl, in splurges.

Mang Pepe asked: "They are all right?" And Jovito looked once more at the smouldering house. "God saved them! God did!" he heard his mother say. "Suppose it happened in the middle of the night, when we were all asleep . . . ." And now she tried—between sobs—to explain to Mang Pepe how it happened, how there was no one in the house but she—and of course the children—and how Tobias was away on the ranch. What would he, her husband, say? And why was he not home yet? Maybe, it was this moonlight; maybe, he liked to see his cows in the moonlight. Of what good are cows?

"You must be quiet!" said Mang Pepe. "It's God's will. Let us praise Him, for all the children are safe. It's only the house, and all the children are safe!"

Jovito's eyes welled with two large tears when he heard the words "children" and "house." His mother had a way of saying them: and Mang Pepe, still another way. She went on trying to explain to Mang Pepe how Tobias—why, she had not wanted him to leave that afternoon! She had not wanted him to go to the ranch at all. Call it premonition, but she had not wanted him to go. What was there to do there? she had asked. Only a few cows to brand, and a corral to repair. That could wait for another day, and so she had pleaded. But, Tobias—no one in all Barok loved cows more than he!

Jovito remembered his first trip to his father's ranch, about eight kilometers away, up the empty riverbed and up the hills, where little creeks wove through the land. It was two years ago since his father took him there, and he remembered the brown and black and dun-coated cows, and how from a distance, as they grazed, they looked like snails on the hillside.

He felt Mang Pepe's hand on his shoulder. "Your father—he may soon be back now. The moon is beginning to set."

This was not exactly true. The moon was still up in the sky, and the moonlight enwrapped the land. The far winds that had sent the clouds racing one after the other had gone, so that the vast dome of sky was now as calm as a sea. It seemed as if the smouldering house could be seen reflected in the far heavens.

Ponso and Jovito watched the serpent-like flames crawling about what was left of the bamboo and wood of the gutted house. A night breeze fanned the fire a little, making round, sprightly, red balls. Fire-threads wound up loops and bends on the rafters and beams.

Several yards away, tethered to a tree, Jovito's milch cow bellowed. It was a melancholy sound. Jovito could see the cow's bright, wide-set eyes in the haze of glowing blaze. He wondered if she would give milk the next morning. For a moment he feared that the fire might have dried up the cow's udders.

He followed Ponso as the latter wandered about with the object of finding whatever articles might yet be saved from the quietly creeping flames. They raked away a pot, a tin can which formerly contained petroleum, the broken half-moon of a lamp shade. Later, they found the round belly of the lamp buried in a heap of flooring, grotesquely blackened and squeezed out of shape.

It was a heart-breaking occupation. Even Ponso himself reacted to the smouldering pile with a sense of personal loss. There was formed in his mind a list of things he had known the Tobias house to contain. Where was Tobias' shotgun, for instance? Where were his books? Tobias had been a schoolteacher before he had bought the farm and turned to raising cattle.

They found the barrel of the gun at last, the wooden butt burned away. It was still hot, and Ponso scorched his fingers trying to touch it. Oftentimes when there was a scarcity of meat on the farm, Tobias had sent him out to hunt—with this gun. Ponso had felt proud putting it on his shoulder and walking up the Barok and into the dense rattan thickets to the east where wild boars had little wallowing grounds.

"He had tucked the gun there near the door," Jovito's mother explained. "Why did I forget it? And why did he forget to take it along with him to the ranch?"

Jovito's mother and Mang Pepe had now taken up the joyless hunt. Jovito's mother, holding the little one in her arms and instructing the other girl Maria to keep out of their way, raked with a stick the portion where the silid had been. She did not have much success. Across the gutted lot, Ponso shouted, saying he had found the meat grinder, the coffee grinder, and the coconut shredder. Ponso had often borrowed these utensils. Also, he found a *bolo*, its blade completely blackened and its wooden handle gone.

Mang Pepe, with a long pole, pushed out of the embers a tin can of salted fish, and another tin can of muscovado sugar. He cried joyfully at this discovery, for he had often come to Tobias' house for a helping of such foodstuffs as these. If one needed anything, in the way of food or money or cloth, one simply went to the house of Tobias. Mang Pepe felt sorry that the salted fish had been prematurely cooked by the blaze and that the sugar had been burned. Still, patiently, at the risk of stepping upon some burning wood, he pulled these tins away from the embers; and when he had succeeded, he began to examine them carefully. When with a bolo he pried open the can of salted fish, hot and salty steam blew upon his face; and Mang Pepe shook his head sadly.

Ponso and Jovito had discovered a pot of rice. Jovito's mother explained it was the rice she had cooked for Tobias, adding that perhaps Ponso could find some boiled chicken which she had kept in a *fiambrera*. Ponso raked away once more. Instead of finding any more food, he found Tobias' carbide lamp for hunting; then some tableware and broken pieces of china.

Jovito's mother and Mang Pepe had piled the trunks and pillows and mats and other things in a corner of the yard near a shed where Tobias had his wooden sugar mill. The house cat darted across the yard and disappeared behind the shed. The fire had not touched this structure and it was here where Jovito's mother started to prepare a bed for the little one. The child dozed off in her arms and even Maria looked sleepy. She spread a mat and screened it to keep off the draft. When this was done she put the little one to bed. "Keep watch over your little sister," she told Maria. The elder girl obediently sat down beside the little one, leaning comfortably on a pillow, against the round belly of the wooden sugar mill.

Jovito's mother then built a wall, utilizing trunks and boxes, in front of the mill shed. Mang Pepe and Ponso helped her gather whatever valuables there were, and those she placed inside the enclosure. There was her small sewing machine, which had no cover, for she had forgotten where it was and during the fire she had been too confused to look for it. Also, she had her cacao grinder, a gift of Tobias. He had brought it home one May, when he had gone to Manila to sell cows. Of course there was her big *aparador*: Tobias had sold a three-year-old bull and had bought this piece of furniture with the money. It was a miracle how she and

Mang Pepe and Ponso had saved it from the flames. While helping the men, her face had struck against the glass and she had been scared to her wit's end by the ghostly reflection of the flames in the mirror; then, too, the glass had been hot and she thought she had burned her cheeks. Hers was the only furniture of the kind in all Barok, and she felt very grateful to Mang Pepe and Ponso.

"Let us rest awhile," she said, resignedly. "Let us rest and wait for Tobias."

For the first time that night, she had uttered her husband's name—a bird that had flown away and had now returned.

"Where are you, Jovito?" she called out, as if distressed. She pronounced his name with love, a kind of tenderness that seemed strange. One would have thought she was dying or was thinking she would die. The glowing embers had lit up the whole yard, even as the moon shone, and cast a ruddy color upon her cheeks.

"Tomorrow," said Ponso, "we shall recover more things."

Jovito was leaning against a trunk, with crossed legs, and had begun to feel terribly tired.

"Tomorrow," he heard Ponso again, "maybe we shall find your milch pail? Or is it only a pitcher?"

"It's only a pitcher," replied the boy.

"It's very late now," said Ponso. "Maybe very soon the moon will set. It must be nearing midnight. Tomorrow, we shall start early and try to find your milch pitcher."

Jovito saw the cat again. It had wormed out of the millshed, then bounced towards him and settled itself at his feet.

The cat stared at the smouldering lot and mewed like a lost one.

It seemed to Jovito that he heard voices from afar—voices of other boys, and voices of men and women, too. The sounds seemed to approach. Yes, now they were there: the boys, those men and women. He could hear the women gasp and say "Ah!" and "Ay!" Also, he could hear the men uttering cuss words. No—they were not addressing his father. They were cussing at some other person, a stranger, a big unbeatable bully, a Wrestler, a Thief, a Wrecker, a Devil. Jovito could not make out what the person exactly was, but it seemed he was something Big, and of the Other World.

Then he saw the people coming. They were not strange faces to him. Jovito could recognize almost all of them. They were from neighboring farms, and some were from the barrio down the river, of course. In the crowd he saw—first, faintly—and then, clearly—with clearness born of memory—his father. The people came in two's and three's and they went straight to his mother. Why they did not go to his father, Jovito could not understand. The picture became confused and in a moment his father was no longer in it. He was shocked by this and he closed his eyes tightly and pressed his back against the trunk. He was not comfortable that way, but it served to calm him somehow.

The voices awakened him. He recognized Mang Pepe's, and then Ponso's. "In the island of Tablas, where I lived as a boy, the *gobernadorcillo*, my uncle—why, he had a house that was also burned." It was Mang Pepe's voice. "And you know, son, it took seven years for my good uncle the gobernadorcillo to recover what he lost. It always takes that long, so the old men say. Eh? What was I saying? Seven years, did I say seven years?" And Ponso did not reply but only grunted a little, as though to say that seven years is a long, long time. Then Jovito heard another voice.

It was his father's. "There are the cows," said this voice. "We shall have to sell some of them in Sumagui, at the lumber camp there. That's the only way. You will come with me, Ponso? To Sumagui?" And Ponso did not grunt but replied: "I promised the boy we shall search for his milch pitcher tomorrow." And he spoke proudly. "The boy?" it was the other voice. "Well, it will not be a long trip. In three days we shall be back." Jovito heard nothing more.

He closed his eyes tightly for fear that if he should open them he would see his father and Ponso and Mang Pepe making plans. He imagined his father standing beside his milch cow, and petting the cow on the back. But his father would not sell his cow, Jovito told himself. There were other cows in the pasture.

He wondered where his mother was. She was not in this picture in his mind. Even so, he did not want to open his eyes lest he would see some distraught or grieved face, lest he would recognize it and knew it was someone thinking of seven long years, someone standing against the smouldering fire, the face ruddy with the mocking glare of the flames. And once more he saw the serpent-like flames creeping, creeping, and eating out the wood and bamboo—and even the earth.

He could feel the warm cat at his feet. Something told him it was not yet dawn, that it was dark for the moon had gone at last. His thoughts were about his mother, but a wave of fatigue drowned him and then he began to dream it was morning.

1940

The Happiest Boy in the World

JULIO, WHO HAD come from Tablas to settle in Barok, was writing a letter to, of all people, *Ka* Ponso, his landlord, one warm June night. It was about his son Jose, who wanted to go to school in Mansalay that year. Jose was in the fifth grade when Julio and his family had left Tablas the year before and migrated to Mindoro; because the father had some difficulty in getting some land of his own to farm, the boy had to stop schooling for a year. As it was, Julio thought himself lucky enough to have Ka Ponso take him on as a tenant. Later, when Julio's wife Fidela gave birth to a baby, Ka Ponso, who happened to be visiting his property then, offered to become its godfather. After that they began to call each other *compadre*.

"Dear Compadre," Julio started to write in Tagalog, bending earnestly over a piece of paper which he had torn out of Jose's school notebook. It was many months ago when, just as now, he had sat down with a writing implement in his hand. That was when he had gone to the *municipio* in Mansalay to file a homestead application, and he had used a pen, and to his great surprise, filled in the blank forms neatly. Nothing came of the application, although Ka Ponso had assured him he had looked into the matter and talked with the officials concerned. Now, with a pencil, instead of a pen, to write with, Julio was sure that he could make his letter legible enough for Ka Ponso.

"It's about my boy Jose," he wrote on. "I want him to study this June in Mansalay. He's in the sixth grade now, and since he's quite a poor hand at looking after your carabaos I thought it would be best that he go to school in the town."

He sat back and leaned against the wall. He had been writing on a low wooden form, the sole piece of furniture in the one-room house. There he sat in one corner. A little way across stood the stove; to his right, Fidela and the baby girl, Felipa, lay under the hempen mosquito net. Jose, who had been out all afternoon looking for one of Ka Ponso's carabaos that had strayed away to the newly planted rice clearings along the other side of the Barok river, was here too, sprawling beside a sack of *palay* by the doorway. He snored lightly, like a tired youth; but he was only twelve.

The kerosene lamp's yellow flame flickered ceaselessly. The dank smell of food, of fish broth particularly, that had been spilled from many a bowl and had dried on the form, now seemed to rise from the very texture of the wood itself. The stark truth about their poverty, if Julio's nature had been sensitive to it, might have struck him then with a hard and sudden blow; but, as it was, he just looked about the room, even as the smell assailed his nostrils, and stared now at the mosquito net, now at Jose as he lay there by the door. Then he continued with his letter.

"This boy Jose, compadre," he went on, "is quite an industrious lad. If only you can let him stay in your big house, compadre. You can make him do anything you wish—any work. He can cook rice, and I'm sure he'll do well washing dishes."

Julio recalled his last visit to Ka Ponso's about three months ago, during the fiesta. He had seen that it was a big house; the floors were so polished you could almost see your own image as you walked; and always there was a servant who followed you about with a piece of rag to wipe away the smudges of dirt which your feet had left on the floor.

"I hope you will not think of this as a great bother," Julio continued, trying his best to phrase his thoughts. He had a vague fear that Ka Ponso might not favorably regard his letter. But he wrote on, slowly and steadily, stopping only to read what he had put down. "We shall repay you for whatever you can do for us, compadre. It's true, we already owe you for many things, but your *comadre* and I will do all we can indeed to repay you."

Reading that last sentence and realizing that he had made mention of his wife, Julio recalled that during the very first month after their arrival from Tablas, they had received five cavanes of rice from Ka Ponso and that later he had been told that at harvest time he should pay back twice the number of cavanes. This was usurious but was strictly after the custom in those parts, and Julio was not the sort who would complain. Besides he had never thought of Ka Ponso as anything else than his *compadre espiritual*, as they call it, a true friend.

Suddenly he began wondering how Jose would move about in Ka Ponso's household, being unaccustomed to so many things there. The boy might even stumble over a chair and break some dishes . . . . He feared for the boy.

"And I wish you would treat Jose as you would your own son, compadre. You may beat him if he should commit some wrong, and indeed I want him to look up to you as a second father."

Julio felt he had nothing more to say, and that he had written the longest letter in all his life. For a moment his fingers felt numb; and this was a funny thing, he thought, because he had scarcely filled the page. He sat back again, and smiled to himself.

He had completed the letter. He had feared he would never be able to write it. But now it was done; and, it seemed, the letter would read well. The next day he must send Jose off.

About six o'clock the following morning, a boy of twelve was riding a carabao along the riverbed road to town. He was a very puny load on the carabao's broad back.

Walking close behind the carabao, the father accompanied him up to the bend of the river. When the beast hesitated in crossing the small rivulet that cut the road as it passed a clump of bamboo, the man picked up a stick and prodded the animal. Then he handed the stick to the boy, as one might give a precious gift.

The father did not cross the stream but only stood there by the bank. "Mind to look after the letter," he called out from where he was. "Do you have it there in your shirt pocket?"

The boy fumbled for it. When he had found it, he said, "No, *Tatay*, I won't lose it."

"And take good care of the carabao," Julio added. "I'll go to town myself in a day or two, to get that carabao back. I just want to be through first with the planting."

Then Julio started to walk back to his house, thinking of the work that awaited him in his clearing that day. But he thought of something more to tell his son, and so he stopped and called out to him again.

"And that letter," he shouted. "Give it to Ka Ponso as soon as you reach town. Then be good, and do everything he asks you to do. Remember: everything."

From atop the carabao, Jose yelled, "Yes, Tatay, yes," and rode away. A stand of abaca plants, their green leaves glimmering in the morning sun, soon concealed him from view.

Fastened to his saddle was his bundle of clothes and a little package of rice, food to last him all through his first week in town. It was customary for school boys from the barrio or farm to provide themselves in this simple manner; in Jose's case, although he was going to live at Ka Ponso's, it could not be said that his father had forgotten about this little matter concerning food.

Thinking of his father, Jose grew suddenly curious about the letter he carried in his shirt pocket. He stopped his carabao under a shady tree by the roadside.

A bird sang in a bush hard by. Jose could hear it even as he read the letter, jumping from word to word, for to him the dialect was quite difficult. But as the meaning of each sentence became clear to him, he experienced a curious exultation. It was as though he were the happiest boy in the world and that the bird was singing for him. He heard the rumbling of the stream far away. There he and his father had parted. The world seemed full of bird song and music from the stream.

1945

Part Three

Children of the Ash-Covered Loam

ONE DAY WHEN Tarang was seven, his father came home from Malig with the carabao Bokal, which belonged to their neighbor Longinos, who lived in the clearing across the river. The carabao pulled a sled which had a lone basket for its load.

"*Harao*—stop!" his father said.

As Tarang ran to catch the lead rope that his father tossed over to him, Bokal flared its nostrils and gave the boy a good look with its big watery eyes, as if to say, "Well, *Anak*, here we are! Have you been good?"

He had been playing alone in the yard, in the long slack of afternoon, and had been good—except that once *Nanay* had said why didn't he go to the hut and play there so that at the same time he could look after his little sister Cris, just now learning to crawl. But that was because Nanay had wanted to go to the shade and pound rice, when what she ought to have done was wait for *Tatay* to help her, or wait for Anak to grow up, even! So what Anak had done was keep silence when she called. And then afterward she was spanking Cris for not taking an afternoon nap; and Tarang heard her calling to him: "You'll see about this when your father comes!" And so he walked to the riverbank and gathered some guavas, and ate the ripe ones as fast as he got them; and now he was belching, his breath smelling of guava. Perhaps his hair, too, smelled of guava, for why should Bokal flare its nostrils that way?

With Cris astride her hip, Nanay came down the hut, saying, "You might give that hardheaded son of yours a thrashing for staying out in the sun all afternoon."

But Tatay only laughed. "Really?" he said, and then asked, "Would you know what I've brought here!"

"What is it this time?" Nanay asked.

Tarang looked at the basket on the sled.

"If you must know, it's a pig!" Tatay said. He had unhitched the sled and was leading the carabao away to the *hinagdong* tree.

"Now don't you try touching it," his mother warned Tarang.

"The boy will have something to look after," Tatay was saying from under the tree across the yard, where he had tethered the carabao.

From down the sled Tarang pulled the basket, and, indeed, two black feet presently thrust out of it. The corner of the basket had a big hole, and now there appeared another foot.

Tatay cut the basket open with his bolo, and the pig struggled out. "It's for you to look after," he told the boy.

Nanay was standing there beside him and, having swung Cris over to her other hip, began scratching the belly of the pig with her big toe.

"Do this quite often, and it will become tame," she said. And to Tatay: "Now if you hold Cris awhile—"

Then she took the bolo and, crossing the yard, she went past the hinagdong tree where Bokal was and into the underbrush. She returned with six fresh ripe papayas; she wanted then and there to cut them up and feed the pig. But Tatay said, "Here, you hold Cris yourself."

He got back his bolo from Nanay, slipped it into its sheath, and hurried down the path to the *kaingin*. Tarang could see the tall dead trees of the clearing beyond the hinagdong tree and the second growth. The afternoon sun made the bark of the trees glisten like the bolo blade itself.

He thought his father would be away very long, but Tatay was back soon with a length of tree trunk which had not been completely burned that day they set fire to the clearing. The fire had devoured only the hollow of the trunk, so that what Tatay had brought really was a trough that the kaingin had made. Now Tatay cut the ends neatly and flattened one side so that the trough would sit firm on the ground.

They all sat there watching the pig eating off the trough. In a short while its snout was black from rubbing against the burned bottom and sides.

"Where did the pig come from? You have not said one word," Nanay said.

"Well, there I was in the barrio. And whom do I see but Paula—when all the time I did not want to see even her shadow."

Tarang stared at both of them, not knowing what they were talking about. Cris sat on Nanay's arm, watching the pig also, and making little bubbling sounds with her mouth.

"We shall pay everything we owe them next harvest," Nanay said.

"Well, there I was and she saw me," Tatay went on. "She asked could I go to her house and have my noon meal there? So I went over, and ate in the kitchen. Then she asked could I fetch some water and fill the jars? And could I split some firewood? And could I go out there in the corner of her yard and have a look at her pigs?

"She had three of them, one a boar," Tatay went on. "And if I wasn't really afraid that I'd be told to fix the fence or the pen, I am a liar this very minute."

"But for a *ganta* or five *chupas* of salt, maybe. Why not?" Nanay asked.

"You guessed right. She said, 'Fix it, for the ganta of salt that you got from the store last time.'"

"Well, there you are!"

"That's the trouble, there I was. But she said: 'For your little boy to look after—if you like. Yes, why not take one sow with you?' And I said: 'For my boy?' Because, believe me, I was proud and happy Paula remembered Anak. She said: 'If you can fatten it, and let it have a litter, then all the better for us.' So I've brought home the pig."

Nanay threw more bits of ripe papaya into the trough. Tarang scratched the pig's back gently as it continued to eat, making loud noises, not only with its mouth but also with something else inside its belly.

"If there is a litter, we are to have half," his father was saying; and then his mother said:

"That is good enough."

"Well, then, feed it well, Anak!" his father said.

"And you said there was a boar in that pen?" his mother asked.

"A big and vigorous boar," his father said.

Nanay smiled and then walked over to the kitchen to start a fire in the stove. When the pig had devoured all the ripe papayas, Tatay got a rope and made a harness of it, securely fastened about the pig's shoulder.

"Here, better get it used to you," Tatay said.

So Tarang pulled the rope and dragged the pig across the yard. His father led the way through the bush, to the edge of the kaingin nearest the hut. There they tied the pig to a tree stump. Then his father cut some stakes to make the pen with.

They did not make a full-fledged pen, only one with two sides, because, for the other two sides, they used the outcropping roots of an old *dao* tree. The rest was easy; it was Tarang who shoved the pig inside when the pen was ready. Afterward his father went back to the hut for the trough.

He fed the pig with ripe papayas as well as green, and the good thing was that Tatay did not become cross with him whenever the bolo had to be used. He would strap it round his waist and go out there in the bush himself. Sometimes he brought home *ubod* from the betel nut or the sugar palm, and the soft portions Nanay usually saved up for supper; the hard parts she allowed him to take to the pig. There was the rice husk, too. Before, it did not matter whether or not, after pounding the rice, Nanay saved the chaff; from the mortar she would take the rice in her wide, flat winnowing basket and, with the wind helping her, clean the grains right there under the hinagdong tree at the edge of the yard. But from now on it would not do to leave the rice husks on the ground. The kitchen wash mixed with rice bran was a favorite of the sow's. For ever so long after feeding time, you could see her wear a brown band round her mouth.

One day Nanay came home from the kaingin with welts across her cheek and over the valley of her nose. Had someone struck her with a whip? Tatay did not seem worried. He laughed at her, in fact; and Nanay had to say something.

"I only went to the thicket for some rattan with which to fix the pen."

"Now which pen?" Tatay asked.

"The sow's."

Tatay said, "You could have waited for us; that was work for us."

"Still, work that had to be done," Nanay said. "And but for the swelling of the sow's belly, what do you think could have happened?"

"We had thought of the swelling of the belly," Tatay said.

"Still I had to get the rattan," Nanay said.

"And hurt your face," Tatay said, touching gently the scratches on the skin.

Tarang also touched the valley of her nose. She continued: "I stepped on a twig. Then a vine sprang from nowhere and struck me."

Tatay laughed over that one heartily. "It was as though you had stolen something, and then somebody had gone after you and caught you!"

"Next time, I leave the pen alone," Nanay said.

But during the days that followed they were all too busy with work in the kaingins to bother with anything else, really. In the nearby kaingins, people had started planting; and so that they would come over to help later on, Tatay and Nanay were often away out there working. That left Tarang alone in the hut, alone to cook his own meals and fetch water from the well near the riverbank; although it was hardly midafternoon, he would start for the underbrush in search of ubod or ripe papayas. Before the sun had dropped behind the forest, he had fed his sow.

He was walking down the path from the kaingin one afternoon when he saw *Tia* Orang in the hut. He had seen her many times before, on days when Nanay and Tatay took him to the barrio, and he was not a little frightened of her then. The old midwife wore a hempen skirt dyed the color of tan bark, which is like brown clay; and so were her blouse and kerchief.

"And where would they be?" she asked the boy.

"Across the river."

"Where exactly? I have come for the planting."

"In the clearing of *Mang* Longinos, perhaps," the boy said. "We are not yet planting."

"Now be good enough to give me a drink of water, Anak," the old midwife said. "Then I shall be on my way."

She reached for the dipper of water that he brought her. She drank, and then, putting down the dipper, tweaked Tarang on the leg. "If I do not see your mother, Anak, tell her that Tia Orang has come. Tell of my passing through, and of my helping in the planting when the time comes."

For a long time afterward Tarang remembered how they spent morning after morning in the kaingin, gathering pieces of burnt wood and piling them up and then burning them again. Some pieces were too heavy to lift, even with all three of them—Nanay, Tatay, and himself—helping together; other pieces were light enough, and he would take them to the edge of the clearing, where his father laid out a fence by piling the wood between freshly cut staves and keeping these in place with rattan.

It was a pity to have Cris left behind in the hut, tied to the middle of the floor, lest she should crawl over to the steps, down the dirt of the kitchen, past the stovebox, then over the threshold, and finally out to the yard; often they returned to the hut to find her asleep, some portion of string wound tight round her legs.

But, one morning, instead of leaving Cris behind, Nanay took her to the kaingin. That was the day Tatay left the hut very early and returned after breakfast with a white pullet under his arm, and then he and Nanay had a quarrel.

"You found the chicken in the riverbed? Is that what you might say?" she demanded.

"I came from Longinos' place, if you must know."

"And that pullet?"

"Look in your hamper," Tatay said.

Nanay pulled out the hamper from the corner and, in the half-light from the window, opened it and looked through her clothes one by one.

"The *camisa* that Paula gave me—it's gone," she said, almost in tears.

"A camisa seven years too worn-out, what does it matter now?" Tatay laughed at her.

"So you bartered it for a pullet—for that *dumalaga*?" Nanay said.

"It will bring luck, have no regrets," Tatay said.

They followed him to the kaingin, but when they reached the edge where the fence was waist-high, Tatay asked Tarang's mother to stay behind. They left Cris and her sitting on a log at the edge of the fence. Tarang followed Tatay past the dao tree where the pigpen was, and the smell of the trough followed him to the middle of the clearing.

Tatay stopped near a tree stump that was knee-high and motioned to him to get no closer, for now he was holding the dumalaga with one hand, letting its wings flap, like pieces of rag in the breeze, and he had pulled out his bolo. No, Tarang couldn't get any closer. Tatay laid the pullet's neck upon the flat of the tree stump and without a word severed the head. Was that a red streak that cut an arc toward the ash-covered ground? Tatay held the headless pullet higher, to let the blood spurt out a long way.

"Go, Evil Spirits of the land! Go, now!" Tatay was saying. "Now this land is ours! We shall make it yield rich crops!"

Tarang looked back in the direction where Nanay and Cris sat waiting, and at first he did not see them. Beyond the clearing's edge loomed the half-dark of the forest, and a cloud had covered the rising sun and changed the morning to early evening.

Tatay had put back his bolo into its sheath and was calling for Nanay and Cris to come.

"Then we start planting now?" Nanay asked.

"You three wait here, for I by myself can get the seed," Tatay said, and walked down the trail to the hut.

He returned with *Tio* Longinos, Tia Pulin and Tia Adang, and they were all of them provided with wooden sticks sharpened at the ends for making holes in the ground. Tarang made one of his own, but he was not good at using it. He was as slow as Nanay, who could hardly bend from having to keep Cris astride her hip. After a while his stick got blunted, and Tatay said he should sharpen it again. Tatay handed him the bolo. But when Tarang started to sharpen the stick, his hand began to tremble. Cold sweat gathered on his brow, and the ash-covered ground seemed raw with the smell of the chicken's blood.

"You and Cris," Tatay said, taking the bolo from him, "you stay in the shade and let your mother work."

And so they looked for the shadiest *buri* palm at the edge of the kaingin. Nanay cut some dry leaves and set them on the ground, and there she also set Cris, and said to Tarang, "Keep your sister from crying, at least."

But, of course, he could do nothing to stop her, and Cris cried herself hoarse. She would not let him hold her; they chased each other round and round, even beyond the boundary of the leaves. It hurt his knees crawling. What stopped her finally was the sound that the wind made as it passed through and over the palm leaves; for it was a strange sound, like that of drums far away.

Toward noon Tatay called everyone together. They gathered in the hot sun near the tree stump where the dumalaga had been killed. Already Tio Longinos and Tia Pulin and Tia Adang were gathered there when Nanay, who had gone to fetch Cris, reached the tree stump.

"Keep out of the way, Anak," Tatay said, for Longinos was setting up a small cross made of *banban* reeds.

He stepped back, but not so far away as to miss Longinos' words to the cross.

"Let citronella grass give fragrance," he was saying, pulling a sheaf of the grass from the pouch at his waist, where he kept his betel nut and chewing things. Likewise, he took from the pouch other things. "Let ginger appease the Evil Ones. Let iron give weight to the heads of rice on this clearing."

Tarang edged closer, using his father's arm, which was akimbo, as a window to peep from. And he saw the bits of ginger and the three rusty nails that Longinos had placed at the foot of the reed cross.

"It's too hot now to work, isn't it?" Longinos said, grinning away his tiredness. His face glistened with sweat, and he led the way, making a new path across the ash-covered ground.

Tarang brought up the rear, and he saw many holes that the sticks had made which had not been properly covered. He stopped and tapped the seed grains gently in with his big toe. He wandered about in this way, eyes to the ground, quick to catch the yellow husk of the grains. They were like bits of gold against the grey of the ashy ground. He stopped and pressed each little mound of grain gently, now with his left big toe, now with his right. Shorter and shorter his shadow grew until it was no more than a blot on the ground, moving as deftly as he moved among the tree stumps and over the burned-out logs.

He heard much talking back and forth afterward about how Tatay had planted the clearing a little too soon, that Tia Orang ought to have come. That they might have waited for her, Nanay said. But what was done was done, Tatay argued.

That afternoon they visited the kaingin. After he had brought the feed for his sow, Tarang followed Nanay and Tatay; it seemed to him that the ground was so dry it could well be that he was walking on sand. Nanay said that ants would soon make off with the grain.

That evening they sat outside, in the yard. They watched the sky. There were no stars. Black night covered the world; somewhere to the west, beyond the mountain range, rain had come. Twice lightning tore at the darkness, as though a torch were being used to burn some dry underbrush in a kaingin up there in the clouds.

They had an early supper because Nanay said that, if a storm should come, it would be difficult to do any cooking in the stove, now that its roof of buri leaves had been dried up and had become loose shreds these many months of the hot season. They went to bed early, too.

"There, what's done is done!" Tatay said, and sat on the mat, cocking his ears.

It was the rain. Tarang thought he might watch it, only it was rather late in the night. He was tired and sleepy still.

Tatay, of course, had rushed to the window, hoping perhaps to see the rain shoot arrows across the yard.

Now Tarang could hardly keep himself from getting up also. He got so far as the window when his mother awoke and called him sternly back to bed. He had to content himself listening to the rain on the roof.

It proved to be a brief rain burst only. Before daybreak it was all over.

"There is work for us to do, don't you know?" Tatay said after breakfast, knotting his bolo string round his waist. "The pig—your sow, understand? With the rains now coming—"

Tarang understood readily that they must have a roof over the pen. He set out eagerly, doing everything that his father bade him. Tatay gathered the buri leaves, and these had to be taken one by one to the foot of the dao tree where the pen was. So while Tatay disappeared in the bush to get some vines for fastening the leaves onto the makeshift beams, Tarang struggled with the leaves. He dragged them through the bush one by one, making the noise of a snake running through a *kogon* field.

They were not quite finished with the roof when the sky darkened again. From afar thunder rumbled; only the storm seemed rather close this time.

It was a long dreary-looking afternoon. It was warm, but he knew that soon it would be raining very hard, perhaps as hard as he had never seen rain fall before. When Tarang set out to gather ripe papayas for his sow, it was already drizzling, and Nanay had to make him promise not to be gone too long.

He came running to the house. The thunderstorm was right behind him. Panting, he strode into the kitchen, unknotting the string of his father's bolo from his waist.

"Mind to look for mushrooms tomorrow," Tatay was saying.

Why, do mushrooms come with thunderstorms? Tarang wondered. All through supper he asked about mushrooms, and how it seemed that with each flash of lightning the million and one mushrooms that grow wild the whole world over raised their spongy little umbrellas an inch or so toward the sky.

The drizzle was heavier now, and an owl kept hooting somewhere beyond the bamboo brakes across the river. Then the calls stopped. Tarang and his father sat there before the stovebox watching Nanay, who was starting to cook rice for supper. Already the real rain was here.

There was the sound of shuffling feet in the yard, and when Nanay looked through the open door, she said, "Why, it is Tia Orang!"

The old woman dropped the frond of buri that she had used for an umbrella in the rain and clambered up the hut. Nanay called out to Tatay, who had gone to the pigpen to see that the roof they had fixed over it was firm enough and would not be blown away should strong winds come along with the rain as they often did.

"The midwife is here," Nanay called. And to Tia Orang: "Now you must spend the night with us."

The other said, "Then, how goes life with you?"

"The same."

"Don't I see a change? Don't I see life growing with you?"

Tarang sat there by the stove fire, idly tending the pot of vegetable stew for supper.

Nanay was saying, "There's nothing to be seen!" And, passing her hand up and down her belly: "Look, nothing at all! Nothing yet!"

"Cris is hardly two, that's why. But—" the old one became a little excited—"but time enough, time enough!"

"Then, let it be," Nanay said.

"And when it's time, I will surely remember to come," Tia Orang said.

Tatay appeared at the door carrying a buri umbrella of his own. He greeted Tia Orang with much show of respect.

"To be sure," he said, "let her spend the night with us," he told Nanay. "Now, is supper ready?" He turned to Tarang, asking, "Anak, is supper ready?"

So Nanay left Cris upstairs with Tia Orang and helped get the supper ready. She removed the pot of vegetable stew from the fire. There were not enough bowls for all five of them, including Cris, and Nanay said Tarang should use the coconut-shell dipper for the drinking water.

"But," Tia Orang asked, laughing, "should I not first of all earn my supper, no?"

Nanay had almost everything ready—the rice, and then a little pinch of salt on a banana leaf, and the bowls of stew, all of these on the bamboo floor.

"If you want to," Nanay said; "do I spread the mat?"

"If you want to," Tia Orang said.

Kneeling on the mat, with one hand pressing Nanay's abdomen, Tia Orang beckoned to Tatay: "Be of help!"

It was as if Tatay had been waiting all this time. He was ready with a coconut shell containing the bits of crushed ginger roots soaked in oil. Tia Orang dipped her fingers into the mess, then rubbed her palms together and began pressing here and there Nanay's sides and abdomen. The smell of ginger root and coconut oil made Tarang sneeze. The shell with the medicine Tarang remembered from the many occasions when Nanay appeared to be ill. Tatay did things like these whenever anyone of them had pains in the stomach.

He had lighted the *lamparilla* and set it on the floor, upon an empty sardine can. In the light, which was yellow, like the back part of a leaf just starting to become dry, Tia Orang's face looked as though made of earth.

Nanay was smiling at her. She lay smiling at everyone, her eyes traveling from one face to the next. A blush reddened her cheeks.

Tia Orang and Nanay talked, but mostly in whispers. Tarang caught only a few words. Then, aloud, the old woman called to Tatay; and Nanay got up and rolled up the mat. She let it rustle softly.

"Let us have supper now," Tatay said.

Wind from the open doorway fanned the kindling in the stove; and because this was bright enough, Tatay put out the lamparilla.

They sat round the plate of rice that Nanay had set earlier on the floor. Tarang felt his hunger grow with each mouthful of rice and he ate heartily, sipping the broth of the vegetable stew, then mixing the rice with the tomatoes and the sweet-potato leaves and the dried anchovies, grey and headless, in his coconut-shell bowl.

Tia Orang talked a great deal. Perhaps to conceal her appetite, Tarang thought. She talked about the old days in Malig, those days when people did not go so far inland as Loob-Loob but stayed most of the time in the barrio or else went only as far as Bakawan. Tarang listened because she spoke of Evil Ones and of Spirits, and he remembered the kaingin and Longinos and the citronella and the nails and ginger root.

"Now there was that man who once lost his arm felling a tree," Tia Orang was saying, "and another, forgetting his reed cross and all those things of the *gapi*, who began to suffer from a strange sickness."

Tarang cocked his ears.

"He began to throw pus instead of water, let me tell you. Do you know what happened, also, to his wife? Well, the woman was with child. And when she was about to deliver, the misfortune came. No child came forth, but when the labor was done there were leeches and nothing else! Fat and blood-red, and they filled a whole wooden bowl."

Nanay stopped eating suddenly. She reached out for drinking water, which was in a coconut shell laid there also upon the floor. Tatay ate in silence, leaving nothing in his bowl. He looked at Tia Orang as if to ask: "Now, what else?"

Outside, it was as though someone with a brightly burning torch were driving bees off a hive up there in the sky. Beyond the western mountains was another early evening thunderstorm.

At the corner where Nanay was spreading a sleeping mat for Tia Orang, the wind brushed the siding of buri leaves. "Mind to gather those mushrooms tomorrow, just as I've said," Tatay kept telling her.

They went to bed very early. Tarang thought he should stay in one corner, far from Nanay. He was a man now, he felt.

He took an empty buri sack, the one for keeping the *palay* in, and pressed it flat with his feet. It made a nice bed on the floor, there against the wall, near the doorstep.

On her mat Tia Orang stirred wakefully, but she could be heard snoring. Many times Tarang awoke, the strange noises in the old woman's nose and mouth frightening him not a little. It was as if she were uttering strange words to strangers, to people who did not belong to the world of men and women. Tarang strained his ears, but he could not catch even one word; yet there was no doubt that she was talking to someone even now in her sleep. She stirred and turned to the wall, and now she was talking to the buri leaves with which the wall was made.

The thunderstorm came closer. For the first time since he could remember, the rain poured with loud thuds on the roof. It must be falling all over the forest, too, he thought; all over the empty river and as far down as the swamps that surrounded the barrio of Malig by the sea.

In his mind, half-awake, Tarang thought the rain was making music now, shaking songs off the swaying treetops on the fringe of the kaingin. Then he heard Tatay get up from bed. Perhaps Tatay, too, heard the music of the rain. Only Tatay was hurrying down the hut, knotting his bolo string round his waist as he slipped past the door.

Tarang thought he could hear something else besides—yes, the sow in the pen, under the dao tree. He listened more carefully. He could hear the grunting. There were little noises, too. A squirming litter, protesting against the cold. Surely, with wet snouts tugging at its teats, a sow could be annoyed. The belly would be soft like a rag.

"That's something to see!" He got up quietly and slipped out the door into the rain.

It seemed that at this very hour the rice grains, too, would be pressing forward, up the ash-covered loam thrusting forth their tender stalks through the sodden dirt. He thought he caught the sound that the seeds also made.

The ground was not too wet. In his haste, Tarang struck a tree stump with his big toe; and the hurt was not half as keen as it might have been, not half as sharp as his hunger for knowing, for seeing with his own eyes how life emerged from this dark womb of the land at this time of night.

1952

Lupo and the River

THE BIG LAUAN log was still some distance upstream. Pisco stood at the riverbank watching it. Already Lupo had gone to the fish trap at the river's mouth. Pisco saw him reach the trap in time to pull out of the water three *hangaray* sticks which supported the bamboo-work. Lupo got a fourth stick out of the mud and shoved the approaching log with it. The log slipped through the opening, carrying the dirt along.

"Let me help!" Pisco called from the bank, ready to push his own *banca* into the stream.

"Go home!" Lupo shouted back. "Get busy elsewhere!"

Soon Lupo had enough of those hangaray sticks out of the way, and the debris from the *kaingins* in the interior—banana trunks, pieces of *hinagdong* and bamboo—rushed freely through. Pisco smiled and walked home.

His father's hut was a stone's throw from the river. It was a small one; it was no different from the other fifteen or twenty huts which comprised the barrio of Malig. Here was the same nipa-shingled wall, the same rooftree with cabonegro stuck into place at the ridge by spear-shaped bamboo sticks. The roof extended over to one side for that portion of the hut called the *sulambi*, or sleeping place, the floor of which dropped about one foot below that of the main room. Nipa shingles also walled in the lean-to, which one entered from the kitchen by way of a three-runged ladder. From the sulambi to the lean-to was another entrance, but this

67

was without stairs of any sort. To enter the sulambi from this side, one heaved over—as though the doorsill were a fence to sit on.

Wet from standing for a long time in the rain, Pisco entered the kitchen. He swung himself over into the sulambi, moistening the doorsill with the damp seat of his denim shorts. It was dark inside; the little room had only one window and it was still closed. The door that led to one side of the house threw in a rectangle of half-light which fell to the floor and then straggled a few inches up the wall. Pisco's foster sister Paula, who was twenty, had just wakened and was still rubbing her eyes as she got up from her mat. He watched her for a moment. She had rolled up her sleeping mat, and was setting it up against the wall, right behind the corner post. As she turned around, her bare shoulders appeared heavyset in the half-light. With her foot she pushed her pillows out of the way, then she took a dress from off a clothesline that hung across the length of the room, and hurriedly put it on, over her loose cheesecloth chemise. The light from the door limned well her large legs. As she walked to the door, Pisco caught a glimpse of the full and firm curves of her breasts.

She must have heard him enter, but before her eyes could meet his— and he knew she could stare at him in such a fierce and frightening way— he had himself looked in the direction of the stove fire. It would seem as if he had simply rushed to the house to avoid the rain which slithered in from the yard.

He began to whistle. But it sounded absurd and he stopped. Still, he couldn't help wondering now how much more womanlike his foster sister would look in better light. Although he was only nine, he wished he could see her with Lupo's eyes. Lupo was almost twenty-five; if he had not married, so people said, it was because the girls were afraid of him. Unlike his sister *Tia* Talia, in whose house he stayed, Lupo did not live a quiet, uneventful life. Tia Talia was the kind of person who would nurse her hurts and grievances in silence. Lupo was ill-tempered; he drank great quantities of *tuba*, which made matters worse. It was a surprise that they had got him to help build and look after the fish trap. Pisco had heard his father say that they were lucky to have him around. It occurred to him now that he knew what kept Lupo coming to the hut again and again. It was not usual for one to set out for the river in the flood and in the rain.

One did those things for certain reasons, and Pisco wondered whether his father also knew. The more he thought of the matter, the more he grew certain that his father had had thoughts of this kind.

The flood swelled that morning and Crispino Olarte acknowledged that Lupo's presence of mind had spared the fish trap from damage. As for him, Pisco said to himself, he missed the crowd that gathered in the hut every morning whenever the catch was brought in.

No less than half the barrio would gather there; people collected near the stove, sat on the bamboo steps, even clambered up the doorsill entrance to the sulambi, and waited for Unday to be done with the partition of the day's catch. On days when the catch was extremely good, people from Bakawan up the river came down in their bancas or took the trail through the swamps; then there in the kitchen they crowded and spilled out into the yard.

Often a length of bamboo, its rind moist with tuba spume, found its way into the kitchen. Numerous *buri* and sugar palms grew in Bakawan, and as a practical method of clearing the land the kaingin-makers collected the palm sap; in this way they killed the trees. Meanwhile, they collected the palm sap in big earthen jars which they set up on improvised platforms atop the trees, and then there they filled their containers and brought the tuba home to the barrio.

Pisco's father hardly missed his share. If no one came he was likely to send Pisco to Bakawan. People knew how it was to go without fish, and they did not mind filling Pisco's container to the brim. At home, his stepmother had always a word or two to say about his father's drinking. Tuba made Crispino many friends, and it was difficult to get one's friends to pay for the fish that they took home with them. Pisco could be sure, however, to see his father hand over a big string of fish to whoever had been so thoughtful as to provide him with his portion of tuba for the day. Sometimes Unday drank a little herself—"Just to make me a little more talkative," she would admit. It was then she did not care any more where the fish went. By now Crispino Olarte had drunk enough to warm, as he put it modestly, the very pit of his stomach. Reminiscences of the Insurrection and of the Constabulary would be then in order; his father's stories never seemed to stale, and Pisco drank also and listened.

If his stepmother Unday had succeeded in keeping his foster sister away from someone who might make her a good husband, then perhaps it would not now be for long. His *Manding* Paula had caught Lupo's fancy. How often he must have seen her knotting her long black hair exactly as the older woman did. How this must have made her look five or even six years older than her twenty. But perhaps Lupo did not mind. From under a coconut tree he would watch her go to the barrio well, which was back of the house where the midwife lived. With wash under her arm and a long bamboo water-container or a jar on her shoulder, Paula was the very picture of diligence. Truly, she needed a husband to protect and cherish her. Pisco thought Lupo could be one such husband.

In a shed outside the fence that protected the well from stray pigs and carabaos, Paula did her washing. There, too, she bathed—leaving the place perhaps two hours later, with her hair lustrous from a shampoo of the juice from pounded *gogo* bark. Sometimes she used lime; its pulp had a scent which, perhaps for Lupo, traveled far. The *patadiong*, now wet and fastened tight under her armpits, hugged her body unembarrassedly. There would be the wash to take home, along with the water-container. Lupo would come round directly, yet as if from nowhere, and then offer to help her. If after the first two trips to the well Lupo did not fill all the jars, he then made a third or perhaps even a fourth trip with the water-container.

It continued to rain the whole afternoon and there was scarcely anything one could do to keep busy. Fortunately, his Manding Paula brought out a winnowing basket heaped with *palay* to be pounded and the chaff saved for the pig that Unday was fattening. The pen was behind the kitchen lean-to and its occupant squealed intermittently. She did not have to tell Pisco to bring to the kitchen the heavy narra rice mortar and two pestles. Usually they set up the rice mortar there in the yard, and the instant Lupo heard the thump of their pestles, he would stop in the middle of a *cara y cruz* or whatever game he might be playing with the other young men of the barrio; even if it happened to be a card game over at Tia Orang's place, he would go straight to the Olarte house all the same. The very moment he arrived, he would pick a heavy pestle from among those under the bamboo steps and proceed to help at the mortar.

It was quite impossible to see Lupo too often at this chore and mistake his intentions.

But now Pisco and his Manding Paula had been pounding the palay for over half an hour in the kitchen lean-to and not a sign at all that Lupo might come. Perhaps it's because of the rain, Pisco said to himself, looking out now and then at the door. A pool had formed at the doorway and one would have to leap over to cross.

Perhaps his Manding Paula suspected what was in his mind, for she said rudely: "Well, if you expect any help, better think again."

"Oh, but wouldn't you want him to come?" Pisco teased her.

"Who? That fellow?" Pisco was glad she did not look offended. "He can't even talk!" she laughed.

This was quite true. Pisco had observed that whenever Lupo happened to be anywhere near Manding Paula, the fellow behaved as if dumb. For that matter, Manding Paula could not look at Lupo directly. Together they would be busy pounding rice and she would keep her eyes to the ground; or Lupo would appear at the kitchen door with a basket of fish on his shoulder and Paula, who would be at the stove building a fire, could be depended upon to turn her back.

That evening, a little after supper—indeed the tin plates they had used were still scattered about the bamboo floor—Tia Orang the midwife paid the Olartes a visit. The rain had changed to a drizzle and the old woman appeared excited over something. She had brought along with her, besides a kerchief with which she protected herself from the drizzle, a basket which contained a black pot; so very sooty it was, one couldn't think it was chicken *adobo*, but it was. Presently Lupo arrived with his father and mother—Lupo and his father Tio Longinos in neat white *camisa de chinos*, and Tia Pulin in a dark starched-stiff cotton skirt and a hempen *camisa*. The two old people had no doubt come all the way from Bakawan in the flood, and Pisco wondered why he had not seen them paddling down the river. They had brought along some tuba, and each of them had carried a frond of buri for umbrella.

"This can only mean one thing," Pisco heard his father tell his stepmother. Then his father whispered something into Tia Unday's ear; and she went to tidy up the house a little before asking their visitors in.

Amidst the clatter of the tin plates, for Tia Unday seemed so clumsy, Tia Orang remarked: "It seems that youth is tongue-tied."

"Very well, then," Pisco's father said, keeping the guests in the kitchen a little while longer. Finally, Tia Unday gave him the signal.

Pisco was about to join them, but his father said: "Go to the riverbank—it seems to me this rain has stopped. See that nobody goes off with our banca!"

Like a hangaray stick at the fish coral, he was being pulled away. Lupo, then, was the big lauan log rushing down? He was looking at him now, smiling.

"We'll need the banca when we go to visit the fish trap sometime tonight," Pisco's father said.

Somewhat nettled, Pisco lingered in the kitchen. He could have done anything to be able to see the matchmaking at first hand.

When the weather had cleared and the river was green again, they added more hangaray sticks and bamboo to the trap, letting its arms spread wider than before. Lupo could not help very much, Pisco's father said, because he was going to be busy building a hut of his own. Although that night no date for the wedding had been set, it was known all over the barrio that Tia Unday had asked that the would-be groom provide a hut for his bride and that for a start they ought to have on hand between the two of them twenty-five *cavanes* of palay.

It seemed that Lupo had acquired a different standing now. He was even more often at home than elsewhere, and when Pisco cooked rice for their noon meal one day, his father reminded him: "Add now an extra chupa. Lupo eats with us."

Pisco set the pot on the stove and fixed the wood in order that the heat would come evenly. Then he walked over to Lupo, who was busy at the whetstone, which was behind the two big water jars. He had been sharpening his bolo.

"What do you think, *Manong*," he began. "The palay will be plentiful this year?"

"The rains must have harmed the crop a little, if that's what you mean," Lupo replied.

He stopped working the blade of the bolo up and down the length of the whetstone and gave Pisco a queer look. "But if you are thinking of the twenty-five cavanes," he added, "then have no worries about that."

After a long pause, Pisco asked: "What are your sharpening the bolo for?"

Lupo ran the blade of the bolo against his thumbnail and, satisfied with it, blinked his big deep-set eyes. What Pisco wondered at was that look he had. Pisco felt uncomfortable noticing how Lupo held the bolo with his thumb and forefinger, gently rubbing the blade. Suddenly he lunged forward, crying "Shsst!" His thumb and forefinger caught Pisco's throat. The boy fell back, trembling.

"Now be off to your work. See that your rice pot boils well," Lupo said, laughing.

The bolo, of course, was for going to the swamps, in the mud and among the mosquitoes; it was for cutting posts and beams and rafters out of *dungon*, *tangal*, and hangaray—and the names of the woods pleased Pisco's ears.

That afternoon, seeing Lupo following Paula to the well, Pisco recalled a remark Tia Unday had made: "About his eating here with us—what will people say?" Paula, who was then in the sulambi, getting together the dirty clothes to wash, had not perhaps heard her mother. Pisco thought his father had looked annoyed then, as if the matter ought not have come up at all. "He works for us," Pisco's father had argued. "A meal or two every day, what does that matter?"

Pisco took a water-container with him, just in case Lupo should wonder what he might be up to. He had not reached the tamarind tree in Tia Orang's yard when he saw him sitting quietly at the midwife's kitchen doorstep. Perhaps Lupo meant to see for himself from that distance that no one came within ten yards of the washing-shed. He himself did not care to get any closer, as if afraid he would see his betrothed in her wet *patadiong* and thus have too soon a surfeit of her.

When Lupo saw Pisco coming, there was nothing the boy could do but walk on ahead with the water-container on his shoulder.

"But I thought I filled all the water jars this morning?" said Lupo, looking quite perplexed.

Pisco lied. "It's water for drinking that we need," he said. The words came to him quite quickly enough.

"What do you mean? Are you saying that I did not fill those jars this morning?"

"It's not that, Manong," Pisco said. His knees felt weak.

"Step over here, then!" Lupo ordered.

Dragging the bamboo container after him, Pisco retreated instead.

"Don't you slip away now, I'm telling you!" the other commanded. "Over here!" His big toe made an "x" on the ground, on a spot not more than one foot from where he stood.

To gain time, Pisco gently laid his bamboo water-container on the ground. He pressed a foot down to keep the container from rolling over and watched the left-over water trickle out of the opening.

"Be quick about it," Lupo said.

Pisco found himself standing on the marked spot. It was as if his feet had moved forward of their own accord. Cold sweat stood now on the nape of his neck, on his temples. His hands seemed to hang limp from his shoulder joints. It was hardly the prize for being too curious.

"Say 'You filled the water jars early this morning!' Say it ten times!"

Lupo grabbed him by the neck and the big callous hands closed in. "You filled the water jars early—" Pisco mumbled.

"Say it out loud; and then ten times!" Lupo insisted, tightening his grip. "Out loud so the whole world will hear!"

As Pisco's eyes began to moisten, a mere gasp emerged from his throat. Down toward the corner of his lips a tear fell and it tasted brackish. "You filled the water jars—"

"Say 'Every one of them, including the one for drinking water!' "

"Every one of them, including—" Pisco repeated. Keeping count with his fingers, he said the sentences again and again: "—the one for drinking water . . . —for drinking water . . ."

Pisco hardly ever saw Lupo idle afterward. In the evenings Lupo stayed sober, too, so that he might work longer and harder the following morning. He began his mornings as always with the filling of the water jars; or, if the woodpile back of the kitchen had dropped to a foot, he cut and split tangal; then he set out for the swamps again.

On a Friday morning he announced he would use the *dalapang*. This was the big outriggerless banca that lay bottomside up behind the kitchen lean-to. It was only for hauling rice that they used his big banca, Pisco remembered. Now it seemed that Lupo had his wood ready—perhaps all that he needed for his hut.

They helped him launch the dalapang. After breakfast he was off, perched like a little boy at the stern, the tip of his paddle hardly reaching the water.

It had meant hard work, not only cutting the wood but piling them piece by piece near some convenient spot on the riverbank, perhaps near one of the three Ambaols. Being without outriggers, the dalapang could go up any of the small creeks that filled the Malig with brackish wash from the swamps. The creeks not being navigable in the ordinary outriggered banca, Lupo had insisted on the dalapang, unwieldy though it was.

Toward noon Tio Longinos Basco arrived from up the river. He had a bolo at his waist—he had come to work.

"Lupo not yet back?" he asked. "He told me to come, to help him."

But Lupo was still in the swamps, somewhere. Tio Longinos was anxious. He had come by way of Ambaol Creek, he explained, for it was here he knew the pile of mangrove wood to be. Lupo himself had told him. From Ambaol Creek, it would be a matter of an hour and then the wood would be in the barrio.

Tia Unday said could Pisco set the tin plates on the bamboo floor for their noon meal? It was a good way to make Tio Longinos feel he was not only welcome but that he was at home, truly.

"This son of mine," Tio Longinos said, sighing, "sometimes it is as if he's like Pisco over there. So restless, and not quite knowing, I must say, what he is about! If it were but October and harvest time now, there would be no end to his saying, 'Father, let us bring down the twenty-five cavanes to the barrio—today, this very minute.' "

Pisco dropped the plates he had brought in from the kitchen. He heard someone out there in the river, yelling.

He ran to the water's edge. But there was nothing in the September sun at this hour toward midday except the green water. And because of the high tide, the water looked greener than ever. Where the tide had reached far up the mangrove-covered bank, on the other side of the river, the trees did not hang their roots over the water's edge any more. The nipa palms held their fronds limp as if they had struggled to stay above water and failed.

Pisco found his father and Longinos standing beside him. "But that's our dalapang—over there—!" he said, pointing to the water, where a thick strip of nipa palms partly concealed the river bend. Half like a crocodile and half like a long black log it looked; and what was strange was that it should be floating but not coming any closer toward where they were downstream.

They could see Lupo's head as he swam in the current. The dalapang had capsized, all that wood had fallen into the water. All that was needed for building the hut—posts, rafters, perhaps even the wrist-sized hangaray sticks for the kitchen wall—the river had claimed. A kingfisher flew across the water, shrieking, and disappeared at the palm-covered bend.

But he succeeded in getting the boat right-side up. As he trod water, he swung and rocked the boat in order to empty it. Tongues of water thrust out from prow and stern, and then disappeared. Lupo must now board the boat to remove the rest of the water. Pisco watched him do this and then saw him scraping out the bottom of the dalapang with the blade of his paddle. The next minute, Lupo was back in the water to start retrieving the wood he had lost, piece by piece. His head now and again looked like a coconut bobbing in the current. Pisco wished he could help, reaching over the side for each piece that Lupo could get back from the river.

Lupo had secured the boat to a mangrove tree, no doubt with a length or two of strong vine. Now it kept turning and turning, as if eager to get caught in the stream, like some dark-spirited and restless creature.

About the first week of October, a peddler came to the barrio of Malig. It was Pisco and his father who took him in their banca from the other side of the river.

"Pedro Aguacil, at your orders," the peddler said, looking very friendly; even his eyes were smiling.

Unlike most peddlers who visited Malig, he did not carry a *palma brava* cane. Neither did he display under his belt the frighteningly long fan-knife one expected of traveling tradespeople.

Pisco carried the pandan-leaf *tampipi* that the peddler had brought along. Upon arrival in the hut where they took him at once, Aguacil showed them his merchandise. Tia Unday left the stove where she was cooking supper, and called to Manding Paula, who dropped the empty pail for hog feed as she stepped into the kitchen and joined her mother.

"Come," Tia Unday said, "perhaps he has something nice for a dress!"

"After all, with her wedding day only to be set—" Tatay said.

"*Si Tatay naman*—oh, Father," said Manding Paula, shy about it all. "Now, Father. What exactly does that mean?"

"Is she the bride?" the peddler said, smiling, his eyes on Paula.

They gathered eagerly round him. He smelled of sweat—from so far away he must have come. A small, wry-faced man, he had cheeks that looked remarkably sharp. His lips were thin, but when he smiled they became quite expressive. A strange look animated his eyes and the small black in them might have been catlike were he less a pleasant-enough person, the kind who could tell one many things about goings-on in the world, about towns he had been to and people he had met.

Aguacil unknotted the string which bound the tampipi. He had come all the way from Pinagsabangan—if only he knew, he said, that there was in these parts a handsome girl soon to be married . . . .

"That's truly nothing to be certain about," Manding Paula protested.

"Then, perhaps, you have some trousers and shirts for my menfolk?" Tia Unday asked. "Something to use so that every now and then they won't look like the river people that they are?"

Aguacil said he was sorry. "Truly my fault—" and he looked as if his regret was great. "But how could I have known? Tell me?"

His own clothes were in the bottom of the tampipi and he dug for them. After the clothes emerged a carefully wrapped package, and what were all these but some holy pictures?

Pisco was disappointed. The pictures were those of the *Nuestra Señora de Buen Viaje*, the *Sagrada Familia*, and the *San Antonio*, the *San Josep*—Tia Unday could identify each of them, and Aguacil said they cost six gantas of palay each. What, then, were six measures of rice compared to the lot of good that could come from having some holy pictures about the house? Pisco listened to Aguacil's pleasantries but without interest.

When, after supper, Tia Unday told her stepson, "Show him where Tia Orang's house is. Perhaps the old woman will want to have a good look at the pictures," Pisco frowned, and said:

"Perhaps the old midwife isn't home tonight."

But Tia Unday was not to be disobeyed. Without eagerness, then, Pisco accompanied the peddler, letting him carry his own tampipi. Tia Unday shouted to Pisco, who had already crossed the yard: "What impoliteness!" And to the peddler: "Let the boy carry the tampipi, Mang Pedro."

But the peddler said it was all right, and took but three of those bow-legged steps of his to clear the yard.

"One must carry one's own burden, is it not?" he called back.

After a week in the barrio, during which time he managed to dispose of all his holy pictures, Aguacil left for Pinagsabangan, going by way of Dias, whence he had come. He would be back in Malig, he promised, perhaps even before the harvest season was over.

Lupo was at his father's clearing in Bakawan at the time of Aguacil's arrival and had remained there ever since. Their kaingin rice was said to look very well; the place must be guarded at night against wild hogs and stray carabaos that roamed around and destroyed the crop. It was everyone's problem, getting the crop in. And when one succeeded, one did not forget the Olartes. The people from Bakawan who came down for fresh fish now brought new rice, their very clothes sometimes exuding its fragrance.

There were those, of course, who were either too busy to come or, as Tia Unday put it, "who had forgotten, because their time of need had passed." And to their clearings Pisco and his father went. "So that you'll know how things are," Tatay seemed to say as he steered the banca up the river in silence. Sometimes Pisco's thoughts were elsewhere. He wondered whether in some way Lupo had arranged for the purchase of Manding Paula's wedding dress. Since Aguacil was coming back, Pisco reasoned, the matter of a suitable dress was perhaps more important than ever.

With empty rice sacks on his shoulders, they visited the kaingins then, and people told Pisco's father: "Ipin, you have the wisdom. You do not work the land; you do nothing but tend your fish corral. But it is as if you've a kaingin right here, beside this one of ours."

"I have no way with the soil, that's why," Tatay admitted. "My father was a sailor, exactly as his father had been before him. I learned to make fish corrals from an uncle, that's the reason. Every bolo to its own sheath, what do you think?"

"True. Then what about Pisco here?"

At this point, the boy would look the other way, shy over being spoken about.

Once his father said: "It is for him to see which suits him best—the river or the land."

Pisco thought about the matter for a long time. It occupied his mind as they trudged along from one clearing to another. The thought followed him on the trail toward the landing in Bakawan. It was pleasant to do the thinking while paddling, the banca smooth in the water, and somehow the little noises which the outriggers and his paddle made in the water seemed something of an answer. Someday he would understand it all completely, he said to himself. At the moment, the answer was somewhat uncertain in the soft drone of the mosquitoes.

When the rice harvest was being threshed, Aguacil returned. One day, he came up the river in a *parao*. The beach was deserted; boatmen poled up the river yelling and shouting, as if in that way they could dispel the heat. There was Aguacil indeed on the parao's deck. Pisco recognized him instantly. But so severe was the heat Tia Unday would not let the boy leave the hut until the parao had come directly in front of the kitchen lean-to. Only then did Pisco run to the water's edge, as though Aguacil had promised him a present.

The peddler did bring two hampers, both of them large ones. In the first were ready-made dresses and undershirts and cheesecloth and denim; in the other were packages of matches and soap. Also, there were two tins of petroleum, contained in a fragrant pine-board crate, that the men from the parao brought to the house. As before, Aguacil stayed with the Olartes.

"Help him if he needs you," Crispino told his son; for Aguacil said he might set up some kind of a stall. A shed, perhaps? The extension of the kitchen roof, propped up so that two benches could be set up under it! There the men might sit around; from a counter, Aguacil would wait upon them.

Two days passed, then three. Pisco hoped Aguacil would say: "Go to the swamp, boy. Get me some wood. And for an undershirt that I'll give you, build me that shed." But Aguacil said nothing of sort.

Instead, he brought the petroleum tins to the house and posted them beside the two hampers, like guards. Whenever the neighbors came to see what goods Aguacil had, he would push the tins to the wall to open the hampers and then display his merchandise on a mat which Tia Unday had given him to use.

The family was not incommoded at all. There was Manding Paula to help Tia Unday. They had underestimated Manding Paula; she liked tidying up the hut and did not mind having visitors about. Lupo had seen a good housekeeper in her. He had foresight, this Lupo.

People from up the river came to see the ready-made dresses, to feel the rough cheesecloth between their fingers, to sniff the gummy smell of denim; and because it was not always that Aguacil was around to talk to them, it was Manding Paula who sometimes attended to them. She opened the hampers herself and discussed prices and terms.

"Do you have the peddler's permission?" Tia Unday might ask.

"Have no fear, Mother," Manding Paula would reply.

Mornings, while splitting firewood in back of the kitchen, Pisco could hear them talk:

"But that would be twenty gantas. What do you say?"

"Five for this undershirt, is that it? Three for the soap and matches? Isn't that a little too much?"

"But it is a bargain!"

"Three gantas for the bar of soap? You call that a bargain?"

"And the matches go without charge! What more can you say?"

On bringing in the wood he had cut, Pisco saw Tia Unday and his father in the kitchen. The two had been listening, too. His father was shaking his head, Pisco noticed.

"Maybe we ought to open a store. We have a shopkeeper right here with us," Tatay said.

"No, not that," Tia Unday said. "But we ought to encourage Lupo—let him set up a store. Let him engage in some small business as soon as the two of them are settled down. 'Open a *tienda.*' Tell Lupo that."

"He'll have the shopkeeper for his shop, true enough," Tatay agreed.

It was said that Lupo's father had threshed sixty cavanes of palay—a good figure, considering that there had been but two cavanes of seed-rice planted. Pisco wondered how much rice would still be left in Tio Longinos' house after the twenty-five cavanes promised for Lupo and Manding Paula had been brought to the barrio.

Now because the work in the kaingin was all over, too, Tio Longinos himself came to the barrio to help his son build the hut. Father and son worked steadily, quietly—"Like grave-diggers!" Pisco heard his father say. But Pisco liked it there in the mornings; he liked sitting around, watching Tio Longinos and Lupo looking so busy. If Tatay, as people in the kaingins had said, had the wisdom concerning the river and fish corrals, Pisco felt certain that Tio Longinos had something of the kind concerning houses and the earth. A *peseta* had been buried with each of the principal posts; the main doorway was to be such that it would face the river and the east; there would be an odd number of steps, never even, for the bamboo stairs. Pisco lingered around, picking up this and that bit of lore, soaking all of them in, as though he were the wick of a *lamparilla.*

"You know how it is done?" Lupo once said.

They were working with the center beam. Lupo had tied it at one end to the center post, and the result was a neat, if elaborate-looking matter of weaving and looping of rattan. Pisco gaped in wonder.

"Go up there, and I'll show you," Lupo said.

Pisco climbed the post, held with his upturned foot one end of the heavy beam Lupo had lowered, bent over and caught the wood with his loop of rattan and pulled. Lupo taught him how to work the rattan this way and that, never sacrificing pattern for strength, never losing your purpose, and yet taking care to make out of something ordinary a beautiful thing. Below, in the broken shade that the roof-frame made on the ground, Tio Longinos worked with mallet and chisel, watching the two. Pisco could not help feeling that it was from him all this wisdom of the rattan had come, and then he thought he saw the father smile quietly all to himself.

From where he was perched, Pisco could see far out along the barrio street in the quivering half-shade of the coconut trees. The peddler Pedro Aguacil was walking home—it seemed he had gone to Tia Orang's. As Aguacil drew nearer, he looked more bow-legged than ever.

"How about going home now and helping your Manding Paula cook the noon meal?" Lupo suggested.

Pisco reluctantly slid down his perch and regarded from below the beautiful rattan work he had done on the beam and post. His reluctance to leave simmered away, as he discovered now for himself from this distance the intricate pattern in rattan he had made. His elation came like a *santol* seed that stuck in his throat. Feeling that way, he thought, he could go anywhere and could do anything Lupo told him.

"Yes, Manong Lupo—yes!" he heard himself saying as he ran home.

When his Manding Paula brought out that afternoon the rice to be pounded, Lupo left his work looking a bit out of sorts.

"There's a pestle for you," Manding Paula pointed to the pestles stacked under the sulambi door.

Lupo took one and began pounding, lifting and dropping the pestle desultorily. Pisco joined, followed by his Manding Paula, who, as she dropped her pestle, kept bending and scraping in with her free hand the rice grains that scattered round the mortar's mouth. It was a broken one-two-three rhythm that they made, and one far from pleasant to hear.

"It's your fault!" Lupo pointed to Pisco. The boy could not answer back.

The rice kept spilling over.

"If that's how the two of you work," said Paula, "I'll have to ask you to stop."

Pisco decided to be a little more careful. Then, after the mortar had been emptied, Manding Paula gathered the husks in a torn buri mat that had been sewn up into a basket. Pisco brought out from behind the kitchen door the old tin pail they used for mixing in hog feed. Manding Paula poured the rice husks into it now, and Pisco picked up a stick with which to stir the mixture. Manding Paula smiled at him.

"There, take it to the pig," she said.

He was walking to the pigpen at the back of the kitchen, the pail heavy in his hand, when he heard them quarreling. By the time he was done, they were shouting at each other in low but angry voices; and he could hear them above the grunts of the pig, its mouth deep in its trough. Thinking it would embarrass him to return to the kitchen, Pisco left the pail in the pen and went to the riverbank. A little later, he saw Lupo with a water-container on his shoulder walking out into the street.

Pisco returned to the kitchen after Lupo had returned from Tia Orang's well. As if nothing had happened, Manding Paula helped Lupo fill the water jar. She held one end of the bamboo water-container against the mouth of the jar so that the water would not spill.

"About my helping Aguaril, what about that?" Manding Paula demanded.

"You must stop it, I say," Lupo answered.

Manding Paula tried to hold the bamboo container more firmly against the jar's mouth. Already Lupo had tilted the container and the rush of the water down the joints of the bamboo left a hollow sound in the air.

"I'll do as I please," Manding Paula's voice was shrill.

"What I say is, you stop!"

"Why, are you my husband already? My master?" Manding Paula let go with one hand and suddenly the bamboo water-container slipped down the round of the jar's mouth and struck the dirt floor.

"Just watch out!" Lupo said, raising the bamboo container and standing it against the corner wall. "I've warned you!"

Lupo was already at the riverbank when Pisco got there in the slow-lifting dawn twilight. At the fish trap, tiny crabs slithered up the platform and down the sides of the *bunuan*. The splash of fish raised sparkling blobs of light on the water.

It was Lupo who got down and Pisco lowered the handnet to him. "Throw all those crabs away! What we want are the fish!" he cried, as he splashed about inside the trap.

Pisco got the paddle and brushed the crabs down the length of the platform. They scattered like pebbles into the water.

"Be ready up there with this catch!" Lupo called.

With him inside, the bunuan looked full. He dipped and rose as if to feel with his hands each and every mudfish and mullet that thrashed and spun around. Bubbles rose and broke on the surface, and finally the handnet came, two hands holding it up, and Lupo shouting: "It's heavy, it's full!"

In order to take advantage of the low tide, they stayed in the river even after Tatay, who had followed them, had brought home the catch. There were several hangaray poles that stood loose in the mud bottom and had to be replaced if the bamboowork could be expected to withstand the rush of the tide at high noon. Then again Tatay came to see that the work was done well.

"What now?"

Pisco saw his father chuckling. It was one of the few occasions when he heard that chuckle. Tatay had found Tio Longinos in the hut, and was asking him: "You offering to barter fish for rice?"

"And how else? That seems to be the way things are," said Lupo's father.

"You, like all the others? What has come to you?"

It occurred to Pisco that perhaps something had gone wrong; he could feel it in the somewhat childish way Tio Longinos spoke.

"It is as if you are some other person. Here your son works and works, and he has a good share—which, of course, he sends up the river to your house. Does he?"

"That's the truth," Tio Longinos admitted. "But today, this morning, it was as if I were a stranger here!"

Tatay laughed, perhaps to make what he might say seem unimportant. "But, *balaye*! How does this happen? How does life make a stranger of you in my house?"

"Ipin," Tio Longinos said, clearing his throat. "You are a sensible person. Now listen. I've been at Lupo's house—working, fitting this bamboo window and that. It's there where some day our two young people will live. It's there where I work, as I've just said. Then I come in here to your house—judging, from the voices of the womenfolk, that fish has arrived. For a man needs fish, even a working man. But I am a busy person, and when I work, I like to finish my work. That portion of it, at least, which I had promised to myself I'd finish. So here I come to your kitchen and I am quite late . . . ."

"I do not understand you at all, balaye. But continue. Your balaye listens intently," Tatay said.

"All right then. Listen, balaye. What happens is, your stepdaughter mistakes me for a customer of Aguacil's."

"Impossible! Paula doing that?" Tatay protested. "I cannot believe it. Shall I call her this very minute?"

"No need for that, balaye. But this I must tell you," Longinos went on. "She asks, shouting from the sulambi: 'What do you want? Soap, matches?' My fault, of course, because I come after those who have gotten fish have all of them gone. Still, I am too dumbfounded to speak. Imagine a prospective father-in-law being treated that way. I do not utter one word in reply. I keep my words, balaye. From upstairs, in the sulambi, this Paula of yours—"

"But she is no daughter of mine, really!" Tatay said, putting his forefinger to his lips, half-whispering.

"All right, then. But still she says, shouting: 'You wait there, there in the kitchen. I'll be with you in a minute. Perhaps you've heard that it is well past harvest-time now, and you can't get goods unless the palay is right there along with you. Have you got the palay then? *Mano a mano*, as they say?' "

"Why, where was Segunda?" Tatay demanded. "Segunda? Paula— where's your mother? And you there, staring like that?"

Pisco saw that his foster sister had heard all, had indeed stepped out of the sulambi to be sure that she caught every word of Tio Longinos' complaint. She posted herself at the sulambi door.

Tio Longinos did not change his tone. Nor did he speak of other things. "There she is!" he pointed. "She'll admit it, if she's honest!"

It was as if Manding Paula was too surprised to speak. She merely stood there, she could not even move. Pisco felt like telling her to go away. Suddenly he disliked her.

"She was standing like that," Tio Longinos continued, in an even tone, "and that means, she knew who it was . . . . God's my witness. What she said I've told you, balaye. Now what am I, an old man—the father of one who might be your son-in-law—what am I to do?"

Then he burst out laughing, as if to say: "There, now!" Since I've unburdened myself, forget what I've said!" On the overturned rice mortar he sat down and pulled out a small buri basket under his rattan belt; from this basket he drew out his chewing things—*buyo* leaf, lime and betel nut. He handed the chewing things to Tatay, who accepted them.

"Well, think nothing of it," Tatay said, giving him three mudfish, so live still they were too slippery and difficult to hold. Tio Longinos picked up a piece of buri with which to string up the fish through the gills.

"Pisco," Tatay said, "give your Tio Longinos a better piece of string!"

And as he was looking for some pieces of buri in the yard, Pisco saw other people from Bakawan arriving in their banca.

His father greeted them warmly: "You've come late! Very late!" Tatay met them in the kitchen, "But let's see what can be done for you."

On account of some customers of Aguacil's, the whole house that evening was astir till quite late. People crowded in the kitchen. At his father's behest, Pisco built a smudge in the yard. After the men had gone and, along with them, Aguacil—who seemed to be pressing some sale— dogs started barking in the street and down the riverbank. Then, above the noise of the dogs, there rose the clear and languid notes of a guitar.

Perhaps Tia Unday was the person most startled of them all. She sat up on her mat, which she had hastily spread after Aguacil's customers had gone. The serenaders were approaching from across the backyard. Pisco looked out the window; the smudge had died.

Now the guitar-player was right by their window, and his father asked: "Will you let him in?"

What could that mean? Pisco asked himself the question, remembering the betrothal. Perhaps, he thought, letting the serenaders come might mean breaking the betrothal. Where could Lupo be at that moment? Perhaps, back there at Tia Talia's? Yes, at his sister's house and sound asleep! What if the guitar should wake him up?

"Paula," said Tia Unday in a whisper. "You'd better light the lamparilla."

Manding Paula brought out the small kerosene lamp.

"Nanay," she said, "perhaps we should open the window."

Tia Unday looked across the room, in Tatay's direction. There was neither consent nor approval forthcoming from his father, Pisco noticed. The lamparilla light flickered miserably. His father's face hardly helped. It was a tired man's face. When he stirred from where he sat in the corner, it was to roll his own sleeping mat, to get it out of the way—a mere concession.

Manding Paula said: "I'll open the window then, Nanay. Please help me," she said, picking up one of the two bamboo props for the window shutter. It hung oddly until, for her portion of the window, Tia Unday had adjusted the prop. That was her part in the opening of the window and a sudden breeze from the river all but extinguished the newly lighted lamparilla.

A chorus of respectful "Good evening's" followed the song. From that moment on, Manding Paula had to sit at the window, holding the lamparilla in her hand.

"They are *constabularios*, Nanay," she told her mother.

After they had sung their fourth song, Tia Unday said: "Ask them in."

Pisco sighed; it was done at last. He heard his father grumbling: "You might just as well."

Profuse "Thank you's" and then the clatter of rifles, as the four men clambered tiredly up the stairs.

They seated themselves on the bamboo floor. Manding Paula set the lamparilla before them, and then seated herself opposite the men. She stared at the lamp, which stood unsteadily, for the bamboo floor slats moved as the men stirred in their places. Pisco noticed they looked at him too, as though fixing in their minds where they had seen him last. He was sure he had not seen them before.

"We have to spend the night somehow," one soldier began.

"Such is a soldier's life," said another.

"My husband there," said Tia Unday, "he was once with the constabularios himself. Only that was long ago."

The conversation was like a banca that had struck, it seemed, a sandbar in the stream; the soldiers tried to push it forward. They had come from Palaon and they had stopped at Tia Orang's, they said. The midwife had wanted to trouble herself about preparing supper, for they must be hungry. But, truly, they had had supper in Palaon. Were they not pushing on to Dias, just ahead? Yes, but the night seemed so restful: there was a moon. They could not pass up this chance, truth to tell, of meeting pretty barrio girls. Ay, soldiers are such lonely people! They ought perhaps to look up someone to serenade, some young girl, a pretty one, if such person could be found! And they had found her? On this point they argued, apparently for sheer argument's sake. It was as though their conversation had run into a whirlpool. Then one soldier poled it out of the danger spot; all four of them were young unmarried men, he revealed. One owned the guitar, had carried it on many a journey like this through the length and breadth of Sipolog Province. He had tied the guitar onto his back and covered his pack with buri leaves when it was too hot on the beach or when it rained. And, truly, all four of them were good listeners. Could Paula favor them now with a song?

The guitar player started strumming his instrument again; they coaxed and begged.

"Let us hear all four of you first," she said, smiling vaguely.

"And then it will be your turn?"

She blushed, half-turning her head, as if to avoid their seeing her face in the flickering light of the lamparilla.

One by one they sang. Then the soldier with the guitar crossed over to Manding Paula's side of the room, clumsily folded his two legs beneath him, balanced the guitar across his lap, and commenced a *pasacalye*. It was one he had not used before. Manding Paula watched his fingers dancing on the fingerboard. Perhaps what specially struck her fancy, Pisco thought, was the seashell ring on the soldier's finger; perhaps she thought of sailboats and distant places. Oh, how tired those soldiers must be, what with their long journey from the South. Yet, of course, they had come with guitar music and the idea that they were begging of her something of great value, a song from her lips, from her very heart . . . . It could touch anyone deeply.

The guitar player repeated the pasacalye, and then from Tia Unday came the shattering harshness: "If you intend to sing, then sing!"

Pisco himself jerked back from his corner near the doorstep. He saw Manding Paula clear her throat before words came to her lips, before the tune could take shape.

Oh, how the beggars make merry
In our town called San Roque,

she sang, and her voice quivering:

Oh, how the blind one
Watches the dancing of the lame!
Oh, how the deaf one
Listens to the song of the dumb!

The soldiers did not return to Tia Orang's hut, where they said they would spend the night, until it was well past midnight. Momently, Pisco expected Lupo to come; it would be no trouble coming from over there, across the backyard, from his sister Tia Talia's house. But he did not come. Pisco peeked through the kitchen door, and found nothing but darkness across the yard, the shadow of the roof of Tia Talia's house slumped in the grey of the moonlight under the coconut trees.

Dogs started barking again as the soldiers, their guns slung loose on their shoulders, walked down the street. Pisco followed them across the yard and down the street. Was that somebody standing there behind a coconut tree? Pisco thought the soldier with the guitar peered into the half-dark himself and then, on finding no one, walked on.

The next morning Lupo appeared at the Olarte kitchen door. Pisco and his father were preparing to go to the trap and they had been indeed rather impatient; Lupo had never been quite so late before. But, well, here he was. Only, what was this he was wearing if not a scowl? And Tia Unday asked: "What do you mean by that Good Friday look?"

Lupo did not say one word.

"Here, you take something warm, both of you," Manding Paula said to Lupo and Pisco, offering ginger tea.

Then Tatay went down to the riverbank. Still scowling, Lupo held the bowl of ginger tea in his hand. Pisco could see Lupo's hand trembling. It could be that the ginger tea was so hot Lupo couldn't take a sip. But also it could be something else; his eyes began to look wet; he blew into the bowl noisily and sniffled, as if he couldn't help it altogether.

"I am going away," he told Manding Paula, putting down his bowl.

"Where?" Manding Paula answered quickly. "To Pinagsabangan? To San Roque, perhaps? Or to the river? In fact, you're already late!"

"Anywhere. What will it matter to you?"

"It's not true," Manding Paula said.

"Just wait," Lupo said.

"Then, perhaps, it is because you want me to cry and say, Oh, please don't go!"

"Just wait," Lupo said again, his eyebrows narrowing.

Except for Pisco, there was no one in the kitchen. Tatay was still at the riverbank; Pisco could hear him bailing out the water in the bottom of the *banca* with a coconut shell. The splashing of the water and the scraping of the coconut shell combined to make a strange sound; it was as if something was being ripped open.

His overhearing the quarrel had made Pisco uneasy. He felt like leaving for the riverbank now; at the same time he couldn't help it if they had started to quarrel while he was still here in the kitchen, looking for a paddle to take along with him to the banca. Now he pretended to be busy with some ropes piled in back of the stovebox. As he stirred, the bamboo siding yielded motes that fluttered in the air. A sneeze caught him, but he stifled it by rubbing his nose. He wished Tia Unday were in the kitchen, too. But then, he told himself, it did not really matter; she could be watching, for all he knew, peering from behind some chink in the sulambi wall.

"Just wait! What do you mean?" Manding Paula demanded. But Pisco missed what Lupo said then. The voice was different, Lupo was not himself.

Pisco pulled out a paddle from under the ropes and got up from behind the woodpile. It was as if that movement had a relation with what he now saw Lupo to be doing, as if he and Lupo were both tied to one rope and someone had jerked the rope. Except that the pull on the rope had pushed Lupo forward. And then there he was holding Paula, drawing her to him, tightly.

He might have thrown back his head at least; but no, he didn't. Pisco forgot thinking about imaginary ropes and wondered why Lupo held Manding Paula so close, no doubt he could smell now the scent of lime and *gogo* bark in her hair. He might have thrown back his head at least, but instead he held her even tighter, and then his tongue was laving her neck and chin. Finally, their lips met; and Pisco shuddered. He imagined Lupo and Paula's teeth knocking together, for it was as if Lupo felt a beastly, uncontrolled urge to bite her. She resisted and managed to turn her head away. Now Lupo had ripped her blouse open, and they tussled for a minute.

Manding Paula, defenseless now, looked limp and weak, her back to the wall. But she did not cry out for help, she only bit her lips and closed her eyes. Lupo suddenly stepped back; Manding Paula managed to turn about and face the wall. Hands covering her face, she began to sob. Lupo caressed her. Her hair, although completely disheveled now, looked soft in his hands. Lupo held her on the shoulder tenderly, and then she lifted her gaze to him. Perhaps something in that look changed him, for instantly he kissed her again. She yielded, holding on to him tightly, her hands digging into his shoulder blades. It was as if she would not let him go, Lupo drew himself away. When he was free, he said, loud enough for anyone to hear:

"There! Who will ever marry you now?"

Pisco rushed out of the kitchen, dragging the paddle behind him. He ran to the riverbank in one bound, crossing the strip of sand from the doorstep to his father's banca at the water's edge.

Whether or not his stepmother had seen what had happened, Pisco couldn't say; but he thought—and Lupo's words kept ringing in his ears—of how Manding Paula's life would be from now on, now at last as Lupo's wife. Surely, Lupo must marry her. But he had dashed out of the kitchen and following the path through the *chichirika* and *sentimiento*, he had crossed to the empty lot where the house he had been making for Paula stood. He would not stop there, Pisco feared. Lupo would run until he had reached the swamp and disappeared behind the *piyapi* trees.

Tatay came hurrying into the kitchen. "What happened?" he demanded, seeing Manding Paula crying. She was standing behind the Y-shaped stand which held the small earthen jar containing drinking water, and she was shaking convulsively. It was as if above the sobs Pisco could hear her saying, "Now, I'm not pure any more!" He thought her trouble was like that of the water-gatherer of the folktale who had broken her jar.

"Now, Paula!" Tatay cried angrily. "Can't you ever stop!" He called to Tia Unday: "Segunda, make her stop! Don't you be making a scandal of it, for the whole barrio to talk about!"

Pisco knew then that his father had understood. "You go down over there," Tatay told him, pointing to the edge of the swamp. "See which trail he's taken."

"Let him alone in the swamp, where he belongs—that beast!" said Tia Unday, coming down from the sulambi, her hair flying about.

Pisco hesitated. He could not see any good in his following Lupo now into the swamp. He stood in the yard, gaping at the sunshine, feeling this might be the first time he would disobey his father.

It was about this time that fish from the corral was ready, and either the neighbors had come for that or they had heard the cries; but anyway they were gathering now in the kitchen.

"What is this I hear mention of my brother's name?" Tia Talia demanded. She had come running from across the chichirika patch, carrying her four-month-old baby astride her hip. Flor and her sister Little Ana had come, too, the latter clinging to the edge of their mother's camisa.

"A beast is a beast, whatever food you feed it with," Tia Unday said.

"Be reasonable, Manang Unday," Tia Talia begged. "Tell us first what this is that my brother's done."

A confusion of voices, of answers and questions, and everyone eager to speak—all but Tatay. To Pisco he had whispered, "Better go fetch the catch yourself," and had sat at the doorstep and remained silent there.

And then started the talk about sending someone to Palaon, to fetch the Justice of the Peace, *Juez* Tupas. Two men from Bakawan had come to see Aguacil the peddler, and Tatay broke his silence finally and asked could these two try and get Lupo. Perhaps, he would stay in the swamps, Aguacil said, repeating what he had claimed a few minutes before: "If only I had been home, nothing would have happened." As if, Pisco thought, Lupo might have paid any attention to the peddler. But, anyway, Aguacil sat near the whetstone and worked on a coconut shell, one of those "over which the moon had passed" and had neither meat nor water. He had found it in the grove two days before. He worked Tatay's bolo up and round the shell, to remove every shred of coir and make it clean and shiny. To Tia Talia, who sat by watching, perhaps wondering why Aguacil could be so much with them and yet so apart, he explained he intended to cut through the hard shell some kind of a slit afterwards; it would serve so well as a container for his pesetas and centavos. Tia Talia stared at him, and Aguacil did not seem to mind; he worked on the coconut shell, engrossed like a child.

Pisco had picked up his paddle reluctantly. Flor made way for him as he left the crowd in the kitchen. Little Ana sidled to the wall and gave him a sidelong glance—rather a startling look, because the girl had a white spot in one eye. It was said to be growing, that already it was the size of a grain of rice, that it might grow so large she would become blind. Yet Little Ana did look at him so, Pisco decided, if only perhaps to say that this would be the first time he would get the catch in the corral himself.

He hurried to the bunuan, each stroke of his paddle bringing to his ears, it seemed, the sound of Lupo's feet in the muddy trail, past the growths of nipa and corkwood. He would be nearing Bakawan now, Pisco calculated. Half an hour more, and Lupo would be at Tio Longinos' clearing, or perhaps he would be up on some buri palm and drinking. It wouldn't take long to get him properly drunk and perhaps barely able to get down the bamboo ladder; and most likely he would be shouting to the buri trees: "I've ruined her already! Who will ever marry her now?"

Pisco asked himself did he really want to see that Lupo and his Manding Paula become man and wife. And his mind kept asking, too, did he pity his Manding Paula now? He was seven when his father married Tia Unday, Manding Paula's mother. She had often beat him up with whole lengths of coconut midrib, if not with the entire swishing broom itself. It had been that way all through that year his father was with the Constabulary and had left Pisco with Unday in Sinukuan. Later, when Tatay got his discharge, the year after his marriage, the family moved from Sinukuan to Malig, traveling across the province by way of the mountain trails. The journey had taken seven days, and Manding Paula, already fifteen then, rode the skinny cow that his father had bought for the journey. Then, pasturing the cow in Malig had been a problem afterward, for there was very little grass on the side of the river where the barrio was. The cow had to be taken across the river to the grass patches in another coconut grove; and every time Pisco forgot to swim the cow over, or whenever he allowed the cow to remain on the other bank for the night, he was sure to receive from either Tia Unday or Manding Paula a tweak in the ear. A good thing Tatay sold the cow to buy some bamboo from Palaon and hire some labor with; somehow this ended, Pisco realized, the "burning" of his ears. At the same time, of course, he had become five—then seven, and then eight. When they got Lupo to help with the fish trap, somehow both Manding Paula and Tia Unday become much kinder people. Pisco's thoughts as he paddled to the bunuan reproduced pictures of his own mother, whom he had heard Tatay call Berta and who had died—Tatay said—when he, Pisco, was only two. A long line of aunts and uncles—in such places as Nawan, Alag and Buhanginan, where Tatay said he spent his youth—moved before Pisco's mind as he paddled and tied the boat fast to a hangaray pole and grabbed his basket and his handnet, and then he climbed up the platform. He was in the water in no more than a minute, and was quietly manipulating the handnet exactly as he had seen Lupo do it before.

Oh, but Lupo was back! His running to the swamp, directly after what happened, had been quite as if only in answer to a call of nature.

On returning from the fish corral, Pisco saw him working on the half-finished house, busy setting up a portion of one wall. Actually, he could not do much for he did not have a bolo with him. They saw him moving about, setting up this hangaray pole and that, putting this one to that side and this other pole to the other side. Sorting them? If he could go back to Tia Talia's house and pick up his bolo, or if someone could bring him a bolo—

But Tia Talia reprimanded Pisco for the thought. "Don't you see a bolo in his hands could be dangerous?"

Still with the coconut shell in his hand, Aguacil nodded: "Yes, true enough," he muttered, although no one had sought his opinion.

Pisco went up to Tatay and whispered. "Lupo's hungry. I'll bring him some food."

Tatay did not answer at once but walked out to the yard, from where they might see Lupo better.

But, by then, Lupo was gone.

"Isn't he that one?" Pisco pointed to a banca that was quietly disappearing behind the palm-covered bend of the river.

"He'll return," Tatay said calmly.

The two men who had been sent to Bakawan returned about noon. Tio Longinos had not seen his son's shadow, and from this fact it would seem that Lupo had gone up some buri tree and drunk tuba and perhaps taken a nap up there for good measure.

All afternoon, Pisco lingered about the beach restlessly. About sundown he saw a parao sailing east from somewhere down Lumawig Point, five miles south of the mouth of the Malig River. Perhaps it had come from Palaon; its sails of buri leaves were dark-grey in the sunset glow. Pisco wondered whether Lupo had meant what he said about going to Pinagsabangan, or somewhere faraway. A spell of loneliness seized him, and he hurried back to the hut to help his Manding Paula pound rice and feed the pig in the pen behind the kitchen.

Impatient for its food, the pig squealed and Pisco thought of Juez Tupaz. Perhaps he could come in a day or so; and if there was going to be a wedding, surely Tia Unday's pig would have to go. No doubt it was for such a day that Tia Unday had raised and fattened the pig, and he remembered now that his stepmother had been so strict about feeding the animal regularly and properly.

Now, who of them at home had had a good night's sleep, Pisco could not say; but he recalled Tatay reminding him about fetching the catch early the following morning and asking where the handnet was. They could not find it anywhere round the house, and Pisco decided he must have left it in the bunuan.

It was not yet light when he set out; he paddled hurriedly. The soft wheezy sound of the crabs crawling about the bamboowork greeted him as he tried the banca to a hangaray pole. But before he could climb up the bunuan there was the handnet, heavy and full, over the side.

"Is that you, *Manong* Lupo?" he asked, breathlessly.

"Go back, quick!" the other said from behind the bamboowork. "Don't bother me."

Pisco emptied the contents of the handnet into his banca and before he knew it Lupo had let the boat loose. "Shall I bring you some food?" he called weakly.

"No, only the bolo," Lupo replied.

"I'll try," Pisco heard himself saying faintly.

But Tia Unday, following a tack all her own, had kept Tatay's bolo, his small fan-knife and axe—everything sharp about the house, all because

Manding Paula kept to herself in the sulambi all this time, afraid that people would see the mark—if any there was—Lupo's lips had left on her cheeks; and it was possible, Pisco thought, that since Manding Paula's shame was great—was greater, in fact, than Lupo's—because it was she, the bride-to-be, who, in effect, was being spurned; because even if she did not love him, she had been pledged to him and now she had been shamed and abandoned; and the hut and the fish corral and the river being the things Lupo now preferred; and because of all this, perhaps Tia Unday feared that Manding Paula might do something to herself.

No word came from Palaon about Juez Tupaz. It was as if in his wisdom the Justice of the Peace had decided that Malig ought to settle its troubles first before even looking toward Palaon for help. The day passed tensely; once more Pisco saw a banca slip past the palm-covered river bend; and although in the brightness of the sun it was not possible to say exactly that that was Lupo's head, that that shoulder was Lupo's shoulder, that that way of lifting the paddle was Lupo's way, Pisco felt sure about him. The buri palm would nourish him, and the river would keep him. He had shamed his betrothed because she had broken her word; and, maybe, in the end the river would counsel him, would tell him what next to do.

The second day was over, and the sound of rice-pounding was over too. Even the occasional barking of dogs was gone. Malig was slipping quietly into evening now. The streets darkened early; in the coconut grove the chichirika and sentimiento bushes looked shapeless.

It was a cool windless night. For November, it was fraught with silence—like a night in Maytime, with everyone in the barrio gone to the clearings up the river for the planting season. Pisco remembered the evening of the soldiers with the guitar, and it seemed he could hear guitar music again. If there was a place whence it might come, this was the swamp: the trees were illumined by fireflies.

Down the bend of the river came a banca, the two persons in it shouting, quarreling perhaps even as they paddled; and one listened to the voices and they were voices that echoed and re-echoed in the mangrove trees. A few more strokes of their paddles, however, and the two became Tia Pulin and Tio Longinos, the woman at the prow and now shouting at the mangrove trees that no wind stirred or rustled:

"Now, what else could they want? The house is being built, soon it will be completed. Our Lupo is no turtle!" And then Longinos, taking a different view:

"But that is the way people are. First one thing, then another! There's the house, yes. Then the twenty-five cavanes. Remember the twenty-five cavanes? Now, they want no wedding set, and then suddenly this sending for the Juez . . ."

And from Tia Pulin: "What does that make of us?"

Tio Longinos: "People to be pulled this way and that!"

Tia Pulin: "As if, then, without thinking heads of our own."

"Be quiet now. Keep your thoughts!" It was Tio Longinos, trying to speak softer, but altogether without control of his voice. "Maybe, the Juez is down there, right now!"

They were coming to a turn and the prow hit sand. It was Tia Pulin who got up first, staggering knee-deep in the water.

"Careful, Longinos," she told him. "After this, never darken their doorstep again!"

The other said, pulling up the banca: "Tonight, what must be must be. But afterwards—"

"This can mean that tomorrow you can bring down the rice. Twenty-five cavanes, no less—" Tia Pulin's voice was strident.

"But what must be must be," Tio Longinos repeated.

Fireflies glowed over their heads as they walked from the river, following the edge of the swamp—taking care, Pisco saw, not to get anywhere near twenty yards of the Olarte hut. And then to Tia Talia's hut they went, stopping for a while in the yard where Lupo's unfinished house stood. From there, across the sentimiento, the old couple made their way to their daughter's hut. If earlier they had uttered their thoughts aloud, with the mangrove and the river listening, they now observed silence. Then, entering Tia Talia's kitchen, they moved about like shadows.

Pisco kept what he had heard and what he knew to himself. It was his secret. Although he wanted very much to tell his father about the arrival of the old couple, he feared that he might be led to reveal other things instead. The idea of Lupo roaming the swamps obsessed him. He imagined that he saw him sitting under a piyapi tree by the river bank and beckoning to him, asking:

"Well, now, can you look after the fish corral all by yourself?"

"Why, then, you are really going away?"

"Truly, I am."

"Is it true, then, about your wish to go to Pinagsabangan, to San Roque?"

"Well, yes. Since you are there and big enough to be of help."

"*Ay*, think of the difficulty in the flood—should there be one."

"That'll be next rainy season, and you'll be a much bigger fellow then!"

The words kept coming, sometimes in whispers, sometimes loud enough for anyone to hear. He imagined himself seeing Lupo go, in the dark, following the trail whence Pedro Aguacil the peddler had come. This was the trail that began at the other side of the river and took you to Dias, from where you could go to Pinagsabangan by parao—or to wherever you wished. And Pisco followed Lupo to the wide world where you lived with such wisdom in your head as Tatay had—and perhaps it was what Lupo had wanted to learn—about the river and fish corrals, or such as Tio Longinos had about houses and the earth.

He had two dreams that night. In the first one, a stranger came down from over Tia Talia's place across the backyard and was holding something in his hand for Pisco to see. It was a bundle and Pisco unwrapped it. A pair of long trousers and a shirt. "Here, something for you!" the stranger had said; and Pisco's leg had jerked in his sleep, and he awoke at precisely the moment his hands felt the weight of the cloth. He slept on, though, and the second dream came. It was full of vague figures and harsh voices and fireflies throwing their lamps into the sentimiento and chichirika. Pisco got up and opened a window wide and looked out. But he saw nothing out there except the night and the river.

To his left among the piyapi trees, the fireflies were burning their lamps as mindlessly as before in the cool and windless air. Would Lupo spend the night in his unfinished house? Later, staggering under the weight of a half-filled bamboo container for tuba that he might have brought down from Bakawan, how he could very well come and ask Manding Paula's forgiveness. If he came, thus, at this hour, no one would see him. No one would hear the stir of the chichirika leaves that brushed his legs dryly—if he but walked home at that hour. He might walk, thus, down the street and the path under the coconut palms and under the arches that their fronds, silent in the listless darkness, formed; and then on toward the beach he might go, to linger there until dawn, for afterward he might see the fish trap which had become so much the heart, as the river was the body, of all these days and nights.

Directly after a streak of white bared the black wall of the sky, as though a door had been opened there to let a visitor in, Pisco left the hut for the river. The air was sodden with the smell of mangrove leaves and tanbark in the brackish water of last night's tide. There was also a burnt smell somewhere, as though all of last night's fireflies had died; and Pisco, lingering at the river for a moment, breathing in these smells, looked around for the banca. At the water's edge, the banca waited. He let the water out with his paddle blade, and he pushed the banca into the stream and headed for the fish corral.

On the platform there lay an empty bamboo container, hardly two joints long. Pisco remembered that it was from here where Lupo had last lowered the handnet to him. The dawn light came fuller now, rippling the water as though it were the breeze.

In the half-light, Pisco saw the body. Broad and bare, Lupo's back had risen from the heart of the trap, clear above the water. The water now rocked him gently.

Pisco pressed his lips and willed himself not to cry.

1953

A Warm Hand

HOLDING ON TO the rigging, Elay leaned over. The dinghy was being readied. The wind tore her hair into wiry strands that fell across her face, heightening her awareness of the dipping and rising of the deck. But for the bite of the *noroeste*, she would have begun to feel faint and empty in her belly. Now she clutched at the rigging with more courage.

At last the dinghy shoved away, with its first load of passengers— seven boys from Bongabon, Mindoro, on their way to Manila to study. The deck seemed less hostile than before, for the boys had made a boisterous group then; now that they were gone, her mistress Ana could leave the crowded deckhouse for once.

"Oh, Elay! My powder puff!"

It was Ana, indeed. Elay was familiar with that excitement which her mistress wore about her person like a silk kerchief—now on her head to keep her hair in place, now a scarf round her neck. How eager Ana had been to go ashore when the old skipper of the *batel* said that the *Ligaya* was too small a boat to brave the coming storm. She must return to the deckhouse, Elay thought, if she must fetch her mistress' handbag.

With both hands upon the edge of the deckhouse roof, then holding on to the wooden water barrel to the left of the main mast, she staggered back to the deckhouse entrance. As she bent her head low lest with the lurching of the boat her brow should hit the door, she saw her mistress on all fours clambering out of the deckhouse. She let her have the right of way, entering only after Ana was safe upon the open deck.

Elay found the handbag—she was certain that the powder puff would be there—though not without difficulty, inside the canvas satchel that she meant to take ashore. She came dragging the heavy satchel, and in a flurry Ana dug into it for the bag. The deck continued to sway, yet presently Ana was powdering her face; and this done, she applied lipstick to that full round mouth of hers.

The wind began to press Elay's blouse against her breasts while she waited on her mistress patiently. She laced Ana's shoes and also bestirred herself to see that Ana's earrings were not askew. For Ana must appear every inch the dressmaker that she was. Let everyone know that she was traveling to Manila—not just to the provincial capital; and, of course, there was the old spinster aunt, too, for company—to set up a shop in the big city. It occurred to Elay that, judging from the care her mistress was taking to look well, it might well be that they were not on board a one-masted Tingloy batel with a cargo of lumber, copra, pigs, and chickens, but were still at home in the dress shop that they were leaving behind in the lumber town of Sumagui.

"How miserable I'd be without you, Elay," Ana giggled, as though somewhere she was meeting a secret lover who for certain would hold her in his arms in one wild passionate caress.

And thinking so of her mistress made Elay more proud of her. She did not mind the dark world into which they were going. Five miles to the south was Pinamalayan town; its lights blinked faintly at her. Then along the rim of the Bay, dense groves of coconuts and underbrush stood, occasional fires marking where the few sharecroppers of the district lived. The batel had anchored at the northernmost end of the cove and apparently five hundred yards from the boat was a palm-leaf-covered hut the old skipper of the *Ligaya* had spoken about.

"Don't you see it? That's Obregano's hut." And Obregano, the old skipper explained, was a fisherman. The men who sailed up and down the eastern coast of Mindoro knew him well. There was not a seaman who lived in these parts who had not gone to Obregano for food or shelter and to this anchorage behind the northern tip of Pinamalayan Bay for the protection it offered sailing vessels against the unpredictable noroeste.

The old skipper had explained all this to Ana, and Elay had listened, little knowing that in a short while it would all be there before her. Now in the dark she saw the fisherman's hut readily. A broad shoulder of a hill rose beyond, and farther yet the black sky looked like a silent wall.

Other women joined them on the deck to see the view for themselves. A discussion started; some members of the party did not think it would be proper for them to spend the night in Obregano's hut. Besides the students, there were four middle-aged merchants on this voyage; since Bongabon they had plagued the women with their coarse talk and their yet coarser laughter. Although the deckhouse was the unchallenged domain of the women, the four middle-aged merchants had often slipped in, and once had exchanged lewd jokes among themselves to the embarrassment of their audience. Small wonder, Elay thought, that the prospect of spending the night in a small fisherman's hut with these men for company did not appear attractive to the other women passengers. Her mistress Ana had made up her mind, however. She had a sense of independence that Elay admired.

Already the old aunt had joined them on deck; and Elay said to herself, "Of course, it's for this old auntie's sake, too. She has been terribly seasick."

In the dark she saw the dinghy and silently watched it being sculled back to the batel. It drew nearer and nearer, a dark mass moving eagerly, the bow pointing in her direction. Elay heard Ana's little shrill cries of excitement. Soon two members of the crew were vying for the honor of helping her mistress safely into the dinghy.

Oh, that Ana should allow herself to be thus honored, with the seamen taking such pleasure from it all, and the old aunt, watching, pouting her lips in disapproval! "What shall I do?" Elay asked herself, anticipating that soon she herself would be the object of this chivalrous byplay. And what could the old aunt be saying now to herself? "Ah, women these days are no longer decorous. In no time they will make a virtue of being unchaste."

Elay pouted, too. And then it was her turn. She must get into that dinghy, and it so pitched and rocked. If only she could manage to have no one help her at all. But she'd fall into the water. Santa Maria, I'm safe . . . .

They were off. The waves broke against the sides of the dinghy, threatening to capsize it, and continually the black depths glared at her. Her hands trembling, Elay clung tenaciously to the gunwale. Spray bathed her cheeks. A boy began to bail, for after clearing each wave the dinghy took in more water. So earnest was the boy at his chore that Elay thought the boat had sprung a leak and would sink any moment.

The sailors, one at the prow and the other busy with the oar at the stern, engaged themselves in senseless banter. Were they trying to make light of the danger? She said her prayers as the boat swung from side to side, to a rhythm set by the sailor with the oar.

Fortunately, panic did not seize her. It was the old aunt who cried "Susmariosep!" For with each crash of waves, the dinghy lurched precipitously. "God spare us all!" the old aunt prayed frantically.

And Ana was laughing. "Auntie! Why, Auntie, it's nothing! It's nothing at all!" For, really, they were safe. The dinghy had struck sand.

Elay's dread of the water suddenly vanished and she said to herself: "Ah, the old aunt is only making things more difficult for herself." Why, she wouldn't let the sailor with the oar lift her clear of the dinghy and carry her to the beach!

"Age before beauty," the sailor was saying to his companion. The other fellow, not to be outdone, had jumped waist-deep into the water, saying: "No, beauty above all!" Then there was Ana stepping straight, as it were, into the sailor's arms.

"Where are you?" the old aunt was calling from the shore. "Are you safe? Are you all right?"

Elay wanted to say that insofar as she was concerned she was safe, she was all right. But she couldn't speak for her mistress, of course! But the same seaman who had lifted the old aunt and carried her to the shore in his arms had returned. Now he stood before Elay and caught her two legs and let them rest on his forearm and then held her body up, with the other arm. Now she was clear of the dinghy, and she had to hold on to his neck. Then the sailor made three quick steps toward dry sand and then let her slide easily off his arms, and she said: "I am all right. Thank you."

Instead of saying something to her, the sailor hurried away, joining the group of students that had gathered up the rise of sand. Ana's cheerful laughter rang in their midst. Then a youth's voice, clear in the wind: "Let's hurry to the fisherman's hut!"

A drizzle began to fall. Elay took a few tentative steps toward the palm-leaf hut, but her knees were unsteady. The world seemed to turn and turn, and the glowing light at the fisherman's door swung as from a boat's mast. Elay hurried as best as she could after Ana and her old aunt, both of whom had already reached the hut. It was only on hearing her name that that weak, unsteady feeling in her knees disappeared.

"Elay—" It was her mistress, of course. Ana was standing outside the door, waiting. "My lipstick, Elay!"

An old man stood at the door at the hut. "I am Obregano, at your service," he said in welcome. "This is my home."

He spoke in a sing-song that rather matched his wizened face. Pointing at a little woman pottering about the stovebox at one end of the one-room hut, he said: "And she? Well, the guardian of my home—in other words, my wife!"

The woman got up and welcomed them, beaming a big smile. "Feel at home. Make yourselves comfortable—everyone."

She helped Elay with the canvas bag, choosing a special corner for it. "It will rain harder yet tonight, but here your bag will be safe," the woman said.

The storm had come. The thatched wall shook, producing a weird skittering sound at each gust of wind. The sough of the palms in back of the hut—which was hardly the size of the deckhouse of the batel, and had the bare sand for floor—sounded like the moan of a lost child. A palm leaf that served to cover an entrance to the left of the stovebox began to dance a mad, rhythmless dance. The fire in the stove leaped intermittently, rising beyond the lid of the kettle that Obregano the old fisherman had placed there.

And yet the hut was homelike. It was warm and clean. There was a cheerful look all over the place. Elay caught the old fisherman's smile as his wife cleared the floor of nets and coil after coil of hempen rope so that their guests could have more room. She sensed an affinity with her present surroundings, with the smell of the fish nets, with the dancing fire in the stovebox. It was as though she had lived in this hut before. She remembered what Obregano's wife had said to her. The old woman's words were by far the kindest she had heard in a long time.

The students from Bongabon had appropriated a corner for themselves and began to discuss supper. It appeared that a prankster had relieved one of the chicken coops of a fat pullet and a boy asked the fisherman for permission to prepare a stew.

"I've some ginger tea in the kettle," Obregano said. "Something worth drinking in weather like this." He asked his wife for an old enameled tin cup for their guests to drink from.

As the cup was being passed around, Obregano's wife expressed profuse apologies for her not preparing supper. "We have no food," she said with uncommon frankness. "We have sons, you know, two of them, both working in town. But they come home only on week-ends. It is only then that we have rice."

Elay understood that in lieu of wages, the two Obregano boys received rice. Last week-end the boys had failed to return home, however. This fact brought a sad note to Elay's new world of warm fire and familiar smells. She got out some food which they had brought along from the boat—*adobo* and bread that the old aunt had put in a tin container and tucked into the canvas satchel—and offered her mistress these, going through the motions so absent-mindedly that Ana chided her.

"Do offer the old man and his wife some of that, too."

Obregano shook his head. He explained that he would not think of partaking of the food—so hungry his guests must be. They needed all the food themselves, to say nothing about that which his house should offer but which in his naked poverty he could not provide. But at least they would be safe here for the night, Obregano assured them. "The wind is rising, and the rain too . . . . Listen . . . ." He pointed at the roof, which seemed to sag.

The drone of the rain set Elay's spirits aright. She began to imagine how sad and worried over her sons the old fisherman's wife must be, and how lonely—but oh how lovely!—it would be to live in this God-forsaken spot. She watched the students devour their supper, and she smiled thanks, sharing their thoughtfulness, when they offered most generously some chicken to Ana and, in sheer politeness, to the old spinster aunt also.

Yet more people from the batel arrived, and the four merchants burst into the hut discussing some problem in Bongabon municipal politics. It was as though the foul weather suited their purposes, and Elay listened with genuine interest, with compassion, even, for the small-town politicians who were being reviled and cursed.

It was Obregano who suggested that they all retire. There was hardly room for everyone, and in bringing out a roughly woven palm-leaf mat for Ana and her companions to use, Obregano picked his way in order not to step on a sprawling leg or an outstretched arm. The offer of the mat touched Elay's heart, so much so that pondering the goodness of the old fisherman and his wife took her mind away from the riddles which the students at this time were exchanging among themselves. They were funny riddles and there was much laughter. Once she caught them throwing glances in Ana's direction.

Even the sailors who were with them on the dinghy had returned to the hut to stay and were laughing heartily at their own stories. Elay watched Obregano produce a bottle of kerosene for the lantern, and then hang the lantern with a string from the center beam of the hut. She felt a new dreamlike joy. Watching the old fisherman's wife extinguish the fire in the stove made Elay's heart throb.

Would the wind and the rain worsen? The walls of the hut shook—like a man in the throes of malarial chills. The sea kept up a wild roar, and the waves, it seemed, continually clawed at the land with strong, greedy fingers.

She wondered whether Obregano and his wife would ever sleep. The couple would be thinking: "Are our guests comfortable enough as they are?" As for herself, Elay resolved, she would stay awake. From the corner where the students slept she could hear the whine of a chronic asthma sufferer. One of the merchants snorted periodically, like a horse being annoyed by a fly. A young boy, apparently dreaming, called out in a strange, frightened voice: "No, no! I can't do that! I wouldn't do that!"

She saw Obregano get up and pick his way again among the sleeping bodies to where the lantern hung. The flame was sputtering. Elay watched him adjust the wick of the lantern and give the oil container a gentle shake. Then the figure of the old fisherman began to blur and she could hardly keep her eyes open. A soothing tiredness possessed her. As she yielded easily to sleep, with Ana to her left and the old spinster aunt at the far edge of the mat to her right, the floor seemed to sink and the walls of the hut to vanish, as though the world were one vast dark valley.

When later she awoke she was trembling with fright. She had only a faint notion that she had screamed. What blur there had been in her consciousness before falling asleep was as nothing compared with that which followed her waking, although she was aware of much to-do and the lantern light was gone.

"Who was it?" It was reassuring to her Obregano's voice.

"The lantern, please!" That was Ana, her voice shrill and wiry.

Elay heard as if in reply the crash of the sea rising in a crescendo. The blur lifted a little: "Had I fallen asleep after all? Then it must be past midnight now." Time and place became realities again; and she saw Obregano, with a lighted matchstick in his hand. He was standing in the middle of the hut.

"What happened?"

Elay thought that it was she whom Obregano was speaking to. She was on the point of answering, although she had no idea of what to say, when Ana, sitting upon the mat beside her, blurted out: "Someone was here. Please hold up the light."

"Someone was here," Elay repeated to herself and hid her face behind Ana's shoulder. She must not let the four merchants, nor the students either, stare at her so. Caught by the lantern light, the men hardly seven steps away had turned their gazes upon her in various attitudes of amazement.

Everyone seemed eager to say something all at once. One of the students spoke in a quavering voice, declaring that he had not moved where he lay. Another said he had been so sound asleep—"Didn't you hear me snoring?" he asked a companion, slapping him on the back—he had not even heard the shout. One of the merchants hemmed and suggested that perhaps cool minds should look into the case, carefully and without preconceived ideas. To begin with, one must know exactly what happened. He looked in Ana's direction and said: "Now please tell us."

Elay clutched her mistress' arm. Before Ana could speak, Obregano's wife said: "This thing ought not to have happened. If only our two sons were home, they'd avenge the honor of our house." She spoke with a rare eloquence for an angry woman. "No one would then dare think of so base an act. Now, our good guests," she added, addressing her husband, bitterly, "why, they know you to be an aged, simple-hearted fisherman— nothing more. The good name of your home, of our family, is no concern of theirs."

"Evil was coming, I knew it!" said the old spinster aunt; and piping out like a bird: "Let us return to the boat! Don't be so bitter, old one," she told Obregano's wife. "We are going back to the boat."

"It was like this," Ana said, not minding her aunt. Elay lowered her head more, lest she should see those man-faces before her, loosely trapped now by the lantern's glow. Indeed, she closed her eyes, as though she were a little child afraid of the dark.

"It was like this," her mistress began again, "I was sleeping, and then my maid, Elay—" she put an arm around Elay's shoulder—"she uttered that wild scream. I am surprised you did not hear it."

In a matter-of-fact tone, one of the merchants countered: "Suppose it was a nightmare?"

But Ana did not listen to him. "Then my maid," she continued, "this girl here—she's hardly twenty, mind you, and an innocent and illiterate girl, if you must all know . . . . She turned around, trembling, and clung to me . . . ."

"Couldn't she possibly have shouted in her sleep," the merchant insisted.

Obregano had held his peace all this time, but now he spoke: "Let us hear what the girl says."

And so kind were those words! How fatherly of him to have spoken so, in such a gentle and understanding way! Elay's heart went to him. She felt she could almost run to him and, crying over his shoulders, tell him what no one, not even Ana herself, would ever know.

She turned her head a little to one side and saw that now they were all looking at her. She hugged her mistress tighter, in a childlike embrace, hiding her face as best she could.

"Tell them," Ana said, drawing herself away. "Now, go on—speak!"

But Elay would not leave her side. She clung to her, and began to cry softly.

"Nonsense!" the old aunt chided her.

"Well, she must have had a nightmare, that's all," the merchant said, chuckling. "I'm sure of it!"

At this remark Elay cried even more. "I felt a warm hand caressing my—my—my cheeks," she said, sobbing. "A warm hand, I swear," she said again, remembering how it had reached out for her in the dark, searchingly, burning with a need to find some precious treasure which, she was certain of it now, she alone possessed. For how could it be that they should force her to tell them? "Someone"—the word was like a lamp in her heart—"someone wanted me," she said to herself.

She felt Ana's hand stroking her back ungently and then heard her saying, "I brought this on." Then nervously fumbling about the mat: "This is all my fault . . . . My compact, please . . . ."

But Elay was inconsolable. She was sorry she could be of no help to her mistress now. She hung her head, unable to stop her tears from cleansing those cheeks that a warm hand had loved.

1950

The Morning Star

THE SAILOR WENT back to the outriggered boat and returned with a lantern. It lighted up the footpath before him and his flat unshod feet. He walked in a slow, shuffling manner, the lantern in his hand swinging in rhythm.

"Can't you walk faster?" the old man shouted from the coconut grove.

Instead of saying something in reply, the sailor shuffled on, neither hastening nor slowing his gait.

"You're a turtle, that's what," said the old man.

As the sailor approached, the lantern light caught the entrance of the makeshift shelter. Then the oval of light completely engulfed the shelter, which was shaped like a pup tent and built of coconut leaves woven into loose shingles. A matting of coconut leaves was spread on the ground; and walking across it, the old man hung the lantern from a ridgepole at the far end. A woman sat in one corner, her back half-turned to the entrance.

"Now if you aren't stupid. Quite like a turtle, really," the old man said to the sailor.

"Ha?" the other said, with a twang.

The old man had expected that; there was something wrong with the sailor's tongue. "And how about the jute sacks and the blankets?" the old man said. "Didn't I tell you to get them?"

"Ha?" came the sailor's reply.

"Stop it!" said the old man, angrily. "If you weren't born that way, I'd give you a thrashing." He waved him away. "Be off! And while you are at it, bring over some water. There's no saying whether we'll find drinking water hereabouts. Would you care for supper, Marta?"

"No, thank you," said the woman in the hut.

"It'll be best to get some food ready, though," said the old man. "We've salmon in the boat."

The sailor had shuffled away, the coconut fronds on the ground rustling softly as he stepped on them.

"Bring over a tin of salmon. And also the pot of rice we have on the stovebox," the old man called after the sailor.

From somewhere a bird uttered a shrill cry; and the old man spoke to the woman again. "If you'll step out of there just a while, Marta . . . ."

"I am quite comfortable here, uncle," she said.

"But you should be walking about, instead of sitting down like that."

"It seems better here," said the woman. But later she said: "All right."

"I'll build a fire," the old man said.

The bird's call came again, in a note of wild urgency. "That's the witch bird. I can tell for certain," the woman said. "They take newborn children away."

"No, it's not the witch bird," the old man said.

He gathered some dry leaves and twigs and in a minute had a fire blazing.

"Still, it's a fine time for having a baby, uncle. Isn't it?"

"It's God's will," the old man said. Marta was laughing at herself. "We'll do the best we can. Walk about, stretch your legs; hold on to a coconut trunk over there, if it hurts you so."

"I'm quite all right, uncle," said Marta.

The fire crackled, and the old man added more leaves and twigs. The blaze illumined the large boles of the coconut palms.

The clear sky peered through the fronds of the palms, but there were no stars. The night had a taut, timorous silence, disturbed only by the crackling of the fire.

The woman walked up and down, not venturing beyond the space lighted up by the fire. She was a squat, well-built woman. Her arms and legs were full-muscled, like those of a man. If she had cut her hair and worn trousers instead of a skirt, she would have passed for a man. Her distended belly and large breasts would not have made any difference.

The old man watched her with unending curiosity. Like him, she wore a field jacket, the sleeves rolled up, being too long. Her skirt was of a thick olive-drab material, made from fatigues that some American soldier had discarded.

"Is that his name printed on there?" the old man asked.

In the firelight the letters "Theodore C. Howard" could be read in white stencils on the back of the drab green jacket.

"Oh, no, uncle," said Marta. "This isn't his. He gave me three woolen blankets, though."

"That's fair," said the old man.

"What do you mean, uncle? Please don't tease me," said Marta.

"Well, others do get more than that. For their labor, I mean. You worked as a laundry woman?"

"Yes, uncle," Marta replied. "But afterwards we lived together. Three weeks. We had a hut near Upper Mangyan. You could see the whole camp of the army from there." With her hands, she held on to her belt, a rattan string, as she spoke. "It pains so, at times. Well, I washed clothes for a living, uncle. That's what I went there for."

"Did you earn any money?"

"No, uncle. I'm never for making money. He said one day, 'Here are twenty pesos,' " she said with a laugh. "He had a way of talking to me and never saying my name, as though I had no name. The others, the ones I only washed clothes for, had a nickname for me. 'Sweet Plum,' I remember. That's how they call me. 'Sweet Plum.' What's a 'plum,' uncle? They say it's a fruit."

"I don't know," said the old man. "In our country, we have no such fruit."

"He would not call me 'Sweet Plum,' even. And, as I said, he wanted to give me the money. 'What for?' I said. And he said, 'For your mother.' But I have no mother, I told him so. 'Well, for your father and brothers and sisters.' But I have no such folk, I told him so. I said, 'Keep your money. I love you, so keep your money.' And he was angry, and he swore and then left the hut. I never saw him again, but he left me three woolen blankets."

The old man listened to the story with great interest, but now that it was over, he made no comment beyond getting up and thoughtfully tending the fire.

"No uncle. You're wrong to think I ever earned money," Marta said. She walked a few steps and returned to the fireside. "By the way, uncle, how much does it cost to go to San Paulino in your boat?"

"That's where you live?"

She nodded.

"For you, nothing. Not a centavo."

"I can give you one of my woolen blankets."

"The trip will cost you nothing."

"Of course, you'll say, 'What a foolish woman she is! To think that she does not know when her time comes!' But truly, uncle, the days are the same to me. The nights are the same. I can't count days and months. Maybe, uncle, I'll never grow old. Do you think I'll ever grow old?"

The old man did not know what to say. A soft chuckle, and that was all.

"And I am going home. Am I not foolish, uncle?"

To humor her, the old man said: "Yes, you are quite foolish. A good thing you found my boat, no?"

"I feel lucky, yes," Marta said. "I must leave, that was all. Maybe, it isn't my time yet. The long walk from Upper Mangyan, and then three days on the beach, before finding your boat . . . . Maybe, this is only the seventh month. How long is nine months, uncle?"

The old man wished he could give a good answer. "Nine months," he said finally.

"I understand. You old men know a lot. Now, don't laugh, uncle. I've been married before, and this man I married was an old man, too. May he rest in peace. Oh, it pains so! Here, right here!" She indicated the approximate location of the pain.

"Walking relieves it, so they say."

The leaves crackled softly on the ground as she trod upon them with her bare feet. She went back and forth, and talked on as if to amuse herself.

"Now, this man was a tailor. You see, I worked as a servant in a rich man's house. And one day, this tailor said, 'You don't have to work so hard like that, Marta. Come live with me.' Ah, you men are tricky. Aren't you, uncle?"

"Sometimes," the old man couldn't help saying. "Some men are, I must say," he agreed readily.

"This tailor, he saw how industrious I was—and, I dare say, I am. Because God made me so; with the build of an animal, how can one be lazy? There's no work you men can do that I can't do also. That's a woman for you! My tailor was pleased with me. I was a woman and a man all in one, and he was so happy he stopped becoming a tailor and took instead to visiting with neighbors, talking politics and things like that." She stopped and then as if suddenly remembering something: "But he left me no child. Oh, he fooled me so, uncle!"

"Well, you'll have one soon, I must say," said the old man.

"As I was saying, I lived with this old tailor. He was a widower and had been lonely, and now he was kind to me. But he died of consumption—he had it for a long time—the year the war started. I went back to the rich man's house where I had worked before. When the Americans came back, I said to this rich man, 'I am going away. Only for a short time, though. I hear they pay well at the camp of the army, if you can wash clothes and do things like that. When I have enough money, I'll come back.' That's what I said. Oh, oh! It hurts so!"

"It's time the sailor returned," said the old man. "Does it pain much?"

"Ah, but pain never bothers me, uncle. Didn't I tell you I am built like an animal? This tailor, he used to beat me. I didn't care. I can stand anything, you know. I chopped wood and pounded rice for him. I was quite sorry when he died. That's the truth, uncle."

She stopped and laughed, amused more than ever, perhaps, at the way she had been talking. The old man looked at her quizzically.

"And you'll bring this baby home to San Paulino?" he said.

"Why, of course, uncle. It'll be so tiny, so helpless—you know. Why do you ask?"

The old man hesitated, but in the end he decided to tell her: "There are places—in the city, for example—where they'll take care of babies like that . . . ."

"But can they take care of him better than I? That's impossible, uncle," the woman said, excitedly. "Oh, it hurts so!—I do like—oh!—to look after him myself . . . ."

The firelight caught her faint smile. She had a common-looking face, but her eyes were pretty and big and smiling.

She had stopped talking. The sailor appeared in their midst, saying, "Ha!"

"Warm the salmon in the fire," said the old man.

He took the jute sacks and the blanket into the shelter and prepared a bed. Outside, in the light of the fire, the sailor opened the salmon can with his bolo and began drinking the soup.

"Can't you wait for me?"

The old man crawled out of the hut, annoyed partly because the sailor had begun to eat and partly because Marta was groaning.

"Don't wail there like a sow," he told her gruffly.

Then he sat before the pot of rice that the sailor brought over.

"A sow doesn't wail so, uncle," said the woman innocently.

The old man said nothing in reply. He and the sailor ate hurriedly, making noises with their mouths.

"Ha!" said the sailor, in that helpless way of his, looking in Marta's direction.

"She doesn't care for food. She said so," the old man explained. And to Marta he said: "If it's too much to bear, you may go in. We'll keep some of the salmon for you. Afterwards you'll be so hungry."

Marta followed his advice, crawling into the hut. Her head struck that lantern that hung from the ridgepole, and for a while it swung about, the oval of light dancing on the ground.

"I'll be with you in a minute," said the old man. "Why you've to let me do this, I don't know." It seemed he had become a different person from the *uncle* Marta knew a while ago; he felt the change in himself.

"Uncle," the woman called from the shelter, "what's a man called when he does a midwife's business?"

The old man was washing his mouth with water from the container the sailor had brought from their outriggered boat. When he was through, he said: "You horrible creature! I'm sure of it! You've fooled me. You planned all this . . . . You're more clever than I thought . . . ."

There was silence in the shelter. From afar the night bird called again, clearly and hauntingly. The sailor, calling the old man's attention to the bird, said, "Ha, ha!" He pointed with his finger at the darkness, but the old man did not mind him.

The silence grew tense, although there were soft noises from the shelter, noises that the movement of feet and arms and body made upon the matting, as if a sow were indeed lying there to deliver a litter. The lantern glow fell full upon the woman's upraised knees. She had covered them with a blanket.

"Uncle!" she called frantically.

Before going in the old man looked up at the sky. There was a lone star at last, up in the heavens. He could see it through the palm fronds. He'd like to remember that. He wished he could see a moon, too, and that he knew for certain how high the tide was at the beach; for, later, he'd recall all this. But there were no other signs. There was only this star.

"I'm so frightened, uncle," Marta was saying, her voice hoarse and trembling. "And it hurts so! Uncle, it will be the death of me!"

"Stop this foolish talk," said the old man angrily. "Pray to God. He is kind," he said.

His hands and knees were shaking. He knelt beside Marta, ready to be of assistance.

"Oh—oh—oh! Uncle, I want to die, I want to die!" she cried, clutching his hand.

When the sailor heard the squall of the child, he said "Ha, ha," with joy. He wanted to see the child, but the old man told him to go away.

"Go!" the old man said, waving his arms.

The sailor returned to his sleeping place and lay as before. The night was warm and restful, and soon he was fast asleep.

The old man joined him under the coconut tree, their feet touching and pointing toward the smoldering fire. Through the palm fronds the old man could see the sky growing light, for soon it would be morning. The star peered at him as before, through the thick coconut palm leaves. It had watched over them all this time.

The old man turned, and using his arm for a pillow, tried to sleep. The sailor was snoring peacefully. The old man could see Marta in the shelter, her legs flat on the mat and the child in a bundle beside her.

The old man fell asleep thinking of the child, for it was a boy. A gust of wind woke him up, and when he opened his eyes, he did not realize at first where he was. He felt glad he had been of help to the woman, and he wondered if in any way he had been unkind to her. He wished he had not called her a sow and had been gentle with her. He sat up and saw the lantern in the shelter.

"Are you all right?" he called, for he heard the woman stir.

She did not answer but sat up, moving in a slow, deliberate way, her shadow covering the child like a blanket.

"It's the witch bird, uncle," she said in a tired, faraway voice. "Did you hear the witch bird? Now he is dead—uncle, he is dead!"

The old man lowered the lantern. It had a faint blue flame. The baby beside her was limp and grey like the blanket wrapped around it.

"You're a sow, that's what you are! God Almighty," he crossed himself, "may You have mercy on us!"

"Believe me, uncle . . . . It's the witch bird . . . ."

The sailor had wakened. He got up and sat hugging his knees and stared at the old man.

"You build a fire, turtle!" the old man shouted at him. "Don't you see it's so dark?"

"Ha!" the sailor said.

1950

The Blue Skull and the Dark Palms

AS SHE STOOD before her class, Miss Inocencio, the substitute teacher, caught a glimpse of him. The roan stallion neighed as though it had sighted a mare in the barrio street. The next moment thick chalk-white dust rose in the air, settling long after horse and rider had disappeared into the heart of the village.

She knew then that in an hour or so the school inspector would come for a visit. She stared at the clock atop the empty bookcase that stood against the thatched wall; it was four o'clock. Leaving her desk, she walked to the window. The afternoon sun reached out toward it, pouring into the room a warm gush of July sunshine.

Then Miss Inocencio did something strange: she looked furtively at the garden outside, that patch of shrubbery and grass where her pupils hoped to plant hibiscus and roses, spanish flags and sunflowers; where the old well stood, its depths long since unplumbed, its water unused. She regarded the abandoned garden as though someone stood there—a man, perhaps her lover—when of course there was no one to be seen; no one to share secrets with, unless this be the blocks of stone that rimmed the well and which now in her mind's ear seemed to say: "True, there's been a war. But we are ready   aren't we?—to start all over again . . . ."

Did the children hear the voice? They looked up at her from behind the desks, and she dropped the pencil in her hand. "You know your respective assignments?" she asked her wards, and several voices answered in a respectful chorus:

"Yes, Ma'am."

"And remember," she addressed the boys in particular as she bent to pick up her pencil, "we must work on the garden today."

This was received with eagerness, and she desisted from telling the class about the school inspector. Already the boys were leaving their seats with much stamping and scraping of feet, re-creating the excitement of last week when the old school garden had presented itself as their common concern. "But we shall bring over our hoes and shovels, Ma'am!"—"And we've seeds, Ma'am; several packages that an American soldier gave us."—"We shall fix the well, too. We shall need water for the flowers!"—"Mind, then, not to touch the water now," Miss Inocencio had said. "It's much too dirty to drink from—that well out there," she had warned them; and from the corner of her eye she had watched her favorite, Leoncio, thirteen, looking at her lips closely as he allowed this modest adjuration to sink into his soul.

Now it was the favored Leoncio who said the first "Good afternoon, sir," when with flared and quivering nostrils the school inspector, tall and erect, stood there at the door. He had come earlier than she had expected. The children said their greeting not too shyly; the visitor smiled in turn and complimented Miss Inocencio on her pupils' performance.

"Thank you, sir," she said, blushing. Leoncio, walking respectfully past the visitor, led the boys out to the porch. "It's their Gardening period, sir," Miss Inocencio explained. "Perhaps you'd like to step in, sir?"

As the visitor crossed the threshold, the sunlight from the window fell upon his cuffless trousers. "Are the textbooks coming, sir?" Miss Inocencio asked eagerly.

"In a week or so," the visitor replied, looking around the room.

"And the new blackboards, too?"

Miss Inocencio was given the assurance that both the books and the blackboards—in fact, all the supplies and equipment she had requisitioned—had been shipped from the provincial capital and were due in the barrio on the next mailboat. "You have done a good job here, Miss Inocencio," the visitor said.

"Thank you, Mr. Vidal," she said.

She walked to the porch with him. "If you wouldn't mind, sir," she said, leading the way, and closing the door behind her.

"For a newcomer in the service, you are doing well," said Mr. Vidal.

"Thank you, sir. You see—"

"I understand. There are things, of course, one just can't manage."

"That's just it, sir," said Miss Inocencio. "If I were a man—well, in an out of the way place like this, it's hard to be a woman, sir."

She felt she had to say it. If Mr. Vidal should find something wrong in the way she ran the school, he would not blame her too readily. As provincial school inspector, he could be strict with her.

"Aren't the barrio people cooperative enough?" Mr. Vidal asked.

"I can't complain about them, sir."

"You'll find things much easier later on—and perhaps for the same reason that you find them difficult now."

She was pleased with this remark. She felt she was making a fair if not indeed a good impression on the school inspector. He would give her an excellent efficiency rating, and perhaps—but, oh, how could she think of it? She was hardly three weeks in the service, and a mere substitute at that. Still, I would like to be well thought of, she told herself. Aloud, she said: "Take the case of the garden, sir." She leaned against the porch rail so that she would cut a charming figure. "I had a plan all worked out." She smiled at him.

"Now what about the garden?"

She persevered. "I had a plan, sir, to spare the children much of the work. The grounds, for instance. It's like an old abandoned ricefield, sir. It's a man-sized job to put things into shape."

In the classroom several girls were busy mopping the floor. The sound that they made dragging and pushing the desks about the unnailed floorboards reminded Miss Inocencio of the makeshift work that the barrio carpenters had done.

"What do you have in mind?" Mr. Vidal said.

"First of all, I want the garden cleared," she replied. "Cleared of wild grass, and fenced. Five hired men can do the work. The well—it's an old one, sir—can be made useful again."

With hands clasped behind him, his heavy leather shoes creaking faintly, Mr. Vidal walked the length of the porch and back again. "I see," he said, and stopped abruptly. "That's a good idea. You have good ideas, and that's what we need in the service. Ideas! You should get a permanent appointment."

"Thank you, sir," said Miss Inocencio. "You see, sir, I'm only thinking of the children's welfare."

"Very good. I should say, though, that the barrio is lucky to have the school opened," said Mr. Vidal. "There aren't enough funds, you know. Well, it's worth the money."

"Do you mean, sir, that this is temporary? That you might close the school, sir?"

"Not that I could close it," said Mr. Vidal. "I have no power to do that. But I can send up a memorandum."

"How dreadful!" Miss Inocencio put her hand over her mouth. "Please don't ever do that, sir."

"Much depends on you," said Mr. Vidal.

"I'll do my best. I promise, sir," said Miss Inocencio. "Did you see the building before, sir? Shortly after the Occupation?"

"No, but I heard it was used as a Japanese garrison."

Now she must tell him. "There was thick soot in one corner, right over there—where the *Ponjap* brewed tea, sir. And, of course, they used desks and floorboards for firewood. Also they had some prisoners here—guerrillas, sir. Among them boys from this barrio, too."

His nostrils quivering, Mr. Vidal looked solemnly around. "Then it was here Mr. Malabanan's son was killed?" he asked.

Miss Inocencio hesitated, surprised at this turn to the conversation. "Yes," she said at last.

"And the family never quite believes it, even now."

"Quite so, sir."

"He was an only son. Did you know him?"

"Pepito Malabanan, sir?"

"That's the name, all right!" Mr. Vidal snapped thumb and forefinger. "The father hasn't given up hope. Nor has old Mrs. Malabanan. Only this noon, at lunch, they were asking me if it was true some guerrillas in the

Panay Regiment had escaped and joined the Regulars. Someday Pepito will be here—that's their belief. Do you think it's ever possible—his being alive, his ever coming home?"

"I can't say, sir."

"The old couple are very kind. And they think well of you," Mr. Vidal said. He started to walk down the steps. "I understand you're joining us at supper. Mrs. Malabanan's making my visit here as pleasant as possible."

"Thank you for coming to our barrio, sir," she said.

On returning to the room to see what her girls had done, Miss Inocencio felt ill at ease. She looked at the window, and watched Leoncio and the other boys cutting the *kogon* grass in the garden. What stayed long in her mind afterwards was Mr. Vidal then turning a street-corner and disappearing behind a tall bamboo fence. He had waved his hands casually, as if to say: "I'm a friend, really. Not an officious school official."

Now that the school inspector had gone, the girls began to chatter like parrots as they worked in the classroom. For Miss Inocencio, this was a relief. The girls seemed unusually gay. Clara, aged ten, began to sing a tune, *The Banana Heart*, swinging in wide arcs across the torn blackboard an old eraser in her hand. The tune had been Pepito Malabanan's favorite no more than it had been that of every youth and maiden in the barrio. Yet Miss Inocencio could well have claimed the song his own. He had serenaded her with a guitar many a time and often sung that plaintive song before her window; this of nights in April and May, in those days before the war. "But I must not think of him any more," she told herself, as she arranged the things on her desk, pulled out her lesson-plan book, and drew the cap off her pen, wondering how best to conduct the next day's class. Certainly there ought to be something new, something no one had done before, something not in the course of study book, which would benefit the children. But would the service allow for originality? Right there before her was the official paper-bound outline; and already it was checking on her thoughts.

The other girls were teasing Clara. "Look at her, Ma'am. As though we had a school program!"

"It's quite all right, girls," Miss Inocencio said.

Whereupon Clara confronted her classmates belligerently, thrusting out her tongue at them. In a minute pieces of chalk, rags, and erasers flew about the room.

"Stop it!" Miss Inocencio cried.

But no sooner had she raised her voice so when contrition seized her. Why shouldn't she let the children alone? Verily, because she felt such a full-fledged woman now and had found a livelihood? Maybe she was begrudging them their innocence. And her next step? To marry and raise a family.

This thought sent her wondering whether Mr. Vidal had a family of his own. Did he have a pretty wife? Two children, maybe—a girl and a boy? And where could Pepito Malabanan be? "I know, Matilde. I should know. I'm his mother. You can't feel what I feel. Pray for his safe return. Our dear Lord will grant it, if we only pray."

Some details of the conversation at school set her wondering whether she had told Mr. Vidal the right things. It was possible, she thought, that the old couple had told him about her betrothal. For what reason, otherwise, should Mr. Vidal bring up the subject? But of course the fault had been hers; she had mentioned the war. "Did you see how the building looked before, sir?" And all owing to an entirely different motive. Perhaps Mr. Vidal had thought she had meant to let him know. Well, then, what would he make of her now? Ah, here's a young woman who's truly in love. Hm! Or would he say instead: How stupid of her! To be quite unable to deal with what's done and over with! What a pity, too, for she's such a pretty creature!

She laid her pen and books away, found no fault with the girls' work and bade them go home. She herself went down to the garden to see what the boys had accomplished during the afternoon.

What had once looked like a bit of wilderness was now cleared land, for the boys had matched their eagerness with industry. Leoncio, who oversaw the work, began to cut the brush that grew in the corner covering the area where the well stood, rimmed all around with blocks of soft stone. There was revealed the notches for the windlass and the grey lichen upon the blocks of stone. Miss Inocencio leaned over the better to see the water below, taking great care not to soil her dress. She held her head for a minute over the dark pit and breathed of its smell. But, feeling rather faint, she had to walk away almost at once. It was as if the darkness into which she had peered was like a pool where someday she would drown.

To shake the feeling off, she walked over to where the boys were gathered, awaiting to be commended for their efforts. They had done enough for the day, she told them. There was always tomorrow, she might have added; but as though of their own volition her feet were taking her back to the schoolhouse. She walked away as if in a trance.

The clock atop the empty bookcase was dead. She looked at it and it said nothing to her. Time could well have stopped. She picked up her books and was startled by footsteps—someone was at the porch. She thought Mr. Vidal had returned, but it was only Clara.

"May I carry your books, Ma'am?"

"But I thought you've gone home," Miss Inocencio said. She piled the books on the desk. "Thank you, Clara. Tell me. Who taught you that song?"

The girl paused and smiled, pleased perhaps over the triumph of her memory. "My uncle Pepito, Ma'am," she said.

"Oh, yes, I keep forgetting." And an access of tenderness for the girl possessed her. "You are his niece, aren't you?" Miss Inocencio said.

They left the classroom together. As they descended the porch steps, they were met by shrill cries from way back, from the garden. A second burst of wild shrieks and Leoncio appeared, running as fleet as deer, holding something in his hand.

"Leoncio!" Miss Inocencio called after the boy. "What's all this?"

But the boy did not heed her. Instead he ran as far away as he could, where the school grounds joined the growths of maguey.

Leoncio could not have betrayed Miss Inocencio more mortally. To hide the hurt, she asked the other boys: "What's that in his hand?"

They watched him in the distance. Standing in the sun, Leoncio turned round and regarded them proudly. He stood alone at the edge of the field as wind stirred the maguey leaves behind him. Then, as though he were bearing a chalice, he walked straight toward them.

"It's a skull, Ma'am," one of the boys said.

The other boys were quick to indict Leoncio. "We told him, Ma'am, not to go into the well."

Upon a sheaf of kogon grass that lay at Miss Inocencio's feet, Leoncio laid the skull gently. They all fell silent for a moment. The boy stared at his feet, like a prisoner in dock. His lips began trembling perceptibly before he could speak.

"It's Magtanggol's skull, Ma'am. Mr. Malabanan's son. That's how they called him."

"What do you know about all this?" Miss Inocencio asked sternly.

"I know, Ma'am," the boy replied. "I know," he repeated earnestly.

The little girl Clara tugged nervously at Miss Inocencio's dress.

Against the yellow-green sheaf of grass, the skull took on a dark blue color, like some piece of metal upon which time had left its mark. There was a haughty anonymity to it; the hollow sockets eloquently suggested no name.

Miss Inocencio bent over to pick up the skull from the cradle of grass where Leoncio had laid it to rest. She could not have explained away why she did so, but the impulse was too strong to resist. The skull seemed heavy, and her hands unsteady. The boys gathered round her in a tight circle. Her hands trembled so, and the skull fell to the ground. It broke in three pieces. Kneeling, she gathered the pieces together.

At half past six that evening, she went to old Mr. Malabanan's house. It was the only frame house in the barrio; its galvanized iron roof, even now in the thickening dusk, rose pale white against the coconut palms.

Mr. Vidal met her at the front steps and his first words to her, as he stood there in the dark, were: "Do you think it would be possible to identify the skull?"

She was taken aback. "I don't know, sir," she replied. She surmised that the boys, on their way home, had spread the news. She had taken the skull, wrapped carefully in a handkerchief, to the schoolroom and had placed it on the topmost shelf of the bookcase. It was with some effort that now she confessed: "I don't know what to do, sir."

"When I heard about it, I foresaw your problem," Mr. Vidal said. "I discussed the matter with Mr. Malabanan immediately. Well, as to whose it is—that's not important, really. But I suggested that an urn be made and appropriate prayers said."

They sat there in the porch, a table with a potted plant between them. "What did Mrs. Malabanan say, sir?" Miss Inocencio's eyes brightened.

"The old mother herself agreed to having a *rosario* said. No one will claim that we educated people are disrespectful toward the dead." Mr. Vidal rested the back of his chair against the porch wall. "I suggested that the priest in the next town be sent for, and as a matter of fact I offered the use of my horse. The matter of interment will be left for the padre to decide."

As he began to rock his chair gently, Miss Inocencio found herself at a loss what to say. She was indebted enough to him: she saw that much. In a kind of chivalry he had anticipated her weakness and spared her some pain.

Three women came up the house and after a respectful "Good evening, Mr. School Inspector," and "Good evening, Lady Schoolteacher," they wiped their bare feet upon the coir door mat, untied their black kerchiefs and filed quietly into the *sala*.

"Don't you think I should join them?" Miss Inocencio asked.

She stood up and was about to go, but Mr. Vidal detained her. "Before I forget, I meant to ask you whether you took a subscription to *Teachers' Journal*. It's a requirement of the service, you understand, to subscribe to at least one professional magazine. In a forthcoming issue, incidentally," Mr. Vidal went on, "I've contributed an article entitled 'The Barrio Schools of Tomorrow.' "

"I shall read the article, sir," said Miss Inocencio.

He got up and bowed as she stood to leave; and, later, as she walked across the sala it seemed to her that he was watching her every step with secret admiration.

The family altar was in Mrs. Malabanan's bedroom, and Miss Inocencio felt embarrassed, for the rosario had already started. More than that, the smell of home-made candles, the old women praying, old Mr. and Mrs. Malabanan kneeling humbly before the fact that was Death—these brought upon her, for she had come on tiptoe, an access of depression. Only a cold hand actually clutching her heart could possibly have produced this peculiar effect. Her lips trembling, she knelt and joined in the prayer.

A waft of wind from an open window sent a chill down the nape of her neck. Then the room began to turn and turn. The walls to her left seemed to be on the point of caving in. Only the altar before her remained steady.

In a trice the grip upon her heart relaxed. Now she could breathe more easily. Tears moistened her eyes, and for no reason at all she remembered the little girl Clara and her song. She looked up at the lighted altar once more, at the image of the Virgin Mary, at the wooden urn with the blue skull. She rose from her knees, resolved to be free of her past. She got up, thinking: "If I am really free, then no one will mind my leaving this room."

She walked away wondering whether anyone would in censure turn around to watch her go. As she had joined them, so did she now desire to quit their company.

The first thing she heard as she crossed the sala was the rustle of the leaves of the coconut palms across the street. Surely, she thought, the palms were waving their fronds in jubilation over her release.

A freedom too easily won? She was panting when she reached the porch. Mr. Vidal was again rocking his chair. Also, he had lit a cigarette. On seeing her, he got up and offered her his chair.

"Thank you," she said, still out of breath. But she did not sit down.

"It's too bad I'm not a praying man. Otherwise, I would have joined you." Mr. Vidal was chuckling softly. Then in a more serious vein: "Out here in the dark, I've been thinking about your work. I realize your handicaps. No professional associations, no books, no magazines. This is a God-forsaken place! What chances has one for self-improvement here?"

She leaned upon the porch-rail and looked at the silhouettes of the palm trees, slim and dark shades against the yet darker sky.

"I was wondering," Mr. Vidal continued, "whether the School Board has sent you to the wrong place. I'll mention the subject in my memorandum."

Mr. Vidal flung his cigarette away, underscoring the finality of the matter. Then he drew her near him, almost as if after having fled from the other room she had been flung into his arms. Momentarily shocked, she felt the hum of the prayers in the other room come to her in a sudden crescendo, as if she had stepped directly upon the path of a horde of angry bees.

"Perhaps you'd consider a transfer to a much bigger school?" Mr. Vidal continued. "There's a vacancy at the provincial capital. Yes, why not?"

The kindness in his voice did not escape her, yet she could say nothing in turn. She became tongue-tied over this prospect of being his protégée.

"Perhaps during the vacation you'd like to attend the Summer Institute?"

He placed his arm on her shoulder—a fittingly protective gesture, she believed, so that the barrio and all its fetishes could not lay their claims upon her any more. She let him draw her to him, warmly, closer.

But she heard herself speaking: "It's very kind of you." It was as though someone were making decisions on her behalf. She started, warily stepped back, and gave a cold firmness to her words: "I must stay . . . ."

There—her tongue had uttered them! And having said them, she let Mr. Vidal hold her hand, when he reached out for it again, but only one minute longer. The dark palms were staring at her.

1950

The Sea Beyond

THE *ADELA*, THE reconverted minesweeper that had become the mainstay of commerce and progress in Sipolog Oriental, was on her way to San Roque. As Horacio Arenas, our new assistant, wanted to put it, the *Adela* was "expected" at San Roque, which was the provincial capital, "in seven hours." He spoke at some length of this particular voyage, looking worn-out instead of refreshed after the two-week vacation we had hoped he would enjoy.

There he was, he said, one of the hundred-odd impatient passengers huddled under the low canvas awning of the upper deck. A choppy sea met the ship as she approached Punta Dumadali, and the rise and fall of the deck suggested the labored breathing of an already much-abused beast of burden. Her hatches were in fact quite full, Arenas said. Hundreds of sacks of copra had filled her hold at Dias. Piled all over the lower deck were thousands of pieces of *lauan* boards from the mills of San Tome. The passageways alongside the engine room were blocked by enormous baskets of cassava and bananas. A dozen wild-eyed Simara cows, shoulder to shoulder in their makeshift corral at the stern, mooed intermittently as though the moon-drenched sea were their pasture.

For the moon had risen over the Maniwala Ranges three miles to the starboard. As more and more the *Adela* rounded the Punta Dumadali, the wind sent the ship bucking wildly. An hour before, all this would have been understandable; it was puzzling, if not thoroughly incomprehensible, now. This kind of sea was unusual, for the Dumadali headland was known to mariners to throw off, especially at this time of year, if at no other, the full force of the *noroeste*. If some explanation were to be sought, it would be in some circumstance peculiar only to this voyage. This was the consensus, which made possible the next thought: that some presence was about, some evil force perhaps—so the talk went on board—which, until propitiated, might yet bring the ship to some foul end. The cows were markedly quiet now. The ship continued to pitch about: whenever the wind managed to tear at the awnings and cause loose ends of the canvas to beat savagely at the wire-mesh that covered the railings, small unreal patches of sea glimmered outside in the moonlight.

It was no secret that there was a dying man on board. He was out there in the third-class section. Whatever relation his presence had to the unpleasantness in the weather no one could explain, but the captain did do something. He had the man moved over to the first-class section, where it was less crowded and would probably be more comfortable for him.

The transfer was accomplished by two members of the crew. They carried the cot in which the man lay and two women, the man's wife and her mother, followed them. Ample space was cleared for the cot; the two women helped push some heavy canvas beds and chairs out of the way. Finally, the two men brought the canvas cot down. The ship listed to the starboard suddenly; and it seemed that from all quarters of the deck the hundred-odd passengers of the *Adela* let out a wild scream.

Then the ship steadied somehow. For a moment it seemed as if her engines had stopped. There was a gentle splashing sound, as though the bow had clipped neatly through the last of those treacherous waves. Either superior seamanship or luck held sway, but the ship might have entered then an estuary, the very mouth of an unknown river.

The excitement had roused the passengers and, in the first-class section at least, everyone had sat up to talk, to make real all over again the danger they had just been through. The steaming-hot coffee which the steward began serving in thick blue-rimmed cups encouraged conversation. The presence of the two women and the man in the extra cot in their midst was hardly to be overlooked. A thick gray woolen blanket covered the man all over, except about the face. His groans, underscored by the faint tapping of the wind on the canvas awnings, now become all too familiar. The mother attracted some notice, although for a different reason; she had a particularly sharp-edged face—brow and nose and chin had a honed look to them. The wife, who had more pleasing features, evoked respect and compassion. It was touching to see her sit on the edge of the empty cot beside her husband's and tuck in the hem of her skirt under her knees. She could not have been more than twenty, and already she wore the sadness of her widowhood. The glare of the naked electric bulb that hung from the ridgepole of the deck's canvas roof accentuated it, revealed that she was about six months gone with child, and called attention to her already full breasts, under a rust-colored *camisa*, that soon would be nourishing yet another life.

It was at Dias, four hours before, where the accident had occurred. Although Dias was a rich port, neither the government nor the local association of copra and rice merchants had provided it with a wharf. The old method of ferrying cargo in small outriggered *paraos* was less costly perhaps, it was even picturesque. But it was only possible in good weather. And already the noroeste had come. The same waves that pounded at the side of the *Adela* at anchor lashed at the frail paraos that were rowed over toward the ship and were brought into position for hauling up the copra. The man, one of the *cargadores*, had fallen off the ship's side.

He would have gone to the bottom had he not let go of the copra sack that he had held aloft and had he not been caught across the hips by the outriggers of his parao. Nevertheless, the next wave that had lifted the ship and gathered strength from under her keel flung him headlong, it seemed, toward the prow of the boat. The blunt end of this dugout pressed his body against the black, tar-coated side of the *Adela*. The crew pulled him out with difficulty, for the sea kept rising and falling and caused the prow's head to scrape continuously against the ship's side. The crew had expected to find a mass of broken flesh and bones, but in actuality the man came through quite intact. He did not start moaning and writhing until his wet undershirt and shorts had been changed and he had been laid out on the cot. There was nothing that could be done further except to keep him on board. Something after all had broken, or had burst open, somewhere inside him.

His family was sent for. The wife, accompanied by her mother, clambered up the ship's side thirty minutes later, to the jocose shouts of "Now you can see San Roque!" from innocent well-wishers in the parao. The shippers, the Dias Development Co., had sent a telegram to the provincial doctor at San Roque, and an agent of the company had come on board and personally commended the cargador to the captain. When at last the fifty-ton copra shipment was on board, the *Adela* weighed anchor.

Now, his having transferred the man from the third-class to the first-class section earned the captain some praise, and the connection between this act and the pleasant change in the weather elicited much speculation. If only the man did not groan so pitifully, if only he kept his misery to himself; if only the two women were less preoccupied too by some bitter and long-unresolved conflict between them. "Don't you think he is hungry?" the mother once asked; to which the wife answered: "He does not like food. You know that." And then the mother asked, "How about water? He will be thirsty perhaps." To which the wife's reply was, "I shall go down and fetch some water." The matter could have stopped there, but the mother wanted to have the last word. "That's better than just standing or sitting around."

The wife got up and walked away, only to return about ten minutes later with a pitcher and a drinking cup from the mess room below. The mother had the pitcher and drinking cup placed at the foot of the sick man's bed, for, as she explained, "He will ask for water any time and you won't be near enough to help me." The mother waited to see what her daughter would make of this; and the latter did have her say: "I'll be right here, Mother, if that's all you're worried about."

The man grew restless. His wife's assurance (she said again and again, "You will be all right!") drew nothing but interminable sighs ("O God of mine!"). Between the man and his wife, some inexplicable source of irritation had begun to fester. "It is in your trying to move about that the pain comes," the wife chided him gently. "We are getting there soon. It will not be long now." Whereupon the man tried to raise his knee and twist his hips under the blanket. The blanket made a hump like one of the Maniwala mountains in the distance, and he let out a wail, followed by "But this boat is so very slow, God of mine! Why can't we go faster? Let the captain make the boat go faster. Tell him. Will someone go and tell him?"

Almost breathless after this exertion, he lay still. The mother, this time as if her son-in-law were an ally, took it upon herself to comfort him. "Better keep quiet and don't tire yourself. The captain will make the boat go faster, surely." And by putting down his knee carefully, the hump that the blanket had made before leveled off now into foothills instead of those high ranges of the Maniwala.

The business of the telegram came after this lull. It was preceded by a prolonged groan, and then the question was there before them: "And did they send the telegram?" "They" meant the Company, of course; in its service the man had enlisted as cargador. If the answer to his question was in the affirmative, then there was reason to say that the doctor would attend to him and put him together again and return him to his work. His wife assured him that the telegram had been dispatched. "So be quiet," she added. "The other people here would not want to be disturbed now. They want to sleep, no doubt," she said, looking about her, as if to solicit the approval of the twenty or twenty-five passengers around—which included merchants, students, and at least three public-school teachers on some Christmas holiday jaunt.

The mother asked about food—a proper question, although under the circumstances perhaps a tactless one. "I am not hungry, Mother," was what the daughter said, firmly. "I'll sit here," the mother offered, in a less affirmative tone than she had been accustomed to use. "I'll do that myself if you are hungry," countered the daughter. "I don't care about food," the mother assured her. "And did I tell you I wanted to eat?" Whereupon the daughter declared that she was not hungry—"Let me tell you that, Mother." The mother alleged that her most loving daughter was no doubt "too choosy" about food, "that's why." She ought to "go down below and ask for something to eat." "Eat whatever you can find," was her solemn injunction, as if to overwhelm her daughter's claim that she was not hungry at all. "Don't worry about me, Mother," the wife added, pointedly. "I don't get hungry that easily." And then to round off this phase of their quarrel, the mother said, loud enough for anyone who cared to hear:

"Maybe it's sitting at the captain's table that you've been waiting for all this time."

The daughter said nothing in reply and the mother did not press her advantage either. It was clear, though, that the meaning of the remark, its insinuation, was not to be easily dismissed. What the mother had so expressed was a little out of the ordinary; the air, as Arenas put it, was rife with conjectures. It was not difficult to remember, he said, that ship officers, or sailors in general, had never been known to endow women their highest value. What remained to be understood was why the mother thought of her daughter in some such awful connection as this.

Five hours later, Arenas said, after the *Adela* had docked at the San Roque pier and the discharging of some of her cargo had begun, the subject came up again. Perhaps the first person to disembark had been the captain himself, to infer from the fact that somebody, possibly one of the mates, had shouted to someone standing on the wharf: "Duty before pleasure, captain!" A jeep of the Southern Star Navigation Co. had pulled up the ramp and then hurried off the mile-long seaside road toward the town, into San Roque *poblacion* itself. The town was brightly lighted, particularly the section along the seaside.

"Now he's gone and we have not even thanked him," said the mother. "And the doctor has not come. How can we leave this ship? Answer that one," she demanded. "You are too proud, that's what. All that you needed to say was a word or two, a word of thanks, surely." The wife remained silent through all this. "And he could have taken you in the jeep, to fetch the doctor; if there was that telegram, and it has been received—" She did not go further. The wife assured her calmly that the telegram had been sent. "So what harm could it have done to have spoken to the captain, to have reminded him, since he would be riding into town anyway?" the mother said; and to this the daughter's reply was the kind of serenity, Arenas said, that can come only from knowledge: "All men know is to take advantage of us, Mother," she said.

Taken aback by these words, the mother searched the faces of people around her for help. She got nothing and she said nothing. The passengers had crowded at the railing to watch the lumber being unloaded. A gang of cargadores tossed pieces of lumber from over the ship's side to the wharf ten feet away while someone chanted: "A hundred and fifty-three—and fifty-four—and fifty-five . . ." and the wood cluttered askew on the fast-mounting pile. The cows lowed again from their corral at the stern of the ship. This blended afresh with the man's groans and with the chant and the clatter of the boards. Meanwhile, the wife talked on softly: "We have arrived, and it's the doctor's jeep we're waiting for and nothing more," wiping her husband's brow with a handkerchief. "Two hundred and three—and four—and five—" chanted the counter, over down below. "This is San Roque now," the wife continued. "A big town it is, with many lights. And with many people." Her husband's brow sweated profusely and it was all she could do with her handkerchief. "And the lights are bright, and so many. Rest now and tomorrow we can see the town," she said softly, folding her handkerchief this way and that so as not to get any section of it too damp with sweat.

It was at this point, Arenas said, that a motor sounded from down the road, followed by the blare of a jeep's horn and the sweep of its headlights. The lights caught the man who was chanting his count of the lumber being unloaded, and they held him transfixed. He called out the numbers louder. The jeep stopped in the middle of the now cluttered up wharf, for what with the stacked rows of copra and the lauan boards from San Tome, there was no space for the jeep to move in. The driver, having gone no farther than possible, turned off his engine and slid off his seat awkwardly; and then approaching the man who was doing the counting, he demanded, "How much longer?" And the other replied, "Possibly until two o'clock—what with the men we have. You know how it is, sir." To which the other said, sternly: "Stop calling me 'sir.' And to think that the captain just told me he'll pull out in two hours, not a second later."

Words, Arenas said, which, although intended for somebody else, did make the wife say to her husband: "They'll first move you over there, to the wharf—that will be solid ground at least—and there we shall wait for the doctor." She had dropped her voice to a whisper.

Across the ten feet of water to the edge of the wharf, lights fell harshly on the piles, on the heads and arms of the cargadores who slid up and down the gangplank with copra sacks on their shoulders, looking like so many oversized ants. To the right was the driver in his jeep; he had not switched off his lights and they flooded the first-class section with their garish glare. "What shamelessness," cried the wife. The jeep's lights singled her out. The driver got stuck between the wall of copra to his left and a new pile of lumber to his right. He was trying to turn the jeep about but did not have the room. The man who had addressed him "sir" had stopped his work, and the clatter of the boards had ceased. Up on the deck, Arenas said, the wife shouted: "What does he want of me? What does he want me to do now?" The mother pulled her away. "She's overwrought. Forgive her," she begged. "And as you've observed, I've been hard on her myself. I don't know why. Why must God punish us so?"

Once more the driver tried to maneuver his jeep and all the time his lights seemed to fix themselves forever on the wife, who, to meet this challenge, sprang away from the ship's railing and rushed down to the lower deck, shouting: "Here, here I am. Take me. What can you want of me?"

It was that way, Arenas said. Two hours later, the man was moved to the wharf, and there behind a pile of copra and another pile of lauan lumber, the wife and the mother waited. Word was abroad that the captain, who had returned from town, had said that he had contacted the doctor. Contacted, Arenas said, was the very word. And wasn't that so revealing?

We didn't know at first what he meant, we told him. Did he want to remind us about the war, the same one during which the *Adela* had swept the mine-strewn sea in behalf of progress and civilization? The word Arenas had used belonged to that time, and he seemed to say, All this because it had been that way at that time. You must understand; you must forgive, even.

But we didn't want him to be apologetic like the mother-in-law he had described; and so, afterward, when he talked again about the subject, wearing that worried look on his face with which we had become familiar, we had to urge him: "Better not think about it anymore."

1954

Part Four

Serenade

"BUT I CAN'T help wondering," said Juan Molino, "what fortune has in store for you!"

The remark had been prompted by the excitement which attended the arrival of the *Tomasa*, an outriggered two-master of which Juan Molino was rather proud. Pilar knew that while he was fond of her, she was readily capable of exasperating him; and the *Tomasa's* affairs provided many an opportunity for that.

The boat had been doing very well, moving copra from the outlying islands to Buenavista. Shippers, like the Rivas y Cia., were fast making profits for themselves and bringing prosperity to the town as well. But was she to be compared then with the *Tomasa* in the kind of fulfillment that she contributed to her father's plans? Pilar thought that this was unfair.

The end of every voyage called for the meticulous but necessary division of the *Tomasa's* earnings between its owner, on one hand, and the *patron* and his entire crew on the other. Today what the patron had turned in was quite considerable. Pilar saw the silver coins, mostly pesos and pesetas, spill out of his purse; and she had helped pick up a few of the former that had rolled off the table. No sooner had her father finished counting the money than the thought of getting herself a new dress came to her, she didn't know why. It had happened before, this mad and intense need to buy and own things—it didn't really matter what they were. Last time she had gotten wrought up over a pair of *zapatillas*; and before that, an umbrella. Tasseled in pink and gold and Hongkong-made, she had been told. And the *Tomasa*, she had been reminded repeatedly, needed a new jib and a new anchor; surely, every centavo would count.

She used to trouble her mother, too, although with hardly any success. Her mother had been less tractable than her father. It was true that Mama kept the money, but it was not she who decided what it might be used for. "Go, ask you father," she would say, which meant that once a peso had reached her purse it was as good as saved. Had she not been that tight-fisted, they would have been less well-off than they were now. Juan Molino, as bookkeeper at Rivas y Cia., received only a modest salary; but Juan Molino, the entrepreneur and proprietor (he had four parcels of land planted to coconuts and from a house on Calle Real rented out to the Chinese merchant Tan Lee came a decent income), deserved Buenavista's respect.

For an easy touch, Pilar knew, the person to go to was her father, and it was money earned by the *Tomasa* that he was particularly generous with. As she had proved again and again, the best time to wheedle a few pesos out of him was on each return of the boat from a voyage.

She waited patiently while her father worked on the boat's accounts. The patron was none other than her own Uncle Isidro. She entertained the members of his crew waiting at the porch, giving them a basket of *atis*. Soon, they were enjoying themselves immensely, shooting out the pits at each other.

Out of nowhere, her brother Lucas bounced into the porch, dipped his hand into the pile of sweetsop, and joined in the fun.

"Aren't you ashamed of yourself?" said Pilar.

"Who—me?" Lucas answered back, asserting his right to sit on the porch rail and swing his feet to and fro, like the *Tomasa* crewman next to him.

"You could at least leave that to them," Pilar said.

"Hsssssiiiitttt!"

The atis pit that Lucas had aimed at her made its mark. The spot at the base of her neck where the black pellet had landed began to hurt.

"Oh, you beast!" Pilar cried.

And she was at the point of pummeling her brother with her little fists when Uncle Isidro began to call out the names of his crew. It was time to give each man his share from the crew's portion of the *Tomasa's* earnings.

Pilar felt it was embarrassing to be around at this juncture. She ran back to her father and said in a whisper: "Just this once, Papa!"

"That was what you said before," Juan Molino said.

"What?" Lucas called out from the porch. "For a new dress again? Or, perhaps, for another umbrella?"

Pilar only stuck out her tongue at him, fearful lest things might get out of hand. "But, really, Papa," she tried again, "this will be the last . . . . Besides, I won't need much at all." When she saw that Uncle Isidro had finished handing out the money to the men, she added: "*Tio* Sid is so kind—look, he's making me a present of two pesos himself. Aren't you, Uncle?"

Lucas had jumped off the porch railing and was all smiles. Uncle Isidro must have given him some money already, Pilar thought. For Lucas and for her, the ploy had worked. Being fond of his niece, Uncle Isidro sometimes gave her as much as five pesos.

But he allowed her only one peso this time. "That should do for the present, you spoiled child," Uncle Isidro said.

Lucas had cleared the porch as agilely as he had emerged minutes before out of nowhere.

"Eighteen and still a child," Juan Molino said. "Here, and let this be the last . . . ."

"Thank you, Papa," said Pilar, almost dancing with joy. Not to be outdone by his brother, Juan Molino had given her three pesos.

And it was well that Lucas had slipped away. He might have received a similar amount, only Papa would have to ask him to account for it. Indeed, to avoid questions later on, Lucas had wisely disappeared.

"And thank you, too, Uncle," said Pilar.

She saw from the look that crossed her father's face that something was wrong. What could he be thinking of? Perhaps, it had something to do with her. Surely, she would soon have to change her ways. She could be forgiven her shortcomings only for just so long.

As far back as she could remember, the family had always had a boat. Her father had often made mention of a *Lucia I*, a two-master with a capacity of three-hundred sacks of copra. Great-grandfather Atanasio himself had been her patron. What a pity that she had to rot in the sun and rain when the old man took ill and died. And so it was something in the nature of a duty that Grandfather Jose built the *Lucia II*, which was so big she managed a burden of five-hundred sacks. Of both *Lucias*, her father seemed to have many pleasant memories. He had impressive accounts about how Grandfather Jose looked after the *Lucia II*, having realized that the merest negligence, of which the *Lucia I* was an example, could change things.

Unlike his father, however, Juan Molino did not acquire the skills of a sailor. It was his brother Isidro who took after Grandfather Jose; and Isidro, having developed into such a spendthrift as to be unable to afford even a dugout of his own, had long abandoned the idea of building a *pasaje* by way of upholding the family tradition. The task had to be Juan Molino's, a challenge to be met with pen and ledger, a tribute to his entrepreneurial spirit. Isidro had to be happy being his brother's patron. Pilar's oldest brother Lucas was already beginning to be their Uncle Isidro's double. He was now twenty-two and, as their father had said, might just as well be handling a boat himself one of these days.

No one could wish for a better boat than the *Tomasa*. Once a year she was recalked and painted; her deck and deckhouse were always kept in good repair. Indeed, the boat was never out of Juan Molino's mind, as his family well knew. The work that kept him busy all day at Rivas y Cia. rated but a poor second in importance. It had gotten so that it seemed their father had become more inclined than ever to take Pilar and her two brothers for granted; worse, because for three years now the family ran a small *lateria* on Calle Progreso. This had kept Tomasa busy since Pilar provided not much help. Lucas, on his part, couldn't keep himself behind the grocery counter more than two minutes without getting bored. He seemed better off out of sight, somewhere with the stevedores or the crew of the *Tomasa*. His brother Jaime had been summarily dispatched to Manila and enrolled at the Ateneo. Small wonder the two-master was a source of satisfaction and escape. The slightest attention paid her was returned with interest; and Pilar's father was not one to miss reckoning things in that manner indeed.

Because the grocery was a modest one and the stock, counter and all, could be accommodated on the ground floor, the Molinos had rented out the first story of their Calle Progreso house. It so happened that a Japanese gentleman, a Mr. Tanaka, was just then visiting Buenavista. Yes, he meant to stay for a while. Yes, he could occupy the two rooms—in fact, the whole floor—directly above the lateria. The Molinos lived across the street; this, in fact, was their third house. And so Mr. Tanaka installed himself, feeling at ease over having a landlord who was head, no less, of one of the first families of the town.

Except when he was out on one of his frequent excursions to the countryside, Mr. Tanaka remained at home pottering about his little kitchen, his wooden shoes making funny noises. He made friends with Pilar Molino soon enough. He showed her little bottles containing silly things—fish and shells preserved in alcohol; soil or pieces of rock in cardboard boxes. He also collected butterflies, smothered them with chloroform and them pinned them down onto layers of absorbent cotton laid out in old cigar boxes. He gathered small blocks of wood, labelling them in his native script. Pilar could only gape in wonder; to be puzzled or overly curious at least did not so much as occur to her.

He had visited many places in the world, Mr. Tanaka said—collecting things. And would he eventually sell them? Pilar's question amused him. What, then, would he do with them in the end?

"Take home," he said. "Then I write book. About plants. About rocks. About butterflies."

Coming home from his expeditions, he hardly stopped at the grocery, as one might expect; and if he did at all, it was only for a minute or two, and then only so as to be able to greet Pilar and her mother. He would then slip away to the back part of the house. There, protected from sun and rain by a generous overhang of the eaves, the steps led to the second story where his rooms were situated. Afterward Pilar and her mother would hear nothing more of Mr. Tanaka for days on end. They might on occasion become aware of his presence on account of the funny sound he made with his little feet on the floor boards, but that bothered nobody anyhow. Pilar's father, for one, did not mind whether Mr. Tanaka was here or there, or up and about. The man paid a handsome rent after all.

On the last day of each month, Pilar went to Tan Lee the Chinese merchant who rented the other Molino house on Calle Real, a street parallel to Calle Progreso. Collecting Tan Lee's rent was a chore that Pilar's father had assigned her several months now. His purpose, she suspected, was to enable her to gain valuable experience in handling money.

Her brother Jaime used to do it but he had great difficulty in bringing home the collection intact. Somewhere along the way he would run into a *cara y cruz* game, which often ended badly for him. Poor Jaime, said Pilar to herself. And to think that the year before he had been made a deckhand on the *Uranos*, their father believing that shipboard discipline might straighten him out. But even there Jaime proved to be an embarrassment; the captain had to send him away. Their father was not unresourceful, however; and thus the Jesuit school in Manila became Jaime's next stop on his journey to reform. There was the money from the Calle Real house; in effect, Tan Lee could help cover expenses. This meant that Pilar had to remain at home— to play the *interna* at La Concordia on an extended vacation. Anyway, she said to herself, Father had written to Manila for a piano.

The thought encouraged her, and she remembered that Tan Lee had always been nice to her. She did not mind his buckteeth which, when he smiled, seemed all that there was to his face. His eyes would flatten out and disappear into mere slits; his nose would crinkle away into a stunted albino bêche-de-mer.

Until recently, Tan Lee paid thirty pesos a month for the house on Calle Real. The amount, however, had to be increased since prices had risen somewhat as a result of the copra boom; and the house now cost Tan Lee ten pesos more. Similarly, Pilar's purchases from the shop had grown. She had fallen into the habit of going to the shop for just about anything she fancied; only recently she took an expensive set of china which Tan Lee had been reluctant to give on credit. How fortunate that his stock did not include silks, linen, embroideries and the like; for he served copra-makers and tenants of coconut groves mostly. Their needs were simple and their pretensions modest.

This afternoon, Tan Lee was as glad as he had always been to show Pilar his books; he was not one to begrudge her a practical lesson or two on money matters himself. And there it was: in her favor was a balance of five pesos and a few centavos. Tan Lee smiled at her as if to say, "What will your father think about that?"

Pilar protested; she understood what the balance meant.

"This is too much, Tan Lee. You add up everything. As a favor," she said, "please include the china in next month's bill, will you? Not in this month's bill, no! Be good!"

"As you wish," Tan Lee agreed, his eyes transformed into mere lines under those thin eyebrows. He began working out the account all over again, manipulating his abacus with the dexterity of a guitar player showing off before an audience.

"There's a real friend!" Pilar said after receiving the money. She thanked him profusely and went on her way.

Her next destination was the Post Office. Mr. Posas was lord and master there, although he was always eager enough to humble himself at her feet. Because of the job he held, he was considered one of the town's most eligible bachelors; however, he had the misfortune of being small and skinny, so much so that at times he reminded Pilar of a field mouse.

But he had been attentive to her, and either he had seen her coming or had expected her appearance this afternoon, for with the help of his telegraph operator Mr. Reyes, and of his letter-carrier, Mr. Posas had tidied up the place. The floor was well swept, the counter without a speck of dust. Even the trash box outside had been emptied, it's contents piled up under the acacia tree across the street, and a smudge heavy with the smell of burning paper and tar rose from it. Pilar had the impression that the sound that the telegraph operator Mr. Reyes made in his little room set off at the back of the office, his steady and irritating tapping at his keys, was like dirt in the air that Mr. Posas would have wished to sweep away too if only he could.

Pilar stepped directly toward the little window at the counter and gave him a friendly greeting.

"It's you!" said the postmaster, breathless with delight. "How may I be of service?"

This was the formula, Pilar knew, by which he assured himself of her esteem.

"Be nice today and send this money that I have with me to my brother," she said. "Be so good as not to make me fill out those horrible forms of yours."

"Very well, very well," said Mr. Posas effusively. "And it is the same amount as before?" He had done her this favor several times already.

"And it is the same address," Pilar replied.

"Delighted!" Mr. Posas said, sneezing, because of the smoke from the pile of burning trash.

Pilar handed him the amount—fifty pesos. It was her brother Jaime's monthly allowance. "Thank you," she said, and then walked on.

It was three by Mr. Posas's clock, she remembered. How nice and kind everyone is this afternoon, Pilar said to herself. In the walk from the Post Office to the town plaza, the acacias gave a cool, pleasant shade.

Directly ahead was the old Spanish church, a gray hulk in the sun. The bell tower was overgrown with grass; it looked so much like a part of the outcropping rock of the hillside directly behind it. The *convento*, which had been built against the side of the hill, stood dilapidated and abandoned. Its roof had been patched up many times over, and now no one seemed anxious to do anything more about it. Such is how things around here have become, so ancient and mean, said Pilar to herself.

Take the town hall, she thought, for it was right in front of her, the old walls showing the large blocks of coral that had once been smoothed over with cement. And to the left was the schoolhouse. How strange that she had only a skimpy memory of having attended classes there as a small girl. What she could remember were last year's dances and, more readily, those exciting box socials she had accompanied the Rivas girls to, an obligatory thing since her father was employed by the family. It was of course true they had been classmates at La Concordia. Who could have told her then that she would have a really long vacation forthcoming?

The schoolhouse had a balcony with some trellis work on it, the original iron railings having disappeared years back, people said, when the building served as barracks for American soldiers. Now at eighteen she would have to believe whatever it was that people told her about those days.

The Rizal monument was a more recent acquisition of the town. It was a ten-foot statue of the national hero in his great winter coat, the two huge novels, the books that had kindled the Revolution, at his feet. There it stood in the middle of the plaza, mounted on a platform around which a concrete fence had been built. And how sad-looking Rizal was! Perhaps, to be quite faithful to Rizal's concern for the country, the anonymous sculptor had depicted him in his most pensive mood, the right foot forward, back turned to the church, the right hand raised to his chin. How could one look so grave as that? But studying the figure again, Pilar thought it bestowed on her a somewhat encouraging if worried smile.

She went past the town hall and the old dry fountain at its steps. For the first time she realized how funny the lions were, lolling out their tongues. And how forgotten, how forlorn La Immaculada was, standing on a sphere, a representation of the big wide world, the continents painted in green and blue, the oceans in lavender, and all peeling off now strip by crinkly strip. The figure of the Virgin itself was cracked all over it; it was a wonder it had not fallen to the empty fountain at its feet.

Pilar crossed the stone bridge from there, and headed for the house at the corner, which was that of Adela Morelos.

The sala rang out with shouts of "Kapaklan! Off to Kapaklan!" when the Morelos children saw Pilar at the door.

"Oh," she said, "but there are so many of you . . . . Now, let's see . . . . We'll take along only those who weren't able to come the last time. How's that? All right?"

Adela, who had put her embroidery away, left the selection entirely to her friend. The lucky ones turned out to be the youngest girl, who was seven, and the oldest boy, who was ten. To the latter, who was called Blas, no restriction could have applied; for Adela would not be able to get her mother's permission for the outing if the ten-year-old couldn't tag along.

When she was seven herself and had been keen about listening to her father's stories, Pilar remembered, Kapaklan had its share of fairies, demons, and dragons. What she liked best was the amusing tale about the dog who bit a man because he killed the fly that had lit upon a piece of ricecake that had come from the woman who lived alone in a hut that was roofed with shingles made out of palm leaves that had been cut by the knife honed on the whetstone that her husband had picked up one day on the road to—to—to Kapaklan! The sequence was more elaborate than that at times, and more confusing than what she could now recall as she and Adela, in the company of the young girl and of the brother Blas, continued on their way.

Yes, in a few minutes they would get there. They had only to cross a little wooden bridge, to the far right of which were the outhouses that made that part of town so unsightly. The proper thing was to walk straight ahead, as if one saw nothing at all, turning neither left nor right but covering one's nose with a handkerchief. A few hundred yards more, and they would take the small side road to the left and would soon be in her father's coconut grove.

For years now Juan Molino had a tenant, or *bantay*, Diego, who looked after it. The place was rocky and as wild with bushes and shrubs as coconut groves were supposed to be in those stories that Pilar recalled from her childhood. More than ever she was certain that the little old men with long white beards lived behind those boulders; a butterfly might be a fairy maiden transformed, a bumblebee a witch. As a little girl she had dreaded the place; its wild shadows haunted her often in her sleep. Only when she was much older did this dread wear off, and then she discovered she could use Kapaklan to advantage. As a picnic place to take her friends to, it was ideal, being so close to town. How unfortunate Diego was on this account! At the rate Pilar brought her friends over, he could hardly make any copra from what remained of the coconuts, because each picnic required harvesting a number of green ones prematurely.

"But we are here scarcely once a month," Pilar would argue.

"It's really nothing to worry about," Diego would say. "Only the trees are not bearing enough this year, and it's a pity bringing down the young nuts the price of copra being what it is these days."

"True enough," Pilar would admit. "But we'll make up for that. Tomorrow, send Lilay over to the house. She'll be back with some clothes and salt and matches. Will that be all right?"

"Ah, since you say so yourself . . . ."

Diego's hut was a low, palm-leaf covered one. Pilar couldn't imagine how Lilay, who was his wife's unmarried sister, could live there with her three nieces and their mother. The latter was pale and often sick; she was thirty or so. Her husband seemed to be always out of sorts, or perhaps hungry for something or other. Thin, narrow-shouldered, Diego had the slouch of a man used to climbing coconuts and bending for hours on end over a plowshare-tipped nut-husker; and—so Pilar observed—he'd give Lilay, who was healthily full-bosomed and twenty-three, an intense, strangely wild look, as though she were coconut meat he had taken great care to dry over a slow-burning fire and now was ready for chopping up and turning into copra for the market.

When they arrived, Diego was in fact gathering the kiln-dried halves of coconut from a platform raised over the fire pit. A warm, pleasant odor exuded from the dark brown meat that had shrunken and almost detached already from its shell.

"It's a whole bunch of young ones you'll need today; that's what it looks like," Diego said, and obligingly began looking for a suitable tree to climb.

In a minute he was up, literally holding the tree trunk in his arms and, as though yielding to a passion, disappeared among the fronds and bunches of green nuts.

Pilar's thoughts returned to Lilay. She wished she could get her to stay in town, but three servants were already with the house on Calle Progreso. She could only be assigned the laundry, and for that she had to go to town three or four times a week.

Today she asked Pilar a naughty, if guileless, question. "When do you plan to get married?" And the way she whispered those words, Pilar could hardly hear anything on account of the noises that Diego made among the palm fronds overhead, and yet she felt certain about what the other meant.

How could Pilar have answered her? Indeed, just then, from out there in the harbor, came the whistle of the *Uranos*. It had arrived from Manila. The three long blasts suggested lonely and long voyages, separation, pain and suffering, sentiments quite unrelated to the twitter of the sunbirds and the trembling of the coconut leaves in the wind.

"Why do you ask?" Pilar said at last, just to be sure that what she thought to be Lilay's reason for being so curious was the right one.

"Because when you have a home of your own," Lilay said, "I'd like to stay with you."

Diego had just then sent down a bunch of green coconuts, and as these crashed to the ground Adela's brother and sister let out shrill cries of delight.

"Now, that's a foolish thing to think about," Pilar said, and sent Lilay for some spoons to scoop out the meat of the young coconuts with. To Adela, she said: "We must be careful not to soil our dresses. Let us hope that Diego's three little girls and their mother have not lost the spoons we left with them—remember?—so that we have something to use everytime we come here."

There were some ten of them, workers from the Rivas y Cia. warehouse and the entire crew of the *Tomasa*. Each had a sarsaparilla bottle in hand, and who would be right there in their midst but her own brother Lucas!

"Tell me!" said Pilar. "What's all this, Lucas?"

But her brother wouldn't tell. Like his companions, he was all smiles—as if to say they shared a secret amongst them that she should discover for herself.

"What's happening, Mama?" she asked her mother, who was preparing to close up the shop although it was still broad daylight.

"Go over to the other house," she said in a mock-serious vein. "See things there for yourself."

The other house referred to was of course the one across the street, and no sooner had Pilar reached the porch when she saw what the men were all smiles about. Her piano had arrived!

It was a gleaming, black German upright with brass candle-holders and a thick, embroidered strip of red felt that covered the keys. Well-oiled coasters allowed Pilar and Lucas to move it easily about the sala, for they had to discover where it could be most advantageously located. Pilar finally decided that it would be best against the dining room wall. The porch would be to the player's back; the lighting would be excellent.

"Now, try it!" her father said, as if to assure Pilar that the piano's presence was a fact of life.

A stool had come with it. Pilar could adjust it to a suitable height. And the sound was beautiful. The action, while firm, only seemed to make the keys all the more soft to the touch. Not to be outdone, however, Lucas shoved his sister rudely away and began picking out a tune roughly resembling "Home, Sweet Home." Everyone laughed, with the result that Lucas was all the more encouraged. He established himself more or less securely on the stool and tried out "Alerto, Voluntarios."

"Please," Pilar begged.

Lucas yielded the stool at last; and before long the neighbors started coming, crowding the sala and the porch. Her mother had arrived herself from the lateria across the street that she had boarded up for the night. She had to pick her way, saying, "Please, allow me . . . ."

It was an occasion worthy of all the amenities. Here was the only piano that Buenavista ever had, with the exception of course of the one that belonged to the Rivas girls. And you did not just go over there to listen to it being played. The town plaza was about the closest you could get to the big stone house. Sitting on one of those stone benches, or on an outcropping root of an acacia tree, you might hear "The Shepherd's Dream" or "Longing for Home." Still this was a treat reserved for vacation time only, when school was out and the girls were back from Manila. And even then, on such afternoons, you couldn't be too sure that it wasn't Don Esteban's wife who had been playing as if to tell the whole world that all was well, that the Rivases had everything.

More sarsaparilla bottles were brought up and biscuits were passed around for the unexpected guests. Young men now hung about the street outside. Juan Molino, sitting by the window, named them off as best as he could. Indeed, in the dusk of twilight, it was difficult to identify everyone.

"But, surely, that must be Mr. Posas the postmaster, Tomasa," he told his wife. "Look over there. Don't you think we should ask him in?"

Pilar, although in the middle of "The Waves of the Sea," had overheard the remark. She wheeled around, the stool screeching. "If you do, Papa," she said, "I'll stop playing this very minute."

"Go on then," said the father.

After about half an hour, he said: "That's the lawyer Mr. Rodrigo, over there at the street corner. Twice he walked up this way and then retraced his steps. I don't know why."

"Don't you think we should ask him in?" asked his wife.

"If you do, Mama, I'll never touch these keys again," said Pilar.

"Go on playing then," the mother said.

In a little while, whom did Juan Molino and his wife see walking arm in arm down the street but Provincial Secretary Morelos and his wife! Adela's parents, no less; they deserved at least a casual invitation. But Pilar had begun the opening bars of "Poet and Peasant" and she was not one to be distracted from this point on.

Lilay, the woman from Kapaklan who came to do the laundry, had a report to make about Mr. Tanaka. She had seen him come home with what looked like a long piece of bamboo reed. She had been busy at her washing, she said, when what would she see but a yellow-green snake, or something that looked like one. It had become rigid, though, as it slithered up the steps. Then she saw it enter Mr. Tanaka's rooms, Lilay said. At this point she laughed, and Pilar asked why. Well, the other said, it took some watching; but she realized that what Mr. Tanaka had brought home was nothing but a length of bamboo.

"What would he do with it?" Pilar asked, used though she was to odd things that Mr. Tanaka collected. What annoyed her was the importance Lilay was giving to this last specimen.

"He's making a bamboo flute, perhaps," Lilay said. "He was busy at it all day."

Pilar refused to give it any meaning. After breakfast she dispatched a servant to ask Adela to come over to see the piano; and in a few minutes indeed a breathless Adela Morelos appeared, announcing her intentions in an endless prattle. She was eager not only to listen to Pilar's music but to try to play herself, although this was the first time that she had come to within an arm's length of so marvelous an instrument.

"First," Pilar said gravely, "you must know solfeggio. Now, if you really want to start . . . ."

And no sooner had they begun when the notes of Mr. Tanaka's flute came, floating like bird-song in the air. "How right Lilay was," Pilar said. "There! Don't you hear something?"

"Is that the Japanese?" Adela asked.

"Don't mind him," said Pilar. "Keep your fingers this way, and relax your elbow . . . ."

But Adela could not keep the flute-player out of her mind. She sat stiff, her shoulders wooden, her arms heavy. "Oh, will I ever learn, you think?" she said pitifully.

"Of course, you will—you will!" Pilar could not have been more encouraging. "Just don't be too impatient with yourself. Let's try again tomorrow."

And what would tomorrow be like? Pilar couldn't help thinking. By being quite casual about it, her father managed to make her not mind her admirers dropping in. Mr. Posas the postmaster came to listen for an hour the next day; and then it was only a short wait before Mr. Rodrigo the lawyer joined him. Both remarked on how readily she had recovered the skills she had learned while an *interna* at La Concordia; and this made her wonder whether her father found an interesting prospect in Mr. Rodrigo, although she couldn't understand why that should be the case. The lawyer had some business to look into in preparation for the visit of the Court of First Instance in a month or so, from what she heard. Mr. Rodrigo was stocky, dark, and pockmarked; he was quite difficult to admire. While you heard nothing about Mr. Posas the postmaster, the people thought well of Mr. Rodrigo. They said he was an *abogado de campanilla*, a lawyer with a bell—a brilliant member of the bar.

"But Papa," said Pilar, when her father remarked that Attorney Rodrigo had paid her three visits and in order that he would become properly bored, she had played "Anillo de Hierro" repeatedly. "How do you expect me to be nice to him?"

"The reason is clear enough," replied the father. "I have heard—and I need not say from whom—that one of these days the Governor, no less, will be coming to pay us a visit on that man's account."

"For what purpose?" Pilar pretended ignorance.

"Not simply to pay us a visit—that's certain," her father said.

"We can be polite and offer the Governor some refreshments. Sarsaparilla and biscuits. Will those do?"

"And what should I tell him then?"

"That business is good, that the price of copra keeps going up. That should please him."

"But that's no reason for all the trouble of coming over . . . ."

"Then tell him anything you wish," Pilar said.

"He'll probably have Attorney Rodrigo for company," said the father.

"What will the governor need the other one for?"

"They are likely to ask for your hand," said the father.

Pilar said quickly, laughing: "Then I'll have a knife ready. And a platter, too." She knew that her father was familiar with a *corrido* that had a narrative sequence of this sort. Her father had once read it to her, and she remembered what the heroine in the story had asked. "Is it the left or the right hand that they want? Which, do you think?"

The father remembered, too. "That, indeed, is in the 'Life and Sad Experiences of the Princess Amalia, of the Kingdom of Palms and Roses.' But it is insolence to treat this matter so lightly," Juan Molino said without a trace of anger that his daughter could detect. "Someday you'll know better."

"Please, Papa," she said. "Don't let any one come on *that* account."

The lessons went on; things went well enough except that Mr. Tanaka's flute came in their way. Adela would be practicing a scale and then on hearing the flute she would suddenly stop as though her fingers had gone limp.

"You forget the fingering so easily," Pilar would remind her.

In the end she had to tell Pilar the truth. "There, listen to him," Adela said. "Doesn't that make one feel lonely? Funny, isn't it?"

Pilar wouldn't admit it, though. "You are being foolish," she said.

Indeed, try as she might, she could not find in the tunes that came across the street anything that could affect her emotionally; she couldn't help wondering what could be wrong with her otherwise eager pupil.

Late one evening, though, when the house was quiet and Mr. Tanaka was once more at his flute, the feeling that Adela spoke of did come to Pilar. So it seemed, anyhow. A quite tangible and lumpy catch in the throat, it made her think of long stretches of wind-washed beaches, of trees bending in the wind.

"Mama," she told her the next morning, "why after all this time have we not asked Mr. Tanaka over for dinner or *merienda*?"

Tomasa was stumped. "That's true, isn't it?"

"Don't you think we should?"

"On what occasion?"

"Nothing in particular. He has been playing that thing. Haven't you heard him?"

"What has that to do with it?"

"He's just there across the street and all by himself," Pilar said.

"What ideas you have," said her mother.

"I think he wants us to have him over," Pilar said, feeling she hasn't really said what she wanted to.

"Then ask him over for merienda," her mother said. "Send Lilay over tomorrow."

Pilar made a modest affair of it, inviting only Adela, the postmaster Mr. Posas and, because her father insisted on it, Attorney Rodrigo as well. Lilay left her washing to help make rice-cakes and some ginger tea.

When at last Mr. Tanaka came with his flute, they were overwhelmed. He was attired in his *kimono*, or something of that sort, and had on his wooden shoes. Half of the greetings and introductions consisted of bowings and grunts, for Mr. Tanaka did not speak Visayan too well. The postmaster and Attorney Rodrigo asked awkward questions about his costume, as if his wearing it had endangered public morality. They were puzzled by the work he was engaged in, they confessed, and they all told him to his face that perhaps he had been up to something beyond the pale.

"I write book about animals of sea and land. Someday, someday," Mr. Tanaka said.

Pilar tried as best she could to play the thoughtful hostess. To this end, limited as their means of communication was, she had to fall back on the flute.

"Play for us something beautiful," Adela said encouragingly.

"What you call beautiful?" said Mr. Tanaka.

"You know, like this—" Postmaster Posas whistled a folk tune.

"Ah," said Mr. Tanaka, smiling. He had large, stained teeth. "I try— yes," he said, raising his flute to his lips. The initial run of notes he produced sounded so plaintive that Adela gaped at him in wonder.

"Better with piano, I think," Mr. Tanaka told Pilar.

To oblige, Pilar tried out a chord in accompaniment, but somehow the expected harmony did not materialize.

"Play 'Anillo de Hierro' then," suggested Attorney Rodrigo.

Pilar did the opening bars of the "Anillo" and they urged Mr. Tanaka to follow, but he succeeded only in making his lips tremble in a silly way.

Attorney Rodrigo found it difficult to restrain himself from laughing. "It's those lips, those eyes of his!" he said, between fits.

"Let him play his own tune first," Postmaster Posas suggested to Pilar. "Then you follow."

"No. That will not be," said Mr. Tanaka, trying all the more to smile.

Attorney Rodrigo let himself go altogether. Pockmarked though he was, his cheeks looked smooth enough whenever he laughed as heartily as that.

"I try, I try," said Mr. Tanaka, raising his flute to his lips again.

Pilar wheeled her piano stool around, resolved to be at least serious and polite. Meanwhile, in the middle of the sala, Mr. Tanaka held forth— dignity and intentness personified. Carried away by the rapture that his own music evoked, he would now and again close his eyes.

"You like, Miss Pilar?" he asked, on completing one number. "You like, Miss Adela?"

The two said "Yes" almost in unison while Mr. Posas and Attorney Rodrigo both looked embarrassedly at each other.

"Now, *sayonara*. Goodbye, I go," Mr. Tanaka said.

Bowing to each one of them, he retreated to the porch and, finally, to the steps, his wooden shoes clattering upon the boards.

When the *Uranos* arrived the next Saturday afternoon, Mr. Tanaka's trunk and boxes of specimens were ready.

"I go Nippon now," he said, bidding Pilar's mother goodbye at the grocery shop.

Tomasa had two servants help him with his things, which were promptly sent down to the wharf, their owner following, to all appearances eager to board the steamer as early as possible.

Juan Molino went to see him after the day's work at Rivas y Cia. and Pilar thought that was very kind indeed of her father. Mr. Tanaka had been, if rather strange in behavior, a good lodger. He had done no one any harm. She wished she had shown him more kindness or had perhaps given him a little more attention, though.

As was his habit, Juan Molino worked on his books directly after supper. Pilar did not feel equal to practicing on her piano that evening; and it was quiet in the house on Calle Progreso, so quiet that she could hear her father's pen scratching away on a page of his ledger. She went up to him and stood, curious, by his side.

"July 7, 1915" she read, admiring the cursive style, the hallmark of her father's penmanship. The page bore the heading "Mr. Tanaka, the Japanese." After drawing a heavy line at the bottom to close the entry, her father added: "Departed for his homeland."

As he was about to put the ledger away, Juan Molino turned his attention to some strange sounds that came from the porch. Pilar herself heard footsteps. A dog had been barking somewhere down the street a few minutes back, and she had thought nothing of it. For a moment all was quiet again, and then there was this voice calling softly:

"*Manong* Juan!"

Pilar recognized who it was instantly. "Is that you, Lilay?" she said. Her father went to the door.

"It's Diego, Manong. I had to come . . . . That Diego's a beast!"

She looked haggard, exhausted. Her dress, one of the cotton things that Pilar had passed on to her, was torn at the back and sleeves.

"Lilay, what's happened to you?" Pilar asked.

But instead of answering, Lilay flung her arms about her and began to cry. "That beast!" she kept saying, as if the word summed up everything she wanted to tell the world.

"You go quietly to the kitchen and get something to eat, if you haven't had supper yet," Juan Molino said, as though food was his answer to everything. "I see that you have brought your belongings along. What does this mean?"

Pilar noticed, too, the little bundle at Lilay's feet.

"I am not hungry, Manong," said the woman.

"Then go quietly to the kitchen," Pilar heard her father say again, perhaps to protect her against whatever blight this was that Lilay suffered from and which she could easily cause to spread.

Then in the throbbing silence of the sala, they sat together, father and daughter, without exchanging a word. Against the dining room wall the German piano stood, its brass candle-holders catching the light, a brooding presence that made the moment alive once more with the music that Pilar knew by heart—"Love and Devotion," "Flower Song," "Poet and Peasant"—music with which she must learn to woo the world into being less harsh and, perhaps, less rude.

1964

Part Five

The Bread of Salt

USUALLY I WAS in bed by ten and up by five and thus was ready for one more day of my fourteenth year. Unless Grandmother had forgotten, the fifteen centavos for the baker down Progreso Street—and how I enjoyed jingling those coins in my pocket!—would be in the empty fruit-jar in the cupboard. I would remember then that rolls were what Grandmother wanted because recently she had lost three molars. For young people like my cousins and myself, she had always said that the kind called *pan de sal* ought to be quite all right.

The bread of salt! How did it get that name? From where did its flavor come; through what secret action of flour and yeast? At the risk of being jostled from the counter by early buyers, I would push my way into the shop so that I might watch the men who, stripped to the waist, worked their long flat wooden spades in and out of the glowing maw of the oven. Why did the bread come nut-brown and the size of my little fist? And why did it have a pair of lips convulsed into a painful frown? In the half-light of the street, and hurrying, the paper bag pressed to my chest, I felt my curiosity a little gratified by the oven-fresh warmth of the bread I was proudly bringing home for breakfast.

Well I knew how Grandmother would not mind if I nibbled away at one piece; perhaps, I might even eat two, to be charged later against my share at the table. But that would be betraying a trust; and so, indeed, I kept my purchase intact. To guard it from harm, I watched my steps and avoided the dark street corners.

For my reward, I had only to look in the direction of the seawall and the fifty yards or so of riverbed beyond it, where an old Spaniard's house stood. At low tide, when the bed was dry and the rocks glinted with broken bottles, the stone fence of the Spaniard's compound set off the house as if it were a castle. Sunrise brought a wash of silver upon the roof of the laundry and garden sheds which had been built low and close to the fence. On dull mornings the light dripped from the bamboo screen which covered the veranda and hung some four or five yards from the ground. Unless it was August, when the damp northeast monsoon had to be kept away from the rooms, three servants raised the screen promptly at six-thirty until it was completely hidden under the veranda eaves. From the sound of the pulleys I knew it was time to set out for school.

It was in his service, as a coconut plantation overseer, that Grandfather had spent the last thirty years of his life. Grandmother had been widowed three years now. I often wondered whether I was being depended upon to spend the years ahead in the service of this great house. One day I learned that Aida, a classmate in high school, was the old Spaniard's niece. All my doubts disappeared. It was as if before his death, Grandfather had spoken to me about her, concealing the seriousness of the matter by putting it over as a joke. If now I kept true to the virtues, she would step out of her bedroom ostensibly to say Good Morning to her uncle. Her real purpose, I knew, was to reveal thus her assent to my desire.

On quiet mornings I imagined the patter of her shoes upon the wooden veranda floor as a further sign, and I would hurry off to school, taking the route she had fixed for me past the post office, the town plaza and the church, the health center east of the plaza, and at last the school grounds. I asked myself whether I would try to walk with her and decided it would be the height of rudeness. Enough that in her blue skirt and white middy she would be half a block ahead and, from that distance, perhaps throw a glance in my direction, to bestow upon my heart a deserved and abundant blessing. I believed it was but right that in some such way as this her mission in my life was disguised.

Her name, I was to learn many years later, was a convenient mnemonic for the qualities to which argument might aspire. But in those days it was a living voice. "Oh that you might be worthy of uttering me," it said. And how I endeavored to build my body so that I might live long to honor her. With every victory at singles at the handball court—the game was then the craze at school—I could feel my body glow in the sun as though it had instantly been cast in bronze. I guarded my mind and did not let my wits go astray. In my class I would not allow a lesson to pass unmastered. Our English teacher could put no question before us that did not have a ready answer in my head. One day, he read Robert Louis Stevenson's *The Sire de Maletroit's Door*, and we were so enthralled that our breaths trembled. I knew then that somewhere, sometime in the not too improbable future, a benign old man with a lantern in his hand would also detain me in a secret room and there daybreak would find me thrilled by the sudden certainty that I had won Aida's hand.

It was perhaps on my violin that her name wrought such a tender spell. Maestro Antonino remarked the dexterity of my stubby fingers. Quickly I raced through Alard—until I had all but committed two thirds of the book to memory. My short brown arm learned at last to draw the bow with grace. Sometimes when practising my scales in the early evening, I wondered if the sea wind carrying the straggling notes across the pebbled river did not transform them into a Schubert's *Serenade*.

At last Mr. Custodio, who was in charge of our school orchestra, became aware of my progress. He moved me from second to first violin. During the Thanksgiving Day program he bade me render a number complete with pizzicati and harmonics.

"Another Vallejo! Our own Albert Spalding!" I heard from the front row.

Aida, I thought, would be in the audience. I looked around quickly but could not see her. As I retired to my place in the orchestra I heard Pete Saez, the trombone player, call my name.

"You must join *my* band," he said. "Look, we'll have many engagements soon. It'll be vacation time."

Pete pressed my arm. He had for some time now been asking me to join the Minviluz Orchestra, his private band. All I had been able to tell him was that I had my school work to mind. He was twenty-two. I was perhaps too young to be going around with him. He earned his school fees and supported his mother hiring out his band at leas‡ three or four times a month. He now said:

"Tomorrow we play at a Chinaman's funeral. Four to six in the afternoon. In the evening, Judge Roldan's silver wedding anniversary. Sunday, the municipal dance."

My head began to whirl. On the stage, in front of us, the Principal had begun a speech about America. Nothing he could say about the Pilgrim Fathers and the American custom of feasting on turkey seemed interesting. I thought of the money I would earn. For several days now I had but one wish, to buy a box of linen stationery. At night when the house was quiet I would fill the sheets with words that would tell Aida how much I adored her. One of these mornings, perhaps before school closed for the holidays, I would borrow her algebra book and there upon, a good pageful of equations, there I would slip my message, tenderly pressing the leaves of the book. She would perhaps never write back. Neither by post nor by hand would a reply reach me. But no matter; it would be a silence full of voices.

That night I dreamed I had returned from a tour of the world's music centers; the newspapers of Manila had been generous with praise. I saw my picture on the cover of a magazine. A writer had described how many years ago I used to trudge the streets of Buenavista with my violin in a battered black cardboard case. In New York, he reported, a millionaire had offered me a Stradivarius violin, with a card which bore the inscription: "In admiration of a genius your own people must surely be proud of." I dreamed I spent a week-end at the millionaire's country house by the Hudson. A young girl in a blue skirt and white middy clapped her lily-white hands and, her voice trembling, cried "Bravo!"

What people now observed at home was the diligence with which I attended to my violin lessons. My aunt, who had come from the farm to join her children for the holidays brought with her a maid-servant, and to the poor girl was given the chore of taking the money to the baker's for rolls and pan de sal. I realized at once that it would be no longer becoming on my part to make these morning trips to the baker's. I could not thank my aunt enough.

I began to chafe on being given other errands. Suspecting my violin to be the excuse, my aunt remarked:

"What do you want to be a musician for? At parties, musicians always eat last."

Perhaps, I said to myself, she was thinking of a pack of dogs scrambling for scraps tossed over the fence by some careless kitchen maid. She was the sort you could depend on to say such vulgar things. For that reason, I thought, she ought not to be taken seriously at all.

But the remark hurt me. Although Grandmother had counseled me kindly to mind my work at school, I went again and again to Pete Saez's house for rehearsals.

She had demanded that I deposit with her my earnings; I had felt too weak to refuse. Secretly, I counted the money and decided not to ask for it until I had enough with which to buy a brooch. Why this time I wanted to give Aida a brooch, I didn't know. But I had set my heart on it. I searched the downtown shops. The Chinese clerks, seeing me so young, were annoyed when I inquired about prices.

At last the Christmas season began. I had not counted on Aida's leaving home, and remembering that her parents lived in Badajoz, my torment was almost unbearable. Not once had I tried to tell her of my love. My letters had remained unwritten, and the algebra book unborrowed. There was still the brooch to find, but I could not decide on the sort of brooch I really wanted. And the money, in any case, was in Grandmother's purse, which smelled of "Tiger Balm." I grew somewhat feverish as our class Christmas program drew near. Finally it came; it was a warm December afternoon. I decided to leave the room when our English teacher announced that members of the class might exchange gifts. I felt fortunate; Pete was at the door, beckoning to me. We walked out to the porch where, Pete said, he would tell me a secret.

It was about an *asalto* the next Sunday which the Buenavista Women's Club wished to give Don Esteban's daughters, Josefina and Alicia, who were arriving on the morning steamer from Manila. The spinsters were much loved by the ladies. Years ago, when they were younger, these ladies studied solfeggio with Josefina and the piano and harp with Alicia. As Pete told me all this, his lips ash-gray from practising all morning on his trombone,

I saw in my mind the sisters in their silk dresses, shuffling off to church for the evening benediction. They were very devout, and the Buenavista ladies admired that. I had almost forgotten that they were twins and, despite their age, often dressed alike. In low-bosomed voile bodices and white summer hats, I remembered, the pair had attended Grandfather's funeral, at old Don Esteban's behest. I wondered how successful they had been in Manila during the past three years in the matter of finding suitable husbands.

"This party will be a complete surprise," Pete said, looking around the porch as if to swear me to secrecy. "They've hired our band."

I joined my classmates in the room, greeting everyone with a Merry Christmas jollier than that of the others. When I saw Aida in one corner unwrapping something two girls had given her, I found the boldness to greet her also.

"Merry Christmas," I said in English, as a hairbrush and a powder case emerged from the fancy wrapping. It seemed to me rather apt that such gifts went to her. Already several girls were gathered around Aida. Their eyes glowed with envy, it seemed to me, for those fair cheeks and the bobbed dark-brown hair which lineage had denied them.

I was too dumbstruck by my own meanness to hear exactly what Aida said in answer to my greeting. But I recovered shortly and asked:

"Will you be away during the vacation?"

"No, I'll be staying here," she said. When she added that her cousins were arriving and that a big party in their honor was being planned, I remarked:

"So you know all about it?" I felt I had to explain that the party was meant to be a surprise, an asalto.

And now it would be nothing of the kind, really. The women's club matrons would hustle about, disguising their scurrying around for cakes and candies as for some baptismal party or other. In the end, the Rivas sisters would outdo them. Boxes of meringues, bonbons, ladyfingers, and cinnamon buns that only the Swiss bakers in Manila could make were perhaps coming on the boat with them. I imagined a table glimmering with long-stemmed punch glasses; enthroned in that array would be a huge brick-red bowl of gleaming china with golden flowers round the brim. The local matrons, however hard they tried, however sincere their efforts, were bound to fail in their aspiration to rise to the level of Don Esteban's daughters. Perhaps, I thought, Aida knew all this. And that I should share in a foreknowledge of the matron's hopes was a matter beyond love. Aida and I could laugh together with the gods.

At seven, on the appointed evening, our small band gathered quietly at the gate of old Don Esteban's house, and when the ladies arrived in their heavy shawls and trim *panuelos*, twittering with excitement, we were commanded to play the "Poet and Peasant" overture. As Pete directed the band, his eyes glowed with pride for his having been part of the big event. The multicolored lights that the old Spaniard's gardeners had strung along the vine-colored fence were switched on and the women remarked that Don Esteban's daughters might have made some preparations after all. Pete hid his face from the glare. If the women felt let down, they did not show it.

The overture shuffled along to its climax while five men in white shirts bore huge boxes of food into the house. I recognized one of the bakers in spite of the uniform. A chorus of confused greetings, and the women trooped into the house; and before we had settled in the *sala* to play "A Basket of Roses," the heavy damask curtains at the far end of the room were drawn and a long table richly spread was revealed under the chandeliers. I remembered that in our haste to be on hand for the asalto, Pete and I discouraged the members of the band from taking their suppers.

"You've done us a great honor!" Josefina, the more buxom of the twins, greeted the ladies.

"Oh, but you have not allowed us to take you by surprise!" the ladies demurred in a chorus.

There were sighs and further protestations amid a rustle of skirts and the glitter of earrings. I saw Aida in a long, flowing white gown and wearing an arch of *sampaguita* flowers on her hair. At her command, two servants brought out a gleaming harp from the music room. Only the slightest scraping could be heard because the servants were barefoot. As Aida directed them to place the instrument near the seats we occupied, my heart leaped to my throat. Soon she was lost among the guests, and we played "The Dance of the Glowworms." I kept my eyes closed and held for as long as I could her radiant figure before me.

Alicia played on the harp and then in answer to the deafening applause, she offered an encore. Josefina sang afterward. Her voice, though a little husky, fetched enormous sighs. For her encore, she gave "The Last Rose of Summer"; and the song brought back snatches of the years gone by. Memories of solfeggio lessons eddied about us, as if there were rustling leaves scattering all over the hall. Don Esteban appeared. Earlier, he had greeted the crowd handsomely, twisting his mustache to hide a natural shyness before talkative women. He stayed long enough to listen to the harp again, whispering in his rapture: "Heavenly, heavenly . . . ."

By midnight the merrymaking lagged. We played while the party gathered around the great table at the end of the sala. My mind travelled across the seas to the distant cities I had dreamed about. The sisters sailed among the ladies like two great white liners amid a fleet of tugboats in a bay. Someone had thoughtfully remembered—and at last Pete Saez signalled to us to put our instruments away. We walked in single file across the hall, led by one of the barefoot servants.

Behind us a couple of hoarse sopranos sang "La Paloma" to the accompaniment of the harp, but I did not care to find out who they were. The sight of so much silver and china confused me. There was more food before us than I had ever imagined. I searched in my mind for the names of the dishes; and my ignorance appalled me. I wondered what had happened to the boxes of food that the Buenavista ladies had sent up earlier. In a silver bowl was something, I discovered, that appeared like whole egg yolks that had been dipped in honey and peppermint. The seven of us in the orchestra were all of one mind about the feast; and so, confident that I was with friends, I allowed my covetousness to have its way and not only stuffed my mouth with this and that confection but also wrapped up a quantity of those egg yolk things in several sheets of napkin paper. None of my companions had thought of doing the same, and it was with some pride that I slipped the packet under my shirt. There, I knew, it would not bulge.

"Have you eaten?"

I turned around. It was Aida. My bow tie seemed to tighten around my collar. I mumbled something I did not know what.

"If you wait a little while till they've all gone, I'll wrap up a big package for you," she added.

I brought a handkerchief to my mouth. I might have honored her solicitude adequately and even relieved myself of any embarrassments. I could not quite believe that she had seen me, and yet I was sure that she knew what I had done; and I felt all ardor for her gone from me entirely.

I walked away to the nearest door, praying that the damask curtains hide me in my shame. The door gave on to the veranda, where once my love had trod on sunbeams. Outside it was dark, and a faint wind was singing in the harbor.

With the napkin balled up in my hand, I flung out my arm to scatter the egg yolk things in the dark. I waited for the soft sound of their fall on the garden-shed roof. Instead I heard a spatter in the rising night-tide beyond the stone fence. Farther away glimmered the light from Grandmother's window, calling me home.

But the party broke up at one or thereabouts. We walked away with our instruments after the matrons were done with their interminable goodbyes. Then, to the tune of "Joy to the World," we pulled the Progreso Street shopkeepers out of their beds. The Chinese merchants were especially generous. When Pete divided our collection under a street lamp, there was already a little glow of daybreak.

He walked with me part of the way home. We stopped at the baker's when I told him that I wanted to buy with my own money some bread to eat on the way to Grandmother's house at the edge of the seawall. He laughed, thinking it strange that I should be hungry. We found ourselves alone at the counter; and we watched the bakery assistants at work until our bodies grew warm from the oven across the door. It was not quite five, and the bread was not yet ready.

1958

The Whispering Woman

As THEY STOOD in the streetlight, Mr. Flores's face notebook-paper buff in the full glare from the lamppost nearby, Mr. Malto caught the strange gleam in his friend's eyes.

"Won't you join me for supper?" he asked. The boarding house was only a few steps away.

"No, thanks," said Mr. Flores.

Mr. Malto thought of other inducements. He remembered the week's batch of *Tribune* which had arrived in the mail.

"I have the Manila papers. Don't you want to see them?"

"Some other time, maybe," said Mr. Flores.

Mr. Malto felt defeated. Perhaps Flores wouldn't even consider rooming with him. What a pity, he thought. One always lodged at Mrs. Bello's; but Flores was different. It was customary to spend one's afternoon at the Rex Bowling Alley, or the Evangeline Drugstore; but Flores preferred walking down to the wharf and watching the sailboats bringing in copra from the islands across the bay. Instead of Mrs. Bello, Flores had this old couple on Calle Real in a tumbledown frame house.

"All right, if that's what you like," said Mr. Malto without resentment.

"See you tomorrow," said Mr. Flores.

Though his chuckle was heartening, Mr. Malto knew that he would never get through to him. And all the time, he thought, he was doing the fellow a favor.

Mr. Malto crossed the landing and hurried up the stairs, thinking: Well, anyway, I'm having the whole place to myself.

It had had its heyday, to judge from the picture album on display in the *sala*. There all of them smiled toothsomely or laughed off the immediate threats that life posed. Oh, you young clerks, schoolteachers, health inspectors, bachelors all, who have somehow found your way here! Mr. Malto felt like saying something unpleasant to every one of them.

There were three daughters, people at the Evangeline Drug Store had said. And from the Rex Bowling Alley crowd, Mr. Malto had learned other things: two of the girls had found good husbands—Fe, a Public Works supervisor; Esperanza, a Weather Bureau man. Mr. Malto did not ask any more whether the two men had been, even though but briefly, Mrs. Bello's boarders. He felt he did not need to know, having been assured that they had prospered in their respective stations.

For Mrs. Bello, who now had only Charity to help her carry on, a poor year loomed ahead. But it need not be a bad one; she had Mr. Malto at least. And Charity, the third and only unmarried daughter, looked intelligent enough. Mr. Malto felt he could count on being well-fed and comfortable and, perhaps, happy. It was sad to see that his friend Flores had no such promise before him.

Tonight supper consisted of beef stew, rice, and two bananas. There was a surprise item, too: a platterful of mackerel in a rich, sweet sour sauce. Charity served, while her mother got Mr. Malto posted on the gossip of the day.

"What? A soldier? He had killed himself?" Mr. Malto asked.

Neither at Evangeline Drug Store nor at the Rex Bowling Alley had Mr. Malto heard about it, strangely enough.

Mrs. Bello had all the details. The poor fellow had put the muzzle of his gun to his mouth and then had worked the trigger with his big toe.

"Woman trouble, maybe," Mr. Malto said.

"Rice, sir?" Charity said, offering him the bowl.

He took only a small portion. He was deeply troubled by the suicide. Was the gun the only remedy? Could it not have been avoided? Mrs. Bello's word for the soldier's trouble was cowardice: Mr. Malto heard her say it clearly.

"Fish, sir?" said Charity. She pushed the sweet-sour dish closer towards him, crinkling the tablecloth and smoothing it carefully afterward so that its flowers, red and yellow, nameless roses of the factory, seemed less unreal. "Mother taught me how to cook it," she volunteered.

"Oh, it's nice," Mr. Malto said without conviction.

There was Mrs. Bello to his right, eager to continue with her story; and being quite fat, she almost spilled from her seat in her earnest effort to lean over, so characteristically her style. This had to be because she could not carry on a normal conversation. Some defect in her throat made it impossible. Instead of talking she whispered.

"Beg your pardon?" Mr. Malto said politely.

The bumble of a bee? The whizz of a wasp, perhaps? He could imagine no sound which Mrs. Bello's whisper resembled.

Sometimes Mrs. Bello put her lips too close to his ear, and a tingle would run up his spine. Throwing her head back later, she might chuckle pleasantly. Then he would say "Oh" as if he understood the indeterminable babble that it all had been.

Well, he would just have to get used to it. He went now to his favorite rocking chair in the sala while mother and daughter, following some self-imposed rule of their trade, hied away to the kitchen to eat their supper. The scratch of his matchstick as he lighted a cigarette underscored the initial clatter of their forks and spoons. His first puff recalled to him the soothing quiet of this very hour the evening before. Tonight seemed different. Up the window to his left, muggy air welled out from the street.

The shell-paned shutters offered a plaque of sky glittering with stars. He knew then that it would be a warm night—if rather the kind you might sit up in, enjoyably, given the right company and some lively topic of conversation.

Had he succeeded in getting Mr. Flores over for supper, they'd be discussing now the Hare-Hawes-Cutting Bill. Flores was an Osrox. By and large, Buenavista belonged to that camp. Mr. Malto thought that he personally belonged to another, that he stood for a more righteous kind of nationalism. The politicians, so far, had not quite organized the party he might join. Now, alone, he could only rock his heavy supper away. He smoked with joyous respect for his package of Piedmont.

Already, Mrs. Bello and Charity were through, it seemed, with supper. He recalled the dead soldier, but rather than listen to Mrs. Bello, Mr. Malto thought, he should be out there in his room, working.

He could hear them moving about the kitchen floor, and once again mother and daughter impinged on his thoughts. They'd perhaps join him under the buzzing Coleman lamp one evening—who could tell? Once he had managed to carry on a conversation with Charity; she had looked all her eighteen years, every day in them, the last ones at a Manila dressmaking school included. That had been an experience which must have surely changed her, although he could not tell in what way. She had sat there, mildly handsome, across the table from him, with the embroidered runner and the flower vase between them; and he had said:

"When will you be opening that dress shop?"

"It'll be up to Mother."

Thus, all over the country, Mr. Malto thought, on some such Sunday evening as this, ineffectual young men were visiting similarly ineffectual young girls and bogging down in a similar mire of dialog.

It could look, though, as if he were one of the young men who paid her some attention, which in fact he had not even thought of doing. Meanwhile, moths nettled the lamp, some falling dead on his hair and others on the embroidered table-runner. Quite simply a ghastly thing, especially with Mrs. Bello there, edging over to whisper—again—something in his ear . . . .

Rather than risk all that now, he hurried away to his room. The dining table stood directly in his way. It was a bother having to turn all around and, as if frantic about something, he reached for the door jamb.

His room looked as good as on that day he had brought in his suitcase two weeks ago. He had had to try the iron bed. He had found it springy enough, and up till now it had not begun to creak. He changed into his pajamas, thinking how things around had not been so bad, really. The food had been good; and his room was fine, any way you looked at it.

Flores—how could he be possibly better lodged and fed? It would be no use trying to get him to live out here, though. Let him alone . . . .

Mr. Malto's work, three pages that must be filled out with plans for the week's Civics and History classes, awaited him at the desk by his bed. But as he buckled down to the task, adjusting the wick of the table-lamp so that the light became agreeably brighter, Mrs. Bello's favorite little stories, which had been whispered into his ear through several delightful meals, came slipping back to him.

She had been full of them. Strange macabre accounts of illnesses and deaths, involving middle-aged men stiffening up in their beds, with strangers standing by, glassy-eyed in their unconcern. She had told him about lonely Chinese shopkeepers drugged with opium in their dens. Drunks, hitting each other with broken bottles, and, their skulls cracked, babbling away with some woman's name on their lips. And they were one and the same story, however varied they appeared.

Not only had they been told to him in the one manner that Mrs. Bello knew, but they seemed to be burdened by the same message. Here was something at once fascinating and dreadful, Mr. Malto was convinced. He felt his thoughts wandering in some direction, near what might be hell or purgatory. A sense of destiny seemed to hang on every word Mrs. Bello breathed. Somehow, too, her stories mixed readily with what he as a teacher knew about wars and revolutions, the murder of kings and presidents of republics, the fall of governments. The thought cut a groove in his mind. He gasped for air but only breathed in the mugginess that rose from the street below.

He had to put his work away. He extinguished the lamp. The house was quiet. No, there were light footsteps outside, followed by the faint clatter of glass. It had become a familiar sound these past three nights. Only, he had not bothered about it. He had often heard his heart thumping, too. Those footsteps had stopped just outside his door, and he had never gone out to investigate. He did not wish to now. It was time for taps; the bugle call would come all the way from across town. He did not want to miss it.

The Constabulary barracks was over down to the south, and the night wind now played tricks with the bugle. It carried the soul-freighted notes over the rooftops and flung them against the wall of coconut-covered hills. The notes rebounded in broken echoes. Then, over the rooftops again the fragments gathered and merged into a great cry of loneliness. To Mr. Malto, it confirmed the death of the soldier. Truth was in every shred of Mrs. Bello's whispers.

She had fixed his bed with fresh sheets, and the pillow now under his head was as soft as the agar-agar bars he had played with as a boy in his mother's kitchen. More thoughtful than his mother had ever been, Mrs. Bello had provided him with a second pillow, an *abrasador* for his legs. He had not quite appreciated the gift before. Now it surprised him that the dutch pillow was as ample as life; he could have convinced himself that it was warm, that in reality it was flesh.

He tossed about restlessly, willing enough to admit that he had debased his thoughts. So this was what it all would lead to—marriage. Who wanted to marry whom? Mrs. Bello? Charity? So this was why Mrs. Bello had encouraged him to give out little confidences about himself. Nine years in the government service and with a little something tucked away in the Postal Savings Bank. He really had no cares in this world, nor perhaps in the next. And in return she had told him about her dear dead, the husband who, living, had been a Constabulary sergeant and a clean man. Although he had captured a bandit, rounded up opium smokers, and caught fishermen with sticks of dynamite in their hands, Sergeant Bello had died in bed. To Mrs. Bello, this was proof enough of grace. Remarry? No, it would spoil things. And she shook her head—her whole whispering body, even. It seemed to Mr. Malto, wiping now the moist feel off his ears, that he could see her fat rippling loose all over her.

He rubbed his ear against the starch-smooth pillow cover, as if to drive off every single sensation which, put together, summoned up all the things Mrs. Bello had told him. He tried to sleep. His legs jerked off the abrasador, and then he fell into the abyss between sleep and waking, and he thought of coffins walking on two short feet, carrying suitcases and looking for fat, smiling landladies, calling, "Flores! Flores!"—although it was he, Malto, in the end, who answered.

He got up in a cold sweat and struck a match. The light was slow in coming. The lamp had a big, round oil container; and this caught the glow and became a concave mirror that tossed back at him a contorted face. He hardly recognized the bleary eyes and the wet-looking nose. It was as if he had mourned the dead soldier, mourned the lost men, and mourned the wanderers who had had always so little time to indulge in their dreams, having been caught by some grim hand—that might also be the big toe— before the moment came when they had to be borne away.

His fear resolved itself into thirst. "A glass of water—water!" he cried, silently but trustfully—to throw off the morbidity, to test himself as quite awake.

He must blame it all on his heavy dinner and the muggy air. As he opened the door, something gleamed in the room; it was as if through those shell-paned window shutters, near where he had sat earlier, some tokens of sifted starlight had fallen.

It was a pitcher of water. A drinking glass stood beside it. There was a catch in his throat when he picked up the glass. The water, as he poured, had that gleam he had caught in Flores's eyes.

Thank you, Charity," he said, softly, to the dark. "Goodnight."

1955

Come and Go

ONE MORNING IN October 1940, Felipe (Alias Philip) Bautista, thirty-six, steward third class, U.S. Naval Transport Service, arrived in Buenavista on the *Nuestra Señora del Carmen* for a brief visit with his family. He had neither written nor sent a wire. He had done so on purpose. To *Nanay*, letters had somehow meant serious money troubles; telegrams had never been anything but ruthless messengers of death. With a notice from the North American Life Assurance Co., of Toronto, in her hand, she once spent an afternoon wandering all over town, seeking out relatives and friends for counsel; for she could not quite bring herself to believe that anyone in the world could possibly have the kindness to offer her two thousand pesos just because Papa had died. Yet that was exactly what the letter said, and she had walked home with a heavy heart, shaking her head, unable to comprehend the disguises of Providence.

Philip had not found this amusing at all, although in a quite longish letter of Perla's that had reached him in San Francisco, she had said that it was. Nanay was now five years dead, Philip told himself. It was pointless to ask what she would say about this visit, but he couldn't help thinking of her. Surely, were she alive, she should wish he had brought along some presents for the family.

Unfortunately, he had bought his ticket on impulse; and realizing that he had no time to shop, he did not even try to get a bag or two of oranges and mangoes from the rowdy fruit peddlers at the pier. The family would understand, he had hoped; and by family Philip meant merely his sister

179

Perla, whom he had not seen in thirteen years, and her husband, whom he knew only by name.

He had not expected any one to meet him at the wharf and, though the crowd was large and the air rang with suddenly familiar greetings in Bisayan, he did find no one there to welcome him. He reminded himself that there were but ninety tons of copra to load up from the Stevenson warehouse; for this he might allow two hours. Promptly afterward, he figured, the ship would weigh anchor for the return voyage to Manila.

A short walk across the town plaza and past the market place, and he was home. And this then was Perla, the "Perls" of those letters he had posted from such odd places at Baltimore, Port Niches, and Vancouver. She had run up to the porch, crying, "Oh, *manong*, you almost scared me!"—and what with the children gathered about her, she looked like Nanay all over, the Nanay of long ago, before he had put the two poles of the earth between them.

"This must be Rebby," he said, holding the feet of the baby that Perls carried astride her hip, exactly as Nanay in her day might carry around a ten-month-old. "Did I scare you also, Rebby?" he asked. Her feet were the softest things his hands had held in a long time.

Jerking her legs, Rebby gave out a shrill, tremulous cry. "But it's your uncle Philip!" said Perls and, turning to him, explained: "She's just now cutting her teeth. That's why she's so bad-tempered . . . . And this is Sid," she added, pulling gently from behind her the little girl who had been clinging to the Mother Hubbard that made Perls look like a long-widowed fishwife. "You be quiet, you!" she threatened, slapping Rebby on the thigh. "You've come on the *Carmen*? It's already six. My, we must have breakfast soon. Ruuuuddy! Ruuuuuuuddddddyyyy!" she called. But no one answered. "He must have gone to buy the bread already. That boy minds his chores."

So this is the family: the thought kept coming like a refrain. And this the house: a three-room frame house set on the side of the rock-covered hill overlooking the harbor. Here it was, complete with the strip of gravelled road before it and the embankment that kept the sea away at high tide. The porch, not yet washed dry by the morning sunshine, had the dank odor that exuded from those rocks and the soursop trees in the yard.

Perls led the way into the *sala* and opened the windows that framed in each of them a view of the wharf and the interisland steamer moored alongside. Beside the Stevenson warehouse rose the hill of copra from where a hundred stevedores or so, like hungry ants blessed with a pile of sugar, hurried off to the ship, the brown sacks on their sweat-soaked and glistening bodies.

Philip wanted to enjoy the scene, for it recalled something from his boyhood. But Perls wanted to show him the room where Papa and Nanay had died. The four-poster with its sagging *bejuco* weave, except perhaps for the torn sheet that Rudy had slipped out of, was exactly as Philip had seen it last. On the floor was a *buri* mat over which a green-and-red checkered mosquito bar hung; here, then, Perls and the two children slept. She had dragged out Rebby and Sid from here to see who had been pounding at the door.

"I didn't recognize your voice," Perls confessed, laughing. "Fermin—that's my husband—is with us only three nights of the week. I thought you were somebody sent over from Agsawa to bring bad news."

"And what does he do in Agsawa? That's on the other side of the island, isn't it?"

"That's where he teaches. He's been banished, you know. And he has not been well. Asthma. Perhaps worsened by his going up and down the steep mountain road."

"I hope he gets better," Philip said, feeling suddenly injured and angry even at how luck had cheated his sister. She ought to have found somehow a much healthier man for a husband. That would have been a relief at least. Philip had no idea of how this fellow Fermin looked, never having seen even a picture of him. The name itself didn't sound right; Philip imagined a thin long-necked creature of forty, with a wheezing in his throat at each gulp of rain-fresh mountain air.

"Friday night he's here. It's a three-hour hike. Then he's back early Monday morning."

"That's difficult," Philip said.

"We can't join him because Rudy's in Grade Six now. Besides, somebody has to stay in this house."

"Perhaps, things will turn out right in the end," Philip said, lamely. He had taken off his gabardine jacket and hung it on the back of the rattan chair.

"I hope so," Perls said.

"And how old are you, Sid?" Philip asked his niece, telling himself: You can't bear the children any grudges. You mustn't, anyway.

"Six," the girl declared, in English.

"You're in school already? Which grade?"

"Two," the girl said, holding up two fingers of her right hand.

"Rebby's really fourteen months now," Perls said. "You will stay till Saturday, maybe? That's three days at least."

"I can't," said Philip. "I must be back, on that boat over there," and he pointed to the *Carmen* quietly sitting at the wharf.

"Then you'll not meet him—Fermin, I mean."

"I'm sorry."

"You can't stay, really?"

"I have to be back on my ship by tomorrow evening. I'm lucky enough to have this leave."

"Why, will there be war? People here talk a lot about it," Perls said. "That's why I keep telling my husband, 'Don't feel so bad about things. This is not yet the worst,' I say to him."

"Maybe, you're right," Philip admitted.

"But we'll be safe here? What do you think?" Perls said, nervously. Philip noticed she kept patting Rebby on the back, perhaps to conceal her anxiety.

"You shouldn't worry," said Philip.

"The war will be far away?"

"Maybe," Philip began, but decided not to continue. The transport *USNS Harold Tilyard Matson* had brought fresh units of the 61st Infantry to Manila, but he couldn't tell her sister that. He had expected her to ask: What then? What will happen? Will you be safe? But Perls was doubtless wrapped up in her own small troubles. Husband away in some God-forsaken station, and with asthma and all that. Rebby undernourished.

Rudy and Sid to keep in school. Old house to look after. He understood the facts, but something rankled inside him. The name Fermin—that was it! It grated in his ears.

A strange mood prodded his thoughts back to those days when he had begged Papa and Nanay permission to go to America. It pained him to remember the trouble he had caused. Winning Nanay over had been difficult. In his desperation, he had resorted to acting like a blackguard in high school, picking fights, insulting the history teacher, openly challenging the principal to a nine-round boxing bout. From all the trouble he had caused, it became quite clear that as a growing disgrace to the family he ought to be away and out of sight.

Raising the money for his fare had not been easy either. It had to be steerage, but even then Papa had to mortgage his five-hectare coconut grove in Bankalanan. It was three years later that Papa died, and to Philip was sent half of the insurance money so that he might return home. The question had not been, Return home to what? but, rather, with what? A year in Hawaii, two summers in Alaska, and, in between, dreary months in the farms of Fresno. His pride told him he could not go back with only stories about the pool rooms in Sacramento for the folks. Nor would they be satisfied with even the choicest secrets of the *sikoy-sikoy* joints of San Francisco.

He wrote fewer and fewer letters. It was only after Nanay's death, he remembered, that he had hit on the nickname Perls. A correspondence began which, if desultory, took account of Fermin and the children, one after another as they came. In some way all of them became, for Philip, more than ten thousand miles away, somewhat real people.

"Come, Sid. Sit here by me," he called to the little girl and made room for her on the chair.

But she drew away. Philip noticed for the first time the dress she wore; it looked like an undershirt that her brother had discarded five years before.

"It's your own Uncle Philip, Sid," her mother reminded the girl.

"Let me give you five dollars," he said, pulling out his wallet. He flicked the crisp note before handing it to the girl. "Buy yourself a dress."

"But Philip!" said Perls. "Maybe you don't have enough yourself."

"Who? Me?" he laughed.

"And what do you say to your Uncle Philip?" Perls pressed the girl.

Sid stepped forward but kept her eyes to the floor. "Thank you, Uncle," she said.

"Bright girl! And here's another five dollars for Rebby," said Philip. "Look, Rebby," he said, touching the little one's cheek with his forefinger. "Tell Mama to buy a dress also. Now don't you forget."

"They do really need clothes and shoes," said Perls. "The Bankalanan coconuts—we paid up the mortgage only three years ago—did not bring in enough last quarter. As for Fermin's salary—Well, you know how that is."

"What about Mama then? Doesn't Mama need anything?" He posed the question to both Rebby and Sid, chuckling, and then looked into his wallet as if counting the bills in it. He pulled out and gave Perls a fifty-dollar note.

"Sid," said Perls, "you better give me your money. You'll only lose it."

"And Rudy? Whatever happened to Rudy?" Philip asked. He felt expansive, relieved of those depressing thoughts, even of the resentments, a while back. "It's Rudy I remember very well." He showed Perls the cellophane leaf in his wallet. "I have been carrying this snapshot all these years. Look, he has Rebby's features—the eyes, especially."

Perls looked out the window, craning her neck in order to see beyond the point where the embankment turned. "Oh—wait—there he is now," she said.

Philip took Sid to the window: she was friendly again. He lifted her up so that she could see her brother coming down the road. "Rudy's almost a young man now," Philip said, seeing the barefoot boy with a paper bag in one hand hugged tight to his chest. He was pleased to see that his nephew had his mother's pleasing features—the oval face, the frank eyes, the full and well-shaped lips.

"Rudy," said Perls, as the boy stopped at the door. "Rudy, do you remember your uncle Philip?"

It was as if the boy was not looking at his mother but at some object beyond. His big round eyes did not blink.

"What have you told him about me?" Philip asked, suddenly vexed.

"Nothing. Nothing much. Except that last year, especially, he kept looking at maps and asking about you. That was when we received your postcard with the picture of your ship."

The reply soothed Philip a little. "Maybe, when he grows up he'll also . . ."

"Oh, no. God forbid!" Perls gasped.

The boy rubbed the soles of his feet self-consciously on the doorsill. Then he walked into the room as if, to begin with, he did not know what to do with the bag of bread he had bought.

"Let me have it," said his mother. "You look after Rebby. I'll prepare our breakfast."

"You were as big as Rebby when—" but Philip stopped. He was about to tell the boy:—when I first read about you. Instead, he showed him the snapshot in the wallet. "Do you know who that is?"

Rudy shook his head slowly.

"But that's you!" Philip said.

"Me?"

"That's you, of course!"

It was only then that Rudy smiled. He carried Rebby awkwardly and then the baby wet herself; he tried to hold her at arm's length. Philip took Rebby then from him and placed her on his chair.

"She will also wet your chair," said Rudy.

"That's all right," said Philip, keeping Rebby steady. "Tell me, what did your Mama say about me?" he asked softly, quickly.

They could hear Perls in the kitchen. A kettle had crashed to the floor, and the smoke from the woodstove smelled damp. The boy smiled.

"Tell me. What did your Mama say about your uncle Philip?"

"That you were bad."

"What else?"

"That you boxed people's ears and then ran away."

Philip laughed. "Your Mama, of all people!" he said, enjoying himself. "Now, listen, Rudy. You'll come with me to America, will you?" He felt he had to make it up with this boy somehow.

"But I'm too young," Rudy said, his eyes brightening.

"No, not now. When you're older. Look, I'll give you my jacket. Will you try it on?"

The boy fingered the smooth gray fabric, unbelieving, then swung the jacket over his shoulders. It fell very loose down his neck and shoulders. In his short pants and with his bony knees and skinny calves, he looked like a scarecrow out of season.

"Maybe next year, it will fit me," Rudy decided, after looking himself over.

"Good," Philip encouraged him. "And here's something else," he said, unfastening the gold watch off his wrist.

"It's for me, really?" Rudy held the bracelet gingerly, afraid that the gold would tarnish at his touch.

"For you," Philip said, now watching the boy wear the timepiece tight up his forearm. "Let's tell Mama all about it."

Rebby could not be kept long on the chair and so Philip had to take her away.

They had breakfast on the low form in the kitchen. Philip found the board damp and smelly, as though fish broth had been spilled over it and the wood had been soaked all over. He sat on the floor and, having rolled up his shirt-sleeves, dunked his bread in the chocolate that Perls had prepared. It was not as thick as he would have liked; and he saw that the long-necked brass pot Perls used had fallen to the floor, an arm's length from the woodstove. There was a saucerful of crisp anchovies that Perls had roasted in an old frying pan. There was also some fried rice. He was glad Perls had not brought out anything special.

"Rudy has a coat to wear when he goes to America. He has a watch, too," Philip said, halfway through the meal.

"It's your father who needs a watch, Rudy," said Perls, from where she sat with Rebby on her lap. Perls fed her with chocolate-dunked bread.

"The jacket doesn't fit him now; but, maybe, later—" Philip began again.

"It's your father who should be wearing things like that, Rudy. He has school programs and meetings to attend. He can use a coat and look better," said his mother.

"I'll let Papa wear it then," Rudy said. "But it still will be mine, won't it?"

"Of course," his uncle said.

"And Papa can use the watch, but it still will be mine," the boy pursued.

"It still will be yours," his uncle said.

"All right, it still will be yours," Perls conceded.

Philip imagined how his jacket would look on his scrawny brother-in-law and wished he had not been so generous to his nephew. He wished the watch would stop ticking the very moment his brother-in-law had it on. He couldn't help asking Perls: "This husband you have, does he take good care of you?"

"How funny you are, Philip," said Perls, putting another piece of bread into Rebby's mouth.

Presently, Rudy got up from the table. Sid followed. Perls was wiping little Rebby's chocolate-smeared face with the hem of the baby's dress when Philip got up and joined his nephew and niece in the sala.

"Look," Rudy cried, dancing in circles before his sister Sid. He had put on his uncle's gabardine jacket again. His arms lost in the long sleeves, Rudy dangled the gold watch, teasing his little sister by letting it touch her ears now and then.

"Mine! All mine!" Rudy said, thumping about like some wild little mountain man. Because Rudy would not let Sid listen to the ticking of the watch, the poor girl was almost in tears.

The *Carmen* let out a sharp hissing sound all of a sudden, followed by four taunting blasts.

"Now we have to hurry," said Perls, running to the bedroom.

After the four blasts, the ship's whistle gave out a long and deep heart wrenching moan. Rudy looked at his watch.

"Quick, put on your school uniforms," Perls said. She had brought out a little white blouse for Rebby and had changed herself, wearing now a pink, newly pressed cotton dress with little prints of sailboats at the hem. There would be just enough time to see Philip off. From the wharf, Rudy and Sid would have to hurry off to school.

A thin silver smoke hung over the ship's funnel, lingering there awhile. Philip was entranced by it. It rose in the air slowly transformed into a white silk ribbon, a piece of bunting for the arch of coconuts that crowned the hills beyond, across the bay. Then, in a trice, it was gone.

"That's right," Philip said, softly, as if to himself. "I really have to get back."

Vaguely, he saw where Rudy belonged. Then, more clearly: Friday was not too far away—soon the boy's joys would be over. Already, Perls could count on adding to her fifty dollars the ten from Rebby and Sid. But then all that money would go for clothes, shoes, and the medicines that Fermin—that horrible name!—needed for his asthma. And food, too.

Philip was frightened by his knowledge of Perls's burden, and he was hurt by his own foolish and futile gestures toward making it seem easier to bear. There was the war she feared, and she had forgotten him altogether. It seemed that his thirteen years of escape from this house had converged upon him for the sole purpose of making him wish Perls had all the strength and courage she needed; and he forgave her the chocolate, her exiled spouse, even the horrid Mother Hubbard. It was not inconceivable after all that someday, out there at sea, he would have to go, like that wisp of smoke, and vanish into nowhere.

1954

The Popcorn Man

IT WAS ONE and a half hours of dust and bumpy stretches ("Sorry, people," their driver would say) and then you had the sun to your left until the turn of the road near San Miguel. This was the chief commercial center in those parts; it was also where a freeway of sorts began, a demonstration piece built under the auspices of an ICA program and which led straight to the U.S. Army camp in the shelter of the Sierra Madre.

By three o'clock you were billeted at one of the quonsets clustered near the Camp Sierra Madre Officers Club, the CSMOC of the marquee. Today a huge sign announced that a two-week field commanders' conference on guerrilla techniques was in progress. In the acacia grove beyond the quonsets, you heard the orioles calling against the throbbing cicada music. You had always thought you could depend on those orioles to turn up if you didn't mind missing once in a while the lilt in their voices.

Thus began the routine of the professoriate of the Sierra Madre Air Force Base University Extension Program. A quick visit to the rest room, and the men in the group joined their women colleagues at the quonset across the yard. The ladies for their part, having discarded their travel-rumpled cotton frocks and changed into fresh ones, would lead the group to the Officers Club for *merienda*. There apple pies were often favored. Oh, but it could well be doughnuts today, although you were not supposed to rub that in. Those doughnuts had served vulgar purposes

189

enough, for anything for a good laugh had become the rule with them; and their attempts at humor had been excessive.

During the previous semester, Miss Elena's favorite had been strawberry ice-cream and Mrs. Dinglasan's pecan pie. Young Assistant Professor Perez had been partial to chicken sandwiches; Professor Leynes, to grilled cheese and fresh potato chips, lettuce and tomato. And then came a discovery: he could manage on popcorn. At his disposal, free of charge, was an entire basketful usually. He had only to reach across the table and he could have his fill, the next moment, of those crunchy, butter-flavored pops. Yes, why not? The CSMOC provided its members with a generous supply, and Professor Leynes was a cardbearing member, as were all the professoriate in the Extension Program. The regulations required it, and you had to get the regulations to work on your side. Professor Leynes's discovery was crucial, indeed. He had now only to raise his arm, bend a little forward, and without so much as a "Pardon my boarding-house reach" prove that many things in this world come free and in abundance.

The merienda was a function that all of them enjoyed if somewhat grudgingly. Too heavy to qualify as "tea," it was, however, too light to serve as "supper." But at best it offered a mirror of their character. Here, instead of saying "Please pass the cream," Mrs. Dinglasan, preferring her own brand of flippancy, could say: "Hello, milk!" Leynes had given up hope that she would ever learn to say "cream." Young Perez, whose subject was Philippine History, had caught on early enough in the game. He had learned to say "Hello, sugar!" During the previous term, Miss Elena, who then taught Economics, had two classes in a row and had particularly no time for a full-fledged meal. She had to resort to fried chicken "to go," but then this type of order was discontinued. She had been obliged to advance her supper to merienda time, asking for steak eagerly only to discover that it worked like a drug. At her first class, she'd turn up sluggish and dull; and at her second, embarrassingly sleepy. She had to abandon the practice altogether. If only she'd try popcorn, Professor Leynes suggested. But Miss Elena would not hear of it. She would have none, she declared, of Leynes's style.

"No offense meant, mind you!"

"That's quite all right," Leynes laughed it off.

But, in truth, he felt rather sluggish himself this otherwise fine afternoon. While drinking his coffee, which came free as well, he tried to be cheerful. "Hello, cream!" he said. But something had gone wrong; he couldn't put his finger on it. The best he could do was empty the popcorn container with determination and vigor.

After the merienda, some twenty minutes later, he retired with his colleagues to the bookshop. Today, as always, they might have been hungry children standing before a display of pastries. For the books could only be purchased with MPC's, which currency only bona fide officers could obtain and use. Browsing was allowed, however; and Leynes was satisfied with that.

Still the injustice rankled; and it stayed with him as he left his companions for the comfort room. There a haggard, fiftyish face stared at him from the mirror above the washstand. Noticing the bags under the stranger's eyes, he moistened his thumb and forefinger with warm water from the tap and gently worked his brow and temples until the soothing feeling went deep down, it seemed to him, to the very hollow of his cheeks.

On the way out, he paused at the weighing machine. A hundred and thirty-two pounds, it said. The job, it might be said, did not particularly agree with him. On the contrary, it exacted a heavy toll on his energies. Here was the result of two years of service. He walked away from the comfort room and proceeded to the main hall of the Club conscious that he produced none of those sprightly steps that the heavy carpet had known before. Only one advantage might be pointed out, he thought; he had been able to keep his weight down.

Freshman Composition, Section A, occupied a corner room at the east end of the last quonset on the row. The entire cluster of quonsets was called Benton Education Center, in memory of a general who had died in a plane crash some years back. It was, by day, Benton School for Camp Sierra Dependents. The room Leynes occupied had been outfitted, accordingly, for Fifth Grade History. A rack off one corner housed a collection of maps called "Rand and McNally's U.S. History in Color." The seats were curved for teenage buttocks; a pink refrigerator stood at the far end of the room, and a huge electric fan favored one corner with a low drone. It was impossible to look around and not imagine a spinsterly blonde demanding to know, smiling: "What and where was the Louisiana Purchase?"

Amidst the customarily indifferent greetings, Leynes entered his room. He acknowledged them perfunctorily and then began the session by passing around for signatures the blue attendance sheet required by Benton Education Center authorities. Muller, Schneider, Brown, Phelps—he ran through the names on the sheet. These were the stalwarts. Hammond and Metallous—why, in two out of six meetings the pair would be absent. But, today, they had turned up; they were as big as life. He remembered Weeks, who had died in a road accident; and Wilson, who had gone on TDY and, unable to catch up with the work, had elected to drop out. There had been others who, before you could become familiar with their faces, simply disappeared without a trace. And there was Harris, handsome and clever Jane Harris, who had been a joy and a pain. A girl from Georgia, she had been quick to see virtue in grammar; but she continued to split her infinitives and refused to see a run-on sentence even if shoved right in her face. And she hedged, equivocated, argued—the times she had flabbergasted him—using every weapon in her arsenal so that her innocence would not be violated. Worse, she chewed gum and popped it every so often like a seven-year-old.

Leynes braced up and said: "We have the Subjunctive Mood for today, don't we? On page 374 of the textbook is a very interesting chart. You probably had a chance to look at it . . . . Well, we shall see . . . . Miss Harris, can you explain how the verb 'to be' is used in the subjunctive?"

The university car collected the professoriate for the short trip to the Officers Club where they took their dinner. The company included Miss Elena now; she had a better schedule this semester.

For the delectation of the company, Leynes was about to say, thinking of young Perez: "Which reminds me that your students have been making a tally of the number of times you say 'Now' in the course of the lecture hour, and I overheard one of them saying you scored seventy-five tonight. No, eighty-three, said another . . . ." But he decided to keep the matter to himself. For Jane Harris occupied his mind. He had had trouble getting her to accept that it was permissible to use the indicative form of the verb in a sentence in the subjunctive mood. She had got back at him, throwing up her arms, exclaiming: "Oh, well, you know the language better than we do!" He had had to explain the point patiently; he was merely making the textbook clear, he had said. And at this juncture she gave him a sullen look. Then, as if by accident, her book fell to the floor, causing a quite unusually shattering noise. She bent over to pick it up, making no effort to prevent a remarkable display of bosom—verily to assuage his annoyance, Leynes said to himself. Guerrilla tactics!

But, of course, he could not be disposed off that readily. "Last week," Leynes said, addressing no one in particular, "they couldn't figure out whether to say 'one of the many who have died,' or 'one of the many who has died' . . . ."

"Neither could I, frankly," said Miss Elena.

"Can," said Perez. "Correction please!"

Miss Elena overlooked that. "And I'm hungry. I bet it's crowded at the Club just now. I hate to be one of the many who will have to wait . . . ."

"There—you got it!" Leynes said.

"Did I?" she said, pertly.

It being Monday, they ordered the special dinner. This was only seventy cents, if you came before seven o'clock. On other evenings, the price was a dollar and twenty-five—quite a drain, Leynes recognized.

And it was so early they didn't have to wait too long to be served. As a matter of fact, judging by standards which the group had become familiar with and learned to accept, tonight's waiters were prompt and polite. Indeed, you couldn't have caught any hint of condescension toward their own countrymen. And the company was nearly done with the dinner when Leynes exclaimed, to everyone's surprise:

"Why, if it isn't that old son of a gun!" And to cries of "Who?"—"Who's it?"—he replied: "C. B. Carlos himself . . . . You don't know C.B. Carlos? He made quite a name, writing those pieces about the Base, about territorial rights, race prejudice, that sort of thing. You'd think he'd be a marked man hereabouts. But, there, take a look—quite the contrary!"

The company was fairly impressed. Two ladies and their officer escorts made up Carlos's group five tables away. In his dark business suit, he was the very image of success.

"We were in school together," Leynes went on, his enthusiasm seemingly boundless. "He's a big shot now. That's what he's become."

"If I'm not mistaken, he made the articles into a book," said Miss Elena.

"A timely subject, certainly. How were the reviews?" Mrs. Dinglasan asked, anxious to contribute to the conversation.

"Raves," Leynes replied. "I'll have to congratulate him, if you people will excuse me . . . ."

Miss Elena and Mrs. Dinglasan waited at the lobby for the party to collect before returning to the Center. As for Perez, he did the intelligent thing; he hurried to the car, to listen to the radio.

When Leynes rejoined them, he said: "Anyone for a bit of nightlife? Carlos is inviting us."

"Why didn't he ask us directly?" said Miss Elena.

"He's delegated that to me," Leynes said.

"No, we can't, can we?" Mrs. Dinglasan demurred. "No, not in a place like this. We school ma'ams might be mistaken for something else."

Leynes did not miss the matronly air. "What prudes," he wanted to say. But already the car had reached Benton Education Center, and they rushed to their classrooms.

Leynes's class was Intro. to Lit.—where Bauer, Montoya, Richards and some ten others were the fairly steady scholars. Hibbet was on TDY, Richards reported. Leynes had hoped that Johnson might turn up tonight. It was to Johnson that he had wanted to explain, at a class meeting the week before, that you didn't avoid reading Conrad's *The Nigger of the Narcissus* simply because of *that* word in the title. Literature was Literature. It served its purpose best by following the doctrine, "Proper words in proper places." It was just too bad that Johnson wasn't in attendance more often. This was one difficulty with the entire extension program. Absences were rampant; and one couldn't be too conscientious about one's work. It was rare that one gave a failing mark. You were only too happy when the required class sizes were met, relieved when each class meeting was over, and gratified when the term itself came to an end. Appointment to the extension professoriate had become an expression of patronage, the regular salary increases having become difficult to get. What a stink the Program would probably raise, Leynes thought, once a typewriter like C. B. Carlos's were to do an exposé . . . .

Carlos was, in fact, already outside waiting in his car. The gesture overwhelmed Leynes. "I'll show you around, I will," Carlos was saying. "You really don't know the place, do you?"

Indeed, he did not, Leynes said; and they were out of the Benton Education Center compound shortly.

Someone in a scooter came abreast of them part of the way. Bauer— Leynes recognized the rider. Bauer had remarked that T.S. Eliot's "Murder in the Cathedral" demonstrated "a case of suicide." That was the young man's phrase for it, an easy conclusion that was nevertheless welcome since hardly anyone had read the assignment well enough to formulate any ideas about it. And now suddenly Bauer, his white helmet gleaming in the dark, slipped away before their very eyes, a young man across whose sky a vision had flashed. Now he was transformed into a nothingness amidst the agitated whir of cicadas in the acacias that lined the road.

Some such disintegration could happen to him too, Leynes thought with a start. It would be his lot unless he could get a grip on things. He now knew why he had become excited over this chance encounter with Carlos. There was a subversive quality to their friendship.

"I'd like to do some writing too," he said.

It came easy, just like that. Leynes was mildly surprised over how he had managed it. And perhaps the announcement might have been dispersed by the music that the cicadas made, wave upon trembling wave.

"What will you write about?" Carlos had caught it.

"This place," said Leynes. "I've had this assignment two years now."

A bolt of lightning struck in the east, momentarily setting a portion of the sky ablaze. As if Carlos construed Leynes's statement as a challenge to the authority behind those newspaper articles, a similar protestation quickly followed:

"I've lived in nearby San Miguel all these years myself. The tons and tons of information I have about this place, about all the people hereabouts . . . ."

Leynes gave it no importance, for he had not meant to question him in any way. "One might write about our being here," he pursued instead, "about what we've to go through here . . . ."

It had begun to drizzle. He held out his hand to feel the rain and thought of the task that such a person as one with Carlos's gifts might set about doing—only to realize the next moment that it was he himself whom he had in mind.

"Is it as bad as that?" the other said.

"We are educational concessionaires here," Leynes replied. "On the same footing as the local barbers and dry-cleaners." He was moved by the phrase he had stumbled on. "Only, instead of the usual goods and services, we vend diplomas."

"Vend, eh?" Carlos chuckled. "I like that."

The visit to Eagle's Roost ("Don't you like the Hawaiian decor?") and the meeting with culturati, like the club manager and the band leader; the manhattan in his hand at The Pago-Pago while couples danced on invisible dimes on the parqueted floor five feet away; the brief look into Lucy's ("You must feel at home here, like I do!") which was the swankiest nightspot in San Miguel, just outside the Army Base—Leynes was struck by the rather harsh quality of life that Carlos opened up for view. By the time the rain had stopped, the excursion was over—though not the impression it created.

In the car that was to physically deposit Leynes at his billet he sat quietly beside his host, feeling uneasy about how to regard him now. For, on one hand, Leynes reminded himself that with some sensitive souls, or so he had read somewhere, no experience could be so trivial as to be lost entirely. Like the rain-washed road they were traveling on, he had soaked all that in. Tonight, it might be asserted, he was being replenished somehow, in the mysterious way Nature does such things. He could be grateful for that. He felt a rash of extravagant fraternal feelings for Carlos such as he had not suspected he was capable of. Yet, on the other hand, something rankled within him, a vast stirring of disaffection. He was particularly troubled by the possibility that Carlos had underestimated him and had thought him to be a person quite different from Leynes's own sense of himself. Such matters must be set aright. Yes, perhaps once and for all.

"It is awkward of me to ask," Leynes began. "But when do you work, C. B.?" There, he had said it at last. "How do you ever get the chance to sit down at your typewriter?" He could not have sounded more earnest, more anxious—more like himself.

"You don't mean all that, do you?" Carlos sounded puzzled. "Imagine me having to be the one to tell you." He put his arm on Leynes's shoulder. "Anyhow, it'll be a long story, if I could tell it at all . . . ."

They arrived at the billet shortly. The car wheels settled on ground that had been made soggy by the overflow from the rain-gutter.

"But I really mean it, C.B. Do you do your best work in the mornings? As most others do—or so we are told?"

"Come now—you must be joking."

Leynes was determined to get an answer. "Do you do your best well into the night like this—in silence like this?"

For, indeed, the quiet was overwhelming. The cicadas were gone, and the two of them seemed to be the only souls abroad. They might well have come to some outpost, to the very frontiers of a world. It was as though he, Leynes, was to do sentry work here—a lookout pressed into service by a most ennobling sense of mission.

"Now, look," said Carlos, his hands on the wheel, "—as one craftsman to another—"

"Yes—" said Leynes with bated breath.

Suddenly the other laughed. "You don't mean to steal my secret, do you?" he said.

Damage enough was done and that word was the cause of it. Whatever it was that he had caught a glimpse of a moment ago was now lost. After an uneasy minute or so, he managed to change into his pajamas. The sound of dripping water, like a child's sobbing, filled the room, which he shared with Perez. He discovered it emanated from the bathroom; a malfunctioning flush mechanism appeared to be the cause. He stood on the bowl cover and fumbled overhead for the offending valve. It was no use. Unaware of the problem, Perez could snore soundly enough, an earnest young man underway like a sleek schooner, off across the gulf of dreams.

For how long had Perez been going full sail while he, Leynes, looked anxiously about, frantic before the facts and illusions of their lives, seeking formulas for self-assurance and success—the kind, anyhow, that Carlos achieved? Leynes sorted out the impressions of the evening as though they had been written on three-by-five centimeter note cards, and whichever way he shuffled or stacked them one particular entry turned up from nowhere:

Leynes, Fermin J. "Fundamentals of
Freshman Composition," *Education in
Review*, IX:3, pp. 225-236.

—his one contribution to scholarship, and, at that, in a journal that usually appeared six quarters late, the forum for either the dead or dying . . . .

Carlos had no reason to thrive while he, Leynes, continued to languish, wasting his energy at bleaching the grammar of U.S. servicemen into a presentable state lest they fail to recognize for themselves the humane, the delicate and the beautiful. Perez, Elena, and Dinglasan—they, too, were in the same trade, the same laundry shop, though specializing in the coarser fabrics, perhaps. There was yet a second crew—a Math instructor, a Geology professor, a P.E. man. They worked the Tuesday-Thursday shift. They had been committed, all of them, to being mere domestics in the academic world, and this was something none of them had counted on. It came as something extra and, considering the circumstances, something to be grateful for. And beyond this there was scarcely anything more to aspire for. Similar limitations were true for Carlos as well; Leynes had no doubt of that. Carlos, too, would discover that. He could soon be asking his own questions. Leynes felt anxious for him about as keenly as he did for himself.

The flush toilet dripped on, an odd affirmation perhaps of what he was thinking. He was in for some troubled sleep. In a trice he saw the man he had always wanted to be, a story-teller whose voice, he imagined, the world could listen to, a maker of fables that explained away the confusions of his time and place. The disguise as a Freshman Comp. and Lit. instructor he would keep, though not that part of it which turned him into a plodding white-collar. He had made every rule of grammar pay, every non-restrictive clause, every colon and comma. He had tried to get at Carlos's secret, had he not? So, then, however you looked at it, he snitched. It had come down to that. And not in terms of popcorn alone. You might say, did not the others snitch also? Did not Miss Elena and Mrs. Dinglasan scrape the saucer clean of butter cubes, and did they not make sandwiches out of those buns and crackers in the breadbaskets? Four cubes to every saucer—"For our midnight snack," they said. Still and all, they snitched as did Leynes himself and to just that level. There had been that morning when he rolled up half a dozen bathroom paper mats and pocketed two tiny cakes of soap. Because you couldn't be sure you'd be assigned to a billet with all the amenities, he had told himself. And how he dreaded athlete's foot!

He heard the car coming, the driver sounding the horn gently. He got up with a start and found Perez packing his bag.

"I was thinking, sir," said the young man, "that you could use a few more minutes of sleep. Did you have a great time?"

"Well," Leynes replied, undecided as to whether to boast or simply seem vague about the experience. "We just about went everywhere," he finally said.

He switched on the light himself, grateful for Perez's thoughtfulness in any case. From the voices outside, it was clear to Leynes that Miss Elena and Mrs. Dinglasan were already in the car.

"Who would have thought they'd be up and about this early?" Leynes said to himself.

Perez heard him nevertheless. "We decided last night," he said, filling Leynes in, ". . . that we might have breakfast down the road somewhere, in some *carenderia* where we could have a real nice and heavy Filipino meal for a change. Fried eggs, rice, sausages, chocolate—and not those buns, waffles and cornflakes they serve at the Club. Aren't you tired of that stuff?"

You would have thought from Perez's expression that the answer would need some soul-searching on Leynes's part. "I can't really say," the latter replied as simply as he could.

Directly after he had got his things together he joined the ladies in the car, sitting between the two of them in the rear. In a minute they were out of the billet area and cruising along the acacia-lined park.

"Going home at this hour is the part of this job that I like best," Mrs. Dinglasan said. "Don't you feel that way, too?"

"I do," said Miss Elena. She was munching something but went on talking. "Sorry, people, I'm always hungry at this hour . . . ."

Those crackers again, thought Leynes. But he couldn't bring himself to being too critical of Miss Elena's habits. He began to feel the chill and so buttoned his shirt at the collar, a precaution Mrs. Dinglasan observed.

"Cold, huh?" she said, kindly.

"Not quite," Leynes said, touched by her interest.

They were now passing quickly through San Miguel town, leaving behind those zinc-roofed houses and boarded-up shops which in an hour or so would come alive with trade from the camp. And then their headlights caught the clusters of grey nipa houses along the road. An open field emerged, then an island of bamboos against the sky, then a peninsula of rice seedlings and a promontory that became all too soon a grove of mango trees. His country, Leynes knew; and not that one back there—where the Carloses triumphed but which diminished him while the cicadas sang their chorus.

From where he sat in front, with the driver, Perez chirped brightly: "Hello, Highway!"

1963

On the Ferry

THEY HAD HAD more than enough of it during the two-and-a-half-hour ride from Manila to the Batangas wharf. No seats had been available except those over at the rear of the bus, which was the part called "Hollywood." It used to be known as "The Kitchen"; and, to say the least, it was hardly comfortable there. But some things just couldn't be helped—like getting to the bus station late, or being unable to keep your son in school. You had to accept all that—well, like "Hollywood."

Except for the bus seats, Mr. Lopez had run through these things before. Now in the comparative comfort of the ferry, he could run through them again. But he didn't care to; and, hoping he could cast them out of his mind, he turned to Nilo.

"Have you checked our luggage?"

The thin bespectacled boy who sat on the wooden bench beside him replied: "Yes, Pa."

"Check again, please," Mr. Lopez said.

The boy got up and peeked under his seat where the *cargador* had pushed in an old suitcase, two boxes of books and magazines, and two grocery paperbags—their *pasalubong*, their homecoming presents.

It was almost sailing time. During the quarter of an hour that they had been on board—"Pa, let's avoid the rush," Nilo had suggested—a steady stream of people from Manila, like them, had arrived on passenger trucks that had raced through the heat and dust. Mr. Lopez had his son occupy one of the starboard benches, hoping that they could have it all to themselves. But, presently, a big party—three elderly ladies and two young girls—joined them, taking the other end of the bench. Tangerine-shirted cargadores followed after them, piling up right in front of the ladies baskets of fruit, suitcases, and groceries in paperbags, too—in the end, shoving these conveniently under the seat. One of the ladies took possession of the spot beside Nilo; and the two others, the far end of the bench, the two young girls posted between them. The latter were plain-looking and dressed in the St. Bridget's College uniform; they were perhaps spending the weekend with relatives at Calapan.

Mr. Lopez, who had been assistant district engineer in his day, had hoped he would not meet any acquaintances from Calapan. That he did not know who the women were pleased him. He was afraid he would only embarrass himself in the presence of former associates in the government service, or even mere business friends. The firm Lopez & Co., Builders, had won many a public works bid in its time and had constructed bridges and river control projects all over Mindoro. But what people would remember, Mr. Lopez feared, was the Bajao Dam. If foreign-owned timber concessions had not denuded, through indiscriminate cutting, the once heavily forested country around Mt. Halcon, nobody would instantly see where the dam came into the picture. But the fact of the matter was that the big flood of December 1956 did wash it away. Contracts had since been difficult to come by.

The cargadores had stopped running up and down the deck. A shudder shook the entire length of the ferry; a whistle sounded and the boat edged out of the wharf and turned toward the open sea.

It was a clear day, unusual for early July. Although Mr. Lopez had made this trip many times before, it had never quite ceased to fascinate him. Today Batangas receded slowly in the mid-morning sun, the dome of the old church and that of the provincial capitol flashing like twin gems of a pendant in its original box of green suede that had been snapped open, the hand trembling for joy.

As the ferry headed toward the Mindoro coast, the view from Mr. Lopez's side of the deck was obstructed by gray canvas awnings rudely flapping in the breeze. He found himself shortly crossing over to the larboard, leaning on the rail. Hardly eighteen years ago, as a young engineer, he had married a girl from St. Bridget's; and it was on a ferry such as this one that the two of them had crossed over to Mindoro. He could not remember, though, whether the two of them had stood at the railings together, their future literally before them, and let some fragment of the Batangas skyline share as well their daydreaming.

Nilo had remained on the bench and had pulled out a magazine from somewhere. The bookworm, Mr. Lopez thought, as he returned to his seat, picking his way through the scattered baggage along the deck. The boy had his mother's forehead and chin; he was delicately built. The eyeglasses added two or three years to his sixteen, but he was very much a boy still. A year away from school—hoping his luck improved, Mr. Lopez told himself—Nilo would be ready for the heavier work of a sophomore engineering student. A sudden recollection of the boy's letters the year before, in which he had described how he had scrimped on food, sometimes limiting himself to a bottle of Coke for breakfast, touched in Mr. Lopez something tender and deep. The appalling fact that Lopez & Co., Builders, had been an utter failure moved him to pity for the boy, for this full year he would lose, for his having gotten himself a bankrupt father.

But Mr. Lopez caught himself, as it were; and, remarking on the magazine that Nilo was reading, he said: "Must be interesting!" He tried to sound cheerful. "What's it? A *Reader's Digest?*"

"It's their copy," Nilo said, pointing to the two St. Bridget girls. He turned the magazine around to allow his father a glimpse of the article he was reading, "My Most Unforgettable Character."

"Who's it about?" he asked.

"Go—e—thals," Nilo said. "He built the Panama Canal." He turned to the two girls and asked: "Isn't that how you pronounce it?"

"Go—thals!" the girls corrected him.

They were surprisingly outgoing, and there was no avoiding introductions now. Mr. Lopez chided his son lightly: "Keeping your friends all to yourself, eh?"

The two young girls called themselves Mary and Rose. The three elderly ladies were aunts of theirs, and the amazing thing was they were all called Miss Adeva and were elementary school teachers.

"Ah," said one Miss Adeva. "What they demand of us nowadays that Science's very much in the air!"

"But we have no vocabulary for Science in the National Language," the second Miss Adeva protested. She was obviously a Tagalog teacher.

"Hmm. Isn't it true that you have to be good at Math these days?" asked the third Miss Adeva, apparently the most innocent of the three.

"I don't know much about these things," Mr. Lopez demurred. "I'm only a businessman now."

"You're being very modest, Engineer," said the first Miss Adeva.

The three ladies were a complete surprise. Judging by their appearance, Mr. Lopez could not have guessed they were abreast with the times and were troubled in their own way by some idea of progress. It was all very heartening.

"Look, Nilo," Mr. Lopez said to his son, "there's a canteen at the other end of the boat. Why don't you run over and get some soft drinks?"

The ladies begged him not to bother. The second Miss Adeva tugged at Nilo's sleeve, urging the boy not to leave his seat.

Meanwhile, Nilo had returned the magazine to the girl called Rose; and, pushing his eye-glasses up the bridge of his nose, he stood up and brought out the coins in his pocket. He counted them unembarrassedly, the two St. Bridget girls unable to hide their amusement.

"You have enough money there, haven't you?" Mr. Lopez asked, ready to offer Nilo a peso of his own.

"It's all right, Pa," the boy said.

"He's such a kid, really," said Mr. Lopez after Nilo had left them. "You go wrong these days, though, if you provide boys with too much pocket money."

"There's a wise father," said the first Miss Adeva.

To merit the remark, Mr. Lopez told the ladies what he felt they needed to know about Nilo. He was an engineering student at UP. "The highest standards, you know," he couldn't help adding.

On discovering that the ladies were very enthusiastic about engineering and that the profession was in their view getting deservedly popular, Mr. Lopez realized he had to say something similarly apposite.

"A wise choice for Nilo," the second Miss Adeva said with conviction.

"Oh, you school people," Mr. Lopez said, still casting about, "—well, you've certainly begun to produce a new type of student these days!"

"Thank you, thank you," the second Miss Adeva said, flattered by the remark.

The third Miss Adeva declared that times had changed; for one thing, education had become too costly.

"Don't I know!" said Mr. Lopez. This was a subject about which he had a direct and personal knowledge, indeed. "And I with only one college student in the family as yet . . . ."

"How many do you expect to have?" the second Miss Adeva asked. "Don't tell us if it will embarrass you . . . ."

"It's nothing to be secretive about, let me assure you, ladies," Mr. Lopez said. "I've three boys, and a little daughter . . . ."

"That's all?" said the third Miss Adeva skeptically.

"Oh, more'll be coming, of course," said the first Miss Adeva.

Mr. Lopez whispered something to her, and lest the two others should feel left out, he said: "What I said was merely that Mrs. Lopez is in the family way."

He was surprised on hearing his own words. One more moment and he could have told the ladies the whole story of his life. But he checked this access of familiarity, judiciously limiting himself to his son's school career.

"He's his mother's favorite," Mr. Lopez said. He told them about Nilo's health, which had always been delicate; and he described his interview with the dean of the engineering college, who had given him a cigar and remarked: "Health's wealth, as well we know, Mr. Lopez," tapping him on the shoulder.

The ladies warmed up to the new subject. They were certain that living conditions in Manila were not particularly wholesome for young people. They complained about the dust and the noise, the crowded boarding houses, and the jampacked movie houses. All these must have contributed to Nilo's poor health, they decided; and Mr. Lopez wholeheartedly agreed.

"But where else can we send our boys these days?" he added, in the tone of one used to generous doses of compassion.

The question made the ladies sad. The first Miss Adeva, in particular, flicked her long eyelashes. "In any case," she said, "a boy such as yours— why, Mr. Lopez, you really ought not to work him too hard."

"That's what his mother always says," Mr. Lopez replied.

"And you must watch out," warned the second Miss Adeva. "Boys his age easily get pleurisy or something like that. I had a nephew, you know . . . ."

And they were discussing this luckless nephew when Nilo returned with seven bottles of Coke clasped together precariously, the straws already stuck into them. The deck heaved under his feet, the bench slid forward. It was all he could do to deliver the bottles safely.

As the ladies sipped their Cokes quietly, Mr. Lopez revealed that Nilo's mother had studied at St. Bridget's. But while this proved to be interesting in itself, especially to the two young ones, Mary and Rose— who asked Mr. Lopez: "Did Mrs. Lopez wear a uniform different from ours?"—the Adeva ladies returned to the problem of Nilo's health, expressing their great concern unequivocally. It was as if Nilo's return from the ship's canteen with the bottles of Coke awoke in them feelings that had long been dormant. He ought never to prefer his studies to his health; no, Nilo shouldn't, they said. The college was right in sending him home for a while. The first Miss Adeva said, addressing Nilo directly:

"You're only sixteen, as your father says . . . ."

It was neither a question nor a statement of fact—to judge by the tone this particular Miss Adeva used. Before the boy—who looked quite puzzled—could say anything for himself, Mr. Lopez clarified the issue concerning his son's age: "Next September, to be exact."

Now Nilo was blushing from being made too much of, and perhaps because Mary and Rose were blushing too. Still on the matter of age, the first Miss Adeva revealed that her nieces were both sixteen also.

"They're twins, you see," she said, as if to explain whatever it was that might be thought of as inexplicable about youth.

The ferry was running into some rough sea, which meant that they had reached the middle of Verde Island Passage. For a good half hour, until the ferry came directly in the shelter of the island, it ran into three-foot waves which occasionally caused the benches to slip again or tilt back against the railings. The Adevas were wonderful sailors, so used they were to crossing the Passage. It was Nilo who looked every inch the poor sailor. Attentively, the first Miss Adeva, who had taken it upon herself to look after him, bade the seasick boy rest his head on the bench, giving him all the room he needed.

"He'll be all right," Mr. Lopez said. "Don't be bothered with him."

"In fifteen years or so—oh, who knows?" said the second Miss Adeva, dreamily. "There'll be a tunnel through here. We'll all be going by train."

"That's one reason we'll be needing more engineers," the third Miss Adeva said.

Now Nilo raised his head off the back of the bench, as if surprised to hear someone speak so confidently about the future. The sea had become smooth again. The sound of falling rain ran through the length of the ferry—a school of tuna, Mr. Lopez saw, caught unawares in the path of the ship. An island, one of three that girded Calapan harbor, swung forward, and the twins cried out:

"A boat!"

Mr. Lopez turned quickly to landward, and there it was. Where the small island rose from a sheet of white sand fringed by coconuts and undergrowth was a sheltered cove, and detached from the shore by a strip of water was a one-masted sailboat, a five-ton *lanchon*.

The Adevas were excited and exchanged all sorts of conjectures, their breaths quivering. One said a leak had sprung, causing the boat to head for safety. The second Miss Adeva said that it sat on a rock right there. It didn't seem to move. The third Miss Adeva declared she could see no signs of a crew. The lanchon had been abandoned. Mr. Lopez wished that the ferry could get closer, although he knew that would be something of an impertinence.

Nilo remarked, just about this time that the ladies had said all they had to say:

"But, Pa," he spoke solemnly, "I can actually see it sinking!"

Mary and Rose sighed. They agreed with Nilo. Watching breathlessly, they clutched each other's arm.

"Pa, isn't it sinking—inch by inch?" Nilo said, almost begging to be believed.

"Why, that's right! Of course, it's sinking!" the three Adevas exclaimed.

"And nobody's doing anything about it!" Nilo seemed terror-stricken. "What could have happened, Pa?"

Mr. Lopez could say nothing. He could not explain this if he tried. He realized what Nilo wanted; he felt the urgency in the boy's words, in his asking to be believed and the derelict explained away. But Mr. Lopez had no explanation to make here any more than for all he had done to conceal his having failed the boy. He knew that he could not lie to him or about him any longer. The time had come when he could protect him no more with excuses and fabrications. How much further could he go? He would run short of college deans and cigars and Panama Canals, and those little half-truths you said about them that made each day pass sufferably. You could fashion make-believe to order; but, oh, not life, complete with its mystery and loneliness. And he had other sons to see through as well, not to mention the young girl now in grade school—and a fifth offspring yet to come. Of one thing he was certain; with all five of them to look after, you could grow hardened enough. And once you've acquired the callousness, Mr. Lopez thought, how dreadful it all becomes. Thank God, he could see that.

The ferry was clearing the channel and leaving behind the island now. He could see that too. The green underbrush, the white beach, the derelict itself—was that the mast that he was seeing now, a bamboo stick stuck in the water?—all these slipped away, and Calapan pier came into view, the zinc roofs of the buildings on the shore garishly white in the sunshine, against the palms on the shoulder of the hill. For a moment Mr. Lopez watched his son Nilo, who stood with his two new friends, their hands on the railing, their eyes shining. A sudden beauty to his being father to this boy possessed him, and he felt that his own eyes were shining too. The deck began to sway—the waves were getting just a bit frisky again—and he sat, steady on that wooden bench and aware of something hard gathering at the core of his being.

"No, not yet," he prayed silently, frightened perhaps by the same terror that had seized Nilo earlier.

But he felt it was already there.

1959

The Wireless Tower

My name is Roberto Cruz.
Honesty is the best policy.
I ought to have a better pair of shoes.
My favorite subject is History, but I like Literature also.
What is a compound sentence?

WONDERING WHAT ELSE to say, Roberto Cruz, the troop scribe, counted the number of lines he had used: he had four more to write on before reaching the bottom of the page. He filled these with the names of his father and mother, and those of his brother and sister, and wrote down also their respective dates of birth. Of the four dates, he had difficulty in remembering that of his father. Bert leaned on the wall boards and tried to refresh his memory. He stretched his legs and waited. A soothing comfort ran down his body, from the nape of his neck to his toes.

He watched the wind bending the grass on the side of the mountain directly before him. He felt he could taste in the wind a touch of bay leaf and somehow of cardamom, too. He was reminded of Mother standing before the woodstove emptying a pot of *adobo* into the candy can which, later, the members of the troop, from Scoutmaster Ponte down, devoured to the last tidbit.

Then, forming a lump in his throat: the day and the month of his father's birth. He was not quite sure about the year. But I'm now fifteen, he reasoned; Father married when he was twenty-five. Bert added the two numbers and finally worked out a solution.

The wall at his back creaked. It was an old wall. The cottage, which was to have served as the home of the caretaker of the radio station, had never been lived in. At Bert's feet the boards were covered with sandlike droppings of woodworm that had lived up there in the ceiling. Bert pulled up his knapsack, which had lain at his feet, and now used it as a pillow. He pushed himself up, and the wall creaked again.

The porch railings were down, like a strip of fence in an abandoned pasture. Nothing obscured Bert's view of the mountainside. It was a pleasant April afternoon, steeped in sunshine. There had been a plan, Bert had heard, to set up a radio station here. Somehow it had not come off. Bert wondered if rust, like the woodworm in the lumber, had heaped rich deposits at the foot of the tower. The structure seemed to hold, though. Already there was a legend about it: lightning had split the rod at the top. It must have been quite a storm. Bert decided he would go and find out.

He put his notebook flat on the floor and made a rough sketch of the tower. He rigged up the drawing with the criss-crossing steel strands which, in the real tower, rose a good hundred and twenty steps heavenward. As he counted, his eagerness grew.

He did not complete the sketch. Hurriedly, he jabbed a vertical line at the top of his steel structure. He marked it with an "X." At the bottom of the page he wrote out a reminder:

> To Whom It May Concern
> I'll be up there.

He signed his name simply, Bert Cruz. He gave his address:

> 27 Real Street
> Buenavista, Buenavista

Then, smiling to himself, he got up and looked for a small rock. He found one at the foot of the small heap which was what had been left of the three-runged steps of the cottage porch. He played with the rock, tossing it with his right hand and catching it with his left.

He walked back to where he had left his knapsack, counting the times he caught the rock in the cup of his left palm. It had held the stone at least five times. His notebook lay beside the knapsack. He picked it up and ran through the pages without looking at them.

Butterflies, birds, fishes, trees and flowers lived like immortal beings in those pages. Bert had an image in the back of his mind of the neat little sentences he had filled the other pages with. He tried to remember when it was that he had gotten into the habit of putting down things that way. He could not remember.

He placed the notebook on top of his knapsack and the small rock on top of the notebook, opened at the page where he had written his message. Then, whistling, he walked down to the yard, over the rickety floorboards of the porch, past the ruins of the steps.

The nearest shaft of the tower was the one to the south and was twenty-five steps away. Four of those shafts rose off a base of perhaps a hundred square feet. Robust concrete blocks anchored each shaft to the mountain. The story was that there ought to have been two towers. People said the second tower was to have risen about five hundred feet farther to the north. There the hilltop leveled off less flatly than here on the south. Bert wondered not so much why this other tower did not get built at all but rather how the mountain would look with the two towers. He imagined the two towers making conversation with the stars. He thought of the words they might have said to each other, like two friends sitting in the dark, rocking their chairs gently, thinking they had all of forever to themselves.

Now the other steel tower seemed almost real. Bert closed his eyes for a moment, afraid to see it in the sunshine standing against the blue of the afternoon sky. Pressing his eyelids, he tried to throw off the vision. He did not want it at all. It wouldn't do to ever get mixed up. He realized that in his notebook he had sketched only one tower.

The line of steps hung on the east side. The first rung was about nine feet off the ground. He had to jump a little to reach the bar. He let go, remembering that he had to roll up his sleeves. He folded the cuffs carefully and got his arms clear up to his biceps. Then he reached for the first bar again. He felt it smooth in his hand. He chinned his way upward, pulling in his hips to get some momentum.

By swinging his legs forward and locking his feet fast behind the big shaft, he was able to let go of one hand and make a good try for the second bar.

The steps were a foot apart. The vertical bars that had held the rungs were a foot wide and ran parallel. Unlocking his feet, Bert caught the swing of his body by slipping his whole arm through and, quickly keeping himself upright on the ladder, until a wee strip of skin between his legs got pinched rather tight. He wished he had rolled up his trousers too, but now that the skin kept hurting he was glad he had not done it.

He realized that he still had his shoes on. It was a canvas pair, all black except for the soles, which were red. He raised his left foot, and knotted and loosened up the lace. He bent over, still safely arm-locked, and pushed the shoe off, tugging from the heel. In like manner, he shed off the other shoe.

This, on hitting the grass, tumbled off miraculously toward its mate. Bert thought this was a sign, an omen or something. He felt that if he had so wished, both shoes might have come together as in a show-window.

But the thought of omens disturbed him. He looked away and saw the portion of the roof where several of the galvanized iron sheets had been wrenched loose by the wind. His eyes followed the rain-gutter cutting an angle with the porch roof. Then his gaze dropped, and he saw his knapsack and the notebook, pale-white, stuck under the weight of the rock.

Without being aware of it, Bert had gained ten more steps. He cleared an additional twenty without looking at the cottage again. Resting, he locked his arms on to the step that came level with his shoulder.

He did not realize how far up he had climbed until he saw beyond the trees on the south side of the mountain the road which led to the town. He followed the road as if he were going home. Suddenly he lost his way in the trees. When he found the road again, it was behind a dark grove of mangoes. The rustle of the leaves seemed to reach him, and somehow this frightened him. It was of course the form that the sound of the wind took, perhaps as it blew past the shafts as if these were broken bits of wire. At this thought, Bert got frightened. He climbed yet higher, though. Something seemed at stake. Feeling numb in the arches of his bare feet, he slipped his leg over one step to rest, as if he were mounted on a horse.

The road passed some bamboos and looked like a strip of tree bark that bunched them up. Then it turned to the beach and went past the town cemetery. The grey walls appeared like the line of barren paddy in a field. Because the tombstones were not uniform, the field did not resemble a strip of riceland. But it well could have, judging from the length and turns of the paddy. The wind was brisk now, and it seemed to bend the things that cropped up the ground and which Bert identified as crosses.

He left his saddle now and diverted his attention to the town slaughter-house which was set on a rock that jutted out onto the blue harbor. There was an interisland ship at anchor, the *Nuestra Señora del Rosario*. The superstructure was unmistakable, hooded though it was with what looked like black canvas. Even the bridge had a forbidding shape. The hull was black too, and the men that crowded on the pier all looked as if they had only heads and no bodies whatever.

The road through the pier area rose black with mottled grey blots where moving objects, which Bert identified as carts drawn by carabaos, ranged in a shadow. The wide canopy of zinc, which was the Stevenson copra warehouse, might have glittered away like a great slab of silver. Actually, a cloud hung low over it, enshrouding the building with sheets of the dullest lead.

Bert looked up once. Huge masses of clouds, odd forms heavy like rocks, and as rugged at the edges, hung in a shelf over him. The wind chilled his back. It did not sing past the shafts now but began, it seemed, to tap the rivets loose. His feet confirmed their steadiness, though. Now the black ship at anchor in the harbor seemed to get smaller and smaller. The crowd at the wharf had begun to disperse, and the dark spots scattered into the town until at last the streets seemed bare.

The wind turned. It came straight at his face now, washing it clean. It was as if intent on cleansing even the dirt behind his ears. It scrubbed his hair and scalp. It rubbed his eyes and cheeks and neck. He felt the sensation of bathing in dry water.

The more steps he cleared the more intense the sensation became. Under his shirt the dry water of wind shrove him neatly. He once saw a movie in which there was a doctor scrubbing his hands and arms interminably. He felt exactly as if he were being cleaned up that way.

Then it came, a searing ache in the balls of his feet. It rose and seized his knees, gripping them as if with clamps. The wind grew still, suddenly. Sweat beaded on his back and across his waist, like a cross. His brow was dry, nothing dimmed before his eyes; but he felt that tears would come any moment. He waited, making three steady steps, locking his arm each time.

He felt like going down. For the first time he did not feel equal to the landscape around. In his giddiness he imagined that the ground rose and sank. He could only look up at the clouds that lay in a shelf above him. An imaginary plumb line was being lowered for him. Suddenly the tip of the plumb line was fastened to the tower. It became the long vertical rod that he must reach. He canted his head, wondering why the rod seemed to move. He suspected it was an effect caused by some fault in his manner of looking.

He could not look long enough, though, to find out what exactly the trouble was. His sweat was heavier now, the pain in his bones had spread to his muscles. His calves knotted in tight bowlines and figures-of-eight. Even his neck was held in some awful knot; or, rather, in that series of knots. He put his chin on one of the last steps, thinking that in that way he could rest. But his teeth began to chatter.

He held his jaw steady. Then after a brief rest his strength returned. He gained three more steps. He counted five more steps achieved that way. Then he began locking in three times in each case; this gave each foot a much longer spell of rest than before. He discovered that he could throw the entire weight of his body alternately on each foot. He felt the pull of the earth coming hard but the lock counteracted that, and suddenly he felt light.

There was nothing now between him and the rod but a narrow ledge. Somehow he had no desire to do it. He searched for the desire, as if he had brought it along like loose change in his pocket. Nothing jingled there. The weight of his seat-beaded back and waist grew heavier again, and he could have slipped earthward from its drag alone. But he had his hands on the edge of the ledge now.

He knew from the tautness of his leg muscles that he had made it. He could feel the base of the steel rod now with the tips of his fingers. He closed his eyes for joy. He reached far out, farther out—for joy.

Thumb and forefinger circled the base of the rod. He wished they would meet, but the rod base was perhaps too large for that. The wind began to sing again. He could feel something like strands of the song at the tips of his thumb and forefinger. An entirely new sensation rose from the middle of his back and settled at the base of his skull. It was made of the wind's song, which came without sound; without a tune, even. And it seemed it would last forever.

He heaved over to get into position for another saddle-rest. His easy success was little short of a miracle, he felt. His hand still gripped the base of the rod; and being able to reach farther now, finger- and thumb-tip met at the rugged edges which rose so many inches up the skin of the rod. Whichever way he turned, the rugged edges followed. He could feel the grit in his teeth and the tang of split metal on his lips. His nostrils flared. He caught the smell of the rock, sun-bleached, born and bred of the sun's heat on steel. It seemed that the rod breathed.

And it was split. This was incontrovertible; he could speak of it without a doubt. His hands could be preaching it; it was gospel talk. He was dazed by the thought.

Something had been drained off his hands so that now it had no sensation left except the anticipation of the feel of the crack and the crevice and the length of the split. He reached again and again; he did not have to search. Each time his joy came heady, and his heart throbbed as if it would never stop.

Bert felt he could not stand it. This was too much to keep for so long. Slowly, and step by careful step, he retraced his ascent. The rock structure of clouds overhead had lifted and soft felt carpets of them seemed to have spread under the sun. He kept his gaze on the town. Now it glowed, roofs and streets and all.

Even the market place and the schoolhouse and the church, which he did not care to see before, emerged as if from shadows and called out to him. He saw the creek that ran past the market place and swept its bed dry to the lee of the harbor, and the pebbles glittered as if they were precious stones. The ship was still at anchor, but it had moved from its original position. Somehow a lid of water quivered between her hull, now an indifferent gray, and the cliff of the wharf. The red band on her funnel and three triangular flags that waved from the main mast caught Bert's delight. The flags seemed to wave to him. The ship offered her white-painted deck to his gaze and the bridge glowed with brass trimmings. Surely, she was on her way to another voyage. Smoke, white and lazy, emitted the message from the stack, and there was a new-looking crowd, well-wishers gathering at the pier. Bert thought they were all umbrellas and hats, and as he cleared more steps he recognized some hands waving and waving.

The last few steps were easy. It was as if his muscles had not tightened up so rudely before. He leaped to the ground and sat on the grass and put on his shoes. Then he walked to the cottage, a little self-consciously—somehow afraid of himself.

He did not wish to hold up his head proudly, he had no desire to get puffed up in any way. He remembered the cemetery and the dark road through the trees he had seen earlier; and he did not care to swing his arms about.

He reached the tumbledown porch and, picking his way carefully, sat beside the knapsack he had left behind. His notebook, with the pencil tied to it, lay as before under the small rock he used as a weight. He put the rock away.

Leaning once again against the old wall, he heard it creak under his weight. Followed a shower of woodworm droppings from the ceiling, some falling on the notebook in his hand.

He laid the page open on his leg and wet his pencil tip again. Without reading what he had written earlier, he set his pencil on a fresh line.

With the next sentence he would have six altogether on the page. It would be better to use a new line.

He wrote: *It is true.*

1963

Part Six

The Tomato Game

DEAR GREG:

You must believe me when I say that I've tried again and again to write this story. The man remains vivid in my memory, alone in his clapboard shack in the middle of a Sacramento Valley tomato field. It is a particularly warm Sunday, in the height of summer. Also, it is the year of my miserable lectureship at Transpacifica University, which caters to the needs of such an industry. Well, it's all because of the ethnic pot. A certain number of offerings oriented toward the minorities, and the university becomes entitled to certain funds. You have read in the papers how Transpacifica gave an *honoris causa* to a certain personage—a prestigious thing to do— which is that, indeed. Look up the word in your dictionary; I do mean what I say. But to return to that summer when, in a fit of nostalgia, I had agreed to go with Sopi (you must know him, of course) to look for countrymen who might be involved in the national pastime of cockfighting. It is illegal here, hence a San Francisco *Chronicle* head, "Transpacifica U. Lecturer in Bloody Bird Tourney Raid" did not seem at all unlikely.

We risked it anyhow and got much more. As in myth, the signs were all over. The wooden bridge, the fork of the road, the large track all around us which earlier had been a tomato field, the rich crop as indicated by the harvesting machine to one side of the field, a menacing hulk . . . . You can see how hard I try. Would that I could have it in me to put all this together.

I can tell you at this juncture that Alice and her young man must be somewhere here in America. I have no doubt about this. I am sure that the old man is very much around too. The likes of him have that power. We can be sure he will prevail.

"With such a man," Sopi said to me afterwards, "pride is of the essence. He tells himself and his friends that as soon as he is able—in twenty, thirty years, shall we say—he will return to the Islands and then bring back a bride. How can you begrudge anyone doing just that?" Which kind of talk makes me angry, and at that time I certainly was.

I am now embarrassed, though, over how we behaved at the shack. We could have warned the old man. We could have told him what we felt. Instead, we teased him.

"Look, *lolo*," Sopi said. "Everything seems to be ready, eh?"

For, true enough, the shack contained a brand-new bed, a refrigerator, a washing machine—an absurdity multiplied many times over by the presence, which Sopi had noticed earlier, of a blue Ford coupé in the yard. "That's for her . . . ." Sopi had said.

We enjoyed the old man immensely. He didn't take offense—no, the old man didn't. "I've been in this all along, since the start. Didn't I make the best deal possible, lolo?"

"Ya, Attorney," the old man said.

"He could have stayed in Manila for a while. Lived with her. Made friends with her at least," Sopi turned to me as if to tell me to keep my eyes off the double bed with the shiny brass headboard. "But his visa was up. He just had to be back. Wasn't that the case, lolo?"

"Ya, Attorney. Nothing else there any more for me," the old man said.

"That would have been too bad. And this taxi-driver boy, will he be coming over too?"

Sopi, of course, knew that the boy was—bag and baggage, you might say.

"That was the agreement," the old man said. "I send him to school—like my own son."

"You know, lolo, that that will never do. He's young, he's healthy. Handsome, too."

"You thinking of Alice?" the old man asked.

"She's twenty-three," Sopi reminded him. I figured the old man was easily forty or forty-five years her senior.

"Alice, she's okay. Alice she is good girl," said the old man. "That Tony-boy—he's bright boy."

As an outsider, I felt uneasy enough. But a fatherly satisfaction gleamed in the old man's eyes. There was no mistaking it. Wrong of you, I said to myself, to have cocksure ideas about human nature.

I saw Sopi in the mirror of my prejudices. He was thin but spry, and affected rather successfully the groovy appearance of a professional accepted well enough in his community. And, at that, with deserved sympathy. Legal restrictions required that he pass the California bar before admission to the practice of law amongst his countrymen. Hence, the invention which he called Montalban Import-Export. In the context of our mores he was the right person for the job that the old man wanted done. Alice was Sopi's handiwork in a real sense, and at no cost whatsoever. Enough, Sopi explained to me, that you put yourself in the service of your fellows. I believed him. He knew all the lines, all the cliches.

I could feel annoyance, then anger, welling up inside me. Then, suddenly, for an entire minute at least, nothing on earth could have been more detestable than this creature I had known by the tag "Sopi." Sophio Arimuhanan, Attorney-at-Law. Importer-Exporter. Parenthetically, of brides. And, double parenthesis please, of brides who cuckolded their husbands right from the start. In this instance, the husband in question was actually a Social Security Number, a monthly check, an airline ticket.

And I was angry because I couldn't say all this, because even if that were possible it would be out of place. I just didn't have the right, I didn't even understand what the issues were. I was to know about the matter of pride later, later. And Sopi had to explain. It was galling to have him do that.

But at that moment I didn't realize he had been saying something else to me. "This Alice—she's a hairdresser. She'll be a success here. Easily. You know where we found her? Remember? Where did we find her, lolo?"

The old man remembered, and his eyes were smiling.

"In Central Market. You know those stalls. If you happen to be off guard, you're likely to be pulled away from the sidewalk and dragged into the shop for a—what do you call it here?—a blow job!"

The old man smiled, as if to say "I know, I know . . . ."

"We tried to look for her people afterwards. Not that it was necessary. She's of age. But we did look, anyway. She had no people any more to worry over." Sopi went on. "She did have somebody who claimed to be an aunt or something. Sold tripe and liver at the Meat Section. She wanted some money; didn't she, lolo?"

"Ya, ya," the old man said. "All they ask money. Everyone." And there must have been something exhausting about the act of recalling all that. I saw a cloud of weariness pass over his face.

"But we fixed that, didn't we?"

"Ya, ya," said the old man.

"Then there was the young man. A real obstacle, this taxi-driver boy. Tony by name," Sopi turned to me, as if to suggest that I had not truly appreciated the role he played. "We knew Tony only from the photograph Alice carried around in her purse. But he was as good as present in the flesh all the time. The way Alice insisted that the old man take him on as a nephew; and I had to get the papers through. Quite a hassle, that part of it. It's all over now; isn't it, lolo?"

"Ya, ya," said the old man. "I owe nothing now to nobody. A thousand dollars that was, no?"

"A thousand three hundred," said Sopi. "What's happened? You've forgotten!"

"So you need some three hundred more? I get check book. You wait," said the old man.

"There's where he keeps all his money," Sopi said to me.

He meant the old bureau, a Salvation Army kind of thing, that stood against the clapboard wall. Obviously, Sopi knew the old man in and out.

"No need for that, lolo. It's all paid for," he said.

The old man's eyes brightened again. "I remember now!"

"Every cent went where it should go," Sopi said to me.

"I believe you."

"So what does her last letter say?"

"They got ticket now. They coming any day now," the old man said.

"You'll meet them at the airport?"

"Ya."

"You've got a school in mind for Tony-boy?" I asked, addressing, as it were, whoever could provide an answer.

Hardly had I said it, though, than regrets overwhelmed me. I should know about schools. The Immigration Service had not exactly left Transpacifica U. alone, and for reasons not hard to find. They had a package deal out there that had accounted for quite a few Southeast Asian, South Vietnamese, and Singaporean students. Filipinos, too. Visa and tuition seemed workable as a combination that some people knew about. A select few. It was a shame, merely thinking of the scheme. But, strangely enough, my anger had subsided.

"Ya," the old man said. Tony had a school already.

"That's why I wanted you to meet the old man," Sopi said. "Help might be needed in that area—sometime. Who can say?"

"You don't mean Transpacifica, do you?"

"That's your school, all right."

"How so?" I asked.

"Eight hundred dollars a year is what the package costs. The old man paid that in advance. It's no school, and you know that."

"I only work there. It's not my school," I said.

"All right, all right," Sopi said. "There's all that money, and paid in advance, too—so this 'nephew,' bogus though he might be, can come over. You understand. We're all in this."

I began to feel terrible. I wanted to leave the shack and run to the field outside, to the tomatoes that the huge harvesting machine had left rotting on the ground. The smell of ketchup rose from the very earth. If it did not reach the shack, the reason was the wind carried it off elsewhere.

"Ya, they here soon," the old man was saying. "Tomorrow maybe I get telegram. Alice she here. And Tony too. You know I like that boy. Tony's a good boy. Alice—I'm not too sure. But maybe this Tony, he'll be lawyer like you. Make plenty money like you," said the old man to Sopi.

"Or like him," said Sopi, pointing to me. "Make much-much more, plenty-plenty . . . ."

The old man seemed overjoyed by the prospect, and I had a sinking feeling in the pit of my stomach. He had trusted Sopi all along; it was impossible not to believe him now. Tony had more than enough models before him . . . .

We had come that Sunday, as I had started to tell you, to see if we could watch a cockfight. When we left the shack finally, Sopi said to me: "To think that that old man hasn't even met the boy."

As we drove down the road toward the fork that led to the wooden bridge, the smell of ripe tomatoes kept trailing us. That huge machine had made a poor job of gathering the harvest; and so here, Greg, is perhaps the message.

Bests.

1970

The Lives of Great Men

IT WAS MANY years ago that I was in Buenavista, one of those strokes of good fortune, you might say (said our Acting Credit Manager's Assistant)—it was the Company that sent me over. You couldn't have thanked the Chief enough for that.

The plane ride, the two hours of grueling heat on the bus, the twelve miles by ferry to the next island—what did these difficulties matter? One must be allowed now and then a little sentimentality. Buenavista was where I learned my three R's. The small barrio called Hinala, now the site of the airport, was where Grandfather took us at the close of each school term. There, before a gathering of cronies, he made an occasion of showing us off. We were specimens of the generation better endowed than his own, a breed equipped for Progress. We could be relied upon, for example, to deliver speeches or recite clever little verses in a language that neither they nor we ourselves really understood. I do not now recall what my cousins' performances were like, but mine were not unremarkable. Longfellow's "The Psalm of Life" was the one piece, for example, that invariably won admirers.

But the poet's homily deceived no one. If Grandfather's friends got the message, they hardly made it known. "Bravo!" they would say, borrowing from Spanish, as if indeed they belonged to the *principalia*, and clapping their hands in the manner of that class. Yet they would proceed with their drinking of the local *tuba*, there being no other beverage they could afford.

As might be expected, Grandfather's friends resumed in the morning the lives that Longfellow had mildly interrupted, setting out as usual for their fish-traps or ricefields. They carried on thus, burdened by no great faith or ideals, their every gesture showing no trace that the lives of great men had influenced them in any way.

This irrelevance did not occur to me then, for the terror that those command performances inspired blocked out everything. Only now and then would rescue materialize in the form of promptings from Uncle Nemesio. He was at that time Hinala's leading citizen, being the incumbent head-teacher at the barrio elementary school. In fifteen years he would be retired from government service and, as one of Grandfather's heirs, become himself a frequent host to many a tuba-drinking party in the barrio.

The flight back took hardly an hour, the palm fronds waving welcome in the *amihan* as we landed. Uncle Nemesio was in the crowd that met the plane. I had of course neglected to write him, let alone wire; and, as it turned out, he had a bad memory. Not until I had given him my nickname did the blank look in his eyes change to one of recognition.

We walked straight away to his house, which was half a kilometer from the airport, beyond the school grounds. It seemed that for this time of the year some festivities had been planned. A bamboo arch had been built at the school gate; strips of colored paper fluttered from the porch eaves. Boys and girls were busy rigging up the unfinished concrete fence with decorative palm leaves. Built in sections about two meters long and a meter high, this fence was in effect a row of concrete slabs stood end to end, each bearing the name of the local worthy who had been opportuned to make a donation. You had the feeling it was a cemetery where true civic-mindedness and generosity lay quietly buried.

The frame house where we used to stay during vacation time now lodged another family—no relation of ours, my uncle emphasized, his lips twitching as he spoke. The property had passed on, in any case, to an aunt of mine, now deceased and survived by a rather improvident son-in-law with no sentiments about the place whatsoever. In short, I should not expect to be put up there for the night.

The property directly across the street from the old place, however, was the portion that fell to Uncle Nemesio as his inheritance, and this consisted of about a hundred and fifty square meters of ground with a nipa house set off by sweetsop trees from the street.

The house was in reality a shack and was oddly appropriate to all concerned. My uncle, now seventy, had become shorter by some three inches, it seemed to me. He had in my aunt (who emerged from the kitchen shed, a cooking pot in her hand) a gnome-like companion. This impression was heightened by her dress, which was of faded orange, and by her long, hemp-yellow hair. Her deep-set and restless eyes were like those that belonged, or so you imagined, to the people of storyland.

"Fedelino is now here with us. He used to work in Hawaii," Uncle Nemesio said.

The reference was to their son, my cousin of forty or so; a bachelor. He had been in that airport crowd, only I hadn't recognized him.

"The two of them, father and son—that's all they do," my aunt said. "You would think that the Governor, or somebody with a basketful of food, or a trunkful of money, was coming to help us out."

The remark sounded like a familiar grudge, its point long blunted from tireless dibbling. In any case, my Uncle Nemesio had by now taken off his shirt and climbed to a bench by the window.

Fastened to the post and to one of the rafters, and thus held somewhat above eye-level, was a small transistor radio. He directed his attention on this object presently, turning this knob and that with great care. He became so overwhelmingly enraptured over the music, it was as though I might as well not have arrived.

Except for the bench and a low table at the center of the room, the floor had hardly any furniture. The table was about two feet square; a glass cover held down a spread of snapshots, my cousin Fedelino's and those of his Hawaiian friends mostly.

The shack itself seemed about ready to fall apart; but quite literally the lives of great men held up its roof and walls together. For here was a gallery of prints of our illustrious heroes such as those to be found on the covers of popular magazines.

Consider the angle formed by wall and roof. The picture frames, which were of various sizes, provided the third side, the strands of twine that fastened them quivering in the wind. From that angle and elevation Abraham Lincoln looked at me pensively at one end, John F. Kennedy at the other. And there were others for good measure. Manuel L. Quezon, swagger stick in hand, standing in his white riding breeches and shiny boots in the middle of a rice paddy; to his right, somewhat farther away, set apart by a wooden beam, Elpidio Quirino smiling benignly alongside Manuel A. Roxas, who wore a solemn, election-poster look; and then all of them together in one picture frame about as large as the others, Jose Rizal, Marcelo H. del Pilar, and Mariano Ponce, an impressive trio in their heavy overcoats, as befitted sojourners in the Europe of an earlier day . . . .

My cousin Fedelino had arrived. "When we saw you," he told me, "all I could think of at once was whether there would be any fish in the fish-corral. I must go and find out this very minute."

He took off the rather sporty knit shirt he had worn to the airport. I had always remembered him as a little boy running about all summer long without pants on. He had a pair of dark blue dacron trousers now.

It was at this juncture that my aunt joined us. "Clothes are all that he brought home from Hawaii. What do his uncles and cousins do but walk off with a piece or two! Very soon he'll be as naked as before," my aunt concluded.

A door led to a small room into which Fedelino had gone to change. I had a glimpse of three matched suitcases of white fiberboard stacked under a bamboo bed. By now down to his shorts, Fedelino slipped out of the room and out of the house.

"The fish-corral used to bring in plenty of catch," my aunt said. "But this is the wrong time of the year. In two months, things could be better though."

I understood then why Fedelino had left without a word, and how I wished he had asked me to join him. As the next best thing, I went to the beach myself. The amihan had ceased fretting the coconut trees; the palm-fronds hardly moved.

In the low tide, the fish-trap looked a good mile or two away. A dark band on the bamboo siding revealed how high the water had been many days before. Golden-red snappers had often gotten the better of my patience here, many years ago. Kalatong Point lay a little to my right on the horizon, a reminder that my memory was not playing any tricks on me.

Legend had it that Kalatong Point was a place where the fairest of women lived, where trees were of the same height and music could be heard in the forest all day long. Once a year, on the eve of the Feast of Santa Catalina, a white ship dropped anchor off the Point. If you believed the story well enough, you might venture forth to some distant city or seek your fortune in some far-away land, and there see your dreams come true. If at the stroke of twelve, midnight of Good Friday, you rubbed your eyes with a certain kind of wax, you might go to the beach afterward and watch the captain's launch heading straight for the shore.

Fedelino presently appeared waist-deep in the water. It was not long before he returned, beaming proudly over his few wrasses and snappers, and he repeated what his mother had said:

"In two months, we'll have sardines and garfish—a whole lot of them!"

We had an early supper. Too tired to go anywhere, I decided to try to get some sleep.

In the bed that I had seen earlier, a girl of ten or thereabouts lay doubled up, struggling through intermittent fits of cough. She must have been there all this time, only I had been unable to distinguish between girl and sleeping mat. Now, upon waking up, and seized by those spasms of dry cough, she was clearly there—real, an identity to be accounted for.

"It's only a bad cold," my aunt said. "She should be up and about by now, but she stayed too long in the sun yesterday."

As I heard this explanation, the girl began rolling up her mat. In a minute, carrying the bundle off with her, she had moved out to the other room.

"Auntie," I protested, realizing what had happened. "Please tell her to come back. Let me sleep anywhere!"

But she wouldn't hear of it. The girl could go elsewhere—that was settled. The spot directly under the bench, for example, would be just right for her. Uncle Nemesio could leave.

"Time for bed," my aunt now told him, as if he were a little boy.

Then she spread a mat for me right where the girl had been. A strange feeling came upon me, something terrible and totally new. Sleep came, in any case. But I awoke with a start, and there was Fedelino at the door. "Better not make any of that noise," my aunt said in a whisper to him. "You might wake him up." And then once more he slipped away. As I tried to sleep again I realized that he had quickly changed to a bright red shirt, or what I imagined to be something of that color.

Faint music was what awakened me for the second time. This must have been past midnight already, and it was as if the Kalatong story was real after all. I could not determine whether it was a string band or a phonograph I was listening to. A third possibility, of course, was Uncle Nemesio's transistor radio.

"Are you awake?" my aunt said. "That's the school benefit dance. Someone came a while ago to fetch you."

"What did he want?" I couldn't imagine having anything to do with a dance.

"To ask if you could join them. I said you were sound asleep," my aunt said. "You were. You were snoring." She gave a little laugh. "A donation for the school is what they're after." She said all this as if she knew in her mind that I wouldn't care for that sort of thing at all. And, no doubt, Fedelino must have agreed with her. "Of course, your cousin's out there," she added. "Things like that are what he likes."

After this remark, she said nothing more about the distant music which now merged with the throbbing sound that the crickets raised in the sweetsop trees.

The bus for the ferry-landing forty kilometers away came about seven the next morning. It pulled to a stop in front of the restaurant across the yard from the local airline office and waited there for other passengers. I had still time for a cup of coffee and a piece of rice cake. A sentimental sort of breakfast, you might say.

"You have a long journey ahead of you. You'll be hungry if you don't eat all that food," was all that my uncle and Fedelino could say when I asked them to join me. There was nothing I could do to persuade them.

And, of course, I had to dispatch as quickly as possible the business I had been sent to Buenavista for, and I was back in good order for the next flight to Manila.

This time my aunt joined Uncle at the airport to see me off. Fedelino turned up, too.

"People asked why you didn't go to the dance," he said.

"What excuse did you give?"

"I said you got too tired from the trip," he said.

That touched me somewhat, and I thought I should pay him back in kind, with my own form of thoughtfulness. This idea came to me quickly and rather took me by surprise—that I was capable of it, that is.

"There's a good chance," I said, "you might make good money here." And I clearly heard myself adding: "If you like to."

He hesitated at first, as if puzzled. "How?" he asked, finally.

"You can start a poultry farm. Then you can ship fresh eggs to the city every day."

But he laughed off the idea. "Oh, we are quite all right here, really. In two months, the fish-corral will be bringing in some money."

"Or, why not start a piggery? Or something! Anything!"

"Last night there was a big tide," Fedelino continued, not minding what I had said. "We had five kilos of wrasses." And then, as if to prove a point: "Besides there's always the income from the coconuts."

Yes, Grandfather's coconuts, I could have said aloud. But something made me keep it all to myself. I could also have said: And, after Hawaii, didn't you learn a thing or two? Have you no ambition at all? Don't you want to be better off than you are now? But my mind backtracked to the evening before, to the music from the schoolhouse. As if rejecting the legend of the tall trees and the white ship off Kalatong Point, I heard myself giving voice to the most gross of all my thoughts so far. I began guardedly:

"What's wrong with the little girl?"

"It's the measles!"

My aunt had overheard me. "If it's catching it that you fear," she said, "don't worry. You're quite past it. You've had it years ago. Don't you remember?"

But, of course, I had forgotten. And I caught her once more with that gnomish smile of hers. Did she know what I had been thinking? I had been mistaken, suspecting that she and Fedelino had been at odds. They might in fact be allies in good standing. Who, for instance, was the girl but a love child? Fedelino's, most naturally! How unfortunate of the girl, had Fedelino's mother—my aunt, that is—not been around to look after her when he was away in Hawaii. And who could the girl's mother be? The seemingly endless questions in my mind only emphasized the distance that had existed between us. All I could do now was to trust that I be forgiven for my coarse efforts at making contact.

But my remorse was short-lived. The plane had already arrived. In the ensuing commotion, I couldn't think of anything worth saying, even by way of small talk that should go with the occasion. All three of them—Fedelino, my uncle, and my aunt—stood at the edge of the crowd that awaited the moment of departure; and from the ramp I waved to them, much in the manner of those great ones whose photographs appear in newspapers and magazines . . . .

That pose (continued our Acting Credit Manager's Assistant) I might have managed well enough then—and now might never quite live down.

1963

In the Twilight

THE SIGN SAID "Marylou's European Pastries," and as we took a table and ordered coffee and croissants it was clear we were eight thousand miles and thirty years away from Panay. All the same, it was twilight once more in the barrio by the river, the quiet only occasionally broken by the shriek of a kingfisher and the splashing of tarpons feeding in the stream.

It was there we took refuge during the last days of the war. Whenever anyone asked, this was what I told them. Of course, I would add a detail or two, depending on my mood.

When the guerrillas brought in the prisoner it was already late in the afternoon. They took over the barrio schoolhouse, as they always did. What would be the fellow's fate? From where we were, on our side of the river, we could hear the guerrillas laughing and singing. Off and on like that; it was weird. Major Godo's men they were, all right. Soon they'd even send for all the barrio girls—frightening the mothers, to be sure. What? A *baile*? Even at this time? Why not? What was wrong with a bit of merrymaking? And they'd send for me, too.

They'd call from across the river: "Music! Hey, you there! Mr. Music! How about some music, Mr. Music?"

For in those days I could do things with the violin. And you couldn't say, My strings snapped! Or, My bow's broken! No one would believe that, knowing how you wouldn't let things like that happen. So we had an early supper. It would be best to get ready.

I thought I heard them calling; but no, something had gone wrong. Dark began to set in, and we went to the river bank and sat there, wondering. What could Major Godo's men be up to now?

It was then we heard the shot.

And this is what I told those who asked. That shot came from somewhere back of the schoolhouse, on the other side of the river.

In America, years later, the barrio vanished. Rightly so, you might say. But that shot—you heard it even better. You heard the echo, clear through the swamps—across the years.

Now the Major was right there with you in the cafe, looking none the worse for wear being past the mid-fifties, like Phil and yourself.

"Drop that 'Major' business, will you please?" he said.

He had had it easy under the new immigration law. He would become a U.S. citizen in three years, he told us proudly.

"Who could have imagined it then?" I said.

Phil's remark was just like him: "I see an entirely new life ahead for you," he said.

"Yes, why not?" I said.

"So you both knew each other during the war?" said Phil.

Long ago, in Manila, he had been Felipe Escondido, of the Ritz Music Makers. Now "Phil" seemed right; it suited the jazz piano player he had become . . . . For that matter, I, too, had become "Dan."

"Remember when we marched right into your barrio, in the middle of your fiesta?" said the Major.

"You visited with us twice, Major," I said, catching the mistake. But it was too late.

"Quit it, will you?" he protested.

"Did Dan, here, already play the sax then?"

I suspected he was pleased we were safely employed, having become union-card holders and all that. The Major had for all his luck still that far to go.

"As Godo, here, will tell you," I said to Phil, "it was the violin then. The second time he and his men turned up they had this prisoner with them."

Phil had often asked me, too, about the war. Now, with the Major there, he would know how true my stories had been.

"Dan remembers vividly how the prisoner died," Phil said.

"You couldn't possibly forget that shot—if you had heard it at all," I said.

"I was supposed to do it," the Major said. "But I couldn't—I just couldn't. We had this messenger from San Paulino with the order . . . ."

"Who did it then?"

I could see that Phil was anxious to get the Major's version.

"Go ahead. You can tell him, if anyone can," I said.

"If you remember," the Major said, "one of the men I had was a fellow named Pungkol."

"The guitar-player."

"If you remember, he had only one ear. On a dare he had trimmed the other off himself. That's how he got his name Pungkol. In San Jose it happened. The men had been drinking and someone had said could this fellow prove he was braver than all the others."

Before I could put in a word Phil said, "Oh, no!" In his shock, he had turned pale almost all at once.

"He had that switch blade always with him, and it was the same one he used there, back of the schoolhouse," the Major said.

"It wasn't you then?"

"Definitely."

"Which shot, then, was that one we heard?"

"You heard nothing, nothing at all. I couldn't do it. I walked away, wetting my pants." He smiled, remembering. "The messenger saw, and I didn't like the look on his face and so gave him a blow."

By this time the coffee was cold in our cups.

"You didn't hear anything," the Major continued. "Pungkol did it with his knife, touching the blade afterwards with his tongue, as if to say that even that—that, too—he could do. But, afterwards, he kept spitting out like this—for days on end, for days—like this—"

Phil covered his face, unwilling to see.

All this was thirty years away, and the croissants on the table looked like wave-washed seashells.

The Major left for his evening shift at Union Carbide, where he worked for Security.

"You two are simply lucky, having gotten to this country earlier," he said. "But this job's only temporary," he said, as if rationalizing. He would not be one to lose hope in somehow making it in his adopted country.

"How do you suppose you can play the sax tonight?" Phil asked.

I had to think for a moment. "No problem," I said, thinking: Work is work, as they say.

"Keep remembering you heard the shot," he said.

"Whoever said I didn't?" *Because over the years it has been that way. Nothing can change that. Nothing must.*

We waited for a while outside "Marylou's European Pastries" for Phil's ride. Then a car stopped in front of us. The door opened, and Phil's wife said to me, "Hi!"

"Hi!" I said also, thinking now about nothing.

Anyhow, we were as far away from Panay as anyone could get.

1978

Appendices

In the Workshop of Time and Tide

I

"Is it a tale of the wars?"

"No," was the reply. "(But) I shall tell you something I saw, or rather something (that) I did not see, this afternoon."

This curious exchange comes from a little-known story by Mariano Pascual which perhaps holds a key to an understanding of Philippine literature and, particularly, of the short story in both Pilipino and English. "The Major's Story," as Mr. Pascual's narrative is called, is in Jose Garcia Villa's *Best Philippine Short Stories 1928*, a pioneer anthology of the Philippine practice of this genre, published by *Philippines Free Press*, itself a pioneer in the promotion and development of Filipino letters in general. The Philippines was in those days a frontier of sorts, although hardly the badlands of literature.

The subject and perhaps the rendering of that literature is symbolically given in "The Major's Story." It concerns a party where a number of girls succeed in persuading one of the many guests, in this instance, the Major, to liven up the occasion with some amusing anecdote.

Our Major obliges; he tells the girls about an incident of no particular significance other than that he could vouch for it. He was on his way home one afternoon, he says, when he spotted a crowd gathering at Colgate Bridge. This was the footbridge over the river Pasig. The crowd, says the Major, included a number of students, two Chinese peddlers, a

Spaniard with a little child by his side, some half dozen Yankee sailors, three women in black who had just come from nearby Quiapo Church, and two laborers carrying a shrieking pig. Soon enough two policemen appeared, one from the north, the other from the south. It was humanity on a small scale. And what was attracting all that attention? A drowned person? A wreck? Someone doing a stunt in the water below?

"The man beside me began it all," the Major tells the girls as soon as he senses that he cannot hold them in suspense much longer. "He had nothing to do, and to kill time he watched the water as it flowed into the sea. People saw him looking into the water, and, being curious, followed him as people will always do."

As an explanation this is plausible enough. But the thoughtful reader might find the Filipino writer in the episode. For the ceaseless flow of the Pasig is what Filipino literature would be all about. At any point in time, one could ask the question, "What, indeed, does the crowd see?"

Writing some forty years later, Francisco Arcellana offered a synthesis of what till then our symbolic Pasig, through time and tide, has offered the observer:

> . . . Wall Street crashed in 1929. What did that mean for us in 1930? Men jumping out of windows of skyscrapers . . . . There was a depression in America. The dole, headlines, the hordes of the unemployed. The Philippines became a commonwealth. Japan invaded Asia. There was a civil war in Spain. The International Eucharistic Congress met in Manila. Italy invaded Ethiopia. The Filipino writer was told to leave his ivory tower. He was told to stay there. They read proletarian literature. They wrote proletarian literature. They debated whether to scab or join the picket line. Germany invaded Poland. And the world that we thought was without end began to end.[1]

Eventually, Colgate Bridge was dismantled and junked. The river Pasig, of course, has remained—although perhaps a bit murkier than before. But for as long as it flows there will be stories to tell, and Filipino

---

1. Francisco Arcellana, "Period of Emergence: The Short Story," *Brown Heritage: Essays on Philippine Cultural Tradition and Literature*, ed. Antonio Manuud (Quezon City: Ateneo de Manila University Press, 1967), pp. 606-7.

writers will be writing them for whoever might care to read, wherever that audience might be.

II

It is not often remembered that the printing press reached the Philippines as early as the last decade of the sixteenth century and that by 1610, a Filipino printer Tomas Pinpin has produced a primer for the learning of the Spanish language. The first known published poem in Tagalog is said to have appeared in 1605. It took almost a hundred years, however, before *Pasyon ni Hesukristong Panginoon (The Passion of the Lord Jesus Christ)*, by Gaspar Aquino de Belen, was printed. Fifty more years were to pass before the emergence of Jose de la Cruz (1746–1829), better known as Huseng Sisiw, who is credited with having written the first verses that dealt with lay, rather than religious, themes. Finally came Balagtas (1788–1862) and his *Florante at Laura* (1838)

> . . . bunga ng pagtatagpo ng tradisyong katutubo at ng impluwensiyang banyaga, at karapatdapat tanghaling hiyas ng panulaang Tagalog ng panahon ng kolonyalismong Español.[2]
> (. . . an outcome of the contact of the native tradition with foreign influences, and [a work which we] must duly esteem as the jewel of Tagalog poetry during the Spanish regime.)

There is more to all those years, of course, than that which might come under "foreign influences." True, the bulk of the formal literature of the period (to distinguish it from the oral) would seem, whether in song or narrative verse, to be mere borrowings from abroad. These were known as the *awit* and *corrido*,[3] the verse forms into which the Filipino

---

2. "Kasaysayan ng Tulang Tagalog," *Landasin sa Panulaang Tagalog* (Quezon City: Pamana ng Panitikang Pilipino, n.d.), p. 1.

3. Many writers use the plural forms, Anglicizing the terms accordingly. *Awit* is Tagalog for "song"; *corrido* is believed to have derived from "ocurrido," meaning "event or happening." It is Tagalog that was used for the narrative verse derived from the European legends and their adaptations.

poet cast the medieval romances and adventure stories that reached him. The material had spilled over from Europe; in Filipino containers they were to remain available for over two hundred years. If early Filipino literature is to be understood, scholars could pay close attention to the awit and corrido with profit.

To the undiscerning, our earliest writers seemed unoriginal and, in refurbishing stories from European lore, limited in their efforts. Here were mere episodes from Spanish chivalric literature and from the Arthurian and Carolingian legends, anecdotes from Portuguese and Italian history latched on at best to incidents from Czech or Persian folklore.

> These stories about queens, princesses and princes, knights, dukes, and counts who lived in a wonderful world of romance where the good were always rewarded and the wicked punished, and where God, the Virgin, and the saints communicated frequently with men through angels and heavenly voices, or even came down to help the heroes and heroines in need, captivated the imagination of a people who as yet knew very little of the outside world. These romances provided a temporary release from the harsh realities of existence. They were, however, the only reading matter that the masses could safely enjoy during a period of strict political and literary censorship.[4]

Some fifty of those stories have come down to us, and in a study by Professor Damiana Ligon Eugenio are analyses and commentaries on both the verse forms and their European analogues. It is research of this kind that might help revise, in the future, the attitude of contemporary scholars toward this portion of the national heritage. Summarily dismissed by some writers as embarrassing scraps of an indeterminable literature, the awit and corrido are, in fact, a mirror upon which the culture of their day is truly reflected. An amazing grasp by the Tagalog mind of the fundamentals of literary art is imaged in them, for example, and it is something to admire.

---

4. Damiana Ligon Eugenio, *Awit and Korrido: A Study of Fifty Philippine Metrical Romances in Relation to Their Sources and Analogues*, Diss. University of California, Los Angeles, 1965.

It was not unusual for the awit and corrido writers to exhibit a disarming humility toward their art; this was exceeded only by their abiding respect for their audience. The romance *Salita at Buhay na Pinagdaanan nang Haring Asuero, ni Doña Maria, at ni Juan Pobre sa Bayang Herusalem*, a work of some four hundred and seventy-five quatrains of unknown authorship, is perhaps typical. The story, according to Professor Eugenio, has analogues in the folklore of Italy, France, and Czechoslovakia. The author begins with a formulaic invocation:

> Oh God, Lord all Powerful,
> Who made and created the whole universe,
> Help now my lips and my tongue
> To be able to narrate an exemplum.

> And all you saints and angels,
> Comrades of God the King of Heaven,
> Bestow grace on my feeble mind
> That I may not err in what I shall say.

> Distinguished audience, what can I
> Say and declare?
> Wherever I look and fix my gaze
> I see that all of you are persons of quality.

> But be it so, distinguished ones,
> I shall begin my story:
> If perchance I omit anything,
> Let your better judgement supply the deficiency.[5]

This appeal to the better judgment of the "distinguished ones" is what today's entertainers might call "audience participation"; the feature, in any case, placed the versifier in direct contact with his public. What he called the awit required twelve-syllable lines, the corrido eight-syllable ones. He worked with quatrains, observing no particular preferences as to which subjects required the awit or which demanded the corrido form. He might

---

5. Ibid., pp. 395-96.

have initially recited his narratives himself; but they were later to see print anyhow, and were obtainable at "sidewalk stalls and brought to the remote barrios by itinerant peddlers."[6] Their popularity was undeniable. Translations appeared and these may have helped immeasurably, in the early development of provincial languages like Hiligaynon and Ilocano, for example, to establish the conventions of grammar and rhetoric so necessary for growth.

The tradition of humble authorship did not, of course, discourage later writers from affixing their signatures to their work. Initials were at times used in the closing quatrain, and with some shrewdness, so as to avoid blunting sentiment for the sake of rhyme. Between veracity to the known turns of a given story and the act of rendering it in some way or other, the latter seemed to have greater value. Thus, in *Proceso*, we find the following subtitle:

> The Life of the Merchant Proceso, and his daughter Maria, in the Kingdom of Hungary, which was derived from a *Cuadro Histórico*, and most laboriously versified by one who is just beginning to write in the common pastime of the Tagalogs.[7]

Francisco Baltazar came from this tradition. Some twelve works have been credited to him; of these only *Florante at Laura*, however, appears to have survived. His predecessor, Huseng Sisiw, is remembered today for *Historia Famosa ni Bernardo Carpio, Doce Pares, Rodrigo de Villa* and others. In Dr. Eugenio's study, only fifteen authors, Balagtas and Huseng Sisiw among them, have their writings fairly well authenticated.

There are probably two hundred of these awit and corrido, according to Professor Eugenio. Earlier scholars, notably Epifanio de los Santos, have left musical scores of a few awit samples. Whatever further study might suggest, it seems clear that the roots of the Filipino story-teller's art are in this material.

---

6. Ibid., pp. 8-9.

7. Ibid., p. 10.

Song, for one thing, is central to the vocabulary of that art. Read as one of the last scenes of Jose Rizal's recorded life, his valedictory poem, "Mi Ultimo Adios," is not lyrical in quality by mere coincidence.[8] Similarly, before the final curtain in Nick Joaquin's *A Portrait of the Artist as Filipino*, we see

> Bitoy (speaking exultantly through the sound of bells and music): October in Manila! . . . The month when, back in our childhood, the very air turned festive and the Circus came to town and the old Opera House!
>
> *(The lights die out inside the stage; the sound of bells and music fades off. The ruins stand out distinctly.)*
>
> Oh Paula, Candida—listen to me! By your dust, and by the dust of all the generations, I promise to continue, I promise to persevere!
>
> The jungle may advance, the bombs may fall again—but while I live, you live—and this dear city of our affections shall rise again—if only in my song! To remember and to sing: that is my vocation . . . .[9]

And then, though quite on a different track, we have confirmation of the same phenomenon from the short-story writers.

> "Was she afraid of Labang?" My father had not raised his voice, but the room seemed to resound with it. And again I saw her eyes on the long curving horns and the arm of my brother Leon around her shoulders.
> "No, Father, she was not afraid."
> "On the way—"
> "She looked at the stars, Father. And Manong Leon sang."
> "What did he sing?"
> " 'Sky Sown with Stars.' She sang with him."[10]

---

8. For a translation, see Nick Joaquin, *Prose and Poems* (Manila: Alberto S. Florentino, 1963), pp. 191-93.

9. Nick Joaquin, *Portrait of the Artist as Filipino* (Manila: Alberto S. Florentino, 1966).

10. Manuel E. Arguilla, "How My Brother Leon Brought Home a Wife," *Modern Philippine Short Stories* (Albuquerque: University of New Mexico Press, 1962), pp. 59-67.

This is from Arguilla's "How My Brother Leon Brought Home a Wife." In J.C. Tuvera's "Ceremony," it appears in somewhat cryptic form but is at the heart of the story:

> "I hate it all here," he said. "In this house. And I can't bear to see you leave again."
> In a rush the words tumbled from her. "I know," she said. "I know." Then abruptly she bent and touched her lips to his face, in the moment when a spurt of song heaved afresh from the night, and then sobbing she fled swiftly from the room.[11]

III

Art does not copy life but rather illumines it by offering for our enjoyment a semblance of it. And the Filipino story-teller has done well enough in this, as the record of his first hundred and fifty years of apprenticeship shows. Hardly can one fault him for being unengaging; and judging from the awit and corrido that have come down to us, he had in fact an intuitive grasp of his role in society.

Competing and authoritative cultures, such as that which informed the civil regime under Spain and the friarocracy that went with it, were never out of the Filipino artist's way. His experience in those years demonstrates what John Dewey was to insist upon as a characteristic of art, namely, its ability to cope with seemingly obstructive matters. In the practice of the awit and corrido writers, invention and a whole-souled affection for the Tagalog language were the tools used to minimize barriers of communication.

Students of the culture, since Father Pedro Chirino's *Relación de las Islas Filipinas* of 1604, have been happily astounded by that richness even before the advent of the verse narrative writers. When the folklore of the world, and particularly that of Europe, became available to the Filipino, the artist in the national community did not appear to require

---

11. J. C. Tuvera, "Ceremony," from *Fifty Great Oriental Stories*, ed. Gene Z. Hanrahan (New York: Bantam Books, 1965), pp. 399-407.

instruction on how to deal with the material; the genius of the race, as it were, took over. We might remember that the long years under Spain were not spectacular for the achievements of that regime in mass education. The authorities undoubtedly saw in the verse-writer an ally, and here commenced the tension in the Filipino experience between art and society.

In dismissing the awit and corrido portion of the national heritage, as some have done, and in relegating this to the heap of unsavory by-products of friarocracy, the banal and uninventive in the Filipino character have been exaggerated. This is unfair to the Filipino artistic sensibility since it was after all very much in control, starting from the years of its formal apprenticeship. Those pious invocations and shy clues to authorship are proofs of this.

They served, to begin with, to dissociate from the art the particulars that story-teller and audience shared and recognized as the nitty-gritty of lived life. They were the story-teller's signals that a narrative was forthcoming and with it a burden of myth and riddle, of fable, some vision of life. And those ritual signatures had a similar, if opposite, purpose. They were meant to restore the audience to the lived life, to the actuality that had been disturbed, or that had been temporarily abandoned for the story's sake.[12] Audience and story-teller both enjoyed a secret, moreover: that the material really belonged to popular history or lore.

The audience knew that the story-teller's boarding-house reach had come up with something for it to share. Painters experience how the quality of sunlight and the nature of shadows in the country where one has chosen to do one's work—say, Italy—influence an artist's development, his style and methods. With the twelve- or eight-syllable line, and the alliteration and assonance in Tagalog, the awit and corrido writers worked diligently, as it were, with their brush, delighting in simply letting themselves be of their time and place. They were earlier Fernando Amorsolos, discovering their sun-drenched tropical landscape.

---

12. See J. R. Rayfield, "What is a Story?" *Journal of the American Anthropological Association*, 74:5 (October 1972), pp. 1085-1106.

The Eugenio study observes that there have been awit and corrido structures that reached from four to more than five thousand lines. Considering the moralistic themes that weighted them, it was remarkable how they did not disenchant the listener or reader but continued instead to hold and win him. We must go to the archetypal nature of those borrowed stories to understand this. For those romances were no mere "histories" or "lives"; they were not topical episodes of adventure. They were, in fact, inherited "deposits" of experience, "banked" answers to life's riddles, motifs of initiations and discoveries. Our awit and corrido writers could not have escaped those, for the imagination and its power to put experience in order would have demanded the performance of them. To our early loss, we did not see this intuitive use that our pioneer workers in the field of the imagination did indeed make of those archetypal images that were as accessible in their day as they are, of course, in ours.

IV

Those archetypes are, as they seem to have always been, informed by that shaping or ordering force. To be aware of this, one has only to recall the tale of the *adarna*—of the sick father who had three sons, and who wanted a magic bird brought to his bedside so that he might become well again.[13] Or consider Balagtas' *Florante at Laura*[14] and its motifs of justice and honor. That political satire has been read into it derives from this archetypal mold that found a particularly revealing parallel in the social reality of Balagtas' time.

John M. Echols has called *Florante at Laura* an "early precursor of the writings of supporters of independence"[15]—an apt description; indeed it was time the writer put his finger on the pulse of the nation. By the middle of the nineteenth century the most important writings were in Spanish, and "the internationally renowned representative of this

13. Eugenio, pp. 372-94.

14. Ibid., pp. 438-47.

15. John M. Echols, *Literature of Southeast Asia* (New York: rpt. Educational Resources/ Asia Literature Program, The Asia Society, n.d.), p. 4.

period," Echols goes further, "is Jose Rizal, whose novels, *Noli Me Tangere* (*The Lost Eden*) and *El Filibusterismo* (*The Subversive*), helped to spark the struggle for independence from Spain . . . His works were ultimately to help bring about his execution before a Spanish firing squad . . . ."[16] We might recall, in this connection, the last work to come from Rizal's pen, mention of which was made earlier: "Mi Ultimo Adios" ("My Last Farewell"). It might have been the song of the mythic adarna bird; for such is the way of archetypes.[17]

Such synoptic remarks by disinterested observers like Professor Echols enable us to recognize the direction that Philippine literature has taken. "Writing in Spanish," he tells us in an all-too-brief note on Rizal, "has not reached such heights."[18] We should not indeed forget that, especially toward the last decades of the nineteenth century, a rising awareness concerning the conditions in the country demanded expression. Spanish, rather than Tagalog, which Huseng Sisiw and Balagtas raised to great levels in their day, was held to be the best medium at this time. Spanish would guarantee access to the ruling elite. Reason and emotion could be appealed to wherever intelligent men might be found. And it is in this context that Rizal's novels acquire a perennial interest. His choice of language was an act of sacrifice; his choice of audience, an expression of idealism. Both sacrifice and idealism were to be reevaluated by another generation, the accruing irony notwithstanding.

At this point in the national literary history, though, Rizal's artistic act has a special meaning. It was an extension of Balagtas's art and a personal response on the novelist's part to yet another European literary convention. Had Rizal followed Balagtas's lead in the use of Tagalog, he might have been held down by the awit and corrido tradition. The fact is that he turned in another direction. He mapped out a new geography for the literature of his country, indicating the procedures appropriate to the exploration of that territory. Three generations of intellectuals

---

16. Ibid.

17. N.V.M. Gonzalez, "Rizal and Poetic Myth," *Literature and Society* (Manila: Florentino, 1964), pp. 32-54.

18. Echols, op. cit., p. 4.

were to go into the terrain, at times flamboyantly flashing their travel documents but only to fail as transients or even as protracted sojourners owing to their inability to distinguish, it would seem, between travel and residence, between the merely naturalized and the native-born.

Rizal's successes derive from his having been a true son of his tradition. Consider his use of the novel form. The awit and corrido, as analogies of the European realistic novel, created a level of rhyme and measure appropriate to a semblance of human experience of archetypal force and blocked off the particular realities of the day. Rizal did likewise, using Spanish and the novel form, the latter already long employed in Europe. He achieved much the same effect as did the awit or corrido writer in terms of creating a virtual world where ideals could be particularized. It was as if he knew all along that his predecessors in the craft of the narrative had drawn enough from the fables of Europe; not it was his turn to tell a tale of a Europe transplanted. Here was his necessary subject; both the convention he chose and his tradition required it. The earlier corrido had rendered glosses on the subject of justice; the awit had lyricized over it. Now he would probe for its truth. Convention laid out the tools of realism on the service-tray before him. In place of the twelve- and eight-syllable lines, which were the versifier's bid for immediacy, he would turn to the resources of scene, dialogue, characterization, of persona and tone—devices already pressed into service by Perez Galdós (1843–1920), Dumas (1802–70), Hugo (1802–85), and Flaubert (1821–80).

The popularity of the awit and corrido among the common people and their heavy burden of pious material must have concealed, for Rizal's younger brothers, the profound artistic advance that has been achieved and possibly the creative resources of the national past as well. Rizal, for his part, had the genius not to miss anything. It therefore became necessary for latecomers to make new discoveries. But the complex role in the national culture that Rizal and his work played concealed the purely artistic facet of his legacy, obscuring leads that could help the diligent and the humble. With the advent of the American regime, a perturbed sensibility began to look about, anxious for indications of roots or beginnings, only to stumble into false starts and ludicrous posturings in hopes of pressing the Filipino experience into acceptable forms. In some cases, as we shall later see, the acceptable meant the vendable. Moreover, events moved at much too fast a clip. Before a freshly remembered event was released from memory and could be articulated, a new one thrust itself forward to overwhelm the mind and trample upon the spirit. The short story in both Filipino and English offered relief from this cultural mutilation.

V

The short story in Pilipino has a less elaborate history than its counterpart in English, although not necessarily a less eventful one. It is unfortunate that the schoolbook trade, like a curse, has encouraged the easy designation of styles and themes and the listing of writers and titles of stories as alternatives to defining the forces that beleaguered the writer and diminished his art. Our account here cannot serve to supply what years of diligent critical attention could have provided. We can only sketch in an idea: the dedicated involvement by some writers and the enthusiastic, if chancy, support by institutions and groups, so that the appearance of the short story in Pilipino, all told, might be recognized as a milestone in the journey of the Filipino toward artistic expression.

What we call *maikling katha*—a short literary composition—could not be anything but new in the literature, considering its formal beginnings in the awit and corrido tradition. The form derives from the *dagli*, brief sketches that Lope K. Santos and his associates published in *Muling Pagsilang* in the twenties. The *salaysay*, or narration, had already been cultivated as well. It may well be that when the salaysay acquired a thematic thrust the dagli came into being. For one thing, length had lost its appeal; and reading matter that could be sold at the patio of Quiapo Church, alongside votive candles in the shape of hearts and crosses, were now things of the past. No doubt, the Revolution of 1896 and the Philippine-American War, which extended to 1904, were more than sufficient explanations for the change of taste in the images of the lived life. What was sought after was entertainment and instruction for the new age. This was the direction of many a publication or journal of the period, and a typical one was *Ang Mithi*. In a literary competition in 1910 sponsored by this magazine, the story "Elias" by Rosauro Almario won first prize, setting a trend in fiction contests.

In 1920, Cirio Panganiban's "Bunga ng Kasalanan" ("The Fruit of Sin") earned the title "Katha ng Taon" ("Story of the Year") in a contest sponsored by *Taliba*. A. G. Abadilla credits Panganiban with having introduced "plot" (*ang banghay*) to the dagli or salaysay.[19] The "orderly arrangement of events, as a function and feature of the literary composition" (*maayos na pagkakatagni-tagni ng mga nangyari, bilang sangkap at haligi ng katha*) was, according to Abadilla, something of a discovery to this generation.

This was an underestimation of the earlier narrative tradition; for the awit and corrido writers were, of course, no strangers to it. What the new writers did manage was a practical use for plot. Whereas their verse-writing predecessors employed plot to mount some tendentious moralizing, the new writers used it to enhance narrative interest, to promote rewards like suspense and surprise. The new writers soon enough slipped into sentimentality, abetted by the lurid prose that had become, alas, the hallmark of popular reading.

And what were their stories about? Abadilla describes their core as follows: "... *ang nakayukayok na kalungkutan, ang inaglahing pag-ibig ng isang mahirap lalo na, ang mga daliring hubogkandila, ang baywang-hantik ng pinaparaluman, at anu-ano pang bunga ng mga kabiglawang pandamdamin at pangkaisipan ....*"[20] (... crushing sorrows, the spurned love of a poor suitor in particular, fingers as shapely as candles, the beloved's waist like that of an ant's, and all sorts of adolescent emotions and thoughts ....") It was altogether an odd image of life, but it was not without admirers.

A readership developed for it in *Liwayway*, a weekly that very early stood for popular writing in Tagalog. It was in *Liwayway*'s pages that the work of the members of the new school almost exclusively appeared. Other weeklies were soon launched and for the first time the writer as a Filipino (working in what today is called Pilipino but which then was

19. A. G. Abadilla, F. B. Sebastian, and A. D. G. Mariano, *Ang Maikling Kathang Tagalog* (Quezon City: Bedes' Publishing, 1954), p. 5.

20. Ibid., p. 11.

essentially the Tagalog of Manila and vicinity) became aware that one could make a living professionally at being a man of letters. Indeed, this was possible through writing fiction, as a craftsman in the language of one's own race.

By 1927, the *maikling katha* was ready for some official accounting. Precisely for this purpose Clodualdo del Mundo initiated his list of the best stories published in the magazines. For nine years he stood watch. Writers were observed to compose their work with more care than before in hopes of making the del Mundo roll of honor, the *Parolang Ginto* (The Golden Lantern).

Another critical observer joined in—Alejandro G. Abadilla, who earlier, had earned a reputation for his poetry. Inaugurated in 1932, Abadilla's *Talaang Bughaw* (The Blue List) exerted pressure on contributors to the popular weeklies and college publications alike. Here was a critic who was keen on craft and willing over the years to keep running skirmishes with those writers gleefully unconcerned with technique.

The practitioners of the maikling katha had much to thank the Abadilla and del Mundo leadership for. In due course, however, the Tagalog scene became polarized. A sharp division between *Liwayway* writers—who were now the old school—and the young blood was all too discernible by 1935, the year of the participation of the academy in the national literary dialogue. For it was then that the National Teachers College offered the use of its facilities for seminars and debates on Tagalog literary issues. The dialogue tended toward dismantling what appeared to be a strong literary fort manned by members of the *Liwayway* camp and their supporters from the staff of similarly minded magazines. The new writers, unable to publish readily in the popular press, were not without ingenuity and enterprise. In the following year appeared the first anthology of the short story in Tagalog, the *Mga Kuwentong Ginto (Golden Tales)*, edited by A. G. Abadilla and C. del Mundo.[21]

The collection contained twenty stories and covered the period from 1925 to 1935. Here the Pilipino term for "short story" seems to

---

21. Manila: Cavite Publishing Co., 1936.

have seen print for the first time. The anthologists defined the form as best they could. Quite apart from the many stories that are already short, they observed, the maikling katha are those that are a class by themselves owing to the attentive regard on the part of their authors for meaning and structure. Each story in *Mga Kuwentong Ginto* could come close, in the estimation of the editors, to what might be called the *sining ng maikling katha* (the art of the short story).

All this had a beneficial effect, as reflected in the work by new writers, many of them still college undergraduates. And from here on, the short story in Pilipino became an open arena for protracted contest between two groups, the old and the young. To the first belonged those committed to the standards set by *Liwayway* and like publications whose survival meant their catering to a large but undiscriminating audience. The writers of the second group had no such loyalties and made no concessions to popular taste. They felt free to experiment with form and to press fresh ideas upon it. The publication of *50 Kuwentong Ginto ng 50 Batikang Kuwentista (Fifty Golden Stories by Fifty Master Story-tellers)* edited by Pedrito Reyes[22] had the effect of placing the innovators in a most advantageous position.

The battle lines seem to have been clearly drawn—although larger issues, then unidentified, began to appear. The *Liwayway* school, it will be recalled, did not particularly recognize a literary past. But it did identify enough with the romantic sentiments that, in the work of the awit and corrido writers, had won popular approval. While dutifully extolling Huseng Sisiw and Balagtas, the *Liwayway* school accommodated itself to the stock situations and cliche ideas that the new public sought. Attempts at new modes and the search for new directions were readily discouraged. Rather than raise the level of the narrative form in any serious way, the *Liwayway* school settled for professionalism in the business of producing popular literature, regarding this as a virtuous gesture suited to the peculiarities of the pursuit of letters in a country without its own sources of newsprint and other paper products.

---

22. Manila: Ramon Roces Publications, 1939.

Its writers rode high on the assets that have accrued to the language through its formal use in the folklore, gains achieved by the chapbooks on the church-patio and through the *sari-sari* store level of distribution. Instead of being sold side by side with votive offerings and from counters with candy jars and sugar-and-peanut cakes, the work of the *Liwayway* writer would now reach its reader by courtesy of a modern delivery service. Printing empires were in the making. What the younger writers could not accept, obviously, was to see literary imagination becoming a tool of wealth and trade. This sentiment was not, however, easily expressed. While mindful of the service that the popular magazines were providing by spreading the idiom to the distant reaches of the archipelago, the younger writers felt that their elders were doing Philippine culture a disservice. In their evolving concept of the theory and practice of the short story, a growing conflict between practicality and idealism was evident.

But the members of the new group were caught up in mundane problems themselves, and the importance of their stand against commercialization was not infrequently obscured by their employment in the very publishing empires that had routed earlier idealisms. The universities and colleges were shortly to provide the country new talent to replace that which by force of circumstances had been weaned away from literature. In this respect the progress of the writers in Tagalog paralleled that of their contemporaries who, using the English language and enjoying the sanctuary of the university, were already writing memorable short stories.

VI

The Filipino short story in English is a reaction against the commercialization of the Filipino's intuitive grasp of his cultural history. We have seen how the awit and corrido writers reached out to Europe and succeeded in keeping a national community stocked with virtual images of life for its edification. When the Filipino mind, owing to an accident of history, accommodated itself to a unique form of the narrative, the modern short story, a similar performance had to be produced by the shaping imagination. This began in the late twenties and early thirties, about the same time that writers in Tagalog were themselves becoming disturbed over the way the literary tradition in the native language was being used. This confluence of awareness by both groups of writers was no coincidence. There was in the maturing Filipino spirit a need for fuller growth.

Although too easy a choice as a common language for peoples otherwise isolated within their vernaculars, English would be acceptable enough as a tool for growth. Its history and tradition, its metaphysics and rhetoric, more than sufficed to serve as serious barriers to the average learner. And this, too, was endurable. As in several countries that were later to be called the Third World,[23] English would serve as the language of government. But what was one to make out of those elements amongst the governed that dared to give artistic expression to their thoughts and sentiments in a school-learned language? Could this be anything but foolhardiness?[24]

At this point, Rizal's adoption of Spanish was simply too fresh in the Filipino memory. Spanish was no *wikang sinuso* for him. It was not an idiom drawn, as the Tagalog would say, from Mother's breast. And Rizal had to borrow not only an idiom but a literary form as well—adding debt upon heavy debt. He did clear the account, at an all-too-punitive interest rate. The writers that were to come, then, after Rizal's martyrdom in 1896, could not quite escape his example. When the learning of the English language moved from the improvised classrooms of the Thomasites to Gabaldon-style schoolhouses and, finally, by the early twenties, to the University of the Philippines and elsewhere, Rizal's example amounted to a challenge. Another generation of inheritors of that restless and durable artistic sensibility in the race had emerged.

The initial efforts at self-identification cannot be recalled without embarrassment. In 1912, Fernando Maramag wondered, for example, if

---

23. N.V.M. Gonzalez, "Imagination and the Literature of Emerging Nations," *Solidarity*, IX: 5, pp. 31-40, and "Holding the Rainbow," *Manila Review*, 1:3, pp. 59-68.

24. N.V.M. Gonzalez, "The Filipino and the Novel," *Fiction in Several Languages*, ed. Henri Peyre (Boston: Beacon Press, 1968), pp. 19-29.

some critic might be found who would tell the nation whether it would be "susceptible to the imaginings of a native Tennyson."[25] The public would thus be "capable of receiving a poet's message with the uplifting sympathy that reaches the divine in man." Besides being a working newspaperman, Maramag was a practicing poet on the scene. Well heard was his call for the man of the hour who would tell the nation "whether the ideals and aspirations of the race" could find full expression in the newly learned language. Maramag stipulated, however, that such ideals must remain "distinctly" native.[26]

Thirteen years later, Jorge Bocobo put the national literary community on the alert. (And this has been the condition of the national scene ever since.) "In what language shall this Filipino literature be written?" Bocobo asked. Already the awit and corrido tradition seemed to have been forgotten. Nor had oral literature been able to win its due. A fresh elitism, as when *ilustrado* and *cacique* tastes prevailed, was in the air.

But like Maramag and other intellectuals of the period, Bocobo had not escaped the national inheritance of artistic sensibility. Besides writing plays, he launched a movement to preserve the national heritage in dance and song. For the present, his thoughts were on writing. "Less and less will it be in Spanish, and more and more in English." Yet all that would be temporary: eventually "the great Filipino novel . . . will not be written in English; it will be in one of the Filipino languages."

However that would be, the next decade found a more unequivocal advocate for English in Salvador P. Lopez, who was confident that the literature would "draw increasing sustenance through the old roots that first grew there [the University of the Philippines campus] twenty-five years ago . . . ." The publishers of *Philippines Free Press* were to issue, in a couple of years, Jose Garcia Villa's pioneering selection of the best short stories in English, from a crop of nearly six hundred that particular year. The *Free Press* was to say, without so much as a smile, that behind its effort to provide support for Filipino writing in English was,

---

25. Loc. cit.

26. Loc. cit.

apart from self-interest, [the desire] to develop a school of Filipino short story writers or authors, partly with a view to the development of some literary genius who might make a name for himself in the United States . . . .[27]

What this meant was that the choice of English—that is, if the writer did have a choice—essentially opened up for him an opportunity that could be overlooked only out of sheer boorishness. Compared to the situation in which Rizal's artistic sensibility achieved its successes, this one was less ideal although it had the advantage of being apolitical; and such illusions and realities as it implied had to be recognized for what they were.

Now becoming attractive as a personal gesture of considerable public value was the act of writing itself, a national ideal that found expression in the Commonwealth constitution, particularly in the provision that defined the role of the state as a patron of arts and letters. Although literature did not count as a learned profession, say, like the law, its practitioners had to congregate in Manila where facilities for publishing were available. Besides the *Free Press*, other magazines and journals took special interest in developing, in particular, the short story—the *Graphic*, *Philippine Magazine*, and weekend supplements to the *Manila Tribune* and *Philippines Herald*, to name but the principal ones. A new anthology had followed Villa's, this one edited by O. O. Sta. Romana, then a senior at the University of Santo Tomas who led, in developing an awareness of posterity, a growing corps of short story writers out of university classrooms and into editors' cubicles and press rooms as fledgling journalists. A civic-minded Philippine Book Guild issued titles by Villa, Manuel E. Arguilla, Arturo B. Rotor; the University of the Philippines student literary annual, not inappropriately named *The Literary Apprentice*, founded years back, now obtained fresh money from the university president's entertainment budget.[28] Because the thirties

---

27. Loc. cit.

28. Elmer Ordoñez, "Remembered by the Clowns," *Literary Apprentice*, XX: 2 (October 1956), p. 58.

were ending, the time had come to make good the state's promise of patronage. Hence the first Commonwealth Literary Awards in 1940.

The stories of Manuel E. Arguilla (who, with his collection, *How My Brother Leon Brought Home a Wife and Other Stories*, won the year's Commonwealth prize for the Short Story in English)[29] were not typical of the work of the period; nor were those by Arturo B. Rotor.[30] But the general excellence of their stories must be regarded as pledges for still more outstanding work to come and, at the same time, as standards that could be achieved by the rank and file through a formal study of the form. Indeed, later writers were to pursue this study abroad. Let it be noted, though, that the short story writers in Tagalog seemed to be moving along, though not necessarily ahead, on their own, striking out more or less on an independent course. At the time of the Japanese Occupation, though, several short story writers in English tried writing in Tagalog (it would be several years still before the language would be officially called Pilipino); and the experiment, apart from having been required by the exigencies of the war, was regarded with considerable welcome.[31]

Largely understood, if hardly admitted or discussed, was the lesson that the two writing groups were each learning from the other. The writer in Tagalog could see what sheer book-learning and formal, if self-conscious, techniques could accomplish; the writer in English saw how inspiration, derived from being able to reach an audience beyond the university campus, could generate material closer to actuality. These were secret lessons, as it were, grasped in the privacy of the artistic conscience. It was becoming possible, in any case, to document Philippine life through the short story—borrowed ostensibly from Edgar Allan Poe, O. Henry and Wilbur Daniel Steele. The Filipino imagination, however, did not seem comfortable with the styles that these writers

---

29. Manila: Philippine Writers Guild, 1940.

30. Manila: Philippine Writers Guild, 1937.

31. Under the auspices of the Manila Shinbunsya, *Liwayway* editors published the anthology of Tagalog short stories *Ang 25 Pinakamabuting Maikling Kathang Pilipino ng 1943* (Manila: 1944).

represent; it favored plotlessness and its ultimate form in the so called "slice of life."[32] This preference was sustained when soon after, the early stories of Ernest Hemingway and William Saroyan, along with those of Sherwood Anderson, began to exert a strong influence on the Filipino writer's sense of form and feel for language. Especially for the writers who chose English as their medium, persistence and discipline paid off.

This success could have been more spectacular had Filipinos been familiar at this time with relevant literary experiences in neighboring countries. The Philippine scene had become too much a client of the American cultural establishment in those years before World War II; the Filipino intellectual was thus deprived of the instruction that cultures close by, in Southeast Asia and South Asia, could offer.

T. Inglis Moore, who had been a lecturer at the University of the Philippines, was to remark in 1947 how similar to that of his native Australia the experience in the Philippines was in regard to the use of the English language for literary expression. This was, of course, not too appropriate a comparison. Australia, after all, had had as an English colony her original stock of native-born speakers of the language. But to Moore the outback that had become a rich source of material for Australian writing had its counterpart in the Philippines, and he sensed an intensifying creativity in the air—the Philippines would soon have its own Henry Lawsons and Henry Handel Richardsons. He was of course to reconsider his enthusiasm when at a later date he wrote:

> When a colonial people has already enjoyed a traditional culture of its own, the conflict between this and the conquering culture of an alien people is comparatively clear-cut. This can be seen in the Philippines after 1898 when the new Anglo-Saxon culture of the American conqueror was imposed upon the Spanish-Filipino one established during the centuries of Spanish rule, and the Filipino then struggled to achieve mental independence from colonialism by the creation of a

---

32. Robert Scholes and Robert Kellogg, *The Nature of Narrative* (New York: Oxford, 1966), p. 13.

national literature. While political freedom has been won, the cultural struggle still goes on. This is the constant theme of the Filipino literary critics.[33]

It is, in fact, the preoccupation of all Third World criticism as well. A complementary lesson could have been offered by Indo-Anglian literature, too. The careers of Tagore and Sri Aurobindo, Mulk Raj Anand, R. K. Narayan and Raja Rao were to be truly relevant to the Filipino shortly. On occasion, then as now, and like Philippine writing in English, Indo-Anglian writing would in fact be required by nationalists to stoke the fires of an idealism that could cause writers to dream and write in their native tongues.

What urged the Filipino writer, perhaps happy enough in his insularity, to persevere in his craft? What drove him to write in English as much as he did? He knew that while he published a few stories, getting a book out would be an entirely different matter, and if he tried the latter, the project would be

... delayed for months, to be squeezed in quickly by the press between run-offs of comic books and political broadsides . . . .[34]

Why give his best producing copy for the

... Sunday supplements which, by Wednesday, may become torches for burning out nests of termites?[35]

The Indo-Anglian writer had experienced all that and much more; what saw him through was, according to C. D. Narasimhaiah, an "inwardness," a familiarity that spills over into total control of the received language.[36]

---

33. T. Inglis Moore, *Social Patterns in Australian Literature* (Berkeley: University of California Press, 1971), p. 93.

34. Leonard Casper, *Modern Philippine Short Stories* (Albuquerque, New Mexico: University of New Mexico Press, 1962), p. xvii.

35. Ibid.

36. N.V.M. Gonzalez, "Holding the Rainbow," *Manila Review*, 1:3, pp. 59-68.

And given that, what had pushed the Indo-Anglian writer yet further on? The promise of audiences? Or

> . . . the challenge of particular dispositions and susceptibilities which can only respond to the possibilities of a medium—in its presence will he feel called upon to give shape and substance to the unwrought urn, the unheard melody and, generally, give airy nothing a local habitation and a name.[37]

All this notwithstanding, the artist quite simply obeys, in Narasimhaiah's view, "his own inner law."

Among Filipino writers that "inner law" demanded, in addition to a surrender to inwardness, an acceptance of historical circumstances and participation as a social being through self-fulfillment. With English, there would be a considerable tradition that he could turn to. In the most practical terms, this meant working with words, which in turn meant working with authoritative dictionaries. This was an advantage that even the writer working in Tagalog did not have. It would be years, through the efforts of an Australian priest who worked all by himself during the Japanese Occupation, before a fairly substantial English-Tagalog dictionary would appear.[38]

Another factor worked in favor of the Filipino writer in English, one which offset his seeming isolation from the larger world of international letters and transcultural issues. This was the not inconsiderable critical dialogue on the scene. The climate for it appeared to be right. Particularly in the fifties and sixties, literary criticism attained a vigorous, self-questioning voice. Such vapid topics as "Can writing be taught?" and

---

37. C. D. Narasimhaiah, *The Swan and the Eagle* (Simla: Institute of Advanced Study, 1968), p. 11.

38. Leo James English, C.Ss.R., *English-Tagalog Dictionary* (Manila: Deparment of Education, R.P., 1965). Printed in Australia under the auspices of the Australian Government, this work covered "more material" than did a similar one undertaken by the Philippine Institute of National Language. The Australian Government, through an arrangement under the Colombo Plan, donated the entire edition of 80,000 copies to the Philippine Government as a "practical token of cooperation" between the two countries.

"Where's the Great Filipino Novel?" were thin disguises for insights into the direction the writers were going. The Abadilla and del Mundo team was preoccupied with the same issues as their brethren working in English, but their scene did not acquire the excitement found where the writers in the school-learned language raised their literary potted plants regularly provided with water from the critical fountains of America and England.

By the late sixties, the high hopes of the *Free Press* had been fairly well forgotten, especially as the beginnings of a trade publishing in English surfaced in Manila. Central to the entire literary activity by now was the need for more reader support: an accounting had to be made as to whom the Filipino writer could reach, and especially in his own country. Leonard Casper, who watched the progress that was being achieved and, in 1962, published *Modern Philippine Short Stories*,[39] had to sound a warning. It seemed apparent to him that for the Filipino writer in English "to write honestly *about* his people, he must risk not writing *for* them."[40]

Ironic indeed as this looks, it cannot be denied that before the bar of literature the Filipino short story writer in English was nonetheless acquitting himself quite well. Commenting on Casper's anthology, Donald Keene wrote:

> Whatever course Philippine literature may take, we are certainly fortunate that there are now Filipinos who can speak to us beautifully in our own language, without risking the terrible hazards of translation . . . . The collection as a whole is of even more importance than the individual excellences. It is an admirable testimony to the emergence of another important branch of English literature.[41]

What was happening then was that while the Filipino writer in English might not be succeeding in getting to his people, from out of his tussles with a language not his own and with a form relatively new in his

---

39. Casper, op. cit.
40. Ibid., p. xviii.
41. Donald Keene, "Native Voices in a Foreign Tongue," *Saturday Review of Literature*, October 6, 1962, p.44.

culture, he was being counted as a contributor to world literature. For perhaps the Filipino short story writer in English was beginning to be the most instructive and unbiased observer of Philippine life, not to say the most accessible one as well. The difficulties of translation and the built-in intramurals among writers in Pilipino—on the issue between purism and contemporary idiom, for example—have cost the latter much time and energy. The Filipino writer in English was spared this dissipation when history offered him a language and a literary tradition. What he had to mind was an inwardness for both. He might have told off his detractors, as Kamala Das did, defining a premise for the survival, if not the continued good health, of Indo-Anglian writing:

> I am Indian, very brown, born in Malabar,
> I speak three languages, write in two, dream in one. Don't write in English,
>> they said
> English is not your mother tongue. Why not
>> leave
> Me alone, critics, friends, visiting cousin,
> Everyone of you, why not let me speak in
> Any language I like? The language I speak
> Becomes mine . . . .
>> It voices my joys, my longings,
> My hopes, and it is useful to me as cawing
> Is to the crows or roaring to lions, it
> Is human speech, the speech of a mind that is
> Here and not there, a mind that sees and hears
>> and
> Is aware . . . .[42]

Beyond the level of words, for that matter, the Filipino short story writer in English was voicing thoughts of his own. We realize this when we understand the kinds of statements that fiction, and particularly the short story, makes. Literary conventions have vocabularies of their

---

42. Narasimhaiah, op. cit., p. 13.

own, and, of course, a grammar and a rhetoric that the writer puts at his disposal. It may well be that the Filipino writer was not quite aware of this, and this is probably fortunate, since more self-consciousness could destroy him.

Although introduced as an exciting discovery in *Story*, Manuel E. Arguilla led the group of writers presented to an international audience in the Casper collection. Now, they could speak beyond the borders of their country. The collection included A. B. Rotor, Francisco Arcellana, Edith Tiempo and many others. More collections by other editors followed. Casper himself supplemented his work in 1962 with *New Writing from the Philippines*.[43] A more than modest beginning in terms of international notice had been accomplished. The record to date is, in fact, rather impressive for an art that could be regarded by some as a country cousin to de Maupassant and Chekhov. The gods have been rather generous.

VII

The brevity of the short story is its essential disguise. This feature enables it to appear almost inconspicuous and to work its other disarming charms on the reader much in the same way the earlier Filipino verse-makers rendered their romances, opening their world of make-believe in the mode of the day. Instead of drawing from the lore of Europe, the story writer today has sought the lore of the modern world, and, working within the limits of the form, he has raised questions about his past and future, as Nick Joaquin has done, or about the ways of tradition as Manuel Arguilla and others have. He has defined certain states of the human condition brought on by war and exile, as in the work of Bienvenido N. Santos in *You Lovely People*;[44] class and status are probed with scalpel-sharp felicity as in the stories of Aida Rivera Ford[45] and Gilda Cordero-Fernando.[46]

---

43. Syracuse, New York: Syracuse University Press, 1966.

44. Manila: Benipayo, 1955.

45. *Now and at the Hour* (Manila: Benipayo, 1957).

46. *The Butcher, the Baker and the Candlestick-maker* (Manila: Benipayo, 1962).

Examples of particular triumphs are too numerous to mention; suffice it to say that the sharpness of its thrust, the revelation of character usually required by the form, or the equally necessary discovery of some idiosyncracy of human life, the focus on an image that becomes an idea objectified . . . these and other skills that the short story brings off, and memorably, have come under the Filipino short story writer's control. Now, having achieved that, he has favored the form, cherishing it in fact above others—the novel and the play, for example—to a point where the muses that preside hereabouts could well be truly jealous.

And the short story has managed to be left alone. Over the years its writers in the Philippines have not allowed it to be commercialized. This trend has also been observed in the American short story. Its writers have been

> . . . left pretty much to themselves, freed from any expectations and preconceptions but their own as they begin to write. It is true that the old-fashioned commodity producers, of the sort who crowded the pages of so many large-circulation magazines now defunct, would be having a hard time of it had they not shrewdly followed their some-time readers into the newer technologies. But the short story in America at the present time, insofar as one may generalize, thrives in its apparent neglect, perhaps even because of it.[47]

The Filipino short story writer in English, and indeed the new generation of writers in Pilipino as well, know this phenomenon from having to live with it. Growth has resulted from the tradesman's indifference and the durability of the artist's sensibility. For what preoccupations could possibly wear that down?

Through good times and bad, through the symbolic floods, through hours of high and low tide at the river Pasig, this sensibility has not denied itself the wonder of expression. There has been no moment in the national experience when the bridge over the Pasig was without those curious ones looking at the water.

---

47. William Abrahams, *Prize Stories 1972: The O. Henry Awards* (New York: Doubleday, 1972), pp. xi-xii.

We must recognize their presence unequivocally. For Art is often surrounded by twilight-cool indifference. It is not difficult for a writer to feel at times that the society he serves is a ward of "catatonic patients who make sure only at the end of their trance that nothing escapes them."[48] In the Philippine experience, that trance has been intermittently broken: the artist does get heard. In any case, "it may not be entirely senseless," as Max Horkheimer reminds us, "to continue speaking a language that is not easily understood."[49]

1976

---

48. Max Horkheimer, *Critical Theory* (New York: Herder & Herder, 1972), p. 290.
49. Ibid.

Glossary

THE PHILIPPINE TERMS in our text, when appearing for the first time in a story, are in italics and then afterwards in roman. They are listed here along with those that have long left the boondocks (like *bolo*, *kaingin*, *kogon* and others) and, happily for all concerned, gained entry in Webster's *Third International*. We have provided some cultural notes when possible.

Abogado de campanilla—An attorney-at-law of considerable reputation. The term is likely to be used by his provincial client, to justify the substantial fee demanded.

Abrasador—A large kapok pillow, designed after the dutch wife and used for more or less the same purpose, although in a different colonial setting.

Adobo—A stew of pork, chicken, beef or a combination of any two of these, or of all three. The dish features a generous use of garlic, vinegar, and soy sauce. It enjoys a reputation as the Philippine national dish.

Aksesoria— Tenement

"Alerto, Voluntarios!"—The first line of a patriotic song that was popular during the Philippine Revolution and the succeeding years.

Amihan—Northwind.

Anak—Son.

Aparador—Armoire.

Asalto—Surprise party.

Atis—The sweetsop tree; also, its fruit.

Balaye—The mother- or father-in-law of one's son or daughter.

Balisong—A fan knife. The name derives from a town in Batangas province where it is handcrafted.

Banban—A variety of reed used for weaving baskets and the like.

Banca—A dugout, usually one fitted with bamboo outriggers.

Batel—A two-masted schooner of usually light draft and modest tonnage, hence an ideal vessel for moving cargo along the southern Tagalog and Visayan coasts. (See *Lanchon.*)

Bejuco—Rattan.

Bodiong—A horn made out of a large conch shell.

Bolo—An all-purpose knife, the Philippine farmworker's faithful companion.

Bunuan—Literally, the place for "piercing through," or "where wrestling is done"; hence, the "heart" of the fish-trap.

Buri—The talipot palm. Its leaves are gathered for use as shingles; when immature and pliant, they may be stripped and woven into mats, sacks, or even into fine hats. The buri is also a source of tuba, or palm wine. Compared to the coconut palm, and, for that matter, the sugar- and the nipa-palm, it is by far the more generous producer of this drink. To find tuba-drinkers gathered atop the buri palm tree is not unusual, although it may be an initially puzzling experience. The buri is anywhere from twenty to fifty feet in height and, for tuba production, is provided with a bamboo ladder. Thus, unless one is familiar with the location of one such tree in the second-growth, walking past a productive buri palm could cause him to wonder how voices could be heard from an innocent-looking cover of tree branches and palm fronds overhead.

Buyo—One of the three ingredients that make up the masticatory popular all over South and Southeast Asia. Also known as the *ikmo*, an entwining vine of the betel pepper variety, it resembles, according to Rizal, the German hop-garden. A portion of the leaf is chewed together with a few bits of areca nut meat (*bunga*) laced with slaked lime. Dedicated users find that as a stimulant, comparable to tobacco; it is, in any case, the reason for their black teeth, and their intermittent ejection of a rich burgundy-colored spit. Since Spanish times, the buyo has made an important contribution to the rural economy.

Calesa (*calesas*, pl.)—The Philippine version of the calash, now generally provided with a fixed, instead of a folding, top. The Spanish word appears to have readily found its way into Tagalog. The two-wheeled horse-drawn vehicle it stands for, however, is slowly but surely becoming a rarity, thanks to the domestication (after World War II) of the U.S. jeep. Christened *jeepney*, this vehicle soon dominated the territory where the calesa driver, the *cochero*, had been the recognized "king."

Camisa—Blouse.

Camisa de chino—A shirt worn by men. It is without a collar; the sleeves are without cuffs.

Cara y crus (or *cruz*)—A gambling game in which a coin is used. To win, a player must name the side of the coin that lands upward on the ground.

Cargador (*cargadores*, pl.)—Stevedore. Also, porter.

Cavan (*cavanes*, *cavans*, pl.)—A unit of measure for rice and corn equivalent to 2.13 bushels.

Chichirika and *sentimiento*—Two wild-growing plants usually found in sandy lots along riverain areas. The chichirika resembles the periwinkle, the sentimiento the coleus. The first has bluish white flowers with petals about two centimeters long; the second tiny buttercup-shaped flowers, light to deep lavender in color. Their beauty has obviously been never appreciated, for they are not potted or in any way cultivated.

Chupa—A measure for rice equivalent to one-eighth of a *ganta*, which, in turn, is one-twenty-fifth of a cavan. (See *Cavan*.) No handier and more readily obtainable chupa measure has so far been invented than the tin can for the 14-ounce condensed milk at the grocer's.

Compadre (comadre, f.)—The sponsor, either actual or nominal, at the baptism or the wedding ceremony of one's son or daughter. These occasions provide families with varied opportunities for strengthening ties of blood and other interests. In any case, families belonging to clearly different economic or social classes find in the *compadrasco* system (as this is sometimes called) a wide range of benefits.

Constabulario (constabularios, pl.)—Constable.

Convento—Rectory.

Corrido—A narrative verse form which, along with the *awit*, was widely used during the Spanish regime for rendering stories from European metrical romances.

Dao—One of several cabinet woods with dark brown markings. The dao tree grows to a considerable size.

Dumalaga—Pullet.

Dungon—An extraordinary variety of hardwood for heavy constructions. It is, in fact, known also as "iron wood," the broad blade of the axe not infrequently a poor match to it.

Estero—A drainage canal. Late eighteenth- and nineteenth-century Manila had a remarkable network of these, the city having risen out the confluence of small estuaries that spilled into the bay. The esteros became the arteries of a lively commerce, in grain, fruit, fowl, and the like, from the neighboring provinces.

Fiambrera—A food container, usually of aluminum or enameled tin, consisting of three or four detachable sections that double as bowls. These are stacked one upon the other and, for convenience in carrying, are locked in place by a lever worked from beneath the handle. It is, then, a tiered lunch box, especially convenient for hot foods and the nearest equivalent to home cooking that an office clerk or schoolteacher might aspire to for his noon meal.

Ganta—A measure for rice or corn equivalent to eight chupas, or one-twenty-fifth of a cavan.

Gapi—That phase in the preparation of the kaingin pertaining to the systematic removal of burned-out material so that the area could be planted to rice or corn, dibbles being used for this purpose. (See *Kaingin.*) The gapi follows the burning of the brush, and is again followed by the *dorok*, a redoing of the area earlier worked out.

Gobernadorcillo—Literally, petty governor. An office in the provinces during the Spanish regime.

Gogo—A tree bark used for cleaning the hair. Antonio de Morga, in *Sucesos de las Islas Filipinas* (1609), claimed that early Filipinos took "great care of their hair, rejoicing in its being very black." They washed it with "the boiled rind of a tree, which is called gogo, and they anointed it with the oil of sesame prepared with musk and other perfumes."

"Harao!"—It is astonishing that work animals observe dialectal distinctions when answering their master's commands. The mule couldn't be expected to come to a halt on hearing its master say "Harao!" Only a carabao owned by a Bisayan farmer would.

Hangaray—One of several mangrove woods suitable for pales or stakes.

Hinagdong—One of several varieties of quick-growing trees easily obtainable in areas that have undergone kaingin cultivation; hence it is a favorite material in the making of temporary houses.

Interna—A boarder in a Catholic girls' school.

Ipil—A hardwood, one of several classed as construction wood.

Juez—The Spanish word for judge is widely preferred over the vernacular (Tagalog) *hukom*. Bisayans particularly favor "juez."

Ka—An honorific, probably from "Kabesa," meaning, "headman of the village." Also, by way of an abbreviation, it stands for "kasama," meaning, "comrade" or "companion." "Ka" precedes a nickname, not the family name. A Mr. Juan Rodriguez would be addressed familiarly as "Mang Juan," or "Ka Juaning" (see *Mang*); or, if the relationship involved justifies a sense of familiarity to the extent that the given name is useful, "Ka Juan." On occasion, "Mang Rodriguez" might be resorted to; but "Ka Rodriguez" is avoided, unless that relationship has soured too badly. What is suggested here is that in the Philippine social context, the honorifics convey delicate nuances and are used accordingly.

Kaingin—This is sometimes spelled with an "-ñg-"; hence, *kaiñgin*. It refers to the area cleared for the planting of rice and corn, and for after-harvest crops like sweet potato and taro. "At close of the dry season," observed Hamilton M. Wright in 1907, writing in his own *A Handbook of the Philippines*, "brush . . . is cut, piled, and burned. The fire consumes all but the larger trees . . . . The burning clears the ground of waste . . . and leaves an amount of ash, the potash salts of which furnish a valuable fertilizing material." (See *Gapi*.)

Kogon—A tall, coarse grass for thatching.

Lamparilla—A small crudely constructed lamp, consisting of a tin container for kerosene and a wick.

Lanchon—A sailing vessel of the catboat type. (See *Batel* and *Pasaje*.) The Dutch Wars and the Galleon Trade left the Filipinos a valuable legacy: the art of boatbuilding. Some of the sturdiest galleons that sailed the seas were the work of Philippine craftsmen; and the batel is a reminder of the skill they attained. On Tingloy Island, in the Verde Islands group, that lies between Luzon and Mindoro, are some samples of boatbuilding skill. The so-called Tingloy batel exhibits a structural strength, symmetry and delicacy of line, and an overall efficiency worthy of the galleon builders of the past. Although in his notes on Morga's *Sucesos* Jose Rizal couldn't but remark on the passing of the Filipino boatbuilder's craft, there yet remains the lanchon to remind us of it, lumbering off shoals and estuaries, heavy with cargo from one riverain or seaside community to some other, plowing the coastal waters.

Lateria—Where canned goods are sold; hence, a grocery store.

Manding—A term of respect and affection prefixed to the nickname of an elder sister. The masculine is *Mandoy*.

Mang—The Tagalog equivalent for "mister," and probably a diminutive for "Mama," meaning, "person." (See *Ka*.) The feminine is *Aling*. In more formal speech and writing, *Ginoo* (m.) and *Ginang* (f.) are used, abbreviated as *G*. and *Gng*., respectively.

Manong—The Tagalog equivalent for the Bisayan *Mandoy*; the feminine is *Manang*. In rural communities age, rather than family relationship, sufficiently justifies the use of either *Manong* or *Manang*.

Mano a mano—A "cash and carry" type of business transaction.

Merienda—Among the middle class, this is merely the afternoon tea. In the lower orders it becomes a light mid-afternoon meal, if that sort of luxury is at all possible.

Municipio—Municipality. Also, the municipal or town hall.

Nanay—Bisayan for "Mother."

Noroeste—Northeast wind.

Palay—Rice in the husk.

Palma brava—The wood derived from the otherwise pulpy and fibrous trunk of the sugar- or areca nut palm.

Pan de sal—The traditional breakfast bread of the Philippines. A crusty, small bun, its size and weight are understood (for these change from month to month) to provide clues on the strength or weakness of the national economy.

Parao—Tagalog for any outriggered dugout of some size. Generally synonymous with "banca."

Pasacalye—Prelude. When providing a singer with a guitar accompaniment, it is customary for the player to do some strumming routines or fingerwork, giving the key in which the melody may be sung. The proficient player does not pass up this opportunity of demonstrating his skill, since it becomes thereafter the singer's show.

Pasaje—A one- or two-masted boat outfitted with outriggers and thatch-covered deck. It is probably the best example of how the craft of boatbuilding has deteriorated; but it is quite clear that the pasaje is adequate to the needs and resources of the communities it serves.

Patron—Boss, foreman.

Patadiong—A wraparound used by women.

Piloto—Pilot, master of a *batel* or *pasaje*. Also, the *arais*. In Southern Tagalog provinces (Batangas, Quezon, Marinduque and Mindoro), *arais* is the term more often used.

Piyapi—A swamp or riverain tree with a whitish bark.

Poblacion—Town site.

Ponjap—This is none other than "Hapon," the Tagalog for "Japanese," pronounced in reverse.

Potro—Stallion.

Principalia—The first families, so called, in a poblacion.

Querida—Mistress.

Rosario—Rosary; the prayers, in the Roman Catholic practice, expressive of devotion to Virgin Mary, consisting of the recitation usually of five decades of Ave Marias, preceded by a Pater Noster each and ended by a Gloria. Also, the beads used for counting this sequence.

Sala—Living room. The term more commonly used, however, is *salas*, which probably helps to distinguish a judge's courtroom (*sala*) from that of a Filipino middle-class parent's formal meeting place for the members of the family.

Sampaguita—The champak flower.

Santol—A fruit, edible either when ripe or green.

"Si Tatay naman . . ."—Literally, "That's quite enough, Father . . .", "Father, please . . .", or some such expression.

Sikoy-sikoy—Bisayan for gambling joints frequented by Pinoys (Filipinos in America).

Silid—A bedroom; a section of a nipa house especially partitioned off for this purpose, although eventually it may become the storage place for goods of some value and, in times of shortages, of rice and corn. (See *Sulambi*.)

Sulambi—Bisayan for that extra room or addition to sleeping or storage space in a nipa house, actually a modest extension of one side of the roof and walled up accordingly; the flooring may be a foot or two below that of the rest of the house.

"Susmariosep!"—Literally, *"Jesus, Maria y Josep!"*

Tampipi—A clothes hamper, usually of pandanus leaves stripped half-an-inch wide.

Tangal—Along with the hangaray and the piyapi, the tangal is another of those swamp woods that cannot possibly be too useful to the Filipino of the coastal or riverain communities. The tangal hardly grows to any remarkable size, being particularly sought after for firewood. Cords of split tangal are loaded on batels or lanchons and shipped to Manila, where the wood is in demand by bakeries and restaurants. The bark of the tangal, incidentally, furnishes the reddish-tan powder that adds body to the coconut-, buri- or nipa-palm tuba.

Tatay—Bisayan and Tagalog for "Father."

Tio, Tia—Uncle, Aunt.

Tuba—Palm wine. (See *Buri* and *Tangal*.)

Ubod—The pith (or "heart") of a palm tree. When extracted from a young palm, the ubod is tender and is eaten raw or cooked as a vegetable.

Zapatillas—Open-heeled slippers, often elaborately beaded, and about an inch or an inch-and-a-half high.

The Author

N.V.M. GONZALEZ is one of the Philippines' most widely known writers. He has gathered here some of his short fiction that have been most often anthologized. The volume, in effect, covers four decades of writing and, for students of Philippine experience, an authentic documentation, one indeed that has already enjoyed considerable acceptance, of a reality verifiable through other disciplines.

In the summer of 1978, the author was invited to the University of the Philippines Writers Summer Workshop as writer-in-residence, returning thus to his country after a sojourn of nearly nine years in the United States. It was this occasion that suggested the publication of *Mindoro and Beyond*; and with this volume, in fact, the University of the Philippines Creative Writing Center began its "Philippine Writers' Series."

For eighteen years, N.V.M. Gonzalez taught writing and the short story at the University of the Philippines. Invited to the University of California, Santa Barbara, and, for a brief stint, the University of Hong Kong, he moved eventually to Hayward, California. During the academic year 1977-78, he was Visiting Professor of English and Asian-American Studies at the University of Washington. He was permanently based, however, at California State University, Hayward, where, as a tenured member of the faculty, he held the rank of Professor of English and served as director of the CSUH Writing Program.

Gonzalez published his stories in magazines in the United States, England, and Australia (*Sewanee Review, Hopkins Review, Life and Letters,* and *Meanjin*) as well of course as in the Philippines; translations have appeared in Chinese, Indonesian, Malay, German, and Russian. The bimonthly *Short Story International,* which presents unabridged "tales by the world's great contemporary writers," has "The Bread of Salt" in its No. 14 (May 1979) issue.

The volume is only partly retrospective, however. For although a selection has been drawn from *Seven Hills Away* (1947), *Children of the Ash-Covered Loam and Other Stories* (1945), *Look, Stranger, on This Island Now* (1963), and *Selected Short Stories* (1964), there are five other stories here hitherto unavailable between book covers. The author has also appended a critical essay, "In the Workshop of Time and Tide," on the art of the narrative as a preoccupation of the Filipino imagination that counts with over three hundred years of history.

The varied lifestyles of both Filipino rural folk and their more sophisticated brothers in the urban areas and in America all come into focus in Gonzalez's stories. Over the years, he has received international critical attention for them. "It is the fully beating human heart, a human awareness and compassion, that N.V.M. Gonzalez has laid open . . . In children and plain women," Leonard Casper wrote (*Panorama*), "he has found his finest centers of sensitivity." Of the story "The Sea Beyond," Constance Glickman commented in a review (*New Writers*): "A work of brilliant ironies . . . with chilling insight we learn how man can overcome the indifference and ruthlessness of nature but cannot conquer these same qualities in himself." Writing in the Chicago *Daily News–Panorama,* Lucien Stryk noted: "Mr. Gonzalez is most telling when he writes of the young, the old, the deprived, and he finds people to care about all over those 7,000 islands of his. He is a very pure writer . . ."

Since his winning a Rockefeller Foundation fellowship in Creative Writing in 1948, N.V.M. Gonzalez received other awards including the Philippine Republic Award of Merit for Literature in English (1954), The Republic Cultural Heritage Award for Literature (1960), and the Rizal Pro Patria (1961).

He was named National Artist for Literature in 1997.